The Tale of a Woods Colt

In the Land of Rob – A Trilogy

G. Mason

This is a work of fiction. The events and characters described herein are imaginary and are not intended to refer to specific places or living persons. The opinions expressed in this manuscript are solely the opinions of the author and do not represent the opinions or thoughts of the publisher. The author has represented and warranted full ownership and/or legal right to publish all the materials in this book.

The Tale of a Woods Colt
In the Land of Rob – A Trilogy
All Rights Reserved.
Copyright © 2015 G. Mason
v3.0 r1.1

Cover Photo © 2015 thinkstockphotos.com. All rights reserved - used with permission.

This book may not be reproduced, transmitted, or stored in whole or in part by any means, including graphic, electronic, or mechanical without the express written consent of the publisher except in the case of brief quotations embodied in critical articles and reviews.

Outskirts Press, Inc.
http://www.outskirtspress.com

ISBN: 978-1-4787-5777-1

Outskirts Press and the "OP" logo are trademarks belonging to Outskirts Press, Inc.

PRINTED IN THE UNITED STATES OF AMERICA

THE TALE OF A WOODS COLT

BOOK ONE OF THE SERIAL TRILOGY
IN THE LAND OF ROB
A SAGA OF THE BLUE RIDGE MOUNTAINS

Fiction is fact distilled into truth.
—Edward Albee

PROLOGUE

In 1876, in the high reaches of the Blue Ridge Mountains, Rob Nickerson entered the world as a woods colt, the euphemism given by morally upstanding people to a child born out of wedlock. As an unwed maiden of the mountains, Lucy Nickerson knew that she and her son faced an unpromising future. Then the quirks of fate and turns of misfortune put her and young Rob under the roof of his natural father, living on a mountain farm under the rugged crest of Ragged Mountain.

As the easternmost major mountain range in the broad Appalachian system, the Virginia Blue Ridge rises like a rampart to divide the Piedmont to the east from the Shenandoah Valley to the west.

Settlement of these lands began in the mid-eighteenth century, with altitude defining the time of settlement and the eventual culture of the settlers. The desirable land lay at elevations mostly under one thousand feet, the fertile fields of the large farms lapping at the foot of the mountains.

In the heights above the prosperous farmland dwelt the mountain people. Most lived in the hollows, the many glens that wended around and between the ancient mountains, where they eked out a living farming marginal land. Further up the rocky ridges dwelt poor homesteaders who were barely able to pry a sparse livelihood from the stubborn hillsides.

The mountain hollows are of three kinds. Lower hollows range to about twelve hundred feet elevation, and are more like coves lying up against the mountains, separated from the open valleys by low hills. The inner hollows are tightly bounded by mountains, and rise to two thousand feet from their juncture with the lower hollows. The upper hollows are mere creases or folds in the mountain slopes that extend up to the ridges at thirty-five hundred feet. The peaks top a lofty four thousand feet above sea level. Social and economic status of the inhabitants decreased as their altitude and isolation increased.

As often as not, the mountain people's eighteenth century ancestors had endured privation in the British Isles, spurring many to flee in desperation by selling themselves into indentured servitude to pay their passage by ship to colonial America. Once released from four or more years of bondage, they migrated in all directions to live in freedom and seek their fortunes in every walk of life.

Some mountain folk were descended from common seafarers who went to sea to escape the strife-torn English-Scottish borderlands. Upon landing in the Virginia colony, they took advantage of bargain land prices to acquire a toehold on the mountain frontier.

Though decended from a British sailor who had acquired large acreage in colonial times, Rob Nickerson's near ancestors were among those of slender means who fell short of the substantial resources needed to buy a viable farm, engage in business or make the arduous journey west to claim land on the frontier in the new United States of America. Instead, they migrated to the Blue Ridge Mountains to settle in the deep hollows and up on lofty heights.

Mountain land was rocky and available at rock-bottom prices, though some who settled the tortured ridges and hollows didn't buy their land. They simply squatted in isolation, with little or no interference from distant absentee owners of sprawling tracts of land. The mountains were well peopled by the middle of the nineteenth century, the hollows and hills dotted with homesteads of humble houses and tiny cabins set in clearings arduously claimed from the forest.

When the Civil War erupted, the momentous conflict had little to do with the mountain people, for though they were *in* the South they were hardly *of* the South. The War of Northern Agression, as the South called it, held no Yankee threat to the mountain way of life, poor as it was with little to lose. Most people living up in the mountains stood near the bottom of the socio-economic strata, and had no real stake in the conflict.

Mountain dwellers had little interest in slavery. The nearest slaves were on the large farms situated several miles away from the mountains. Those few slaves that had ever been brought into the hollows were long gone by the time the War Between the States broke out. Many of the mountain people had never seen a slave. Divergent interests and pockets of union sympathy further isolated them from loyalty to the Confederacy.

By the latter half of the nineteenth century, lowlanders tended to view mountain people as inferior, and disparagingly called them *mountaineers*. Ardently independent, mountain folk possessed a stubborn streak of resistance to meddlesome authority. Ensconced in the isolation that suited them, they were considered by valley people to be wild and woolly.

The trilogy, *In the Land of Rob*, depicts mountain culture and portrays the interplay between lowlanders and the highland folk as it spans the ninety-four year true-to-life saga of colorful mountain man Rob Nickerson.

The Tale of a Woods Colt begins the story, taking Rob from his conception through his adventures as a young man seeking his future in the Shenandoah Valley, where an ill-fated romance lands him in prison.

The Call of the Whippoorwill carries Rob from his luckless valley sojourn back to his mountain milieu, where he eventually falls into a double life. He is caught up in the forced eviction of over five hundred mountain families to create the Shenandoah National Park, after which he despondently finds himself at the portals of old age.

The Crags of Old Rag concludes the trilogy with the illiterate Old Man Rob doing his best to cope with the modern world that swirls in around his mountain home.

THE TALE OF A WOODS COLT

"All happy families resemble each other; each unhappy family is unhappy in it own way." Leo Tolstoy. Anna Karenina.

PART ONE
LUCY

ONE

1876

The Birth

The cabin door burst open to reveal the looming form of a stout woman, her silhouette backlit by the pale sun. Lucy stiffened at the sudden rush of cold air, but then recognized Aunt Tilly and leaned back on her bed with a sigh of relief.

Aunt Tilly stepped into the room, pushed the door shut behind her and stood with her shoes firmly planted on the pine-planked floor, surveying the dimly lit scene.

A smoky wood fire smoldered in the stone fireplace. A single small window admitted a feeble ray of light. A tin lamp sat burning on a wooden table. A small spinning wheel occupied a corner. On wall pegs hung an old double-barreled shotgun. Jesus looked down from a frame on the wall. The simple room held no other adornments.

"Bile water," ordered Tilly, in a commanding voice.

She tossed her old coat into the corner and, with a nod to the worried looking woman at the fireplace, let out a robust, "Evenin', Hannah."

Aunt Tilly had arrived in force at the Nickerson home. A horse of a woman with lively eyes, her moon face beamed ruddy good health, except for lips shrunken into her nearly toothless mouth. She was a take-charge type who had midwifed her mountain neighbors for over two decades.

Standing in her coarse and tattered attire, Tilly cut an imposing figure. One of the toes on her sockless feet showed through a hole in the leather of the high-laced shoes. A bonnet that once had been white, a shabby black long-sleeved blouse with fluffed shoulders, and a rough gingham skirt covered her head to foot. Sturdy and solid, she was, in the local jargon, "a good lifter."

"Tilly, I'm powerful glad you's h'yar. She hain't got much longer," said Hannah Nickerson from her seat on a crude chair, the bottoms of her bare feet facing the fire and showing the hard leathery soles of a mostly shoeless existence. In contrast to Tilly, Hannah was rail thin, with mousy brown hair pulled severely back to a tight bun. Her face, drawn taut by a hard life of continuous worry and work, was showing the strain of motherly anxiety.

Hannah immediately swung the black iron kettle in over the fire and laid a couple more logs on, punching the glowing embers up under the vessel. The fireplace served as cookstove and sole source of heat.

"Her pains been a-comin' on right smart this evenin', Tilly," said Hannah through lips so tight they were only capable of a thin smile whenever the burdens of life allowed.

Lucy–Lucinda Nickerson–lay in rags on a rustic plank bed with a cornhusk tick for a mattress, her belly bulging under a dirty blanket. Her sweaty, drawn face showed the strain, but she was relieved to now be in Aunt Tilly's able hands.

Lucy's pains had started before dawn. Right after breakfast Hannah had sent the four other children away for the day, putting Otis, the oldest, in charge...

"Otis, take Jenny, Richard and Mazie up to Uncle Elwood's. You hear me now?"

"Yassum," said Otis, with an adolescent crack in his voice. A strong and wiry boy, he usually worked with his father, Festus, in the arduous effort of winkling a bare subsistence from their rough mountain acreage. But Hannah saw to it that Festus wasn't working this day.

"Then git right on over to Tilly's and tell her Lucy done got the pains."

"Yassum."

"Then git back to Elwood's. You stay up'par till Daddy come fer you, you hear?"

"Yassum."

Tilly and Ernest Foster lived a mile up the trail, and Uncle Elwood wasn't far from there. Aunt Tilly had no training as a midwife, but there were no trained midwives in that mountainous corner of the county. She had a natural talent and was trusted to handle most of the births in the highlands that rose above the tiny community of Nabors Mill, Virginia.

The nearest doctor was in the village of Sperryville. But he was only willing to come seven miles up the mountain by horseback if a life was in danger. The Nickersons and most of the mountain people couldn't afford a doctor anyway. They couldn't afford a midwife either, but Aunt Tilly didn't demand a fee. If someone could pay, she'd ask for fifty cents. Otherwise, she accepted whatever was offered in trade. Tilly had delivered Lucy and the other four Nickerson children.

The hill and hollow dwellers thought Aunt Tilly had the calling to be a midwife because she'd never had her own children, as though it were an alternative outlet for maternal instincts. Calling her Aunt Tilly made her an honorary family member.

Everyone knew to call on Aunt Tilly when labor pains began, just to let her know to be ready. She didn't come right away, though. She had plenty of work at home and couldn't spend all day waiting by the birth bed. First-birth labor could last a day or a couple of days. The family was expected to take care of housework and tend to the expectant mother. "Come fer me once't the water's broke," she always instructed. Only when the birth was imminent did Tilly come to her patient.

Through the morning hours, Lucy's contractions had become more frequent. With each spasm, Hannah took her daughter's hand in hers and soothed her with words of encouragement.

Festus, a dour man and unkempt, ignored his daughter as he sat with a little jug of corn liquor cradled in the crook of his arm, sullenly staring at the fire through dark eyes peering out from sunken sockets. At Hannah's insistence, he had put off work and was attired in his good clothes for the birth—collarless shirt, vest stained by tobacco juice, baggy woolen trousers, loose suspenders and scuffed boots.

Not yet forty, Festus looked a rugged fifty. Under his scraggly hair stretched a gaunt, leathery face that sprouted week-old stubble around his sullen mouth that defaulted into a droopy frown. His upper lip twitched irregularly, signaling his cranky and crotchety mien. His head still held a few tobacco-stained teeth that were seldom seen because he never smiled.

By early afternoon, Lucy's contractions were closely spaced and increasingly painful. Then her water broke.

"Festus, git on up'par and fetch Tilly," said Hannah. "Lucy hain't got much longer."

Usually given to grousing, Festus pushed himself out of his chair without a word, put on his crumpled hat, grabbed his threadbare coat, took a few wobbly steps and ducked out the door.

Out in the yard, Festus looked back at his humble abode and pulled on his coat. Beyond the one low room, the little cabin extended only to an upstairs loft, a porch on the front, a lean-to on the rear and a mud-mortared stone chimney at one end. Cramped and totally lacking in convenience, comfort and sanitation, the rudimentary hovel was a typical dwelling in the high reaches of the Virginia Blue Ridge.

"Women's business," he muttered to himself, turning toward the rough footpath.

Festus saw no reason to celebrate the birth. He felt cursed that his daughter was adding another mouth to feed at his table. Regular nips from his jug had taken the edge off his consternation by the time it fell to him to go fetch the midwife. He hurried up the trail to the Foster cabin and found Tilly coming in from the barn with a pail hanging from her fingers.

"You best come on down," he croaked, in his raspy closed-mouth way of speaking. "It's a-comin'."

Tilly carried the pail inside and came back out with a bag of rags under her arm. Festus saw her back down the trail to his cabin, then found his fishing pole and disappeared. He was a good husband. He wasn't like some others who couldn't be bothered with the "nonsense" of fetching the midwife. Still, he drew the line at attending the birth. Childbirth was strictly women's business. He'd have no part of it.

Hannah Nickerson had born eight children, with five still living. At sixteen, Lucy was the oldest, and now becoming a mother herself...

Tilly tied on her tattered apron and sat down beside Lucy, taking the girl's hand in hers. "You goin' to be fine, child," she reassured, in her best soothing voice. "Let me look in now." She checked Lucy's cervical dilation and made sure the baby's head was down. A breech birth would mean trouble. She then laid out her rags. It might be another half hour.

Tilly turned to Hannah and asked, "You supposen you goin' to have ary more children, Hannah?" Only thirty something, Hannah looked a haggard forty-five.

"Hain't no way to know, Tilly. I reckon I'll have many as I'm supposed to have."

"Womens always holts up best what don't have too many, Hannah."

"I hain't got nothin' to do with it, Tilly. Yer goin' to have yer number," said Hannah, reflecting the fatalism prevalent in the mountains.

"Some womens can stop," said Tilly.

"It's up to the Lord," declared Hannah.

"Dicey Simpson, she done had six," said Tilly, persisting. "I done tolt her she best not have no more lest she die. Her man, he done vow he hain't agoin' to let her die. He sleep in a separate bed now, and she hain't had no more, neither," said Tilly, making her point.

Hannah sat quietly in her homespun dress and a course sweater of no defined color, staring into the fire without responding.

THE TALE OF A WOODS COLT

But Tilly kept at it.

"Ritchie, he thinks a heap of Dicey. Some womens reckon they man's got to always be satisfied. But Ritchie, he a mighty good husband to Dicey," she said, hinting.

"I cain't say nothin' like that to Festus!" protested Hannah.

"But he might…"

"He won't hear of it!"

"Hannah, womens got ways of sayin' without actual sayin'."

"It's just manners fer a woman to obey her man," insisted Hannah.

"Wahl, I'm just a-sayin', Hannah, you best not have no more neither," said Tilly.

"Wahl, I hain't had none fer about six yahrs. May be I hain't goin' to have no more children. May be I *cain't* have no more, Tilly."

"Wahl, could be that…"

Lucy shrieked, grimacing at the sharp pain of a contraction, pulling Tilly back to her patient.

The contractions started coming quickly. With each one, Tilly coached Lucy, who did not need coaching. Natural forces were in charge.

"Poosh."

Lucy's face contorted in a paroxysm of pain. Between contractions she breathed heavily, rolling her eyes in the agony of giving birth and the ecstasy of giving life.

"Poosh, Lucy!"

Lucy screamed with another strong contraction.

"Poosh harder!"

Lucy cried out again, but with a little less pain as the baby began moving.

"POOSH!"

Tilly wiped Lucy's brow with a rag. "Yer doin' good child, yer doin' good."

Hannah took over holding Lucy's hand, which Lucy gripped and squeezed tightly with every intolerable contraction. Presently the baby's head appeared.

"It's a–comin', it's a–comin', cried Tilly. "Poosh! Poosh!"

"Ah..AH..AHHHH!!!" screamed Lucy, her pain spiking at the final push; the head was out, and then the shoulders. The baby, all slick and red, slid into Tilly's waiting hands.

"It's a boy!" exclaimed Hannah with shining eyes and a rare grin. Her voice was a dam breaking, releasing a flood of pent-up apprehension. Childbirth was a regular and ordinary occurrence, not something to make a big to-do over. Still, Hannah was charged with anticipation, and not a little anxiety. Things could easily go wrong.

After carefully cleaning the quivering newborn's nose and mouth, Tilly held the baby up, the tiny feet kicking and tiny fingers curling. She gently smacked the little bottom, inducing a hearty scream and the first breath of life. Only then did she tie off the umbilical cord, cutting it with a small knife pulled from her apron pocket. She dipped a rag into the kettle of hot water and held it up to cool. She gently wiped the infant clean, swathed it in more rags and laid the newborn in Lucy's arms with a sense of relief that the birth had gone smoothly.

Despite the primitive conditions and lack of sanitary methods, Tilly rarely lost a mother in childbirth. If a woman dies giving birth, mountain people accept it with stoic fatalism. If a woman's time to die has come–she will die. "It wahr her time to go," they would say. Still, the midwife took special pride in her high success rate.

The birth was over; there was no birth certificate or written record.

Tilly picked up her remaining rags and stood up to leave. "She strong but best give her three, four days in the bed," she said to Hannah, turning toward the door to go.

Hannah rushed up and grabbed her arm. "You done brung my first grandchild into this world!" she gushed in a flood of relief. "I cain't thank you enough, Tilly!" It was one of the few times Hannah showed strong emotion.

"I just done what I do," replied Tilly, with a professional air of mission completed. "I just done my callin', Hannah."

She stepped out the door, off the porch and headed up the trail in the dimming light.

Dusk had deepened nearly to darkness by the time Festus appeared on the path into the yard, the four children straggling out behind him. "*Git* on down h'yar now!" he barked in his coarse voice. Three fish hung from his hand.

Hannah stood hunched over the fireplace, boiling up a pot of turnips and cabbage, frying a skillet of fatback, and baking ashcake for supper. Looking over her shoulder at her husband and children filing through the door, she announced, "It's a boy."

Jenny and Mazie, grinning and giggling, looked over at Lucy. No one said anything and Hannah didn't expect much excitement. Gaining and losing family members was a regular occurrence. Life and death were predestined. "You cain't do nothin' to change it" went the saying. Few families went two years without one or the other.

"H'yar's some fish fer supper," were Festus' only words as he handed over the brook trout, which Hannah quickly cleaned, filleted and fried.

Hannah knew Festus would take little notice of the new baby. He'd taken little interest in the birth of his own children and now here was Lucy with a baby and no husband. In his coarse way, he'd made his view clear. "A girl orter git her a man afore she git's her a child," he had grumbled. "Trouble is, iffen she gits it in her head she goin' to git it in her ass, because hain't hardly nary a man that gon' say no."

Hannah looked over at Lucy lying on the bed in exhausted contentment with her little one nuzzling her nourishing breast. Only Hannah felt any actual excitement about the birth, though the two girls were showing amused interest. She saw Festus throw a quick glance Lucy's way as he took his seat at the table.

Each of the four children went over to the bed for a curiosity look at their new nephew.

Jenny asked, "Can I holt him?" Lucy detached her infant from her nipple and gently handed the little rag-wrapped bundle to her sister's cradled arms. "He so itty bitty!" cooed Jenny.

Little Mazie peeked up over her sister's arms. "Why he so *red*, Lucy?" she wanted to know, as the miniature fingers clenched and the tiny mouth erupted in discontent.

"They always red the first day," said Lucy, retrieving the infant and reconnecting him to his supper. The siblings all found their positions on the table bench to connect to their own suppers.

Hannah served up the food in clayware table bowls, with a bedside plateful for Lucy. Table grace was not part of the Nickerson meal. They were religious in the sense of believing in the Lord and His control over life, and in the hereafter, but not in the sense of prayer and worship, or petitioning, or even giving thanks.

Festus helped himself by stabbing fish, vegetables and fatback with his knife and plopping each in turn onto his battered tin plate. He sprinkled salt across it all. They had no other spices or condiments.

Then the children dug in, forking food onto their bent and dented plates. Hannah filled her plate last. Dessert was dried apple slices soaked in water, with a little honey she'd saved for special occasions.

Festus wiped his sleeve across his mouth and looked across the table at Otis. "We gon' cut fahrwood most the entahr day tomorrow, boy."

Then Hannah caught Jenny and Richard's eyes, "I'm sendin' the both of you up to Tilly in the mornin'."

There was no more table talk. There wasn't much to talk about. Supper was about eating. Late winter meant a lean diet of food stored from the previous harvest. They still had ample salted fatback and some smoked pork from the hogs butchered the prior fall. A supply of potatoes and turnips remained in the damp root cellar and the loft held enough corn, but the cabbage had dwindled and only one cask of dried apple slices remained. Their cow had been bred and was now dry. So today's fish was a special treat.

Dinner lapsed into dead time. They had no books, not even a Bible. None of them could read. There was nothing much to talk about, not even the new baby. Life was about getting by today, not reflecting on the past or envisioning the future. Some mountain families had a fiddle, banjo or mandolin, and the talent to entertain themselves, but not the Nickersons.

Hannah and Jenny washed out the dinnerware, leaving little Mazie to gravitate back over to Lucy and the baby. Festus and the boys sat staring into the fire; their eyes had begun to droop by the time supper cleanup was complete.

"Let's git on up," said Hannah, announcing bedtime. Day was done and the next morning began at dawn, so up they filed to the sleeping loft. Bed was a cornhusk tick on the floor, and heavy blankets, each shared by two children. Hannah and Festus, having given up their first floor bed to Lucy, slept up with the other children.

The Nickersons and all the near neighbors could neither write nor spell their names, and could only count and figure by using fingers, which was how Hannah kept track of the children's ages. Some mountain people lost count of exactly how old they were, not because they couldn't track the years but because it didn't matter much to them.

TWO

The next morning
The Nickerson Place

Hannah rose just before first light, swapped her nightshirt for her usual dress and sweater, and then felt her way down the dark narrow steps.

She laid a couple of logs on and blew the dying embers into a fresh fire, then swung the kettle and porridge pot in over the new flame. She slipped out onto the porch, grabbed a wooden water bucket with each hand and stepped barefoot down onto the cold earth.

The crowing of their rooster and the calls of chirping birds enlivened the nippy dawn air. The first glint of light showed in the downhollow sky as Hannah padded along the path across the yard and down into the woods above the hog pen. She stopped a ways below the spring, sat the buckets down and disappeared behind a massive boulder. They had no privy—the big rock provided enough privacy.

She reappeared, took up the buckets, continued up to the spring, filled them both and, with arms stretched tightly downward, lugged the fresh water back to the cabin. She poured half a bucketful into the porch basin, then took the rest inside and topped off the kettle just as Festus was stepping off the stairs, clutching his well-worn britches.

"Mornin'."

"Mornin'," she replied, not looking up as she poured water into a metal tub.

Festus, covered by his course gray long underwear and the maturing stubble on his face, took hold of the newly emptied bucket and stumbled out the door. He found another empty on the porch, stepped off into the sharp chill and quickly made his way out the path past the pigsty and into the woods, pausing below the spring. He dropped the buckets and ducked behind the huge rock.

He emerged after a minute, snatched up the buckets and continued to the spring where he filled them and toted the water back to the cabin, pouring it all into the tub by the smoky fireplace.

Festus had pulled on a pair of gray ducks—his heavy canvas workpants—and was buttoning up his shirt when his two boys appeared on the stairs in their raggedy homespuns, rubbing their eyes.

"You boys bring me back three buckets," said Hannah from the fireplace.

Otis latched onto two buckets and Richard took one. The pair trooped out the path, sat the buckets down in the woods and went behind the big boulder. The rooster had crowed a couple of times before the two materialized back on the path. They got their water and delivered it to the porch just as Festus splashed a double-cupped handful from the basin onto his face.

It was his shaving day and the boys lingered to watch the delicate routine. Their father pulled his razor, brush and soap mug from a high porch shelf, dribbled in a little water, whipped up a soapy froth and brushed the lather onto his face. They watched with rapt attention, toward the day they'd draw the razor over their own skin. Festus propped a small broken mirror on a shelf, unfolded his straight razor and leaned in close to the mirror.

He proceeded to pull the skin tight with his free hand and carefully slide the thin, sharp blade down the surface of his cheeks, dipping the soapy razor in the basin with every stroke. He lifted his face to stretch the skin and stroked his neck, pulled his lower lip into his mouth to short-stroke his chin, and finished on his down-stretched upper lip, taking care not to nick it when it twitched.

"You boys thinkin' that you gon' see a li'l blood, is you?"

"Nosir," said Otis.

"Look all you want but I hain't about to put no cuts on my face."

Sometimes he did, though, and drew a little blood, which always got the boys' keen interest.

Festus tossed the soapy water off the porch and sloshed in some fresh to flush the basin. Then off he went toward the little log barn to feed the family mule and cow. The boys struck out for the woodpile to take up their next chore.

Inside, Mazie stood next to Lucy, watching the little one nurse, and Jenny stirred the porridge pot at the fire, the two looking like ragamuffins in their gunnysack dresses. Just then the boys piled through the door with armloads of firewood.

"C'mon, Mazie," called Jenny, picking up the empty water bucket. They stepped out into the morning light and traipsed into the woods below the spring. After a stop at the rock, they continued up to the spring, dipped out a bucketful of crystal clear water and hauled it back, with little Mazie gripping one side of the handle, doing her best to hold it up.

"Let's go git the eggs, Mazie," said Jenny after they'd splashed morning water on their faces. Off they dashed to the chicken coop.

Water was always needed, so no one came back from the woods empty handed. Clean, fresh water was the precious gift of the mountains. Every cabin sat near a reliable spring.

In short order, Hannah had the table set with a breakfast of home-roasted coffee, rolled oats porridge, fried eggs and scrapple with ashcake and gravy.

"How my li'l darlin's doin'?" she asked, nestling Lucy's plate of food on her daughter's lap.

"He been real good, Mama. He just the perdiest li'l thang!" said Lucy, beaming as she handed her newborn to her mother for cleanup and a burp.

After sopping up the last of the gravy on his plate with a biscuit, Festus smacked his lips and proclaimed, "Yass indeed, that thar's some fine eatin', Hannah."

It was the closest he ever came to a compliment, but she knew how he felt. He genuinely appreciated her contribution to family welfare. Despite his grumpy demeanor, he considered her to be his equal in making their way through life's challenges and necessities—as long as he thought he ruled the roost.

Hannah, cleaning up breakfast dishes, dispatched two of the children. "Jenny and Richard, you two git on up and help Aunt Tilly and Uncle Ernest, you hear now?"

"Yassum."

"And pick me some creasy sallit on yer way back," she called from the porch as the two children shuffled out across the yard, with the older Jenny leading Richard. Land cress, the first fresh salad green of the season, was appearing in the corn patches.

Ernest and Tilly Foster lived by subsistence farming, but they had no brood to help with all the work. Neighbors would send their own children to help the Fosters with tasks and chores, partly as payment for Tilly's birthing services and partly out of sympathy for her lacking children of her own.

Sitting on the porch pulling on his worn boots, Festus barked a command to Otis, "Git the axe and crosscut saw, boy!"

"Yassar." Otis tied his second bootlace and trotted off to the shed, while his father went to harness up the mule.

Festus seemed a stern and sour man but he was not prone to anger. A thing had to fester in him to arouse his ire, and it took a real provocation to rile him. He'd holler at Otis whenever he wanted something done, but the boy knew the loud words weren't yelled in anger. His father had never actually beaten any of the children.

Festus took the axe from Otis and led the mule up into the forest, with Otis trudging behind carrying the logging gear—the single-tree over one shoulder, with the log chain looped over it, and the crosscut saw balanced on the other shoulder.

Inside, Hannah turned to her youngest. "Mazie, carry this h'yar bucket of ashes to the garden and meet me down by the chickens," she said. "You hear me child?"

"Yass, Mama."

"You goin' to help Mama clean out the coop and git it on the garden."

"Yass, Mama."

Little Mazie lugged the ash bucket out the door, leaving her mother alone with Lucy. Hannah sat herself on the edge of the bed and peeked in on the tiny newborn.

"You been thinkin' about a name fer yer li'l boy, darlin'?"

"Yass, Mama."

Hannah got up, stoked up the fire and left the cabin, leaving Lucy lying placidly in the dim stillness of the room. Her sleep had been interrupted during the night to nurse the baby, who was now snoozing serenely. With her newborn nuzzled against her breast, Lucy looked drowsily around the tranquil cabin; the dust motes floated lazily in the scant sunlight coming through the window, luring her toward delicious sleep.

In time, her eyelids drooped and she drifted off into the nebulous place between the conscious and the dream, where visions floated back into the past. Her drift of mind carried her memory back nearly a year to the day when, after a harrowing courtship confrontation, she had walked away from her childhood, and to the father of her child…

The first warm days of spring heralded prime courting season in the mountains.

Courtship typically involved a young swain visiting a desirable girl's home, hoping for an invitation to sit and chat for a spell. This was his chance to gauge her temperament and to impress her that he was worthy and would make her a good husband. After a visit or two, they were talking–mountain jargon for courting. Several more visits would lead to hand holding, then to embracing and kissing, upon which betrothal was assumed by one and all.

A couple of up-the-mountain types of questionable character had already been nosing around the Nickerson place, trying to get Lucy to come out and talk. Mature for her age, she wanted nothing to do with either of them. She saw too much boy and not enough man. And she was resolved to be selective in choosing a husband.

By custom, a visitor would stand just off the porch, to be announced by the dogs or a cry or two of "Yee-ar." The young bucks sniffing around Lucy were either too shy or too proud to take the forward step of approaching the cabin, hat in hand, in the usual way. They would stand alone at the edge of the yard, staring at the cabin and hoping for a word of welcome.

If one of them showed up with a friend, they were nearly always pretty well lit with liquor. They'd holler for Lucy to come out, and were often boisterous, as if they needed to impress each other more than her. Then Festus would shoo them away with his glowering look and menacing growl, though one had given him a good cussing.

One day a couple of especially ornery drunks appeared outside the cabin and made a ruckus. The two Nickerson hounds bayed for a few minutes and then retired, leaving the inebriates standing at the edge of the yard.

"Yee'ar Lucy! Come on out and talk a spell!" called one loudly.

"We just wants to talk with you, Lucy!" hollered the other.

Hannah peeked out the window.

"It's them rascally Fisk boys," she said with a scowl. "And they's perty well liquored up."

The Fisk boys were standing a ways out from the cabin, almost at the woods. The Nickersons stayed inside and didn't respond. They didn't like obstreperous drunks and they especially didn't like two rowdy drunks together.

Swigging from a small jug of corn liquor they passed between them, the two outside stood barefoot, swaying a little, their ragged shirtsleeves rolled halfway up their forearms and tattered britches cinched to their skinny frames with rope belts.

"You gon' hafter talk to *somebody*!" reasoned the older boy.

"Why hain't you talkin' to nobody?!" protested the younger one.

The older Fisk boy was interested in Lucy and the younger was there to support his brother. Of the many Fisks in the area, that one family was a troublesome lot. No one thought much of them. They made bad corn liquor and drank it all themselves. And they were known to steal whatever wasn't nailed down.

"You cain't hide her forever!" cried the older, turning his appeal to the parents.

"You hain't got no right to keep her away from us!" accused the younger.

Festus peered out the window. "Them sorry Fisks gon' be trouble."

"You best let that girl come on out!" warned the older boy.

"We don't want make no trouble!" assured the younger.

"Them boys is a-thinkin' yer keepin' Lucy from 'em," said Hannah to Festus.

Festus looked back out the window.

"Reckon I best run 'em off afore they gits theyselves ary more liquored up."

He stepped out on the porch to confront the brothers.

"Lucy hain't agoin' to talk with nary one of you! You best git on, now!" he hollered.

The prospective suitor and his sidekick, with clenched fists and dark frowns, were visibly angered.

"We hain't movin' till you lets her talk to us!" yelled the older.

"We stayin' right h'yar till we sees Lucy!" cried the younger.

The hair stood up on the back of Festus' neck as his brow furrowed, lip twitched and curled, and his face flushed with anger.

"Lucy don't want talk to you boys!" he snarled. "Now *git* offen my place!!" he ordered loudly, jabbing out his arm with a finger pointed toward the path.

"*Damn* you, ol' man!!" screamed the older boy as he reached down, picked up a stone and hurled it at Festus. The younger followed with another stone. One hit the cabin door and the other caromed off the porch post, grazing Festus' forehead.

Festus fled back into the cabin, florid, furious and bleeding. Hannah and Lucy looked fearfully at the murder in his eyes.

"I'm goin' to *kill* the both of 'ems!!" raged Festus as he grabbed his double-barreled muzzle-loader from the wall. A trickle of blood reached his eyebrow.

"No! Daddy, no!! Don't shoot em!!" cried Lucy, dropping to her knees and throwing her hands to her face. "Please don't *kill* em, Daddy!!" The terror in her eyes said she knew he'd fire with no additional provocation. She wanted no part of the Fisk boys, but she didn't want them shot.

"Hit 'em in the legs, Festus," said Hannah in a determined voice and with a steely look in her eyes, suggesting she also feared Festus would actually shoot to kill.

Stones banged off the cabin wall and door as Festus rammed powder, shot and wadding down the gun muzzles. The children were wailing as he pulled back both hammers and put caps on the firing pins.

Hannah and Lucy, with hands on blanched faces, moaned in terror as Festus jerked open the door. A rock flew into the room and he charged out with his gun cocked and the stock to his shoulder—ready to fire.

"I done got a bead on you, boys!!" he yelled, with an eye aimed straight down the barrels and fingers closed on the triggers. "Now git *outin* h'yar and *don't* come back or I'll blow a hole right through the *both* of yous!!"

The two Fisk jaws dropped and stones fell from their fingers as the boys stared at the business end of Festus' gun. The fierce demonic look on his face said he wasn't bluffing.

The two trespassers stood still as statues in the tense moment. It was their dignity or their lives.

Festus' fingers tightened on the triggers. He stepped forward, jabbing his gun at the air. "Now *git!!*"

The suddenly sobered Fisks stepped heedfully backwards, turned and slinked away into the woods.

Festus lowered his gun and went back inside where Hannah and Lucy were heaving sighs of relief. "One more word and I'd have kilt 'em dead," he growled as he unloaded the weapon. Hannah rushed to wash the cut on his head.

The tense episode left Lucy shaken. She felt chained to childhood and trapped in the cabin. She'd never gone anywhere alone. Errands and excursions were always with a parent or sibling. As the oldest, she'd been like a second mother in her home but was still a child to Hannah.

THREE

The Dinkins Place

Soon after the incident with the Fisk boys, Lucy's Aunt Sarah came calling. In the morning sunshine, she sat in a cane-bottomed chair on the porch with Hannah and Lucy. After some pleasantries and small talk, she looked intently at Hannah and came right to it.

"Hannah, my Nellie done come down with the wheezes somethin' terrible," she blurted, with distress etched across her face. "She in the bed and cain't hardly stand up." Nellie was Sarah's oldest daughter.

Hannah's brow furrowed. "Lord! That's about the worstest wheezes she ever done got!"

"I hope to *tell* you!" exclaimed Sarah, drawing and exhaling a nervous breath. "She done always had the wheezes but she hain't never been like this, Hannah. She cain't do a thang, and I hain't got no one atall can go be with her."

Sarah looked at her sister with pleading eyes. "Truth be tolt, I'm more'n a mite afear't fer her," she admitted, looking earnestly to Lucy, who was sitting on the porch steps biting her knuckle in concern for her sick cousin.

"Dear Sarah, I wish't we could help, but we cain't handily keep up with our ownselves, what with all the work here on the place."

"But Hannah, I hain't got no one to send down and you got…," She looked at Lucy again.

Hannah took the hint. "Wahl, I reckon I can let Lucy h'yar git on down fer a spell," she said, looking expectantly at her daughter.

Lucy's eyes lit up at the proposal. "Course I can go help Nellie!" she said wholeheartedly, bringing relief to the faces of mother and aunt.

Lucy was perfectly willing to go help her cousin. It was an opportunity to get out of the cabin and dodge annoying young men. She was a lively and comely girl with a buoyant disposition, a shapely figure, a broad smile and straight teeth. Pert and pretty, she was bound to soon attract more than a few young fellows.

A bud ready to burst, Lucy's instincts yearned for freedom to flower. She welcomed the chance to get away for a while as a blooming rose welcomes a place in the sun.

Aunt Sarah stood up to leave and clasped her hands at her bosom. "Lucy, can you git on down thar in the mornin' and stay on a week or two?" she asked, with urgency in her voice.

"Yassum," agreed Lucy, standing up. "I most surely can."

Hannah got to her feet. "She can and she will, dear Sarah."

Sarah took her sister's hand between her palms. "I knowed I could call on you fer this, dear Hannah," she said thankfully, with her eyes closed and head wagging slowly. Then, pinching up the fabric on each side and she lifting her dress a little, she stepped heavily down the porch steps and hurried up the path for home.

The next morning opened bright and cheery, matching Lucy's spirits as she slipped into her store-bought print dress, stuffed a few garments into a tow sack and set out for the Dinkins place. She wouldn't likely encounter any of those bothersome boys, especially the rowdy ones. They all lived higher up the mountain, and she was headed down.

Nellie and Morgan Dinkins lived with their four children in a log house about two miles away, near Nabors Mill, a more prosperous community. The Dinkins farm encompassed eighty acres of mostly rocky land with a year round stream for the animals, and a strong spring to supply water to the house. The place included some cropland, a small hay field, a couple of acres in apple trees, and the rest in rough pasture and woodland. For the Dinkins, it translated into a horse, a mule, a milk cow, several head of beef cattle, half a dozen hogs and turkeys, a coop full of chickens, some saw timber, ample firewood and plenty of hard work.

Though marginal land, the Dinkins spread yielded an assured and reliable level of self-sufficiency a couple of notches above the Nickersons, whose acreage higher up was smaller and rougher. The place was all Morgan Dinkins could keep up with, the children being too young for heavy farm work. It produced plenty for the family table plus some cash income each fall with the sale of corn, apples, a couple of calves and several hogs.

With springtime in her heart and a spring in her step, Lucy made her way down the Broad Hollow path for a mile, and then followed a rutted road over a low hill for another mile, toward a stream flowing across the road.

She felt as though she'd been released from captivity and was bursting forth into a free and open life. She'd broken the cocoon and fluttered fresh as a butterfly off into the bright world, brimming with youthful spirit and promise. Everything seemed to expand and Lucy expanded with it.

A warm breeze floated up the hollow, wafting across white dogwood blossoms and dainty redbud florets. The roadside was strewn with a full palette of wildflowers, the whole scene a riot of scents and sunshine.

Lucy cut a radiant figure as she bounced along barefoot at a jaunty pace. The full flower-print dress sheathing her slender form gave her the look of a moving clutch of native blossoms, as she made her way with skipping feet and a dancing heart, shedding her childhood with every step

Reaching the bottom of the hill, she waved across a rail fence to Haywood Hobson as he lurched along behind his mule, plowing a corn patch.

" Mornin' , Haywood!" she called ebulliently. It was the flower of perky young femininity that called to farmer Hobson, feeling enough the woman to hail him by his first name.

"Holt on now!" The plowman reined his mule to a halt and ejected a side shot of brown tobacco juice into the freshly turned earth.

Stopped behind his plow, Haywood looked over the crossed rails. "Why, Lucy! Whar you off to in yer flowerdy dress, girl?" he asked in his sonorous voice and with a grin that revealed a couple of missing teeth.

"I'm a-gittin' on down to Morgan and Nellie's," she said. "Nellie done got the wheezes right bad and I'm goin' down to set with her fer a week or two."

"Wahl, you mighty good to be a-doin' it, Lucy. But settin' with her hain't gon' help Nellie much."

Lucy looked puzzled. "What I orter do then, Haywood?"

"What you orter do is take on the work. Around the house and all."

"How I gon' do all that?"

"Yer lookin' up to a woman's work, and you gon' have that li'l Janie to help. I'm thinkin' yer good fer it, Lucy."

"Reckon I am," said Lucy tentatively.

"And you orter figger on more'n a week or two."

"Reckon I can, Haywood."

"I know you can. And you tell Nellie I'm goin' to say a prayer fer her." He turned and commanded, "Git up!" as he snapped the mule back into action. Haywood Hobson was a little more religious than most of those further up in the mountains.

Lucy continued on to the stream, a freshet of sparkling water burbling from the forest and flowing across the dirt road into open pasture. Just beyond lay the rocky lane that followed the stream up to the Dinkins place.

With her sack in one hand and the other outstretched for balance, she hopscotched across the rippling brook on dry rock tops and skipped on to the lane. She paused to pluck a fistful of wildflowers. *Nellie goin' to feel better with daisies by the bed,* she thought.

Making her way up the lane, Lucy came to a wall of stacked

fieldstone, and then into the open where large, neatly stacked stone piles spotted the landscape. The house sat above the spring, where a steady flow of water issued from the base of a huge spreading maple tree. Looking below the spring and beyond the barn, she noticed Morgan plowing a field with his horse.

She passed the gum tree beehives and several rough-planked outbuildings that bordered the yard, and continued through a scattering of fruit trees—peach, pear, plum, cherry and quince. Her eye was drawn to the tidy rows of young vegetable plants in the big garden beside the house, and the neat apple orchard that ranged out behind it. Beyond the orchard, rock-studded green pastureland stretched uphill to a verdant forest backdrop that climbed steeply to the top of Hot Mountain.

Pausing a ways out, Lucy held the house in her gaze. A tidy log dwelling anchored by two well-laid stone chimneys, it was twice her family's tiny cabin. A half-story loft topped the two first floor rooms, a lean-to extended the rear and a sitting porch spanned the front. *Haywood, he's right,* she thought. *I got to take on the house work fer Nellie.*

Before approaching the house, Lucy looked back the way she had come. Crossed split rail fences zigzagged over the entire spread, completing the scene. The picturesque homestead had fertile soil but was rough and hard to work. The place was no farmer's dream, but was picturebook pretty and productive enough to provide for the Dinkins family.

Two skinny hounds bounded off the porch and loped over to announce Lucy's arrival. With their noses in the air, the dogs stood in front of her and bayed halfheartedly before trotting off to resume relaxation, having discharged their duty as homestead sentinels.

Lucy stepped up onto the porch that was littered with a pair of cane-bottomed rockers, a bench, a basin and a couple of buckets. A handloom occupied one end. She slid the wooden door peg and slipped inside to the aroma of baking biscuits.

The sick bed had been moved into the main room from the bedroom beyond, crowding the table, chairs and benches a little closer to the iron cookstove. On the bed lay Nellie, her wan face drawn and haggard. Only in her late twenties, she looked old beyond her years. Her lowered eyes and labored breathing, and the tin cup nearly slipping from her fingers, made Lucy think she was asleep. But she looked up and smiled weakly.

Lucy spoke first. "I done come on down to be with you, Nellie," she said, as she arranged the flowers in a cup and placed them on the bedside table.

Nellie's eyes brightened. "You a good girl, Lucy. You the onliest one, 'ceptin' my mama, what done come to set with me," she said feebly. "Lucy, I'm havin' the awfulest spell of the wheezes. I cain't hardly git up, and I cain't do nothin' atall."

Lucy eased onto the edge of the bed and took Nellie's limp hand. "I done come to stay with you until you gits better, Nellie. I'm goin' to help you and the family until you up and offen this bed."

Nellie smiled weakly at the welcome news. "My Janie, she a good li'l mama's helper but she hain't up to all the work," she said softly. "And Morgan, he been helpin' a li'l, but he right busy gittin' the crop in the ground. And he hain't got no hand fer the cookin', no how."

In the faint light, a pot and a kettle simmered on the stovetop, and biscuits baked in the oven. Nellie had been directing Janie in preparing the mid-day dinner, the main meal. The child had gone to the garden to gather early spring greens.

Little Janie, the oldest of four but only ten years old, came through the door with a basket of mustard leaves in one hand and a bundle of cookstove firewood in the other. Her mother motioned her over to her bedside. The girl deposited her load and approached slowly.

"You remember my cousin Lucy, child?" Nellie glanced toward Lucy.

"Yassum," said Janie, her shy eyes meeting Lucy's.

"She done come down to help us until Mama gits better. Now git

THE TALE OF A WOODS COLT

Mama another cup of Jimson."

This happy news put a smile on Janie's face. She took the tin cup from her mother's fingers and dropped in a few dried leaves, over which she poured hot water from the kettle. She placed the steaming cup beside the daisies at the bed.

Nellie's strong potion was smoke-dried Jimson weed,[1] a native herb used as the sovereign remedy for the wheezes. As with all herbal medicine, it was considered fully effective only when taken on the full moon. As the moon was waxing, Morgan had gathered some of the weed where it grew by the barnyard, and hung it above the stove to dry. Then it was administered to Nellie on the full moon, which was today. She sipped the foul and bitter brew with a wrinkled nose.

"I cain't hardly git it down, but I has to have it," she said, in resignation. "It's the onliest thing what'll cure my wheezes. It makes my head turn. I don't know which from whether."

Jimson on the full moon'll most sartainly git her past the wheezes, thought Lucy. It was a comforting thought.

Lucy immediately took over cooking duties, and sent Janie out to the spring for a bucket of water. She cut the stems from the mustard leaves and put them in a pot to boil with a chunk of fatback. *Li'l Janie, she fer sure glad to see me*, she thought. *We gon' git on just fine.*

The staple of the meal was smoked ham, a slab of which lay on the stove shelf. Lucy spooned a little lard into the iron skillet, sliced the ham and set it to frying. Once the ham was out of the pan, she stirred some flour and water into the meat drippings for a thick gravy.

Janie came through the door with her shoulders tilted and an arm stretched tightly under the weight of the wooden water bucket.

"Lucy! I done dip the water in the bucket when ol' frog, he done jump right in!" she exclaimed. "I done throwed him out with my hand!"

---

[1] Short for Jamestown weed, a native plant named for the 1607 Virginia colony whose members discovered the weeds hallucinogenic and poisonous properties.

"Wahl, you done right good, Janie," said Lucy, amused. "Whar's ol' frog now?"

"He down in the branch now, whar I throwed him."

Hmm, thought Lucy. *Ol' frog, he might had somethin' scare't outen his tail end into the water.* Then it occurred to her; *the drinkin' water done been set out. I'm gon' bile this h'yar bucket fer dishes.*

"Set it right thar by the stove, Janie."

Nellie chuckled softly in mild amusement at Janie's frog adventure and then drained her cup.

Without being called to dinner, Morgan had come in from the field and put his horse in the barn pasture. With no clocks or the ability to tell time, he had the mountain farmer's keen sense of sun time.

He trudged up from the barn, calling the children in from various diversions. "C'mon now and git yer dinner!" He poured a little water from the porch basin on each of their hands, then washed his own and splashed a double handful on his face.

Morgan followed the three youngsters in, stooping his lanky frame through the low doorway. As his face came back up, he saw Lucy at the stove finishing the cooking.

"How do, Miss Lucy," he said politely, removing his straw hat. Morgan had accorded her the status of young adult commensurate with what he saw her doing—preparing the meal for his family. He had expected to help Janie finish and serve the food. It wasn't man's work but he was a good husband willing to pitch in during his wife's illness. Seeing Lucy at the stove was a welcome surprise.

" Mornin', Morgan. I done come on down to help Nellie while'st she got the wheezes."

"I'm mighty glad to see you, Lucy," he said, with his crooked smile and easy demeanor, his intent blue eyes meeting hers. "I hain't much at cookin' and, besides, it's women's work."

Lucy just smiled and turned back to her task.

Morgan, an energetic man in his mid-thirties, was clean-shaven, had most of his teeth and was considered, in the local jargon, good to look at. He had bought the farm from Arnold Nabors right after he and Nellie married. Most of the eighty acres was rough land on the fringe of Arnold's large and more productive estate. But the price was right at two hundred fifty dollars, with Arnold holding the note for the entire amount. Morgan had managed to pay it off in ten years by thrifty living and hard work.

The Dinkins' position—geographically, economically and socially—was between the abjectly poor neighbors living higher on the mountains and the modestly comfortable ones occupying the land just below theirs. No one around Nabors Mill, even those possessing large acreage, would be considered well off. It was all marginal land, fertile but much of it hilly, rocky and hard to work.

After tipping his hat to Lucy and absorbing the good fortune of her arrival, Morgan stepped over to his wife, looked approvingly at the empty cup, sat down on the edge of the bed and took her hand in his. "Nellie, you goin' to git past the spell," he said gently. "You hain't goin' to suffer much more. Ol' Jimson goin' to make you better."

She lifted her eyes to his and smiled weakly. "If the Lord's a-willin'," she said in a labored voice.

"Yass, and I just thanks the Lord fer sendin' Lucy on down. It wahr the Lord's doin'," Morgan said, with eyes cast upward. "The Lord and ol' Jimson goin' to take care of you now, Nellie," he said, meeting her weak gaze.

Lucy was glowing at Morgan's comment. He rose, stepped over to the stove and said, in a teasing tone, "Lucy, yer lookin' mighty handy with that stove, no older'n you is."

"Wahl, Morgan, I just might be a mite older than I actual is," she replied, adding a sly smile to her repartee as he pondered the paradox.

"Wahl, it don't make no never mind to me. I'm just glad you knows how to cook," he said appreciatively. "I'm a-willin' but I just hain't got no head fer cookin' and I hain't got no hand with the stove neither," he said before taking his place at the head of the table. The children all slid onto the side benches.

Lucy served up the food: potatoes from the big pot, greens from the small pot and ham slices with a plate of biscuits, plus a boat of gravy. There was butter, buttermilk and fresh milk. She fixed a plate for Nellie and placed it at bedside before taking her own seat at the table.

The children took their father's lead in cupping their hands. Though with no experience of prayer in her own home, Lucy followed by putting her palms together.

Morgan, clasping his meaty farmer hands together, said the table grace. "Thank you, Lord, fer this h'yar food and fer our home and fer our family. Thank you fer sendin' Lucy and please take away my Nellie's wheezes, amen."

The Dinkinses were religious only in a simple way. A large picture of Jesus with a halo looked down upon the room. There was a pair of other religious pictures on the walls. One showed heavenly rays of light beaming down through billowing clouds to enlighten the sinners on earth. The other depicted Adam and Eve being driven from the Garden of Eden. There was no Bible. None of them could read.

The healthy appetites of people who live by continuous exertion soon demolished the dinner, except for Nellie's. She wasn't hungry and Lucy had to coax her to eat half her plate.

Following dinner, Morgan stepped out onto the front porch. The lord of his manor, he stretched his long frame out on the floorboards for a nap, as was his habit. The smaller children went outside to play, leaving Lucy and Janie to clean up the dinnerware. Mercifully, Nellie drifted off to sleep.

In time, Morgan woke and got to his feet. He stretched and, with his arms dangling from his slack shoulders, ambled off in his clodhopper boots, back down to the field to continue his task of getting the corn crop in the ground.

While Morgan toiled in the field below the barn, Lucy and Janie took on the household and homestead chores. Together they went down to the spring where Janie filled a bucket and Lucy pulled a couple crocks of yesterday's milk from the spring box.

"Janie, I'll git to churnin' the butter, and you git in fahrwood and peel the taters and turnips fer supper."

Janie lugged the water up to the kitchen and then loaded the wood box by the cookstove while Lucy put the crocks on the porch and skimmed off the cream. The skimmed milk went into the slop bucket and the cream went into a butter churn, a bucket-sized cylindrical wooden device made of white oak, with a couple of paddles on the inside and a handle on the outside to turn them.

Lucy was sitting on the porch cranking the churn handle to separate the cream into butter and buttermilk. Janie came out carrying a knife, a pot and a pail of potatoes and turnips, and sat down beside her.

"Lucy, I been so scare't fer Mama," she said, paring a twist of skin off a potato. "She hain't never been this bad off afore."

"You and me and yer daddy gon' to take good care of her, Janie."

"Ever night I been afear't she might go to the Lord when I'm sleepin'," said Janie, her face clouding with worry.

Lucy paused her churning and took Janie's hand in hers.

"Now Janie, yer mama gon' get better soon," said Lucy, with a reassuring hand squeeze. "Bed rest and ol' Jimson gon' fix her right up. I'm sure of it," she said, taking hold of the churn handle again.

"I'm glad you's here, Lucy. So me and Daddy don't have to worry so much," said Janie, as she took another potato and turned it against the sharp blade of her knife.

"And I'm gon' stay long as it takes fer Nellie to git well and up offen the bed," assured Lucy, continuing the tiring task of turning cream into butter. "It's like churnin' this butter, Janie. You keep at it until it's done."

After dropping the last peeled turnip into the pot, Janie dumped all the peelings into the slop bucket. "Time to go feed the chickens and turkeys," she said, disappearing inside with the full pot in her hands.

Janie fed the birds by scattering feed grain on the ground, causing them to dash about pecking it all up, and pecking each other in the competitive frenzy. The poultry were free to forage all over, so the grain was extra food to increase egg and meat production.

Lucy was using a wide wooden spoon to stir the butter in fresh water, a washing that she repeated several times to prevent souring, when Janie came back out on the porch to help pack it into wooden molds.

"What meat you think we orter have fer supper?" asked Lucy.

"We hain't had no chicken since Mama got sick."

"Then we gon' have fresh chicken on the table," declared Lucy.

Janie wasn't old enough to be using an axe, so it fell upon Lucy to kill the bird. They corralled a cackling hen into the coop where it fluttered frantically but was soon grabbed by Lucy. Gripping both legs and a wing, she walked the squawking fowl over to the chopping block.

The children, seeing the impending translation of a live being into their supper, gathered round the execution arena. The killing tools were a short gum tree log, set on end as a chopping block, and an old axe that was too worn for other uses. The act was simple in concept but tricky in practice. The axe had to land squarely on the feathered neck, which was connected to a moving head.

Decapitating the chicken required skill in aiming and timing. Leaning over, Lucy laid the bird on the block. She held the body with her left hand and the axe in her right, with her hand choked half way up the handle. She could hold the body still but the panicked head thrashed about, making the neck a moving target. With the blade poised above the victim, she paused for a moment to let the creature calm a bit.

"Ary one of you wants to chop off this h'yar chicken head fer me?" asked Lucy teasingly, looking at the children.

The little Dinkinses shook their heads and took a collective step backwards.

Down swung the axe... Tchock! Off went the head in a spurt of blood.

The children sucked in a startled breath. They'd seen it often but that moment of death still held a morbid fascination.

The executioner released the headless bird to frantically dash in random directions, to the great amusement of all. Its adrenaline depleted, the chicken soon collapsed. Lucy took it into the house and dunked it into the pot of boiling water on the stove. Scalding the bird made the feathers easier to pluck out, a job that was done outside by Janie. The naked carcass then went back to Lucy for gutting and cutting.

Lucy and Janie were a team. Lucy was old enough to seem grown up to Janie, but young enough to make Janie feel just a little more grown up herself.

But their bond would soon be strained by the unforeseeable.

FOUR
Dalliance

Lucy's first week with the Dinkinses stretched through a second, and then a third and into a fourth. Nellie, her lungs still wracked by illness, was improving—but slowly.

Evening approached and it came time for Lucy to milk the cow, a familiar chore, for milking had been her job at home. The light brown Jersey cow stood placidly at the fence gate bars above the barnyard. She was a prized possession that grazed the rocky hill pasture with the beef cattle, but was conditioned to come in at milking time. So there she was, waiting patiently at the bars.

Lucy picked up the enameled metal milk bucket and a small wooden pail of water, pattered down the porch steps and took up a quick pace to the pasture gate. She slid the four bars to the side, let the cow out onto the path to the barn, put the bars back up and followed the animal on down, its neck bell dinging with every plodding step.

She tied the cow's bell collar to an iron ring in the barn and poured out a ration of grain into the feed box. After splashing water on the udder and teats, and wiping them down, she positioned a three-legged milking stool beside the animal and slid the milk pail in under the udder.

In the manner of milkmaids for centuries, she squatted on the short stool and, with hands in rhythmic alternation, squeezed all four teats in rotation—squeeze, squirt, shish; squeeze, squirt, shish until the udder was empty and the pail full. She poured a little milk for the cat, which was waiting eagerly at its pan, and untied the cow to spend the night in the barn.

Lucy had just unlatched the barn door and stepped one foot out when she heard the stable door open on the other side of the barn. She glanced back to see Morgan leading his horse in. He looked up, his eyes meeting hers for a long moment. She broke a shy smile, to which he responded with a slight tilting nod of his head.

She latched the door behind her, turned and started up the path to the house as a pleasant sensation washed over her.

Lucy took care of the milk out on the porch, pouring it through a strainer cloth to remove bits of straw and dirt that had fallen off the cow. Half the milk went into a jug with a bung stopper, and the rest she poured into a crock to let it separate. It would take a full day for all the cream to rise to the top. She finished by toting the crock and jug down to the spring box, a tight wooden cubicle fitted into the cold spring water just where it issued from the earth. There she paused and looked back toward the barn, intrigued by Morgan's intent gaze.

Lucy put the milk in, immersing the jug and crock in water inside the small box. The cool water kept milk and cream fresh for several days, and the box kept the creatures out. Nighttime would bring out the opossums, raccoons and bobcats, foragers that liked nothing better than to get at some fresh cream. She hurried back up to the house to prepare supper.

Morgan came up from the barn and went to playing tickle with the children on one end of the porch. On the other end, the hounds lay flat out on the floorboards, sedated by the heat.

Inside, Lucy and Janie sweated over the hot cookstove, preparing supper. Cooking was a juggling act; they had to keep the firebox stoked, lift the round stove lids to shuffle the fiery coals beneath and shift the pots and pans around on the flat iron top for a steady temperature, plus bake corn pone in the oven.

Beside the stove sat the skimmed milk bucket, collecting all the cooking waste and table scrapings. This became hog food. The dogs got leftover corn pone and gravy, along with any bones and meat scraps. Not a particle of food was wasted.

"Janie, fix Mama another cup of Jimson," said Lucy, seeing that cooking was under control. The full moon had returned, prompting another herbal treatment. Three cups during the day was the acknowledged dose, taken before meals.

"Lucy, you want I should fetch another bucket of water?"

"They's enough hot in the kettle fer yer jimson. Then go fetch another bucket and put it on fer dishes."

Janie flicked some of the dry leaf into a cup and poured steaming hot water over it. "H'yar Mama," she said, holding out the cup.

Nellie sipped at her bitter elixir. "Least ways I hain't got no worse't," she said, crediting the first round of the weed taken four weeks earlier. "This h'yar orter pull me on through."

Janie grabbed the wooden bucket and made for the door.

"You look out now, lest ol' frog jump right down yer dress!" teased Lucy, pulling a chuckle from Nellie and a blush from Janie. Lucy instinctively knew the importance of keeping spirits up in this time of family stress. Nellie had been sick for six weeks.

Returning from the spring, Janie hauled the full bucket, sans frog, up the porch steps.

"Janie, pour a li'l in the porch basin; that's a good girl," said her father.

Morgan washed his hands and splashed his face on the porch before coming in. He nodded politely to Lucy, who met his glance with a demure smile, keeping her hands in motion on the stove. Morgan took a seat by Nellie.

"I done got the last bit of the plantin' most all done, and I even done had time to fix that paster fence I been layin' off fer months," he said, holding her hand in his.

"That's right good, Morgan. You hain't gittin' much behind time like we wahr a-fearin'," murmured Nellie softly, taking a final sip of Jimson.

Morgan, sweaty in his blue shirt and brown ducks, sat with Nellie for a quiet minute, hands joined, his eyes meeting hers in a silent embrace.

Lucy and Janie had choreographed the meal—frying chicken,

boiling peas, new potatoes and greens, baking corn pone and stirring up a batch of gravy such that it was all finished at about the same time. She turned to Janie and said, "Call 'em in!"

Janie popped her head out the door and yelled "Supper!" The three younger ones washed hands and filed through the opening. They didn't have to be called twice.

Morgan said the table grace and everyone dug in heartily. Even Nellie managed to nearly finish her plate, after which she fell asleep. *Her appetite gitten' better*, thought Lucy, with satisfaction.

"Supper wahr some kind of fine eatin'," Morgan said, licking the last of it from his lips. "Lucy, you and Janie been doin' real good," he said as he stood to leave the table.

Twilight lingered long into the evening. Morgan took up his seat in the porch rocker to rest his tired bones and contemplate the next day of work.

After supper, Lucy took charge. "Janie, you clean up and I'll go slop the hogs," she said as she scraped the final table scraps into the skimmed milk and added some feed meal to the slop bucket.

The hog pen, a board-fenced enclosure that lapped across the stream to supply the animals with fresh water, lay below the spring. The hogs had trampled and wallowed the lower end by the stream into a fetid muddy mess and a pig's paradise. A wooden plank trough lay along the upper fence. The animals were fed by pouring the slop over the boards into the trough without having to enter the pen. Hogs fly into a competitive feeding frenzy when the slop bucket appears. Going into the pen with the bucket can be dangerous.

Lucy took hold of the bucket and slipped through the door onto the porch.

"Lucy, take care with that big ol' boar hog," said Morgan. He'd bought a boar the day before to breed the sows. "Don't git yer hand in too far."

Lucy paused at the top of the steps.

"Ol' boar hog hain't goin' to git nary one of my hands. I need both my two hands to take care of you and the family, Morgan," she replied confidently, hoping he would see her as a competent young woman, not just a girl trying to escape childhood.

Full bucket in hand, Lucy made her way down to the pen and poured the contents over the fence into the trough, setting off much squealing and jostling among the grunting and snorting porkers as they slurped up the slop as fast as they could.

She sauntered back to the porch and lingered, sitting on the steps below Morgan, imbued with the calm tranquility of the dying day. The fading sunset yielded to a growing gleam in the east where the full moon breached the horizon. In the cloudless, windless sky of the evening star, the bird of the twilight broke the stillness from the forest edge with its haunting call.

"Hwip-poor-*hw'ill*" "hw'ip-poor-*hw'ill*" "hw'ip-poor-*hw'ill*"

They sat in serene silence. The smoky orange moon rose and climbed and brightened to a beaming yellow, suffusing the homestead in a surreal pale glow. In time, the whippoorwill went quiet. Morgan and Lucy rose in unison to go inside.

They stepped into the dim room in the feeble light of a solitary oil lamp burning low at Nellie's bedside. She lay deep in peaceful sleep, and the children slumbered in the loft above. Morgan quietly latched the door behind him.

Lucy slept on a cornhusk mattress on the floor at the foot of Nellie's bed. Morgan took a few steps up the stairs and paused. Lucy felt him taking a long look at her as she snuffed the lamp. With a warm glow in her heart, she curled herself on the course tick and pulled a blanket up around her.

Lucy rose before dawn, filled Nellie's water cup and went about firing up the cookstove. The iron cookstove was a luxury compared with cooking on the Nickerson's open-hearth fire. She dipped a couple of corncobs in coal oil, stuffed them into the firebox and lit them off with a match struck on the black iron stovetop. In went some sticks of wood and on top she placed the water kettle. Then it was down to the spring for two buckets of fresh water, one for the porch basin and the other for breakfast.

She grabbed Nellie's chamber pot and scooted out to her morning toilet before the family crowded the facility. The Dinkinses were a bit more refined than the Nickersons. They had a pit privy by the barn, a one-holer with a plank seat and no door.

The sky hinted at light when Lucy paused on the porch to wash; then she was off to the barn for morning milking and to turn the cow loose into the pasture. After that, she strained the milk and toted the crocks to the spring box. Only then did she go in to start breakfast.

Morgan came down the stairs toting a chamber pot in one hand and his shaving kit in the other. He slowed as he passed Lucy, who was fussing at the stove.

"Mornin'," he said, looking over and flashing her a smile on his way out.

"Mornin', Morgan." She didn't look up. She was pleased by his attention but discomfited that he hadn't first gone to his wife's bedside.

Dressed in their homespuns, the children filed down from the loft and out the door to line up down at the privy, and then return to wash up on the porch, where they liked to linger and watch their father shave. He had whipped up a soapy froth in his mug, brushed it on his face, and was now carefully drawing a straight razor down his cheek as he leaned into a small mirror hanging by the door.

"Janie, fetch in another bucket of water," said Lucy when the girl reported for duty.

Nellie had awakened and was sitting up in bed, sipping water when Morgan came back in and sat down next to her.

"You lookin' a mite better this mornin', Nellie."

"I'm feelin' a sight better, but I hain't breathin' no better," she said weakly.

"Wahl, ol' Jimson always takes a spell to do its good," he said, counseling patience.

"I reckon I just got to bide the time," she allowed.

"Breakfast now," called Lucy, drawing the family to the table set with fried eggs, scrapple, milk, gravy, cold beans, hot biscuits with butter, quince jelly, milk and home-roasted coffee. Even Nellie cleaned her plate.

After washing the breakfast ware, Lucy and Janie divided up the chores. Water was hauled and the floor was swept. Fowl were fed and eggs were gathered. Ashes were carried out and stove wood was loaded in.

Dinner was prepared and the family fed. Nellie was made comfortable. The chores were nearly done. Then it was milking time.

Morgan appeared with his horse at the barn just as Lucy was inside wiping down the cow's udder. She looked up to see him step through the barn door. He had come in early. *He most likely got some other chores to do*, she thought.

"Lucy," he said, nodding a greeting.

"Morgan," she said, smiling. She was glad to see him.

Morgan proceeded to wipe down and groom the horse, while Lucy scooped feed into the cow's box and sat down to milk. She glanced over to see him taking a long look at her. She quickly looked back to her task and started squeezing the cow teats, shooting jets of milk into her pail.

Morgan found a pitchfork and climbed up into the loft to toss down some hay for the horse. After a couple of tosses, the sound of the pitchfork ceased. Lucy felt Morgan's gaze from above, behind her. She kept on milking.

Finally she couldn't resist. She looked around and up to see Morgan staring silently down upon her. He broke a sheepish grin and swung back into his pitchfork. She flushed and turned back to her milking.

The horse was fed and the cow was milked. Morgan descended

the ladder just as Lucy stood up. They took a step toward each other.

"Let me carry the milk bucket fer you, Lucy," he said, reaching down and lifting the pail, his arm sliding against hers. She quivered at the strange wave rippling through her.

"Thank you, Morgan," she said, trying to seem steady and collected.

They departed the barn and started up the path side-by-side, his arm swishing against hers. A warm flush fell over her that shrank the minute down to mere seconds.

"H'yar you are, Lucy," said he as he lifted the milk pail up onto the porch. "I gots me some wood splittin' to do," he said. He disappeared around the end of the house. Lucy fetched the strainer cloth and poured the fresh milk through it to the sound of Morgan axing cookstove wood back at the chopping block.

Morgan came in and sat with Nellie before supper. "Nellie, you hain't lookin' so peaked today," he said optimistically.

"Ol' Jimson done me right good, Morgan."

"You best take yer bed rest and eat all yer vittles, now."

"I'm goin' to be up offen this bed afore too long," she said hopefully.

"Lucy and li'l Janie, they done got the women's work under the full control," he said. "Hain't no need fer you to come up offen the bed till yer feelin' up to it."

"How you gittin' on in the field?"

"I done got all the weed chopped outen the corn. I'm goin' to scyze the hay tomorrow. I'll be dogged iffen I cain't git it all cut afore dinner," he said optimistically.

Supper was served a little late that evening. Morgan withdrew to the porch rocker to enjoy the soft close of day. Lucy and Janie cleaned up. Nellie fell asleep. The four children retired. Lucy felt drawn to the porch to be with Morgan, but resisted. She was a bit frightened by her feelings from the afternoon, so she sought refuge in sleep.

Morgan lingered much longer, alone on the porch in his rocker. The moon was well risen by the time he rose and went inside. He struggled with conflicting inner voices as he stood looking down upon Nellie and Lucy, both in serene slumber. If only life could remain so placid. He climbed the stairs and spent a restless night of fitful dreams.

The next day dawned bright and clear. After breakfast, Morgan pulled a scythe from the tool shed and set off toward the hay field, with the long handle laid over his shoulder and Lucy weighing on his mind.

He gripped the wooden handles and waded into the waist-high grass, sliding the curved blade back and forth in long rhythmic strokes, his muscles tensing and relaxing, his body swaying with every forward thrust, in a reverie of motion.

Warm sweat poured from his brow and body, dripping from his face and soaking his shirt. The hours collapsed into minutes. He lost track of time. Just as he strained to swing several mighty strokes, Lucy's call snapped him back to the moment.

"Yee'ar!! Morgan!! Dinner!!"

Morgan paused and, with his stilled scythe blade resting on the ground, lingered to catch his breath and survey the results of his exertion. He'd cut most of the field. He turned his tired body toward the barn and ambled down to where he rested the scythe against the sideboards, and then made his way up to the house.

After dinner, Morgan put down a folded feed sack for a pillow and stretched out for a nap on the porch floor, putting his straw hat over his face.

Presently Lucy came out and sat in a porch rocker to mend a tear in Janie's dress. Rocking slowly, she hummed softly as she stitched on the patch.

He came awake to her soothing notes. Lying with his eyes closed in the fullness of her presence, warm waves stirred a pleasure in him.

In time, Lucy rose and withdrew inside, breaking Morgan's spell. His pleasant desire subsided and he rose to face his afternoon of toil. He devoted the balance of the day to cutting the rest of the field, and then to using a broad wooden-toothed rake to pull the dried morning cut into long windrows. He worked with a mesmerizing rhythm, imagining taking Lucy into his arms with every stroke, with every reach and pull.

Morgan was most pleased with himself. He had cut the entire field and raked the first half of what he'd cut. He was leaning on his rake and admiring the results of his efforts when he heard the dinging cowbell. He looked back to see Lucy trailing behind the animal, as it plodded toward the barn. He took in a long drink of her, until she disappeared behind the front barn door.

He laid the rake and scythe over his shoulder and started for the barn. His horse and mule had not worked that day. They were out to pasture, needing neither grain nor grooming. He would find something else to do at the barn. *I might's well sharpen up the scyze*, he thought, giving himself an excuse to be near the milkmaid.

Morgan stepped through the rear barn door, rake and scythe in hand, to see her wiping down the cow's udder in the dim milking stall, arousing him to imagine her stroking him. He found a whetstone and dragged a stool as close to her as he dared. Her smile beamed approval, so he eased himself down with the scythe blade on his lap.

He commenced rhythmically stroking the hard steel blade; she put her hands to the soft warm teats. The shhh-eeww of his sharpening and the shish-shish of her milking seemed to merge, sending a rush of desire through his body. He glanced at her. He was barely minding his task and he thought she was barely minding hers.

When the milk pail was full, they rose. He turned away from her to put away the whetstone. "Let me carry the pail, Lucy," he called over his shoulder.

She stood unwavering as he approached. Her allure drove all else from his mind. He paused, and then drew slowly closer as she met his gaze with liquid eyes and parted lips. His arms begged to wrap her lithesome body. Time stood still.

"We best be a-gittin' on up," she whispered, breaking his spell.

His body quivered as he reached down and lifted the pail. He stumbled a bit as he followed her up the rough path, his eyes drawn from his own footsteps to her fluid motion. From the porch, Lucy took the milk pail and went in to get supper underway. Outside, Morgan disappeared.

Inside, Lucy was distracted. She fumbled as she and Janie pulled supper together, spilling some beans and she nearly let the corn pone burn.

She touched her arm to the hot stove. "Ow!"

"Lucy!" cried Janie.

"Hain't nothin'," said Lucy quickly. "Hain't nothin' atall."

Lucy rubbed lard on her burned forearm. It wasn't a bad burn—just a streak of red—but she felt embarrassed to seem so clumsy.

"I'm just not myself this evenin'," she remarked to no one in particular, hoping her distraction wasn't too noticeable.

Lucy avoided looking his way when Morgan came in and sat with Nellie.

"How's my Nellie doin' today?" he said, stroking her hand and arm.

"I hain't too bad. I done slept right smart," she said softly, with a peaceful smile and serene eyes, enjoying his touch.

"Wahl, I done got all the hay cut. I'll git it all loaded in tomorrow evenin', once't the dew done dried off."

"That thar's a mite much fer one evenin', Morgan."

"I'm goin' to git Lucy to help, and git it all in afore supper," he said. Lucy's ears perked up.

"Lucy, you good to help me git the hay in tomorrow evenin'?" he called over his shoulder.

Lucy's pulse quickened at the prospect of spending an afternoon doing man's work with Morgan.

"Why sure, Morgan," she said, looking at Janie. "Long's Janie can handle the supper."

THE TALE OF A WOODS COLT

Dense air hung heavily on the morning, the warm humidity a portent of a late thunderstorm. Morgan spent the early hour nailing up some more planks on the hog pen where the boar had rooted under it and almost gotten out. Then he went to the barn to prepare the wagon and harness for the afternoon task.

The dew had dried by mid-morning, so he used up the time before dinner to pull the rest of the cut grass into windrows. On the way in to eat, he retrieved the horse and mule from the barn pasture and positioned them in the stable.

Inside at the stove, Lucy gave Janie some instructions.

"Bring the cow and pails to the barn. Then you got to do most all the supper because I'll be helpin' yer daddy git up the hay this evenin'. Can you do it?"

"Yass, I reckon," said Janie, nodding tentatively and looking challenged.

After dinner, Lucy, tingling with anticipation, stepped out onto the porch with Morgan, he in his canvas ducks and straw hat, and she in a course dress, old sunbonnet and worn shoes borrowed from Nellie. From the woodline came the melancholy call of the mourning dove.

Hu-huuu, Hu-huuu.

"Ol' rain crow's a-callin'," she said.

Hu-huuu, Hu-huuu.

"Might come on to stormin' afore supper," he said. "We best git right to it."

Cradling a jug of spring water in each arm, they hurried down to the barn where Morgan hitched the two draft animals to the hay wagon, tossed on a couple of pitchforks, and led the rig out from the open end of the building.

She climbed onto the wagon and took her place beside him on the bench seat. He flicked the reins and they were off with a lurch and a wobble, rolling out toward the field.

He stopped the wagon between two windrows, hopped off and started pitching up forkfuls of the dry grass onto both sides of the flat bed. Her job was to fork the hay around such that it stacked up evenly in a stable heap that would not topple off as the load swayed back to the barn.

Morgan moved the wagon down the rows until it was filled, which was when the pile was so high that he could no longer toss forkfulls to the top. Then it was back to the barn where he pulled in under the open side to unload. Morgan stood on the stack and pitched hay up into the mow where Lucy forked it around into even layers.

They gulped swallows of water from the jugs and then went back for another load. Their only rest was in riding back and forth, and the momentary water breaks. In the barn for the second time, Lucy picked up a water jug-and felt Morgan's presence behind her. She could hear him breathing. She did not turn around. Her blood was pulsing and a current coursed up her spine.

She gasped as she felt his strong hands gently wrap her waist, his palms flat below her navel. As he gently pressed himself against her, her breath quickened and a rush surged through her. He released his hold and she turned to face him; a quiet moment passed before they mounted the wagon and rolled back out to the field in silence.

Morgan had just topped off the fifth load and paused to wipe a sleeve across his sweaty brow, when he took notice of something at the edge of the woods.

"Poplar leaves done turn't up," he said, pointing. "Wind's a-comin' up the country. Rain's a-comin', sure as shootin'."

He looked up at Lucy. "Hain't even two more loads out h'yar," he said. "We most surely goin' to git it all in."

After hurriedly unloading in the barn, they rode the empty wagon back into the hayfield, facing dark clouds looming in the southwestern sky. The two bent feverishly into their work, energized in the electric air of the gathering storm.

THE TALE OF A WOODS COLT

"Wind's a-pickin' up," he gasped, panting heavily. "Won't be long now!"

Lightning flashed in the distance as they topped off the load, followed by the low rumble of thunder as they started back in at a pace faster than prudent. They both stayed on the wagon now, furiously pitching the hay up into the mow.

"Hain't but less'n half a load left!" cried Morgan. "Let's git it all in!" He flicked the team to a brisk speed, racing back out to the field. As he lashed the reins to spur the animals on, Lucy clung to the seat with one hand and to Morgan's shirt with the other while the empty wagon careered wildly out to the last windrow.

Over at the next mountain, jagged forks of lightning split the sky, followed on by deep booms of thunder. They scrambled to toss on the last of the hay, under the roiling black turbulence of an angry sky rushing in overhead.

He glanced at the menacing squall bearing down. "We best git on smartly! It's a-comin'!" he cried, the two of them clambering hastily up onto the wagon seat. "Giddup!!" he yelled, lashing the reins against the skittish team.

Claps of thunder overtook them during the wild dash to the barn. Clinging to the seat and to Morgan, Lucy looked back to see dazzling lightning slicing the air and sheets of rain sweeping the far woods, the thrashing gale tearing at the tree tops. She was charged with the excitement of racing the onslaught and flushed with the exhilaration of jostling against Morgan, the mad swaying and jolting nearly bouncing them out of the seat.

He pulled the wagon to a halt just at the open side of the barn, to let man and beast catch a breath. Sitting side-by-side, they relaxed and laughed in relief at outrunning the charging storm. In that moment she felt his hand slide onto hers in a titillating clasp.

Falling from high in the boiling clouds, the storm gust swept over them in a rushing refreshment of cool air that brought instant relief to all four sweaty beings.

As the cloudburst closed in across the hay field, Morgan reached for the reins. But before he could pull in under the roof, the sky exploded with a sudden bolt that struck like a cannon shot. The deafening ka-BOOM!! sparked the skittish animals to jerk the wagon forward into the open barn bay with a lurch that flopped Morgan and Lucy back onto the mat of hay, sending his straw hat and her bonnet flying.

In that instant, Lucy found herself bosom to breast in an ardent embrace, his lips pressed to hers. The deluge struck and battered the barn roof, but did nothing to douse the passion on the wagon. Time vanished in the incessant barrage of flashing and crashing, the driving downpour pummeling the barn relentlessly.

Trembling hands fumbled buttons and fabric. Her dress went up with a rip, and his pants came down; they drew together, chest to breast, in a blaze of desire.

The tempest ripped all around them. Torrents of rain flooded down the roof and cascaded from the eaves, enveloping the barn in sheets of water splattering loudly against the earth.

She closed her eyes and felt him come over her and against her, as another fierce bolt and thunderous ka-boom struck nearby. On her back in the warm hay, she spread her legs.

A blinding flash rent the crotch of a close tree in an earsplitting blast. A splatter of hail rattled the roof above. Lucy winced at a stinging twinge, her body tightening at the sharp crack of lightning, then releasing to a warm fullness, tensing and relaxing; rising and falling, and surging to a rushing crescendo.

On their backs, panting and dripping, they lay in a soak of shared sweat. The pounding was over. The fury had subsided and the deluge diminished.

The horse, the mule and the cow stood patiently, waiting.

Sliding their sweaty bodies off the hay, they washed themselves with jug water, arranged their clothes and went back to work. She milked while he unhitched, fed and groomed the two animals.

The storm had died to a distant rumble but the rain kept on, pelting them as they hurried up to the house. They came through the door soaked, dripping and…drained.

"Lucy! Daddy!" cried Janie as she ran to Lucy's side, taking an arm with both hands. "Lucy, it wahr the awfulest storm! I wahr so scare't, I liked to died!"

Morgan went to Nellie.

"It wahr a terrible storm, Morgan. We's a-fear't you two done got struck by lightnin'," she said, with a good deal of relief in her voice and face.

"We just barely done got the entahr field loaded in the barn when the storm hit," he said with satisfaction. "We's in thar when she broke loose." He looked toward Lucy. "Li'l Lucy thar, she a right good field hand and right handy with the hay fork," he said. He stood and went up to the loft find dry clothes.

Everyone was afraid of lightning and thunder. Janie had trembled through the tempest, gripping her mother's hand. The other children had crawled under her bed and whimpered all through the raging wrath of nature.

Morgan came down and Lucy went up to change, and returned to the stove.

"Lucy, I done got the supper cookin'," said Janie. The two of them completed the meal and got the food on the table.

"Janie, carry Mama's supper to her, now. H'yar," said Lucy, handing over the plate of food. Lucy didn't feel composed enough to approach Nellie. *I dast not look Nellie in the eye just yet*, she thought. One glance might spill out an entire confession.

Morgan was with Nellie. "Nellie, you hain't so wheezy this evenin'. Soon's yer strength's up, you goin' to be up on yer feet," he said, encouraging her as she propped herself up in bed.

Janie slid the plate onto her mother's lap.

"I hope yer right, Morgan. I cain't hardly stand bein' in the bed no more."

Morgan took his place at the supper table, with little to say besides grace. After supper, Janie washed up the dishes and Lucy went out to slop the hogs. Nellie was resting easily and Lucy was keen to avoid revealing her own uneasiness.

Lucy came back in, sat the empty bucket by the stove and said, to no one in particular, "Wahl, I best be a-mendin' my dress what got ripped on the wagon." She retrieved the wet garment, found needle and thread and stepped out on the porch, where Morgan was in his rocker. She sat on the bench sewing as he rocked slowly. Nothing was said.

The rain was gone, but damp, still air hung heavily about the place. A breath of foggy mist drifted up from the sodden ground into the cooling dusk. Gentle dripping was the only sound. The curtain of darkness soon fell across the scene.

"Good night," he said, rising.

"Good night." Lucy lingered in the black silence.

She turned in late, and struggled with her conscience into the wee hours. She twisted the thing over in her mind and looked at it from every angle.

Lucy reminded herself that she had come to help the family, not disrupt them. But, she reasoned, they'd not be disrupted if they didn't know. Still, it wasn't right to take up with him, especially when Nellie was down. *But I hain't actual took up with him*, she told herself. She had no intention of getting between Morgan and Nellie.

Yet guilt still stalked her and denied her sleep. It just didn't seem right to serve his manly needs when her cousin couldn't. Then she looked at it from a different slant. Nellie couldn't serve his needs just now and she could, so wasn't that helping? *Iffen Nellie knowed, she gon' be scare't I'm tryin' to take away her man.* But she had no intent to lure him away so there was really nothing to be afraid of. And didn't serving his needs count toward helping the family?

Turning restlessly on her cornhusk mat, she tussled with both sides of the thing, both condemning herself and excusing herself. She finally resolved that she was helping each of them in every way she could. She had not pressed herself on Morgan. She had responded to him. *Besides, it wahr his doin'*, she told herself. With that, she found peace with herself and fell asleep.

Morgan slept soundly. And he felt no conflict as he sat with Nellie the next morning. The idea of a discreet dalliance interfering with his family life hadn't entered his mind.

He was a man who'd stand by his woman. He wasn't one to chase other women, but he wouldn't push them away either. In his mind, a man is a man and it wouldn't be manly to refuse a willing woman.

I hain't goin' to say no, but I hain't goin' to worry no womens what do say no, he thought. *But iffen they's right thar and they's a-willin', then I'm dang sure goin' to be a-willin' too. Thar hain't nothin' wrong with it, long as hain't nothin' said about it to stir up no trouble.*

Reasoning that he had not forced himself on Lucy, Morgan believed that everything was in its natural order. *Besides, it wahr mostly her doin', bein' willin' and all,* he told himself.

Morgan and the children took their places at the breakfast table. Lucy served a plate to Nellie, with whom she felt a new bond—and more than a little nervousness.

The day passed and then it was milking time. Lucy followed the cow into the barn, where Morgan was waiting.

They fell into a hungry embrace and scrambled up into the haymow. He dropped his britches, she lifted her dress and they fell into the hay, hearts pounding and blood pulsing. Her legs went high and wide, her hands pulling him into her. When it was over, the evening resumed. Milking. Supper. Bedtime.

FIVE

The Next Day
Discovery

All was routine until the delights of the haymow. At milking time, Janie went to the privy by the barn. She then decided to visit the milkmaid. She eased the barn door open a little and slipped inside.

Standing fixed for a moment in the dimness of the smelly chamber, she listened and let her eyes adjust to the low light. Beside its feed box stood the cow, but there was no Lucy.

Janie cautiously stepped in a bit further. She heard sounds from above. Two people. *Like I done hear't Mama and Daddy in the night time once't*, she thought, sensing she was trespassing into a mysterious and secret adult world.

"Lucy?" she called feebly, timidly.

The sounds stopped.

She braved a raised voice. "Lucy?!"

Nothing.

I orter not be in the barn just now, she told herself, gripped by the anxious feeling that she had intruded into forbidden space. She quickly tiptoed out and scurried up to the house, trying not to think about what she thought she had heard. *I best see how Mama's a-gitten,* she thought. *Mama might be a-needin' somethin'*, she told herself. *Time to git supper on*. Her racing mind reached for any distraction from knowing what she thought she knew. *Daddy and Lucy!* She started fumbling with the pots and pans.

Back in the barn, Lucy hastily milked the cow and hurried up to the house. When she went in with the milk bucket, she saw Janie at the stove and threw a quick glance at her eyes, searching for a sign.

Janie studied the stove.

"Janie, I'll bring you some milk fer the gravy soon as I strains it," ventured Lucy uneasily, feeling sick. *What she done hear't? What she know about such thangs?* Her tormented mind begged for an answer.

"Yassum." replied Janie, without looking up.

Lucy stopped. There it was–the sign. They were no longer a team. Janie had just inserted a generation between them.

Lucy tried not to show her dread as she went back out to strain the milk. *I don't know what Janie know about mans and womens,* she worried silently. *How much Nellie done see'd in Janie's face?* she wondered fretfully. *How much she actual done tolt Nellie?* She felt she was holding a powder keg with a lit fuse. *I cain't just set out h'yar on the porch,* she thought, as the last of the milk went through the cloth.

Lucy went back in to get it over with. She sat by Nellie, their eyes level. Nellie was sitting on the side of the bed, feeling much improved. She was able to get up and move about a little and to speak without laboring.

"Nellie, you lookin' a whole sight better today then you wahr yesterday," said Lucy, braced for whatever.

"I'm a-feelin' a whole sight better'n I wahr yesterday," said Nellie, looking straight at Lucy with a serene smile. "Won't be fer long now that you can git on home, Lucy."

Lucy saw no additional clue in Nellie's inscrutable countenance. *Wahl, least she didn't git down on me,* she told herself, easing her anxiety. Lucy pondered Nellie's remark about her going home soon. Was it about feeling better or about a worn out welcome? What did Nellie know or suspect? *If she do know, she hain't lettin' on,* she reasoned. Some private time together might reveal more.

Then Lucy had an idea. "Wahl, Nellie, I'm a-thinkin' we's goin' to git you all washed up and into a clean dress tomorrow, and git a fresh cover on the bed," she proposed hopefully.

"Lucy! My, what goodness done got in to you, pamperin' me so?"

Hmmm, thought Lucy. Were those words of pure appreciation, or was there a little suspicion woven into them? Lucy turned it over in her mind and decided to leave it alone. But it made her nervous. She stood and turned to help Janie get the supper on the table.

Morgan had made himself scarce. He was worried about what Nellie might have learned from Janie. He stepped inside just as the children were called in to eat, and took his place at the head of the table. Nellie was able to sit at the other end, shifting Lucy around to a side bench.

"Thank you, Lord, fer the vittles and fer our home and fer our family, and thank you fer sendin' ol' Jimson to heal my Nellie. Amen." He then tucked into his supper a little faster than usual.

Janie picked at her food, eating little and attracting her mother's notice.

"Janie, you hain't hardly ate nothin'. You gittin' sick, child?" Nellie reached over and felt Janie's brow.

"No, Mama. I just hain't hungry atall." She rose, scraped her plate into the slop bucket, picked up a water pail and went out.

Silence overtook the supper table. Morgan said nothing other than, "Pass me that cabbage" and "pass me them 'taters."

"What's wrong Morgan? Cat git yer tongue?" asked Nellie, her humor returning.

Morgan looked up, trying to read her face for signs of any suspicion. He had no idea what Janie understood and what she may have said. "Wahl, I suppose I'm just thinkin' right smart. Uh, about the farm and all," he said as he pushed back from the table, stood up and withdrew to his rocker on the porch.

That left Lucy inside with Janie and Nellie. She uneasily joined Janie in cleaning up but she knew better than to try breaking the girl's sullen silence, as they went through the motions.

Back on her bed, Nellie lay in a lax state of body and expression that offered no further signal to Lucy. *Iffen I can just git through this evenin'*, Lucy thought, *without Janie sayin' or showin' somethin'*. She tried to think of how she could busy herself right up until bedtime, without having to be in Nellie or Janie's presence.

"I best be sloppin' the hogs, and I see the butter's gittin' low. I reckon I'll churn some up," she said to the two of them, looking at neither. Churning could take as long as one wanted, until the cream ran out.

Janie went out to join the other children, moving Lucy to grab the slop bucket and swing out the door right on the girl's heels. She didn't want to press her luck. Dwell time alone with Nellie right now might be risky.

On her way back from the hog pen, Lucy fetched a milk crock from the spring box and deposited it on the porch. She went through the door and, in continuous motion, plopped the empty slop bucket by the stove and grabbed the fresh water bucket with one hand and the churn with the other. "Got to git that thar cream churned up," she said to the furniture, as she slipped back out the door.

Morgan sat rocking faster than usual, such that the rocker squeaked a bit. Lucy placed the churn on the porch edge, dipped the cream in, sat down on the top step and commenced turning the handle. A whippoorwill started up its evening call.

Finally the day died. The children went to bed and Nellie fell asleep. Morgan slowed his rocking, Lucy finished her churning and the whippoorwill closed shop for the night. A loud silence fell across the porch, as neither of them spoke.

Lucy washed the butter and scooped it into wooden molds, exhausting the last peek of light. Morgan rose and, without a word, stepped through the doorway and turned in. Lucy lingered on the porch a while, to be sure she went in to a sleeping family. She would spend a restless night on her pallet at the foot of Nellie's bed.

The early hot spell that had settled over the area continued the next morning, a Saturday. Lucy awoke early from a fitful sleep. She lay on her tick pondering how to manage the day. Having promised to freshen Nellie, she finally decided to make it an all around cleaning day.

Laundry and bathing were more or less monthly events at the Dinkins place, and both were overdue. Lucy thought to make a special contribution to family morale, and maybe subdue the awkwardness in the bargain. *Iffen I can just git 'em to feelin' a mite better,* she thought. She got the project get under way first thing.

"Morgan, can you set the wash kettle up fer me?" asked Lucy while lighting the stove, as he stepped drowsily off the loft stairs, pushing an arm into his shirt sleeve. "I'm goin' to wash up all the clothes and covers," she said, as he put on the rest of his shirt. He went out without a word, sat on the porch and pulled on his boots.

Morgan dragged a huge iron kettle from a shed, along with three iron rods and some hook chain. He pulled it over and went about setting the thing up near the rail fence on the leeward side of the yard. He set the rods in a tripod about six feet high and hung the kettle from three chains under the tripod.

Next he carried over armloads of firewood and put several chunks under the kettle. This usually marked the end of his role on washday, but he wasn't his usual self today. With a bucket in each hand, he shuttled up enough water to half fill the kettle, and lit the fire under it.

Nellie set Janie to collecting the family wardrobe and mattress ticks. "Carry 'em out and put 'em in the kettle, that's a good girl." Janie got herself and her siblings into their gunnysack garb and sent them off to the privy. She went up to the loft and shook cornhusks from the ticks. After stumbling two armloads down the narrow steps, she shuttled the covers and clothes out to the yard kettle where she used the battlin' board, a paddle-like stick, to push and stir the fabrics into the warming water to soak.

After breakfast, Lucy turned to the children. "Cousin Lucy and Janie goin' to scrub ever one of you, soon's I wash yer mama." The three children looked at their older sister, who nodded. They looked at each other, rose in unison and fled out the door.

Morgan went out. Bathing the family was women's business.

Feeling up to light activity, Nellie was on her feet in her nightshirt, helping Lucy and Janie clean up. The three worked in concert, yet none uttered a word until Nellie said "Janie, slip on out and stir the kettle."

Lucy found herself alone to bathe Nellie by the stove. She poured hot and cold water into two basins while Nellie undressed. Bathing used homemade soap and rags steeped in hot water. Lucy wanted to do something special for Nellie, so instead of having her stand at the basin, she seated her and went about scrubbing, rinsing and wiping her from top to bottom.

Lucy was working on the arms and back when Nellie spoke.

"You sure knows how to make a body feel good, Lucy."

Lucy wondered if she'd just heard a double entendre. *Hope she just talkin' about her ownself,* she worried, working her way around to Nellie's breasts and belly.

"I wahr once't as good to look at as you are now," said Nellie. "But havin' four children pulls you down and spreads you out."

Lucy started working on the legs, hoping there was no more to what Nellie said than she actually said. She didn't need to deal with any jealousy. She dipped and soaped up a rag, and handed it to Nellie to wash her own crotch.

"Women's always wonderin' if their man's still gittin' satisfied the way he once't wahr," confided Nellie, pulling the dripping rag up between her legs and making Lucy uneasy. *This hain't soundin' good atall,* she fretted to herself.

Lucy traded the soapy crotch rag for a fresh rinse cloth, and stepped behind Nellie to dry her back.

"Course now, iffen his wife wahr thar fer him, and thar warn't no other woman thar, then he orter ...," Nellie spoke as she stroked the warm rinse rag between her legs.

Lord, oh Lordy! Lucy was alarmed. She felt something coming that wouldn't be pleasant. She kept on patting down Nellie's back from behind.

"... orter just be happy with her and not go gittin' the eye fer no one else," said Nellie. "And that's just how my Morgan is."

Lucy relaxed—a little—as she dried Nellie's belly and bosom. Was Nellie treading on the very edge to torment her? Or was she just confiding her feelings, woman-to-woman?

"Thar now Nellie, you's just like a new woman!" exclaimed Lucy, elevating a simple wipe and dab bath into a full rejuvenation. She patted Nellie's legs and feet with dry rags, pulled a second nightshirt over her head and wrapped a blanket around her. Nellie stretched out on the bed to rest.

Lucy stepped out on the porch and called to Janie. "Let's call in the children now," she requested in a friendly tone, trying not to rub Janie the wrong way. They filed through the door as Lucy pulled a large metal tub from behind the stove. It wasn't big enough to lie in, but two children could stand in it and be washed together.

"Shuck off them clothes, now," said Lucy. They dropped their sack clothes and two stepped into the tub to let Lucy wash and Janie dry them. Janie washed down and dried the third child and then pulled their ill-fitting garments over all three while Lucy changed the tub water.

"Yer next, Janie."

Janie just stood there, arms to her side and eyes cast to the floor. "I can do my ownself," she muttered.

"Course you can, Janie. I didn't mean to say..."

"And I can fix the dinner my ownself, too."

Lucy took the hint and went out to work the laundry. *Lord! I'll hafter be careful with her!* she thought. She was stirring lye soap into the kettle when Morgan appeared, leading the mule carrying a two-bushel sack of corn he'd flopped across its back. He hitched the animal to the porch and went inside, with barely a glance at her.

Janie, looking like a ragamuffin in the tattered burlap gunnysack dress she'd put on after bathing, was marshalling the necessities for cooking dinner.

Morgan went up to change into his good clothes, then stopped at Nellie's bedside.

"Would you be needin' somethin' else from the store, Nellie?" He was feeling a little more at ease in her presence than he had the night before.

Saturday was store day, or rather store days were on Saturday, since Morgan usually shopped monthly. The Dinkinses, with a toe in the cash economy, shopped at the Nabors store, the one closest to their home. He always picked up the usual—green coffee beans, sugar, salt, pepper, coal oil, lime for the privy and nails or other hardware.

"Git a box of matches, and somethin' fer the children," said Nellie.

Lucy was still stirring the wash kettle in the yard when she saw Morgan emerge and step off the porch. He tossed his work pants on the laundry pile and untied the mule, whereupon man and beast disappeared down the lane.

Lucy wanted to talk to Morgan, but could see he was reluctant. She didn't know what it might take to set off a scene with Nellie, and Morgan must now also have the same concern, considering his reticence. If only she knew what Janie had said to Nellie or what Nellie had intuited from Janie and Morgan's faces? *Womens can see the entahr thang right thar in the face, and the mans cain't see nothin' atall*, she reminded herself uneasily.

Lucy stuffed his pants into the nearly boiling kettle and spent the next half hour stirring and churning the hot mass, while turning the morning over in her mind. She pulled fabrics out one at a time and went about rubbing and kneading them arduously on the washboard, worrying all the while if there was any more to come from Nellie.

The Nabors store and gristmill sat at the intersection of two rocky roads, right where the flat land reached in between low hills and lapped at the foot of the mountains. An area of modest farms, the place itself was called Nabors Mill, or just Nabors.

Several well-populated hollows opened into Nabors, making the modest community the commercial center for a swath of mountains. And Nabors was about as far off the mountain as the most isolated mountaineers ever ventured.

The Nabors general store was everything a country store should be. It wasn't large, but it stocked a little of everything. The inside was one big display, with shelves and racks and hooks holding goods on all sides, and more piled on the floor and hanging from above. Folks could buy seed and fertilizer for their gardens, and they could buy the staples they couldn't grow for themselves. They could buy a pound of salt or a horse collar. If they needed some nails, a glass windowpane or a roll of tarpaper, they could get them at the Nabors store.

And it was more than a store. Anyone could send and receive mail. The store was a social center. The front porch was the nexus of news about everything and everyone, until the winter chill drove the gossip circle inside to cluster around the potbellied stove. Hearsay and rumors were common currency, and flowed as steadily as the creek on the other side of the road. More secrets were let out at the Nabors store than at a cathedral's confessional, the difference being that at the store the confidences were always about someone else. Few shoppers came and went without trading some tittle-tattle.

Morgan hitched his mule to the mill porch, slid the hundredweight sack of corn onto his shoulder and carried it in. Inside stood a slim and rail-straight man in a bushy white moustache and red suspenders, supervising the action and lugging a few sacks himself. More salt than pepper in his curly hair hinted mid-fifties.

" Mornin', Arnold."

" Mornin', Morgan. Just the one sack today?"

"Yup, just the one today." said Morgan, flopping the sack onto the mill floor.

"I'll have it fer you right soon then."

"I'll be over to the store, thar," said Morgan.

Arnold Nabors owned the mill, the store and over eight hundred acres of surrounding land. Despite possessing the area's dominant estate, he lived in the modest home of his boyhood, a century-old cabin of squared chestnut logs that sat just across the creek.

He was the youngest of eight, descended from German immigrants who'd come to colonial Virginia in the previous century. He'd grown up poor but ambitious, advancing his fortunes by marrying Ellen Huffman, whose family's substantial holdings dated back to another German pioneer.

Arnold was the chief man in this end of the county—actually two counties, as the Madison-Rappahannock county line cut through his spread. His energy, business acumen and thriftiness would have elevated him to the status of a minor baron, had it not been for the mediocre quality of land and the poverty of many of the people in and around his fief.

The mill was modest, about the size of a middling barn or a large house. The two grinding stations were simple in their operation. Each station consisted of two round wheel-like whitish stones, each nearly four feet wide by nine inches thick and encased in a circular wooden box. The two stones, lying flat with one on top of the other, ground the grain between them as one rotated against the other. The ground meal spilled out at the edges from grooves cut into the stone faces, whence it dropped into a short chute through the floor to the room below, where it was bagged.

The entire creaking mechanism was turned by a fifteen-foot wood and iron overshot water wheel, connected to the millstones by a linkage of wooden axles and shafts turning pulleys with wide drive belts. Not a pleasant place to work, the noisy and dusty interior was roasting in summer and freezing in winter.

When Morgan came up the store steps, he found his neighbor, Haywood Hobson, on the porch bench leaning back against the clapboard wall, with his feet sticking out in front of him, his thumbs hooking his suspenders and his cheek bulging with a tobacco chaw.

"Mornin', Morgan," said Hobson in his deep, resonant voice, nodding and turning his head in continuous motion to shoot a splat of tobacco juice into the dirt off the end of the porch.

"Mornin', Haywood," said Morgan with a nod. He removed his hat and entered the store.

The interior was dim, requiring a pause for his eyes to adapt. A pair of clerks stood behind the counter, serving customers. The shelves behind them ran floor to ceiling, and were loaded with goods. Barrels and crates of commodities sat about, sharing floor space with racks of clothes and harness items and hardware. A cold pot-bellied stove sat alone in the rear, waiting for winter.

Morgan waited his turn before stepping to the counter.

"What'll it be fer you now, Morgan?" asked the clerk.

Morgan, possessed of the good memory of the illiterate, recited, "Pound of green coffee bean, three pound sugar, box of salt, shaker of pepper, sack of lime, two can coal oil and a box of matches." The clerk jotted it all down on a sales slip.

The store clerks, Arnold, a couple of preachers and a few dozen others were the only ones around Nabors who could read and write. Morgan, being profoundly illiterate and nearly innumerate, was more typical. He could not sign his name and he knew no arithmetic beyond counting to twenty and adding ten to equal thirty, forty and so on. His knowledge of weights and measures was by experience only.

"And give me four of them likkrish ropes thar, Shelby," he added, remembering Nellie's request.

The clerk gathered the goods to the counter where Morgan stuffed it all into the extra sack he'd brought along.

"Somethin' else fer you now, Morgan?"

"That thar's the last of it, Shelb."

"Comes to 82.6 cents[2] on account, Morgan," totaled the clerk, turning the sales slip around on the counter and sliding it toward his customer. Morgan couldn't read it but he knew he wouldn't be cheated, so he took the offered pencil and clumsily marked an X on the bottom of the slip. The clerk took back his pencil and completed the formality by writing "his mark" with an arrow pointing at the X, and signing his own name. The sales slip was thus converted into a legal instrument of debt.

No money had changed hands. Few had any money that time of year. The clerk posted the sum to Morgan's account in a ledger book. Accounts were settled each autumn after farmers had sold whatever surplus they'd produced. They could also barter at the store. Many were illiterate dirt farmers like Morgan but they were extended credit at the Nabors store. No interest was charged. Only the deeply impoverished upper hollow and ridge dwellers were limited to cash & carry or barter.

Morgan stepped out onto the store porch with his full sack, and sat down next to Haywood to await the milling of his meal.

"Hot, hain't it, Morgan?" said Haywood in his baritone, opening with the standard warm weather line.

"A mite hot. How's yer crop comin', Haywood?"

"Just got the last of my corn in yesterday. How's Nellie gittin' on with the wheezes?" asked Hobson, ejecting another line of foul tobacco spit.

"She a whole sight better'n she wahr a few weeks back, Haywood."

"I done hear't you got you some help fer her."

Morgan was puzzled, wondering how Haywood would have heard that.

---

[2] Goods were routinely priced in mils – 1/10 cent – a practice that continues today with motor fuel. There was no mil coin at that time. Payment totals were rounded up to the nearest cent.

"Mighty good to have that Lucy Nickerson down to help, Morgan," said Haywood, with a wry smile.

Morgan was surprised. *How'd he know 'bout Lucy?*

"I done see'd her comin' down the road, what, about a month ago? She done said she wahr goin' down to help you and Nellie," divulged Haywood.

"Wahl, we's powerful glad she done come on down. She mighty handy at the stove, Haywood," said Morgan, composed but ill at ease with Haywood's tone.

"Wahl, I'd be mighty happy my ownself to have li'l Lucy come take care of me," said Haywood with a wink and pulling a grin that reached across his round face.

Morgan felt the wink and the grin hit a little too close for comfort, so he changed the subject. "Powerful storm t'other evenin', warn't it, Haywood?"

"Yassar. My children, they liked to died with all the lightnin' and thunder."

Just then Arnold signaled Morgan from the mill door. "Reckon I best be a-gittin' on up, Haywood," he said, standing up.

"Be good, Morgan!" called Haywood after him, as he stepped down and across the road to collect his sack of meal.

The mill operated differently from the store. It was neither cash nor credit. Instead, the miller kept one sixth of the grain or meal as payment for grinding. Morgan flopped the sack of meal across the mule's back, tied on the store goods sack, unhitched and started up the road.

Lucy had poured out the soapy wash water and was straining to carry two large buckets of fresh water up to her laundry, when Morgan and the clopping mule came up the lane. She wanted to get all the rinse water into the kettle so it could be heating up while they ate dinner.

THE TALE OF A WOODS COLT

Morgan hitched the mule to the porch and stepped over to the kettle, picking up both buckets.

"How much more you be needin?" he asked, his first words to Lucy all day.

"Uh, about six buckets'll do, Morgan," she said, appreciative of his help and pleased he'd finally said something to her.

Without further words, she stoked the fire while he carried and poured in the water. Then he threw the sack of cornmeal over his shoulder, grabbed the bag of store goods and went inside.

The mid-day meal passed in an uneasy quietness, after which Morgan took up his napping position on the porch and Nellie came out to enjoy the fresh air. Lucy was busy stirring the rinsing laundry when Janie emerged onto the porch.

"Janie, go help Lucy lay it out," ordered Nellie from the rocker. She looked down at her dozing husband. "Look at him takin' his ease," she remarked. "I hain't never see'd no menfolk of no kind do no washin'." Morgan was unmoved.

Lucy was beginning to lift the laundry out of the hot rinse with the battlin' board and flop it onto the rail fence to drain and cool when Janie went over and started stretching and spreading the fabric out on the rails. Lucy snuck a quick glance. *Wish't I knowed how li'l Janie and me can go back to like we was afore...* She let the thought trail off.

SIX

The Same Day
The Gimlet Eye

Before all the laundry on the fence had dried, it was milking time. Lucy went to fetch the cow, leaving Janie sitting on the porch steps looking sullen.

Lucy and the cow arrived to find Janie waiting at the barn door. Lucy felt a lump in her throat as she asked, "Why you down to the barn, Janie?"

"Mama done said come on down and help you with the milkin'," said Janie grudgingly, looking sideways.

Lucy felt a twinge of alarm. Two panicky thoughts streaked through her mind. *Whar's Morgan?* She threw a quick glance toward the barn pasture, where Morgan had taken the mule. *What's Janie goin' to say once't we's in thar?*

Lucy led the cow in, with Janie following. She glanced around the interior with trepidation, and then relief. She was worried that he would be waiting for her in there, but he was nowhere to be seen.

The next worry was Janie and what she might ask about.

"Can you pour two scoops of feed in the feed box fer me?" she asked Janie, as she positioned the stool and pail.

"Yassum."

Janie dug deeply into the feed bin and spilled a scoopful into the box at the cow's nose. Then another scoopful.

Lucy commenced milking in nervous apprehension as to what the girl might say next. Then she had an idea. "Janie, you wants to larn how to milk?" she asked. "I'll larn you how."

"Yassum."

"Pull the stool over and set beside me."

Janie situated herself, looking interested.

"You takes yer thumb and yer finger and you pinches the top of the tit. That thar keeps the milk down in the tit. You see?"

"Yass," replied Janie, studying the hand on the teat.

"Then you squeezes the tit." Lucy demonstrated and a strong stream of milk shot out into the pail.

"See h'yar how I keeps the top pinched when I squeezes the bottom?"

"Yass," said Janie, nodding.

"Thar now, you do it. Pinch the top, squeeze the bottom."

Janie pinched the top and squeezed the bottom, but no milk came out. It had looked easy. "Why no milk come out, Lucy?"

"H'yar now, let's try again," said Lucy patiently, as she wrapped her hand around Janie's on the teat. She squeezed the hand, which squeezed the teat. That made the difference. Pinch-squeeze-squirt; Pinch-squeeze-squirt. But then there was the matter of aim. Janie was milking, but it went everywhere but into that pail.

"Yer a'milkin' Janie, but let's git it in the pail," said Lucy, chuckling at the wild squirts of milk. "H'yar." Lucy put her hand around the Janie's to tilt the teat. Soon she had the hang of it.

"Yee'ar!" cried Janie excitedly, looking up with a wide grin on her face. It was a two-fisted job; left–right, left–right, shish–shish, shish–shish. It didn't take long to fill the milk pail.

Lucy felt a weight lifted from her, as the two of them carried the pail of milk up the path. Two hurdles had fallen. She was back in Janie's favor with no embarrassing questions asked.

Nellie was still in the rocker. Before they reached the porch, little Janie called out, "Mama! Lucy done larn't me how to milk! I done milked the entahr pail!" she exclaimed excitedly.

"That thar's mighty good of Lucy," said Nellie, nodding approval. "Now on, the milkin's goin' to be yer chore, Janie."

Lucy was the last to turn in that night. As Nellie slumbered, she sat alone in the dim light of the oil lamp, recounting the day's events with satisfaction. Then she heard a plaintive voice from the stairway.

"Lucy, I cain't sleep," whimpered Janie.

Lucy tiptoed over and whispered, "C'mon now. I'll sang you a song." She took Janie's hand and led her back up into the loft.

The other children were sprawled out in deep sleep, and Morgan lay on his back, snoring peacefully. Janie curled up with her head in Lucy's lap.

Lucy started to sing very softly.

> *Grasshopper settin' on a sweet potater vine*
> *'Long come another and says "It's mine"*
> *Yeller bird sangs in a sycamore tree*
> *Red bird sangs in harmony*
>
> *Yawnin' in the cabin and yawnin' on the floor*
> *Go to sleep on the count of four*
> *Under the covers and wiggle in the bed*
> *Time to say goodnight to a sleepy head*
>
> *The li'l frog jump from log to log*
> *Butterfly lands on a baby hog*
> *The hoot owl waits fer the light o' the moon*
> *Ol' fox listens fer the owl to croon*
>
> *Yawnin' in the cabin and yawnin' on the floor*
> *Go to sleep on the count of four*
> *Under the covers and wiggle in the bed*
> *Time to say goodnight to a sleepy head*
>
> *Bumble bee flies to the honeycomb*
> *Queen bee says "it's time to come home"*

THE TALE OF A WOODS COLT

The buttercup closes its petals and sides
Li'l cub bear starts to rub his eyes

Yawnin' in the cabin and yawnin' on the floor
Go to sleep on the count of four
Under the covers and wiggle in the bed
Time to say goodnight to a slee..py h..e..a..d

Janie was in dreamland. Lucy slipped downstairs and turned in.

The next morning, Nellie was out of bed and on her feet, preparing breakfast and directing Janie. Though not fully recovered, she was feeling stronger and was weary of being laid up.

It was the day of rest, the Lord's Day. They did not attend church, though. Like Lucy, Morgan and Nellie had grown up believing in God, and in spirits and in the hereafter. But unlike their early forebears who had settled the area, they had no regular religious practices. Just after Morgan and Nellie had married and settled down, an early Brethren Elder had passed through on his mission.

The Elder had given them the three wall pictures, and had attempted to provide some religious instruction. But the Bible, source of all wisdom and authority, was useless, for neither Morgan nor Nellie could read a word. He had tried to teach them some simple prayers and parables, and to memorize a few lines of scripture, but made frustratingly little progress. Both Morgan and Nellie were from families further up in the mountains, where many had long ago lost interest in worship or church.

The preacher couldn't even bring them around to believing in sin and salvation, or in everlasting heaven or hell. The best he could do was to get them to acknowledge Sunday as the Lord's day, a day of rest, and that the departed have gone to be with the Lord. All the couple remembered from the encounter was a basic table grace that Morgan adjusted to suit the needs of the moment.

Being Sunday, Nellie added smoked bacon and apple butter to the breakfast menu. After breakfast, Morgan pulled his gun from the wall and went off to hunt squirrel, which meant sitting near a walnut tree waiting for a squirrel to come dig up last year's buried nuts. It wasn't prime hunting season, but he wanted a squirrel to complete Nellie's recovery.

Lucy went out on the porch with Nellie to relax and bask in the warm late morning air. She settled on the steps, leaving the rocker to Nellie. They were watching the children play when Nellie spoke.

"Wahl Lucy, I sure hope you finds you a man good as my Morgan."

Lucy didn't respond. Was Nellie hinting, fishing or just musing? She hoped this wasn't to be the confrontation she dreaded. She stared out to the yard.

"You do think the world of Morgan, don't you, Lucy?"

This didn't sound good. Lucy could feel Nellie's focused gaze. The showdown was coming. She couldn't decide whether to risk the full punishment or say something to try to steer it off.

"Yass, I thinks that Morgan's a mighty fine husband to you, Nellie, and a good daddy to the children," she said, meeting Nellie's eyes while trying to sound detached from Morgan. She looked away under Nellie's steady gaze.

"Now I hain't sayin' Morgan hain't got no faults," said Nellie, rocking gently.

Nellie seemed to be changing tack. Lucy fretted and tried not to show it. This line had the potential to turn Morgan back toward her. She looked back at Nellie, who spoke again.

"You cain't expect him to be nothin' but what a man is" she said, rocking and rocking, and looking intently at Lucy.

Lucy averted her eyes again. *Lordy lord,* she thought, feeling Nellie closing in on her.

Nellie went on. "And you cain't expect him to do nothin' but what a man will do," she said, rocking and rocking.

Lucy shifted uneasily on the step. *This hain't gon' be good*, she said to herself, feeling targeted and oppressed under Nellie's inscrutable gaze.

"And you cain't expect a man to say no to all temptation."

Alarmed and feeling cornered, Lucy flicked her eyes nervously about, avoiding Nellie's.

"And iffen somethin' sweet wahr right thar afore him..." The rocker stopped.

Panic raced through Lucy. Sweat beaded on her brow. She was trapped. She could feel Nellie's eyes boring into her.

"And iffen durin' the while the sweet thang come right up against him," said Nellie, leaning forward.

The accused capitulated, feeling as if her head was on the chopping block, guilty as charged. *H'yar it comes*, she thought miserably.

"And iffen thar wahrn't another body thar to see it." Nellie's hands gripped the armrests as if about to pounce on Lucy.

Lucy sucked a breath and braced for the blow. The axe of condemnation had been raised.

"But then, my Morgan's a sight better'n most ary man," said Nellie, leaning back.

A rush of relief surged through Lucy. She sensed a reprieve coming.

"And he hain't got no faults what'd take him from me and the children." Nellie resuming her rocking.

Lucy felt pardoned. She was still tormented by not knowing for sure what Nellie knew versus suspected. But she felt she was being let loose and was expected to take advantage of it.

"Wahl, Nellie, reckon I best be a-gitten on back up home, now with you up offen the bed and doin' so good," said Lucy. *I orter leave afore dinner*, she thought. *While'st I got the chance.*

"Lucy, you was mighty good to come on down and nurse me and take care of *ever* one of my family," said Nellie, keeping up the strong hint that had run through the encounter.

Bam!! All heads turned toward the woods. Presently Morgan emerged from the trees with his gun in one hand and a bloody gray squirrel dangling by its fuzzy tail in the other.

"Janie! Git over h'yar and skin out this squirrel," he called as he strode across the yard and and handed over the limp, furry rodent. Janie scooted inside with it.

"I done kilt a squirrel fer you, Nellie," he said, looking up at her from the yard. "It'll fix you right up, good as new."

Squirrel was considered to have medicinal qualities. It was a good supplement to any treatment specific to an ailment, and was equally effective at any stage of the moon. In the local lore, squirrel was "good fer what ails you."

"Morgan, Lucy goin' to be gitten on home, now that I'm up on my feet and about to eat me some squirrel," announced Nellie, studying Morgan intently.

Morgan showed no reaction to the news. He turned to Lucy.

"Wahl Lucy, it's been mighty good havin' you h'yar," he said politely, with intonation that carried a subtle note of intimacy. "When you headin' back up home?"

"I'm fixin' to git goin'."

"Hain't you gon' stay fer dinner?"

"I best be a-gittin' on directly, Morgan."

Morgan propped his gun against the porch.

"Wahl Lucy, I hope that you sees fit to come back see us right soon," he said.

"I suppose I'll see y'all again afore too long, bein' how we's kinfolk," said Lucy, looking at her cousin Nellie.

Janie came out. "I gots the squirrel all skin't, clean and in the pot, Mama. I'm goin' to do the milkin' with Lucy this evenin'," she declared, with undisguised pride.

"Lucy 'bout to git on up home now, Janie," said Nellie.

Janie looked dejected. "Cain't me and Lucy do the milkin' just one time?" she pleaded.

"Lucy, she hain't gon' stay 'til milkin' time," said Nellie. "She 'bout to leave right now, soon's she gits her thangs." Nellie looked at Lucy.

"Janie, I knows yer up to doin' the milkin' all by yer ownself," said Lucy, standing up. "I knows you can do it." She went in to collect her few belongings.

The moment of departure was at hand. Janie stood with one bare foot on the other and an arm wrapping the porch post, looking glum. Morgan stood silently in the yard, expressionless and motionless. Nellie rocked gently on the porch with a look of serenity on her face.

Lucy went down the steps and turned.

"Come back to see us, Lucy," called Janie, wistfully.

Then Nellie spoke.

"Morgan, hain't you goin' to see Lucy down to the road?"

Lucy was taken aback. She looked at Morgan and then at Nellie, who was rocking slowly with a sweet smile that gave no clue. Did she know or didn't she know? Did Nellie know and was just being generous and understanding?

"Uh, uh, I...yass," stammered Morgan. "Yass I am, yass I am."

They walked in silence. At the road they turned to each other. His hands found hers and their eyes met.

"Iffen I didn't have Nellie, I'd be askin' fer yer hand, Lucy."

"I'm hopin' I can find me a man just like you, Morgan."

With misted eyes, Lucy turned and made her way up the road.

Morgan stood still, his gaze fixed on her until she passed from sight.

Lucy's life at home was now but a distant memory of an ancient time. She had been gone a month. She gave no thought whatever to what would come next.

SEVEN
1878
The Greatest Man

Robert E. Lee Nickerson. Lucy had named her boy the day he was born, over two years earlier. There were other Roberts among the many local Nickerson families. But there was no other Robert E. Lee Nickerson.

Lucy was of the highland people in Virginia's Blue Ridge Mountains. Little Robert was born to those hills and hollows and to the ways of the folk who inhabited them. News, politics, history and the cash economy mostly stopped at the foot of the mountains. Most mountain people had never heard of Abraham Lincoln. But Robert E. Lee was the exception. Everyone knew about Robert E. Lee.

Young Lucy held a mother's high hopes for her child. She knew he would not face much discrimination among the highland folk, but she was soberly aware that he certainly would anywhere beyond these impoverished mountains and hollows. She was keen to provide her son any advantage she could. A name connoting respect was all she had to give him. So she launched her boy with the most honored name in all of Virginia.

Robert E. Lee was the greatest man in the world. Lucy had heard Morgan Dinkins say so back in the spring of 1865. It was one of her earliest childhood memories, listening to Morgan and her father talking proudly of Robert E. Lee. The Nickersons had been visiting the Dinkins after Morgan and Festus were mustered out of the Confederate Virginia Militia. The Civil War had just ended...

THE TALE OF A WOODS COLT

...Five year-old Lucy squatted on the Dinkins porch, amusing herself while Morgan and Festus sat sharing a jug of white mule, the local home made corn liquor, and discussing the defeat of the Confederacy between swigs.

The two had joined the Confederate Virginia Militia when the war broke out. It was a local self-defense force that had stationed lookouts on hilltops to watch for Yankees, and had ridden patrol to scout for spies and saboteurs. Morgan had a horse, so he had ridden patrol. Festus had pulled sentinel duty on a nearby mountaintop.

The militia had not been attached to the regular Army of Virginia, so Morgan had not joined in the tremendous cavalry battle just twenty-five miles away at Brandy Station. Neither man had seen any action at all. The closest the war had come to Nabors Mill was a cavalry skirmish at Sperryville that was over as fast as it had begun.

So the boozy porch discussion was about the war in general, rather than actual experiences. Like all the folk around there, they were ardent supporters of the South, owing more to being part of the South than to belief in Southern causes.[3]

Sitting on the porch, Morgan and Festus had become increasingly adamant, with every swallow of hooch, that Robert E. Lee was the greatest general of the Confederate War, and would have been victorious had the South been able to provide adequate materiel and logistics.

"Ol' Bobby Lee, he most sartainly would have whupped them thar Yankees good, up'par in Pennsy Vania, iffen only that he had enough pervisions and wagons to feed the army," Morgan declared.

"He dang sure would have won the entahr war, iffen he had enough powder and shot," echoed Festus, "and vittles and shoes and such."

"Gen'ral Lee wahr the greatest gen'ral what ever did live," proposed Morgan.

---

3 People of the eastern Blue Ridge largely supported the confederacy, unlike the predominant Union sympathies of Virginia's western mountains that led to their secession from the Confederacy and the formation of the State of West Virginia, and unlike the Unionist far southern mountains that saw large Union army enlistments from Kentucky, Tennessee and North Carolina.

"Yassar. He wahr the onliest one what could have done it," seconded Festus.

As the whiskey went down in the jug, Robert E. Lee gained stature. The greatest general quickly became the greatest man of the south, and then passed through being the greatest man in America to being the greatest man in the entire world.

Finally the jug was drained of the last drop, and a wobbly Morgan proclaimed, "Yashar, ol' Bobby Lee'sh the greatesht man what ever did live! Yash indeed. Hain't nobody can touch him!"

The slurred words made an indelible imprint on the mind of the very young Lucy...

...The mountain forests hinted at the rich palette of colors to come later in October. Two and a half year-old Robert E. Lee Nickerson was walking and talking and getting into everything. But Lucy had a helper, in the form of her little sister.

"Mazie, look after li'l Robert now while'st I help Mama in the garden."

Lucy usually detailed Mazie to keep the toddler out of trouble, an assignment the eight-year-old relished. The girl was finally elevated from being the family baby to the important post of junior assistant mother.

But Lucy hadn't been elevated at all. She resented that her mother still treated her as a child. She felt oppressed at being under Hannah's thumb, and it grated on her.

"I'll turn up these h'yar taters and you pull up them thar turnips," directed Hannah when they arrived at the garden.

When they finally flopped their root sacks on the porch, Hannah gave Lucy another order. "Holt on now, let me pick out some fer supper," followed by another, "Thar now, carry 'em on down to the cellar."

Lucy did as she was told. Hannah, to Lucy's consternation, was mother to all, lumping Robert in with her own children. Lucy was piqued at being the deputy mother to both her siblings and her own child. She felt she should be accorded adult status but was reluctant to confront her mother. *I cain't say a thang lest Mama git down on me again about havin' no husband,* she thought, lugging the sack into the dank, dark root cellar under the cabin.

Hannah was, indeed, deeply concerned about Lucy's shrunken marriage prospects. "Thar's good boys out thar, Lucy," she'd reminded her daughter. "When you goin' to talk to someone, Lucy?" she'd say, nagging. "I just wish't you'd find yerself a good man."

Lucy had long since grown tired of hearing her mother harping on it, and pestering her as if any man willing to take her would do.

Then there was her father. Lucy had to endure all of his complaining. "The longer it goes on, the less chance she got," railed Festus regularly to his wife, as if badgering Lucy should fall to Hannah, not him. Then he'd say something hurtful to Lucy anyway.

Lucy stashed the potatoes and turnips in the cellar and went up to join Hannah. She was very worried about her future but it was her intolerable present that plagued her mind and gnawed at her spirit as she and her mother prepared supper.

Lucy had given good riddance to the young fellows who no longer came courting. She had little Robert now. That dropped her from the top of the eligible maiden list to near the bottom. Being a widow would have moved her up a notch, but she wasn't a widow. She was the mother of a woods colt, a bastard.

Her good looks alone were not enough to attract the better sort of eligible young men. The several others that had come calling were layabouts, rejected by other desirable girls for habitual drinking, gambling, or for being shiftless and lazy. She'd turned them away for the scruffy knaves they were, an act that stuck in her father's craw.

To Festus, the natural progression of life had stalled under his roof. He would even consider one of those rascally Fisk boys now, if it took that to set the social order straight.

Early October blessed the Nickersons with a full crop and fine harvest weather. Festus and Otis came in from cutting and shocking the corn patches. The women set out the supper and the family convened around the table in the smoky dim light. Festus helped himself, then Otis, Richard and the rest of them.

Meals at the Nickerson table usually passed in silence. It was just as well. Anything Festus said was complaining. Anything Hannah said was nagging or worrying. To Lucy, the less said the better.

On this evening, Festus had that bilious look, and Lucy knew what it meant. She felt his anger building with his every bite of food. *Oh Lord, Daddy 'bout to lay in to me now*, she warned herself. *He got that hateful look in his eye.* Like the condemned before a firing squad, she braced herself for another castigating blast from her father.

At length, he wiped a sleeve across his mouth, furrowed his brow, shot a hard look at Lucy and, in his gruff voice, growled, "Tain't right fer a girl to live at home with a child and no man. Don't you like no mans atall?"

Lucy didn't answer.

"Somethin' got to be done to git you a husband."

That did it.

"Wahl, Daddy, them mans what done come around hain't what I'm a-lookin' fer," she said. "They's thinkin' I'm needin' me a man just because I gots me a child. I hain't needin' no man like that." She was well vexed by his vitriol. It burned deeply into her, because she was so frustrated by her own situation. She strained under the dual burdens of worrying about her future and warding off her parents' condemnation.

She stared at her plate and picked at the food left on it.

Festus persisted.

"You actual *is* needin' you a man *because* you gots the boy," he said, looking about to get all riled up. He let a minute pass.

"I'm thinkin' you orter be a-gittin' on down to the church Sundays," he suggested, switching from griping to directing. "You might find you a good man down thar." He was suggesting a last resort, referring to a Primitive Baptist church by the creek in Dinkins Hollow, a couple of miles below the Nickerson home. The church was well attended by the inhabitants of that lower hollow.

"Wahl, Daddy, I don't wants just *ary* man," she insisted, standing up to him but losing all appetite for the rest of her dinner.

Festus didn't take that very well.

"You hain't looked fer no man atall!" he retorted loudly, and pounding his fist.

"But Daddy..."

"The bigger that thar boy, the smaller yer chance," declared Festus, glaring at her.

Hannah intervened, leaning over toward Lucy.

"You orter have you a man, Lucy. Li'l Robert orter have him a daddy," she urged, making the oblique point that Festus would not be serving as Robert's father.

Lucy felt the pressure, but saw that her mother had forestalled her father's escalation into a tirade.

But then Hannah pressed the issue.

"Lucy, do git on down to the church Sundays and find you a good man. They's some good mans goes to church," she exhorted sympathetically.

Lucy shot back. "Wahl, maybe I *orter* be a-gittin' down to the church so's I can bring the Lord back up to *this* h'yar home!" she snapped. She sprang up and left the table in a huff.

Lucy had grown touchy to their frequent needling, mostly because she believed it herself. She took umbrage at being the oldest child again after her sojourn as a young woman. She was made to feel like Robert was her little brother rather than her own child. She needed a permanent break from her childhood. Robert was no longer a baby. He was a little boy and a good daddy for him was her urgent dream.

EIGHT

The Next Morning
The Funeral

The next morning Festus and Otis returned to their corn cutting. Hannah dispatched the next oldest children to the Foster place. At first, it seemed an ordinary day in the mountains.

"Jenny and Richard, git on up to Tilly's now. Jenny, you help Aunt Tilly and Richard, you help Uncle Ernest. Git on now, both yous." Hannah hadn't sent any children up to help the Fosters since Tilly had delivered Robert, and she was feeling remiss.

Barefoot in their homespuns, the two disappeared up the forest path under a leafy canopy just showing the reds and yellows that would soon blaze into full autumn glory.

The Nickerson cabin sat on a level shoulder of land part way up the steep-sided Broad Hollow, a mis-named fold in the mountain that harbored only half a dozen families. The Foster cabin was close to a mile on up, at the head of the hollow where the pitched terrain flattened out somewhat.

Jenny and Richard traipsed up the path through the woods and approached the Foster cabin from below, just as Aunt Tilly stepped off the porch.

Jenny, thirteen and in charge, stepped out ahead of her brother, toward Tilly.

"Mama says me and Richard suppose to help you and Uncle Ernest today."

"Wahl now, that's mighty good of yer mama, child. You can help me dig up the sweet taters and the turnips. Richard, you can git on out to the patch and help Ernest with the corn."

"Yassum."

Richard found Ernest leaning into his work of swinging a corn knife to slice the stalks off close to the ground. He looked very much the mountain farmer in a sweat stained shirt that hung slack on his thin frame and was tucked loosely into worn ducks held up by black suspenders. His shabby boots dug into the soft earth as he rhythmically whacked his way down a row of corn.

Ernest set Richard to shocking, the job of stacking the stalks in an upright teepee shape that was narrow enough to reach into and pull out the ears at a later date, once the shocks had fully dried.

Tilly and Jenny had no sooner started turning the tubers up out of the earth when a pair of small figures appeared on the path above the cabin. A girl of about ten and a younger boy walked up to Tilly.

"Mama says she done got the pains," said the girl.

The words grabbed Jenny's attention.

Tilly nodded. "I'll be right h'yar the entahr day," she said. "Now Lylie, the two of yous git on back up'par and tell yer daddy to come fer me once't the water done broke. You hear me now, child?"

"Yassum." The small pair turned and retraced their steps, hurrying out of sight.

Lylie was Elliott and Pearl Hawlins' oldest child of three still living. This would be Pearl's sixth birth, so the midwife would likely be called to duty within a few hours.

Children were the communication system in the mountains. They were sent out as family emissaries with messages or requests and, in fine diplomatic form, were always careful not to re-word or paraphrase their instructions. It was "Mama says," or "Daddy says" or "Granny says," followed by the message spoken verbatim. They always went in pairs, the younger being the understudy.

Jenny had absorbed the scene attentively. Her memories included the births of little Mazie and Robert, but she had been sent away with her siblings and was anyway less concerned with the business of birthing babies back then.

But now she was feeling a stirring interest in such things. She looked at Tilly, hoping for an invitation to tag along. She was too reserved to ask, but her curiosity was already engaged. Questions about childbirth tumbled through her head. *What it gon' look like? What it gon' feel like? Is it goin' to hurt right smart? What else come out, besides the baby? What end come out first? How big it gon' be? Might be she'll have two! What Aunt Tilly actual gon' do?*

Leaning on her digging fork, Tilly stood studying her young charge, as if seeking a glimpse into the girl's mind to help her make up her own.

Jenny felt her entire self rise up under Tilly's deliberating gaze. Her eyes lifted and widened, her chin came up and her body lighted upon its feet, as though the force of anticipation reduced the force of gravity. Her eager interest must have moved Aunt Tilly.

"Wahl, I suppose you can come along with me, iffen you wants to."

Jenny felt a rush of excitement, as she released her breath and broke into a broad grin.

"Yassum! Yass I do, Aunt Tilly!" She felt giddy at the prospect of crossing the great divide, from the small sphere of childhood into the broad world of womanhood, even if only as an observer.

They went back to their digging, but Jenny could barely keep herself focused on the sweet potatoes and turnips.

"Wahl, we best be a-gitten the dinner on," said Tilly, swinging the heavy potato sack over her shoulder. Jenny took up the smaller turnip bag and they trudged over to the cabin, flopping their harvest onto the front porch.

Inside, Tilly stoked up the cookstove where she already had a pot of white beans and fatback simmering. She handed a wooden water bucket to Jenny.

"Slip down to the spring and fetch me up a pail."

Tilly was whipping up the last of the food when Jenny hauled the bucket through the door.

"Set it thar by the stove and set out the table, now; that's a good girl."

Tilly had sliced and fried some cabbage and bacon, then stirred some flour and sweet milk into the bacon drippings to produce thick gravy. Leftover cold corn pone completed the menu.

"Call 'em in, now, and pour some water in the porch basin."

Jenny took the water bucket and stepped out on to the porch to see that she didn't have to call them in. Ernest and Richard were already coming up the path. The two of them splashed their faces and washed their hands before going in to their places at the table.

"How you comin' along in the corn patch?" asked Tilly.

"We done right good fer one mornin'," said Ernest, running long bony fingers across his head of thinning gray hair. "Richard h'yar a right good li'l shocker, no bigger 'n he is." He looked over at the boy's beaming face.

"Wahl Ernest, you still a right good corn cutter, olt as you is!" teased Tilly.

Earnest gulped down a cup of cool water, smacked his lips and played along.

"Hain't no man no whar in the mountain can keep up with me cuttin' the corn," he declared in a droll tone befitting his leathery bassett hound face and long ears. Ernest was one of those mellow even-tempered sorts with no hard edges and no extremes, a man who lacked passion for any particular thing, besides his wife.

Tilly changed the subject. "Li'l Lylie Hawlins done come down and said Pearl got the pains. I reckon I'll be a-handlin' the birth afore the evenin's over."

Ernest looked over at Jenny quizzically.

Tilly must have read his thoughts. "Jenny h'yar's goin' up with me, case I needs help," she said, answering the question he hadn't asked.

Ernest looked back at his wife without comment, but skepticism was arranged all over his face. Children did not attend births.

"About time now she larn't about family thangs," said Tilly. "She's more'n willin'. I done see'd it in her face."

That was enough explanation for Ernest. He stayed well clear of Tilly's midwifery. He sopped up the last of his gravy with a chunk of corn pone, popped it in his mouth, licked his lips and pushed back from the table.

"Why you and Aunt Tilly hain't got you no children?" asked Richard with the innocence of a ten year-old.

"Shush Richard!" cried Jenny, flushing.

Ernest was taken aback and paused for a moment. "Wahl boy, reckon the Lord, he got his reason why we don't got none," said Ernest. "Hain't no fault of Tilly's."

Jenny saw a tear form in Tilly's eye.

"We wish't we done had us a boy and girl just like the both of yous," said Tilly. She had delivered both of them. "But we never..." She looked over at Earnest, as the tear streaked down her cheek.

His eyes met hers, releasing a current of appreciation. He picked up on her words.

"We never had us no children, but ever baby she done brung in is like her own," he said. "And they hain't no man in the mountain that got no better woman than Tilly."

Tilly composed herself. "Ernest means he eats right good," she said with a chuckle. "I love him."

"By God, Tilly, you always sets a fine table of vittles," he said. "What with ever other thang you gits done, I supposen I done gots me the best dang wife in all the hollers."

Tilly smiled and he rose. Richard took the cue, stood up and followed Ernest out to resume labor.

"Let's git the last of them taters outen the ground," said Tilly, piling up the dishes for later.

They were half way down a row of sweet potatoes when a burly figure appeared, striding down the path at a motivated pace. Tilly looked up to see Elliott Hawlins.

"Tilly, Pearl's water done broke. Can you come right on up?" he said, his words wrapped in urgency. "It won't be long now."

"Sure 'nough now, Ellitt." She toted the sack of sweet potatoes to the porch, disappeared inside and came straight back out with her apron and rags bag in hand, to where Elliott was fidgeting to get going.

"C'mon now." She motioned to Jenny, drawing a perplexed look from Elliott, who was not about to ask questions or wait for a lengthy explanation. Jenny leaped forward and the threesome lit out smartly up the path to the Hawlins cabin, with Elliott leading and Jenny, her anticipation building, bringing up the rear. Seeing the two in rear silhouette, Jenny thought Elliott and Tilly looked nearly the same. He was a tad short, stocky and thick of arm and leg in a muscular way, giving the appearance of being well planted to the ground.

The Hawlins cabin was like most of the others thereabouts—squared chestnut logs chinked with mud, stacked stone chimney, rear lean-to and a front porch.

Jenny stopped halfway up the cabin steps when Elliott paused on the porch, took Tilly's arm, drew his face close to hers and half whispered, "Pearl done said she hain't been feelin' no kickin' lately." He let a few beats go by and then, with his chin tucked down in a serious look, "She's a-fear't it's dead and…I'm a mite scare't myself."

"Now Ellitt, how 'bout you stay right close here?" suggested Tilly.

He pulled back and straightened himself. "I hain't a-goin' no whar," he announced. "I'm goin' to set right h'yar till it comes." He took up position in the porch rocker that put him closer to a birth than any man of the hollows had likely ever been.

Elliott's words had sent a twinge of apprehension through Jenny. She looked up at Tilly, whose face showed no sign of alarm. The midwife gave a hand signal and Jenny followed her through the door.

The inside was like Jenny's home, except for having a small iron cook stove. Pearl lay on the bed, grimacing and moaning with every painful contraction. Her look of distress had spread to her mother, Rosie.

"Set the water to bilen'," said Tilly, as she moved toward Pearl. Rosie stoked the stove and added water to the already hot kettle, as she studied Jenny from the corner of her eye. Jenny stood by the door, feeling uneasy under the mother's silent quizzical gaze, wishing she could shrink herself into obscurity.

"She h'yar to help, case I needs it," explained Tilly. The midwife sat, taking Pearl's hand in hers and putting her other on the bulging belly.

"I hain't been feelin' no kickin', Tilly. I'm powerful worried."

"Wahl, sometimes it gits so big it hain't got no room to kick no more."

"I'm just scare't it done died," said Pearl, her voice edged with fear.

The midwife didn't say anything as she checked the baby's head position. The contractions were strong. There was nothing to do but let nature take its course.

Jenny stood silently, transfixed by the scene before her.

Pearl screamed, seized by a contraction.

"Poosh! Pearl. That's it. Poosh hart, now!" coached Tilly emphatically.

Jenny winced with Pearl's every agonizing contraction. Then she received her first assignment.

"Jenny, wash yer hands and dip these h'yar in the kettle water," said Tilly, handing over a clutch of rags from her bag. "Holt 'em up and squeeze 'em out. Holt 'em till I asks fer 'em."

Presently, the top of the baby's head appeared.

Her rag task done, Jenny edged closer to the bed where Rosie, her face tense with apprehension, sat gripping her daughter's hand. The midwife crouched at the ready.

"Big ol' poosh now, Pearl!"

"AH AHH! OHH!! OHH!!!"

The baby slid out into Tilly's hands. Her face fell.

THE TALE OF A WOODS COLT

Rosie sucked a gasp and let out a shocked cry of anguish.

Jenny stepped back, drew a quick breath and threw her hands to her mouth.

It was dead. It was a baby girl and she was dead. Pearl saw it in all three faces.

"It's dead! Oh Lord! It's dead!! Lordy! Lordy! It's dead!"

Rosie clutched her daughter's hand between her palms. "Oh darlin'! It's over. It's all over now, darlin'," she lamented. "It wahr the Lord's will. It's done over now."

Pearl was inconsolable, sobbing on and on.

And it was not over.

All the afterbirth came out, but Pearl was bleeding heavily.

Tilly wrapped the stillborn in a blanket, placed it on the table and went to trying to stanch Pearl's bleeding with the warm rags.

"Hand me all of 'em!" she called, turning toward Jenny.

Out on the porch, Elliott sat rocking and nervously puffing his cob pipe. When he'd heard his wife cry out he'd jumped up and started for the door but stopped. *Must be just regular fer 'em to scream like that*, he thought, trying to calm himself. He sat back down, packed a fresh pipe, lit it and anxiously drummed his fingers on the rocker arm.

Rosie came out to him.

"It wahr born't dead," she said, in a depressed monotone.

"We's a-fear't it wahr dead," was his only reaction as he rocked and puffed his pipe.

Inside, the midwife was holding a bloody rag compress to Pearl, and hoping for the best. She looked quickly at Jenny. "Run now and git me two buckets of water!"

Spurred by Tilly's solemn face and the gravity in her voice, Jenny grabbed a couple wooden buckets, raced out the door, skittered down the steps and scurried down the spring path, startling Rosie into rushing back in to Pearl's side.

Blood-soaked rags had made a frightful pile when Jenny struggled through the door with the buckets to hear Tilly speak. "The bleedin' done slowed a mite," she said, sounding desperate for a hopeful sign. She turned her head and Jenny saw the urgency that belied the optimism. Tilly motioned toward the bloody pile. "Jenny, squeeze 'em out in the bucket and give 'em back to me." The midwife was desperately resorting to a cold compress.

A doctor lived in Sperryville but it would be three hours to walk there, plus two more hours return trip on horseback, assuming he was home. It would all be over, one way or the other, well before then.

Jenny felt fear rising as she squeezed the blood from rag after rag, wrung and then cycled them back to the midwife. Pearl looked so pale and weak.

"Holt me, Mama." pleaded Pearl in a feeble, shaky voice. "I'm scare't."

Rosie leaned closer, anxiously clutching her daughter's hand. "You hain't gon' to suffer much longer, darlin'," she comforted, moving their conjoined hands up and down hopefully. "Yer goin' to be alright."

Jenny kept the cold rags moving. Tilly's grim look said time was short.

"Mama, I'm so colt. I feel so colt," whispered Pearl, her face wan and gray.

"Oh my darlin'! Oh Lord, my darlin'!" cried Rosie fearfully. "Don't take her from me!" Her eyes filled with panic.

A lump rose in Jenny's throat at seeing a life slipping away before her eyes.

Tilly was clearly alarmed as she grabbed all available rags and, hunching over her patient, applied them as a tight compress in a desperate attempt to stop the bleeding.

"I cain't stop it!" she cried in anguish. "I cain't stop it!"

"Mama, yer so far away." The feeble voice was nearly inaudible. "Yer so far away."

"Oh Lord no! Please! Lord no!" begged Rosie.

Jenny felt utterly helpless, as a veil of horror fell across her being.

Tilly's grave countenance confirmed the obvious as the last glimmer of life drained from poor Pearl's face.

The midwife sat up, her shoulders sagging and arms limp in stunned capitulation to the loss of her patient, friend and neighbor.

Rosie wailed as she hovered over Pearl's lifeless body. "My poor baby! My poor baby done gone!" she cried out in grievous disbelief. "Oh Lord, you done took my poor baby!"

Jenny stood with her hands cupped over her mouth, staring in shocked disbelief at the stilled, colorless and strangely vacant form that just moments before had been a familiar living human being.

Tilly spoke in a breaking voice. "Best git him in h'yar now, Jenny," she said, as she reached a finger up and eased Pearl's eyelids down, then brought the lips together.

Jenny found enough legs in her living nightmare to ease out the door and approach Elliott with trepidation.

Elliott was already out of his rocker and pacing the porch, more and more convinced, with every long passing minute, that something was going wrong. Now Jenny's ghastly expression and weak, uncertain utterance confirmed it.

"Aunt Tilly says you best come on in."

Childbirth was not a man's place but he could barely contain himself and, at Jenny's words, ducked quickly in through the open door with her on his heels.

He took two steps and froze, his eyes riveted on Pearl. Seeing his stricken face, Jenny began to cry. Rosie and Tilly rose up and turned toward him with tears flooding down their cheeks.

"She done took to bleedin' real bad, Ellitt," said Rosie. "Tilly done her best, but it kept on a-comin' and thar wahrn't no stoppin' it."

He stepped forward on unsteady legs to the bedside, paused and then eased himself down onto bended knee. Sudden grief overcame his stoicism. "P-Pearl, Oh Pear-r-l, Oh Lor-r-d," he moaned, his voice cracking. He lingered, her hand in his in a fond caress, weeping softly.

At last a small peace descended to his aching heart; he drew the blanket up over her.

He rose and turned to the midwife. "I knows thar wahrn't a thang more you could have done, Tilly," he said softly, slowly shaking his head. He then gently lifted the bundled blanket from the table and left the cabin.

Jenny stepped outside to see him pull a shovel from the shed and go about the sad task of burying the tiny one at the forest edge, in the small dignity of a slight rise of land.

Tilly came through the door, sack in hand, and joined Jenny on the porch. Neither spoke as Tilly started for home. She trod somberly down the path, with Jenny following in numbed silence.

By and by, Tilly found it in herself to say something. She sat down on a fallen log, placed the sack beside her and rested her hands on her knees, staring at the ground.

"I onliest had one other born't dead. And thar wahrn't but three womens done died in my hands," she said. "And that thar's been nigh on twenty yahrs, now," she added, hoping to temper the shock Jenny had just suffered on her first venture into the world of women and childbirth.

Tilly had thought her curious young assistant would view a birth with utmost interest, and would find it instructive. She had no expectation at all of exposing the child to the dying side of life. Stillborns were rare and birthing deaths uncommon, despite unsanitary conditions and lack of prenatal care. Tilly had midwifed numerous births with only a few difficulties.

Sitting on the log, Tilly worried. *"What this gon' do to her?"* she asked herself. She feared that witnessing a wrenching tragedy, one she would likely never encounter again unless she took up midwifing, would ruin Jenny. Tilly felt an urgent need to reassure her and quell any aroused fears that could cripple her outlook on motherhood, and a future family of her own.

Jenny just stood there in the filtered light of the afternoon sun, looking down and scuffing her feet in the dust, saying nothing.

"This h'yar wahr about the worstest in my entahr time," said Tilly, trying again to bring Jenny back.

Jenny stared at the ground and said nothing.

I hain't gittin' through to her atall, thought Tilly. She changed tack. "And you can come with me again, iffen you wants to." She looked at Jenny, trying one more time to reach her, and hoping for a chance to supplant today's horror with a normal birthing experience.

Jenny silently avoided Tilly's eyes.

This here hain't the right time, thought Tilly. *It's too soon after.* She rose and led the way in miserable silence, with Jenny lagging back a few steps. Things couldn't have gone more wrong, and Tilly felt responsible for Jenny's trauma. The walk down seemed interminable.

Jenny sat herself on the Foster porch steps, while Tilly went to hail Ernest and Richard in from the corn patch. When they appeared, Jenny noticed Richard looking questioningly at her. But then she had been with Aunt Tilly to a birth and that was women's business, so she didn't expect questions, and there weren't any.

To Jenny, Richard sounded far away when he spoke. "We's best be a-gittin' on down home now."

Jenny heard Ernest speaking to her brother in a distant voice. "Wahl, I do thank you fer shockin' up the corn. You done some good work today, boy."

Tilly chimed in. "Yass, we's mighty glad to have the two of you's up to help us," she said, sounding to Jenny like a surreal echo.

Jenny saw Tilly biting her lip, and looking at her. She felt nothing but numbness.

She stood up and started after her little brother, then paused to look back and see Tilly standing with folded arms, furrowed brow and tight lips, watching her leave. She turned and followed Richard down the path.

Approaching home, Richard veered off on a different interest. Jenny went straight for the door. She burst in to find her mother and Lucy organizing supper. Mazie and Robert looked up from their play corner.

"Mama! Lucy!" Jenny broke loose, her face dissolving into a gush of tears and crying. Hannah and Lucy looked at each other in alarmed puzzlement, and then back at Jenny, who burst out with it between choked sobs.

"Aunt Tilly and me… we was diggin' sweet taters….when Pearl done got the pains… Tilly, she done took me along to help… and it wahr born't dead!"

Hannah and Lucy froze, stopped still with mouths agape, stunned speechless.

Jenny fell to convulsive gasps, and blurted out the rest of it. "Mama, Pearl's baby wahr born't *dead*!!" She went to wailing uncontrollably until she got half a grip on herself and went on. "And… and Pearl she done got to bleedin' and…. Aunt Tilly, she tried to stop it…. and she cain't stop it! She cain't stop the bleedin'!"

Lucy and Hannah threw their hands to their mouths in horror.

"Pearl she kept on bleedin'… and Aunt Tilly's a-tryin' but she cain't do nothin' atall. Pearl, she done died!! She *dead*, Mama!"

Hannah and Lucy dissolved into gushes of sobs and tears.

"Oh Lord! She so young!" cried Hannah. "Lord, so *young*," she cried, throwing both hands in the air and shaking her head back and forth in anguish.

"I cain't hardy believe it!" exclaimed Lucy. "I just cain't believe poor Pearl done gone!" she cried, her fingers at her tear-streaked cheeks.

The sobbing went on and on, with Hannah wrapping her arms around poor Jenny. Lucy buried her face in her hands. All the bawling infected Mazie and Robert, who erupted and blubbered in unison.

When the weeping had weakened to sniffling, Jenny stepped in to help with supper. All three were still sniveling when Festus and the two boys filed through the door. Red eyes and somber faces told them something was wrong.

"Pearl done had her baby, and it wahr dead," said Hannah.

Festus stopped, his eyes fixed on her.

"She got to bleedin' somethin' awful and now she done died too." His face fell.

"Thar wahrn't a thang Tilly could have done to stop it. Jenny wahr up'par and done see'd the entahr thang," she said.

Behind his stolid countenance, Festus reacted to the disaster with grim sorrow. Death came regularly, but unexpected death was still jarring.

"Let's git the supper fixed so we can git on up'par to the wake afore dark," he said to the women. Then he turned to his oldest.

"Otis, take Richard and git on down to Morgan and Nellie, and tell 'em about Pearl," he said. He sat down, put his head in his hands and spoke to the room.

"They's gon' be all broke up about it," said Festus dolefully. "Ellitt, he's Morgan's bestest friend, and Nellie, she thought the world of Pearl." Elliott and Morgan had grown up on the mountain and had been boyhood chums, a friendship that had endured.

As she put ashcake in the fire to bake, Hannah thought, *I cain't let Jenny go back up'par and see Pearl laid out dead.* And it occurred to her how indiscreet and awkward it would be to have Lucy and little Robert in the room with Morgan and Nellie. She looked at Lucy.

"Lucy, can you git on down and call on the preacher man fer the funeral tomorrow? Jenny can look after Robert. The three of yous can come up in the mornin' fer the funeral."

"Reckon I can, Mama," said Lucy, relieved that she need not face Nellie with Robert that day.

Up at the Hawlins place, Elliott had removed a door and set it on chairs to be the laying out board where he and Rosie placed Pearl's body. Rosie went about the grievous necessity of washing and dressing Pearl, and Elliott struck out along the Hazel road to summon Pearl's sister and to spread the sad news. He finished the day with the dolorous task of fashioning a pineboard coffin.

By the time the sun dipped below the mountain, a cohort of relatives and close friends began arriving at the Hawlins cabin, with supper in their hands and grief on their faces. The assembled mourners feasted on the spread of victuals and then shared stories, remembrances and reminiscences in celebration of Pearl, until deep into the night. Most of them found a place for a few hours sleep, though Elliott and Rosie, Morgan and Nellie, and Hannah and Festus stayed up into the dawn.

After early breakfast, Rosie dispatched children and grandchildren as messengers to invite all the neighbors living within two or three miles, and to arrange for a wagon to carry the coffin. Elliott and Morgan took up picks and shovels and went to dig the grave.

The Hawlins place sat at the edge of the Hazel country, a plateau-like area spread across several flattened high ridges, named after the mountain that anchored one side and the eponymous stream draining the area. The burial ground lay less than half a mile away.

The heavens blessed the mourners with a bright Indian summer day. With the welcome autumn sun softening a crisp morning chill by noon, the crowd congregated at the Hawlins cabin for the service. Most Hazel country and Broad Hollow dwellers came, as well as some from Nickerson Hollow, a long and wide hollow that dropped down from the Hazel ridges. The men always snuck in plenty of corn whiskey, for they did not work on funeral days.

Pearl lay in a plain board coffin resting on four chairs in the middle of the cabin's main room. The bed had been moved outside, and the table to the porch, to make room for a crowd inside the tiny cabin.

Everyone mixed pleasantly, except that Lucy kept a distance from Morgan and Nellie, barely flicking a glance their way. She occupied herself with everyone else. For their part, Morgan and Nellie snuck curious but discreet looks at little Robert.

It was widely known that Morgan was Robert's father. The one number the women knew best was nine months, the time between Lucy's sojourn with the Dinkinses and Robert's birth. But neither Festus nor Hannah bore Morgan any grudge. Nor, apparently, did Nellie. Little Robert was accepted reality, though his paternity was never a subject of discussion in either family.

The other highlanders viewed Robert's origin as a circumstance of life. They referred to Robert simply as "Morgan's other boy," with no moral judgement. But down below, on the more piously Christian side of the adjacent lower hollows, Robert was euphemistically called a woods colt, and seen as the illegitimate product of moral turpitude.

Festus edged over and had some private words with Morgan, who snuck a look at Lucy, standing at some distance across the yard. In a bit, Morgan found Elliott for a discreet chat, after which Elliott took Festus aside for some confidential talk.

Jenny stuck to Lucy, keeping her distance from Tilly and stubbornly averting her eyes from the midwife's entreating, almost pleading gaze.

The Primitive Baptist preacher had come up from Dinkins Hollow to say the service. He stood on the porch with the mountaineers arrayed across the yard in front of him, all looking up to him with rapt attention.

He started in. "The Lord giveth and the Lord hath taken away."

The preacher read scripture, expounded on the need to prepare for death, followed by a farewell to life. "She has left life's troubles behind." He moved on to the predestination of coming and going, his words holding the gathered mourners in his sway.

He looked out at them and spoke, pausing for a response after each sentence.

"This were meant to be," he intoned. A voice in the crowd affirmed. "She done lived her days."

"It were intended fer her to die," he said. Someone responded with, "It wahr her time to go."

"The Lord has called her home," he declared, with an arm stretched out and palm open to the sky.

"She done passed to the other side," called out two in unison, casting gazes upward.

"She safe in heaven now," he proclaimed.

"She better off at rest," said a voice.

The interactive crowd was spellbound. The women moaned, and the men looked more mournful with every nip they tipped from the passing jugs.

The open drinking in front of him reminded the preacher of how needy these people were of salvation and absolution of their sins. Many of the isolated upper mountaineers had lost the tradition of church and religious practice, and he was concerned for the souls of those gathered before him. So piety and godliness compelled him to change tack and pray for their salvation.

"Let us pray." The preacher bowed his head and closed his eyes.

"Dearest Lord," he started, then went on with the usual, and finished with, "And Lord, let these sinners come to meetin' to pray and worship in your holy name…"

But they didn't consider themselves sinners. They saw no reason to worship or pray for salvation

"…and scripture says repent and ye shall be saved… "

But they couldn't read, had little to repent and perceived salvation to be a given.

"… and let them be saved and enter into your kingdom in heaven…"

They were too concerned about today to worry about eternal life in the hereafter. Their salvation was assured by belief in the Lord alone, not by their life's works.

"…in Jesus name, amen."

The preacher raised his head and opened his eyes. The yard in front of him was empty. They had all drifted away.

It was enough religion for the mountaineers to know the Lord controlled life and death. They saw no need to worship Him and perceived no connection between a moral code and a place in heaven. They would pray for whatever they wished in the affairs of life, but always knew that God put His hand in only when and where He wanted. Everything was predestined. Salvation was theirs by their faith alone.

Elliott sipped sparingly from the jugs. The poor man was quiet and reticent, still stunned with grief. He believed, like all the others, that death was preordained and beyond human influence, but his loss was great and it had hit him hard.

Like Tilly's Ernest, Elliott and Morgan had felt a much greater intimacy with their wives than some, for whom marriage was a practical arrangement with less deep feeling, though separation and divorce were rare in the mountains.

Using two poles, Morgan, Ernest, Festus and several other sturdy men bore the pineboard casket to the wagon which, pulled by a plodding steer, made its way to the burial ground with the entire company trailing behind.

The women and girls cried as they went, with Pearl's mother the loudest; "My poor Pearl!" she wailed, throwing hands into the air. "My baby done gone! She done gone ferever!!" she shrieked, then collapsed in sobs into Hannah and Tilly's arms.

Some of the men were well enough lit with liquor to be staggering unsteadily, with the others draining out the last from their jugs. The boys lagged and shuffled along behind, feeling aloof from the grieving crowd and not really wanting to be there.

The cemetery lay upon a rising knoll with a sweeping view out across peaks and hollows, where the mountain mantle of forest was just coming ablaze into autumn brilliance, as though the spirits of those interred there could be inspired by nature's grandeur.

They placed the coffin at the graveside and lifted off the lid, setting off a new round of grief, the moans reverberating eerily off surrounding hills. Mourners lined up and filed by to pay last respects, with some dropping to their knees to kiss Pearl's lifeless gray cheek. Once

Elliott and Rosie had passed, Festus nailed the lid shut.

The bearers lowered Pearl into the grave, with her feet facing east in the age-old practice. The preacher recited the lines—"ashes-to-ashes, dust-to-dust."

It was over. Pearl was fully laid to rest. As the crowd slowly dispersed, Jenny went over to Tilly, who took her into her arms, both shedding uninhibited tears. "That's right. Let it all out," sobbed Tilly. "Just let all of it come on out."

The ceremonial and communal feeling of the funeral proved a catharsis for Jenny, liberating pent up sorrow and grief in a cleansing cry.

Festus and Morgan shoveled in soil to fill the grave. In the custom of the mountains, they heeled the two shovels into the earth with handles crossed, to signify the end of labor on this earth. Elliott planted oblong fieldstones upright on the grave, the larger at the head and the smaller at the foot.

NINE

The Set Up

The heavy frosts of late November signaled hog killing time. In the six weeks since Pearl's funeral, Lucy had noticed that her parents no longer pestered her about finding a husband. She had no idea why, but she welcomed the relief it gave her.

The Nickersons had two hogs ready to butcher. From an early spring litter, they had reached prime weight to provide a year's supply of pork.

The Hawlinses were coming down to help. Hog butchering could be a cooperative endeavor, and a social occasion for two families to work and visit together. With sixty rocky acres each, the Hawlinses and Nickersons managed to produce barely enough to keep a cow, a mule and themselves through the winter. Everyone had some chickens but many neighbors in that upper region had no cow or mule because they couldn't grow enough to feed the animals through the cold dormant season.

But hogs were different. A family of hogs was let loose to roam the mountain forests, feeding on a variety of wild nuts and whatever they could root up. The hogs would be fed at the home pen a couple of times a month–just enough to keep the semi-wild porcines coming back to the homestead.

People seemed to mostly know who owned which hogs, though disputes sometimes did arise. It was the open range system. It wasn't exactly legal, but it worked for the people on the mountains. Acorns made the meat bitter and darkened the lard, so the hogs would be penned and fed corn for about a month before butchering.

Saturday dawned gray but dry, with a nip in the air. As early light crept into the homestead, Festus and Otis came out of the cabin, sat on the porch steps and pulled on their boots. After visiting the big boulder and spring, they returned four full water buckets to the yard. Setting up for hog butchering was a project. The yard was the slaughterhouse.

"C'mon boy and help me git the kettle and all out h'yar," ordered Festus, starting toward the barn. Otis was at his heels. They lugged a very large iron kettle to the front yard and suspended it by three chains fastened to a tripod of iron rods.

"Thar now." Festus was satisfied with the setup. "Now the table and barrel."

Hannah and the two older children came out just as father and son emerged from the barn, each with the end of a rough plank tabletop under one arm and a sawhorse under the other. They went back to get the big barrel and four long wooden poles.

"Jenny and Richard, carry me some fahrwood over h'yar," called Hannah. She was on her knees lighting a fire under the kettle, next to which Festus and Otis had positioned the open top barrel under three long poles they'd set up teepee style.

Lucy, having consigned Robert to Mazie, came onto the porch with two wooden water buckets in hand to join the busy scene.

"Lucy, afore you totes that water, how 'bouten you gives me a hand with the tubs," her mother requested.

Lucy noticed immediately. Her mother's words and tone were unmistakable. It was a request, not an order.

"Why sure, Mama!"

She felt suddenly relieved that her mother had not commanded her like a child. She didn't know why, but the change was obvious and welcome.

They proceeded to pull various smaller vessels and butchering utensils from the tool shed and place them in an organized array on the table. These included a washtub, a waste tub, lard buckets, cheesecloth, bell scrapers, a boning knife, a butcher knife, a handsaw and a hatchet—everything needed to convert pig into provisions.

Jenny and Richard brought over armloads of firewood to where Lucy was stoking the fire under the big kettle, and had set up the smaller lard kettle. "Stack it all right thar," she said, pointing to the upwind side. She then grabbed the buckets and headed down to the branch, a hundred yards away. Hannah had gone back inside to marshal additional butchering utensils.

Lucy hauled the full buckets into the yard and, pouring the contents into the big kettle, threw a glance at Mazie following little Robert here and there. Robert was making it his job to wander about exploring everything within sight and hearing.

Ready to go for more water, Lucy paused and let her eyes follow her little fellow as he scampered around to whatever caught his attention. Her heart yearned for him. *What I'd give to have my own home and a daddy fer him*, she thought longingly, as she turned and headed for the spring.

Hannah emerged with a collection of kitchen gear in her arms, dumped it all on the table and turned her attention to managing the fire, leaving Lucy to tote the many buckets needed to fill the kettle. The big kettle was a prized possession, used to boil laundry and soap, in addition to hog-scalding water.

Wisps of steam were rising from the kettle when the Hawlinses arrived, filing down the path with Elliott in the lead and Rosie following with the children. She had stayed on to keep house and take care of her three grandchildren after her Pearl had passed on.

"Mornin', Ellitt!" hailed Festus from across the yard.

"Mornin', Festus. How do Hannah and—Miss Lucy," greeted Elliott, turning to the sweating Lucy with a polite nod and smile. The two women nodded their hellos to Elliott and Granny, and the day together was underway.

"Let's go git 'em," rasped Festus, shooting a stream of tobacco juice to the side and picking up a heavy hammer.

Kettle water was nearly at a boil when Festus, Elliott and the boys, carrying a lug pole and some cord, approached the hog pen.

The two men slipped through the board gate into the muddy, squalid sty, panicking the animals into racing about squealing and banging themselves into the sideboards. With outstretched arms they cornered a raucous hog, to the boys' great entertainment.

"I'll go fer the front and you grab the hind end," said Festus.

The creature's squealing stepped up some decibels as it tried to bolt and was fallen upon by its captors.

"Holt him down! Holt him down!" cried Elliott, jerking the rear legs out from under the kicking animal. Festus got his knee on the neck and quickly whacked the hammer hard on the forehead, stunning the animal. They bound the front and rear feet and dragged it out.

Next they tied the cords to the lug pole, suspending the captive beneath. The hog topped two hundred pounds, so it took the four of them to shoulder the pole back up to the yard where the women had partially filled the scalding barrel with hot kettle water. They rested one end of the lug pole on the plank table and the other on a stout crotched stake, leaving the unconscious hog hanging upside down.

The impending execution drew the children from their amusements to gather around the suspended victim. Killing a hog was nothing new to people who lived close to the earth and produced most of their own food. Hog butchering was an annual event. Still, the actual killing transfixed the young in a gruesome fascination at the sacrifice of a living being.

Festus picked up a large butcher knife and, holding the handle out toward the gathered children, croaked, "Which one of yous wants to stob this h'yar hog fer me?"

All eyes widened and all heads wagged negative. He broke a snaggle-toothed grin at his own tease, then turned and without hesitation slew the hog by plunging the knife straight in above the breast bone, severing the jugular. The creature let out a brief death jerk and a gush of blood into the pan that Hannah held under the wound.

Festus had earlier fastened a small block and tackle under the tripod top and strung a rope through it attached to a single tree, a short stout wooden bar normally used to connect a draft animal to its load. He tied each hind foot to a ring on the end of the single tree, spreading the rear legs apart. Elliott hauled on the rope, raising the carcass to an angle allowing the last of the blood to drain. Then he hoisted it up under the tripod, suspending the incipient pork upside down above the steaming barrel.

Festus picked up a shovel, dipped the blade into the barrel water and pulled it out. He carefully watched the water dry on the wet blade. "Too hot," he declared.

Hannah stepped forward with a bucket of cold water and poured some in. Festus stirred the barrel and repeated his shovel test. This time it dried a little more slowly. "Lookin' good," he announced. "Ease him on down now, Ellitt."

Elliott let the rope slip slowly through his fingers to lower the dangling dead animal head first into the hot water. Scalding the hog made scraping off the hair feasible–but it had to be done just right. The hot water was well below boiling and within a narrow temperature range. Water too hot, or too much time in the water, would set the hair and it wouldn't scrape off. Too cool and the hair wouldn't slip.

Lucy noticed that Elliott wasn't paying much attention to the hog scalding. He seemed distracted and glanced her way occasionally.

Festus used a stick to hold the carcass fully under water and, after a very few minutes, rasped, "Let's haul him out fer a look." Elliott got his hands back on the rope and hoisted the dripping pig up into cool air.

Hannah, with a round bell scraper in her hand, stepped over to the steaming carcass and scraped a bit of hair. "It needs a li'l more time." Down it went to scald just a tad longer. After barely a couple minutes, Elliott hauled it out of the barrel and Hannah confirmed that the hair slipped readily.

"Git a holt of them thar front feet!" barked Festus to the boys, as he and Elliott latched onto the rear legs and unhooked the hog. "Swing it up on the boards, now," he said. They grunted as they hoisted the hot steaming carcass onto the plank table.

The women stepped right in to scrape off all the hair before the skin cooled off.

"It's a-scrapin' down real nice h'yar," said Grandma Rosie.

They worked quickly, using bell scrapers to avoid cutting the skin. They scraped out the bristles, roots and all. After scraping came the gutting.

The men shifted the tripod away from the barrel and hoisted the hog back up under it, letting it dangle above a metal tub on the ground.

Lucy watched her mother whet a kitchen knife and step up to the carcass.

"Now let's git it opened up."

Hannah slit the skin and sliced the belly fat from crotch to sternum, taking care not to puncture the gut. She cut a circle around the anus. Festus came forward with the short handsaw to cut through the breastbone. Then it was back to Hannah.

She tied off the anus to contain the putrid contents, carefully cut loose the large intestines and the slippery mass slid out, plopping into the waste tub. She separated the small intestine and placed the twisted gut on the table. Next she pulled out lungs and liver, heart and kidneys, stomach and bladder; all the organs were used, most of which went into sausage and scrapple.

"Otis!" called Hannah. The boy appeared from somewhere.

"Carry the tub down in the brush and dump it out t'uther side of the big rock." He grabbed the tub handles, waddled through the yard and stumbled down into the woods. Various wild night scavengers would later make short work of the offal.

Festus picked up a full bucket and tossed a couple flushes of water into the body cavity, readying the carcass for conversion into cuts of pork, a job to be performed by the three women.

With a boost from the boys, Festus and Elliott swung the hog back onto the table. They swapped the big scalding kettle for the much smaller rendering kettle, and went off to fire up the little smokehouse in preparation for hanging up the hams, shoulders and some other cuts to smoke dry.

Grandma Rosie grabbed the big butcher knife and cut the neck to the bone all the way around; with a quick twist, she snapped the neck and separated the head, which she dropped into a bucket, to be cut up and processed by Hannah.

She then proceeded to clean out, flush, strip and scrape the small gut into sausage casing. Very little of the hog was not kept and used.

Lucy, using knife and hatchet, separated the major cuts—hams, shoulders, loins—and trimmed off small meat to be saved for sausage.

In a while, Hannah paused, turned to Rosie and asked, "Reckon yer goin' to handle the renderin'?"

This caught Lucy's attention. She was interested in perfecting this useful technique and there was no one better to learn from than Grandma Rosie, who enjoyed a well-deserved reputation as an expert at rendering lard. Not everyone could do it properly; it was the highest of skills. If not done just right, the stuff became rancid and unusable.

"Can I help you with the renderin'?"

"Course you can, Lucy."

The two went about cutting out the fat, starting with the very pure leaf fat from the gut cavity. Then came the layer of fat under the skin, which they cut up with the skin left on.

"H'yar's the tricky part," cautioned Rosie as she added the fat, little by little, to the barely boiling water in the lard kettle, and shuffled the fire to keep the correct temperature.

"You cain't put the fat in too quick," said Rosie. "And you gots to keep the water bilen just a little."

Bits of skin cooked crispy—the cracklins—rose to the top and were removed as a delicacy.

"Thar now. It hain't bilen no more," said Rosie pointing at the kettle. "All the water done biled off. It's ready to pour off now."

Lucy had studied the procedure intently. The lard was rendered when the water was all boiled off, leaving only fat.

"Git the cloth on them pails, now," directed Rosie. Lucy placed the lard pails on the table and stretched cheesecloth across the top of one. "Holt her tight, now." With Hannah's help, Rosie poured the kettle contents through the taut cloth, straining the hot liquid fat into the bucket, where it would congeal into a white solid and remain until used.

They went on until the several pails were filled. Once all the fat was poured and strained, Rosie stepped back to admire the product. "That thar's some mighty perty lard, Lucy," she bragged proudly.

Prior to refrigeration, meat, fruit, vegetables and other foods were preserved by making them too sweet, too sour, too salty, too dry, too alcoholic or too smoked to harbor spoiling bacteria. The hog meat that wasn't smoked was rubbed with salt, except for some kept fresh for immediate consumption. In the chill of the season, fresh meat could sometimes last for a couple of weeks, if protected from raccoons and other scavengers. Though nearly all the hog was used, the two dogs still got some chew bones from the slaughter.

Lucy gripped a ham with each hand and carried them over to the smokehouse, where Festus and Elliott were sitting and chatting. They went silent as she came within earshot.

"Just set 'em thar on the rock step, Lucy," said her father. She wondered what they were talking about.

Festus and Elliott enjoyed a discreet visit and a few nips from the jug. Festus pushed a chaw into his mouth and Elliott packed and lit his cob pipe, the two of them talking over some private matter. Then it was time for the second hog. They rose and went back to the hog pen for a second round of entertaining the children.

THE TALE OF A WOODS COLT

Jenny's job was to prepare dinner for everyone. She had acquired an avid helper in the form of little Lylie Hawlins, who pitched right in without being told or asked.

"You help yer granny with the cookin' up home, Lylie?" asked Jenny.

"Yass. I helps ever day. I wants to git big so's I can take care of my daddy. My mama done gone to the Lord."

Jenny turned away from Lylie. She didn't want the child to see her tears. She didn't want to have to explain. "Lylie, run to the spring and git a bucket of water fer me," she said, hunched over the stove with her back to the girl. This would give her time to compose herself.

Dinner consisted of the usual fare, plus fresh pork liver. The table didn't hold them all, so the meal was served in two sittings. Men and larger boys usually sat first table; women and children sat second table. However, this day Hannah had directed that Jenny and the five smaller children eat first, after which Hannah shooed them all out of the cabin.

"Jenny, look after the children outside," she ordered, flicking a hand.

Hannah set out the second table. As usual, Otis and Richard wolfed their food and disappeared. When the adults had nearly finished, Hannah nodded to Festus and Rosie, whereupon the three rose in unison and found something to do outside.

Lucy was suddenly left alone with Elliott, sitting across the table from him. He leaned toward her, resting on his forearms with hands clasped together, nervously biting a lip. Lucy felt bewildered; then it dawned on her that she had been set up with him.

Elliott was a steady man who seldom showed joy or anger. His emotions stayed within a narrow band bordering on melancholy. He wasn't shy. He just didn't have much to say, but when he spoke, it was straight to the point and sincere. His was not contrived sincerity.

"Lucy, I been a-wantin' to talk to you." He ran his hand back through his dark hair like a finger comb and took a deep breath.

Lucy was puzzled.

"I knows I'm a mite older'n you are, but I'll most surely undoubtedly make you a good husband, Lucy."

Lucy was taken aback by the sudden marriage proposal. Most second marriages in the mountains were between widows and widowers, sometimes with the sister or brother of the deceased. Lucy knew Elliott would be looking to re-marry, but she'd not figured herself in the picture. She was dumbfounded.

"Wahl, Ellitt...." She paused. She felt him looking at her intently. "Wahl, I just don't know what to say." She felt his earnest urgency, and didn't want to torment him with prolonged suspense. She believed Elliott would be a good husband and that she could make him a good wife. But she hesitated, not feeling up to a final and immediate commitment to a man with three children.

"I just don't know, Ellitt..."

"I'll understand iffen it's about me being a sight older'n you," he said forthrightly.

She looked down at her lap for a minute of contemplation.

Elliott was a plain man, plain in all ways—plain looking, plain thinking and plain talking. His square head and shaven face held slightly undersized features except for the long forehead—an imbalanced but honest visage that looked across the table at Lucy with hopeful eyes.

"Hain't you, Ellitt," she said, looking up at him. "I just hain't fer sure about bein' mama to four children."

"Lucy, I'm sartain my three goin' to take to you straight away."

She drew and let out a deep breath.

"You goin' to be a fine wife, and li'l Robert thar goin' to be just like my own child," he assured her, perched as he was on the edge of anxious suspense.

She gazed past him and chewed her thumb, struggling with the decision. A silent stretch of eternity passed before she looked into his eyes and spoke.

"Yass, Ellitt, I'll make you a wife."

He leaned back, released a relieved sigh and broke a grin. She cracked a small smile and they both stood and stepped out onto the porch to find Festus, Hannah and Granny standing still in the yard, three frozen statues with faces looking toward the cabin in keen anticipation. The couple's smiles spread to the trio in the yard, bringing them to life as they joyously realized that expectations had been met.

Festus produced a jug and sat down on the porch with Elliott for a celebratory nip. Lucy joined the two women for the balance of the butchering, and then tidying up all the mess.

"Like I done tolt you, Ellitt, you done come to the right decision h'yar," said Festus. "Lucy hain't got nary a bad way to her."

Elliott nodded approvingly.

Festus went on as if he needed to close the sale. "She the workin'est li'l thang, and she mighty handy with the cookin'."

Elliott's eyebrows lifted with a slight tilted nod, as though feeling luckier with Festus' every word.

"And besides, Ellitt," said Festus, leaning into Elliott and keeping his voice low, "a girl like that can make a man feel like a man," he said, with a sly wink and a wry smile.

Elliott's narrow mouth stretched into something between a smirk and a grin. The two cemented their new kinship with generous swigs from the jug.

The women went about their lard, headcheese, sausage-stuffing and salt-rubbing tasks with excited chatter.

Rosie turned to Lucy.

"Lucy, I hope to tell you, that thar Ellitt goin' to be a mighty good husband to you. He's a good man and a good pappy to the children," she said. "He hain't got nary a mean bone in him."

Lucy listened attentively.

"All he do is work hart, 'ceptin' when he's a-coon huntin," said Rosie, as if to dispel any second thoughts Lucy might have about marrying Elliott.

Elliott was as reliable as rain. He went about all his affairs in a deliberate way with interest but no fervor—with one exception. He was passionate about raccoon hunting.

Lucy nodded approvingly. 'Coon hunting, drinking, gambling and shooting matches were the mountain man's main sports. The first was the least bothersome to the women.

"And besides, my Pearl would have wanted it this way," said Rosie, with a hand on Lucy's shoulder and a tear in her eye.

Lucy's misty-eyes traded empathy with Pearl's grieving mother. They drew into a tight hug that completed the new family bond.

Keeping her hands busy, Hannah took it all in with giddy excitement, grinning and beaming like a barnyard cat at its cream. Hopes and dreams had come true.

The meat was hung in the smokehouse, the kettle and barrel rigs were stowed away and the excited dogs got their scraps, as the gray afternoon waned.

The day had been a dance of dissection that had divided two beings into an inventory of edibles, and had released a profusion of rank odors—from the hog pen, from the scald water, from the carcass offal, the rendering kettle and the sausage stuffing. Hog killing day was not entirely pleasant, but was always productive and memorable.

The Hawlinses assembled for departure.

"Wahl, we's best be a-footin' it on up home," said Elliott to the group, but with his eyes fixed on Lucy. He and Rosie looked pleased as they turned to go.

"We's all goin' to git on up'par to yer place next Saturday, Ellitt!" called Festus, raising his hand in goodbye. It was with the satisfaction of a most successful day that the Nickersons lingered and watched the Hawlinses disappear around a bend in the path.

The mood around the Nickerson supper table that evening was lighter than it had ever been. There was even a bit of talk. Festus looked at Lucy. "That thar's the bestest man you could have got," he pronounced, with a note of accomplishment in his voice.

"Yass, Daddy."

Hannah seconded. "You hain't agoin' to have nary a worry in this world, darlin'."

"Yass, Mama."

It was not excitement but relief that carried Lucy to bed that night. She had made her decision for the good of all. Her burden lifted, she fell easily to sleep.

Attraction. Infatuation. Affection. Passion. Love. The emotions of courtship are luxuries not always afforded people living close to the earth, close to the edge and close together. Expedience ruled the present and predestination ruled the future.

Lucy was a little different. She sensed instinctively that a body did have some influence over events and outcomes. She wanted her boy to have every promise and prospect she could provide. In her circumstances, this was the best she could do for him.

TEN
A Week Later
Paradise

The day opened clear and crisp in the stark mountains, their dormant trees bare of leaves but for the usual brown stragglers on the white oaks and beeches. The sun crept up and cast its light through skeletal wood to dapple the forest floor. The Nickersons gathered themselves for the hike up to the Hawlins place.

Lucy had made her decision and had no regrets, yet she felt a trifle lonely and sad as she quietly stuffed her small wardrobe and a few personal items into a tow sack. Hers was to be a one-way trip up the hill to a new life.

Hannah got them started. "Jenny, tote Lucy's poke, now. Mazie, you stay up h'yar with Mama."

They all set off up the trail, with the two boys charging up ahead and Festus leading the others at a measured pace. Lucy bounced little Robert along on one hip and then the other, and Jenny carried Lucy's sack over her shoulder until they traded loads half way up.

Arrival at the Hawlins yard found the same scene as at the Nickersons a week earlier. The butchering array was fully laid out and set up. Lacking help from larger children, Elliott and Rosie had beavered since dawn to get everything ready.

Elliott's eyes went straight to Lucy, and hers to him, as she sensed his warm welcome to her new home. He ran over to shoulder her sack.

"Come over h'yar to my children, Lucy," he said enthusiastically, taking her hand in lead to the porch where he had staged his three youngsters. His attentions made Lucy feel more appreciated than ever before. With Grandma Rosie and the Nickersons looking on approvingly, Elliott introduced his brood to their new mother.

"Lylie, Eddie, Sue–Lucy h'yar's yer new mama. Yer first mama done gone to the Lord. Lucy's yer new mama." The three glanced shyly at Lucy. "Daddy wants ever one of you to mind yer new mama and do what Lucy say. You hear Daddy now?"

"Yass Daddy," said Lylie. The other two looked at their sister, then said the same. The three of them stared at their feet in timid uncertainty, unsure of what changes to expect and how to react to Lucy taking their mother's place.

"Now Lylie, take Jenny on in to git the dinner fixin's goin' and all."

"Yass, Daddy," said Lylie, looking to Jenny, who put Robert down into Mazie's custody and scurried up the steps. The two disappeared inside.

The ballet of butchering began and ran through the day, with a noon intermission. By the time the sun had dipped toward the far ridge, all parts of the pigs were in their proper places and all the gear was stowed, bringing the curtain down over the scene of slaughter.

Festus announced, "Wahl, we's best be fixin' to git on down home."

It was the signal for the Nickersons to bid goodbye. They all stood in the slanting last rays of sunlight, facing Lucy and little Robert. As the evening chill fell across the mountain, Lucy went from Mazie to Jenny to Richard and Otis, giving each a warm hug and a few words of parting.

"Mazie, me and li'l Robert gon' miss you somethin' awful," she said, leaning down to hug her little sister, then rising to face Jenny. "Don't fergit to come see us time to time, you hear now?" The girls sniveled farewells, with a tear or two in their eyes.

Lucy turned to her brothers, who stood stolidly and a little uneasily. "You be good now and do what Daddy tells you," she said, wrapping her arms around each of them. The boys were wooden, discomfited by being hugged, but managed to mutter a sincere goodbye to their big sister.

With all the relief of a mother seeing her stray child getting back on life's track, Hannah embraced her daughter and bestowed fond hopes and wishes. "Ellitt goin' to be a fine husband to you, darlin', and a good daddy to Robert," she assured, holding Lucy's head to her shoulder for a moment and then extending her to arms length and, looking her daughter in the eye, added, "And my li'l girl goin' to be a mighty fine wife and mama."

"Oh, Mama, I don't hardly know what to say," sniffled Lucy, pulling herself to another tight squeeze for a long moment, then dabbing her eyes.

Then there was Festus. Lucy turned and stood uneasily before her father.

"Daddy, I knows what you done fer me, and I got much oblige to you fer it."

He hung his head and scuffed the dirt with his boot toe, ill at ease and at a loss for words. Finally he looked up and found it in himself to bid her a parting sentiment.

"Iffen you ever needs somethin'—ary thang atall—just call on yer mama and yer ol' daddy," he uttered, his sunken eyes looking this way and that, as if meeting her gaze would release some emotion he was holding back. He turned to go.

"Let's git on, now," he called out.

Lucy picked Robert up and watched her family troop down the path until out of sight in the dimming light. Robert looked a little bewildered and almost alarmed to see the familiar faces vanish from his view. He might have burst into tears had he not been resting on his mother's hip. Elliott stepped up behind his betrothed and put his hands lightly on her shoulders.

Grandma and the children had gone inside, where she and Lylie produced the supper. They didn't expect Lucy to get into housework on moving in day.

Early darkness had closed in over the gray naked forest, and a nippy stillness had settled upon the mountains by the time Grandma tucked the three children and herself to bed in the loft. Elliott and Lucy were left downstairs by the fireside in quiet contemplation, he puffing his cob pipe and she rocking Robert to sleep in her lap.

Looking down at the sleeping child unlocked Elliott's thoughts. "Morgan and me, we done come up together up h'yar on the mountain, and we still the bestest friends. That boy's goin' to be just like my own child to me."

Lucy felt sure that Robert now had the good daddy she'd yearned for. The niggling urgency and corroding anxiety that had beset her had now given way to the warm comfort of relief and contentment. It was with a sense of security that she looked to Elliott. "I'm goin' to be as good a mama as I can be to yer three, Ellitt."

His hand found hers and there seemed no need for further words, as the fire died to last embers.

Lucy lifted little Robert and put him under a cover on the pallet she had laid out at the foot of the bed. She and Elliott modestly turned away from each other, disrobed themselves and pulled on nightshirts. They slipped nervously under the bedcovers and lay motionless for a quiet moment, until he broke the spell by tickling her underarm.

"Hee, hee, hee; quit that Ellitt. Hee, hee, quit it now," she giggled, feeling her abashment melt away. They snuggled into a close embrace of gentle nuzzles and caresses. She felt his hand slide down her belly and his palm slowly rub her pubes, and then his fingers went between her spreading thighs. He eased over, and in. Suffused in pleasure, she let her eyes come closed.

First light revealed a white fuzz of frost covering all things outside, and a shivering chill pervaded the inside. Rosie was up early, lit the grease lamp, fired the stove and then, chamber pot in hand, went out into the raw morning for a visit to the necessary.

Warmth seeped slowly through the room, bringing the cabin to life. Elliott and Lucy stirred from the bed and the children dribbled down from the loft, rubbing their eyes. They each studied Lucy for a minute, as though the new day required them to once again record her presence as their new mama.

That Sunday morning would mark the change of command at the Hawlins cabin from Rosie to Lucy. After dressing and ducking outside for a minute, everyone went about chores. Elliott and Lucy went out, she to milk the cow and he to feed his mule and turn it out to the season's last grass. Rosie dispatched Lylie to the spring and Eddie to the woodpile. At seven he was big enough to carry in stove wood. Little Sue occupied herself with Robert, whose arrival had promoted the four-year-old up a step from being the family baby.

Rosie rustled up the breakfast, at the end of which she looked to Elliott and Lucy. "Wahl, reckon I best be a-gittin' myself on up home," she said, getting the children's attention. She went up to gather her things, leaving Lucy and Lylie washing up the cooking and table ware.

I just hopes I gits on with Lylie h'yar good as I did with li'l Janie Dinkins, thought Lucy hopefully, wanting the family merger to go smoothly and happily.

Grandma Rosie leaned over to hug each of the children. "Mind yer new mama now, you hear?" She picked Robert up and drew a shy giggle with a tickle under his chin. Then, leaning close to Lucy's ear, she said softly, "Lucy, you gots you a good hart workin' man thar and a fine li'l family to take care of now. You call on me iffen yer needin' ary help atall."

"Yass, I will."

Facing Elliott, Rosie declared, "Ellitt, you done found you the bestest woman you could have got. You best treat her with the love and respect you gave to my poor Pearl. You hear me now?"

"Yass, I most surely will, Rosie."

They all stepped out onto the porch into the chill to bid Grandma goodbye. Elliott said, "Lylie and Eddie, the two of you git yer shoes on and see Granny on home now." Rosie lived over near the head of Hazel

Hollow, about a half hour walk.

Lucy and Elliott lingered on the porch letting the new sun warm their faces, she surveying the new place and he basking in her presence.

Though not as steep, the Hawlins place resembled the Nickerson place, but to Lucy it couldn't have been more different. Two months before she had been the chafing child of a carping father and nagging mother. Now she was the wife of a caring and affectionate husband, and the mother responsible for four children. In a day, Lucy's life had been transformed from the one she had come to loathe to the one she had dreamed of. So it was with a good deal of satisfaction that she looked out over the humble homestead from the sunny porch of her new home.

Elliott eased closer and put his arm around her waist. "In the mornin' we'll git on down to Wash'tun and do up them marriage papers."

The next morning a damp mist clung to the peaks and ridges, waiting to be driven off by the climbing sun. The happy couple got into their good clothes.

Lucy put Lylie in charge of the cabin and the children for the day. "Lylie, you goin' to be a li'l mama to the children today. Daddy and me's goin' down to town and we hain't comin' back till late in the evenin'."

"Yassum."

Lucy and Elliott set out early, she in her white bonnet and he in his black vest, downhill on foot in worn out shoes. He carried two small jugs of white mule and some of the money he had earned picking apples, and by selling a small farm surplus. After descending mountain trails they picked up a rough dirt road, putting eight miles behind them by the time they reached Sperryville.

From there they hitched a ride on one of the freight wagons plying the turnpike. Six massive horses pulled them the remaining six miles to the town of Washington, Virginia, the county seat of Rappahannock County. Wagon teamsters would pick up mountaineers if they had a jug in their hand, expecting to share a few nips. Elliott surprised and delighted the teamster by giving him one of the small jugs.

They hopped off the big wagon and went straight to the clerk's office. The Clerk of Circuit Court officiated and recorded marriages. Elliott had been there once before and it was, anyway, easy to find. Washington—called Little Washington to distinguish it from Washington, D.C.—consisted of two grist mills, two taverns, four general stores, two main churches, a couple more small ones and some four hundred fifty souls in residence.

The clerk looked up from his desk when the couple came through the door.

"We wants to do up the marriage papers," announced Elliott.

"Yes, very well then." The clerk stood up, pulled a form from the file and placed it on the counter between himself and them.

"What's the name, now?" he asked, looking at Elliott.

"Ellitt Hawlins."

"Very well." He dipped his pen into the inkwell. "Then that's E-l-l-i-o-t-t H-a-w-l-i-n-s," he wrote. "And your age?"

"What?"

"How old are you, Mister Hawlins?"

"Wahl, I'm right about thirty-eight yahr, I reckon."

"Uh, yes. Thirty-eight years old then." The clerk penned 38 on the paper.

"And your address?"

"Hain't got no address."

"Where do you live?"

"Up'par in the Hazel country."

"Well then, that address would actually be Nabors Mill," he entered on the form. The clerk looked at Lucy. "And your name?"

"Lucy. Uh, Lucinda Nickerson."

"Yes, that's L-u-c-i-n-d-a N-i-c-k-e-r-s-o-n , and how old are you, Miss Nickerson?"

"I'm right at eighteen," responded Lucy, accurately.

"Yes, of course you are," he said, knowing she might or might not be, but seeing no need to add in the complication of parental permission. He wrote 18.

"And where do you live?"

"I lives with him."

"Nabors Mill, " he said and entered, and then turned the form around to face Elliott.

"Sign your name right here on this line, Mister Hawlins." With his finger at the line, the clerk offered his pen.

"Um. Uh, I cain't do it. I cain't write."

The clerk had assumed as much, but thought it the lesser embarrassment to act as though Elliott could write rather than as though he couldn't. He had a sense of civil service to all citizens and did not want to seem condescending to the mountaineers.

"Well then, just put your mark here, like this." He demonstrated by writing an X on a scrap of paper.

Elliott took the pen and, with a clumsy hand, made his X mark.

"Now you, Miss Nickerson."

"I cain't write neither."

"Make your mark then, just like his."

She marked the paper, whereupon the clerk wrote *his mark* and *her mark* by the X's, signed himself as the witness and the form was complete.

Being a good Methodist, the clerk had simple wedding vows that he preferred to use in civil ceremonies.

He faced Elliott. "Do you, Elliott Hawlins, take this woman to be your lawful wedded wife, to have and to hold, from this day forward, for better and for worse, for richer and for poorer, in sickness and in health, to love and to cherish, until death do you part?"

"Yassar, I do."

The clerk turned to Lucy. "Do you, Lucinda Nickerson, take this man to be your lawful wedded husband, to have and to hold, from this day forward, for better and for worse, for richer and for poorer, in sickness and in health, to love and to cherish, until death do you part?"

"I do."

"Then by the authority vested in me by the Commonwealth of Virginia, I pronounce you man and wife." He paused a moment, looking at Elliott. Then, with a glint of humor in his eyes, he said, "You may now kiss the bride."

The newlyweds stood there looking puzzled.

"I.. yes. Uh, well, you're now lawfully married Mister and Missus Hawlins, and that will be ten cents."

"Thank you, judge," said Elliott, slapping a dime on the counter.

"You're welcome, Mister Hawlins. I'm just the clerk of the court, though."

Elliott and Lucy stepped out and walked a block down to the road to hail a ride back to Sperryville, giving the teamster the second jug for his kindness. They stopped at the general store in the village before beginning their trek back up the mountain. Elliott had some money left over after recently paying off his account at the Nabors store.

The small village of Sperryville boasted two general stores, a school and a small hotel. Sitting at the junction of two turnpikes, one from the town of Warrenton, and the other running from Culpeper west over the mountains to the Shenandoah Valley towns of Luray and New Market, the stores offered a larger variety of goods.

Elliott took advantage of the infrequent visit to do a little shopping. Winter was coming on, so he chose new boots and Lucy picked out a pair of high-laced shoes. They guessed at Lylie's size and bought her shoes one size larger. The other children wore hand-me-downs, when they wore shoes at all, which was only in the snow or the coldest weather. In the mountains, shoes were a luxury to be conserved.

Elliott noticed Lucy fingering a small oval mirror on a handle, looking at herself. She looked up to see him watching her and blushed with a shy smile.

"Go on and set the lookin' glass thar with the shoes," he said, with an amused grin, motioning her to include it with the purchase. Lucy was tickled. A gift seemed entirely in order. It was their wedding day.

"Comes to four dollar eighty-four cent, with the mirror," said the clerk.

Elliott dropped his last silver dollars onto the counter, and fished coins from his pocket. He knew that a nickel was five pennies, a dime was two nickels and a quarter was five nickels. But it was beyond his ken to add up the coins to a total. He just spilled them all out onto the counter and let the clerk count out the eighty-four cents.

"Four dollars and eighty-five cents. Your change is an Indian Head." The clerk completed the transaction, pushing the excess coins plus the Indian Head penny back to Elliott.

The two plopped down on the store's porch bench to pull on their new footwear.

"I hain't never had no *new* shoes afore, Ellitt!" Lucy exclaimed, beaming at her newly shod feet and her newly wedded husband.

Off they strode in their new footwear, walking the back road along the base of the mountains, to the smell of fallen leaves and of wood smoke hanging low in the cooling air. As the sinking late autumn sun reached for the high ridges, they turned onto the trail up the mountain, to be home by twilight.

"Oh Daddy! Oh Lucy!" Lylie was thrilled to step into new shoes. They were a little too long, which was good. Shoes had to last several years. Lylie would not come to call Lucy Mama, as the other children would.

After supper, Lucy showed Lylie the mirror. The girl twisted it to different angles, peering at herself gleefully. "You can use it ary time you wants," said Lucy. She was beginning to feel like a partner with little Lylie. It reminded Lucy of her month with Janie Dinkins three and a half years earlier, and turned her thoughts fondly to Robert.

ELEVEN
Joy and Sorrow

Winter loomed. Early December was devoted to preparing for the cold and dormant months. In the mountains, every increase of one hundred feet in elevation equates to being twenty miles further north. Winter up in the Hazel country brought the biting cold and snowfalls of middle New England.

Mountain dwellings were always in need of repair, and the Hawlins cabin was no exception. New mud needed to be daubed in where the old had fallen out between the logs, and between foundation and chimney stones. Several roof leaks demanded repair and it was time to replace a porch step or two.

Hand-split white oak or chestnut roof shingles were long lasting, but everyone nursed extra time from them by patching up the frequent small nuisance leaks. American Chestnut also made superior fence rails so Elliott, whenever splitting rails, would also cut and set aside several round chestnut blocks from a large tree. The blocks, sections of tree trunks a couple of feet long, would dry for a year. Then he'd split them into the shingles to fix the old roofing on the cabin, corn crib, barn and sheds.

A mild day heralded the end of autumn. The afternoon saw Elliott sitting on a stool in the yard, using his maul and frow to split roof shingles from a round block of chestnut. He placed the frow blade edge on the block of wood and then smacked the back of the blade with the wooden maul, slicing off shingles, one at a time.

Lucy sat on the porch, her leathery bare foot pumping the spinning wheel pedal, twisting out a strand of yarn, the homespun from which women made cloth on small handlooms.

"Ellitt, don't fergit that leak up'par against the chimley," she reminded him.

"Yass indeed, they's about four places I got to fix up'par," he said. "I done laid it off and laid it off the entahr yahr, but I'm goin' to fix 'em all today."

Lucy took her foot off the pedal. "I'm a-thinkin' I gots me enough yarn h'yar to make somethin' fer everone," she said to herself, studying the output of her spinning wheel.

Elliott rose from his stool, gathered up a pile of new shingles, balanced the load on his shoulder and carried it over to his homemade ladder leaning against the porch roof. He'd put one foot on the bottom rung when Lucy looked up to see him wobble a little under his load, jerking the ladder a bit. She hopped up and reached for the ladder.

"H'yar now, let me holt the ladder fer you," she said, planting her feet on the porch edge with her hands on the ladder rails. "Cain't have my man breakin' no leg or nothin'," she said teasingly.

Steadied, he went up the ladder and flopped the shingles onto the roof, and looked back down. "Now you mind yer spinnin' thar, woman. Cain't have you pinchin' no finger or nothin'," he countered with a wry smile, before he heaved himself onto the roof and went about fitting the shingles in where needed to replace the bad ones.

Lucy went back to her spinning, reminded of the contentment she felt with her new life, and her growing love of her husband.

A deep cold snap just before Christmas put the Hawlinses inside, sitting close by the fire. "Good day fer easy settin' down work," said Elliott. "Got plenty of corn to shell out," he said, as he picked up another ear of corn and used the heel of his hand to rub the kernels from the cob.

Lucy busied herself with sewing and mending and Lylie sat at the table using a little hammer and her nimble fingers to crack out black walnuts. Black walnuts were collected in October and dried until the husks fell away. Walnut was a delicacy by virtue of the difficulty in cracking out the meat from the thick hard shells.

The harshest winter weather kept them indoors. They only ventured out to feed animals, collect eggs and fetch water or wood. They had dried the cow in preparation for early spring calving, so there was no milking.

The upper mountain people had developed a form of semi-dormancy to sustain them through the coldest days. They'd sleep twelve hours through the long night and then sit sedately by the cabin fire or stove, with only the minimum activity necessary to take care of basic needs.

On milder winter days, Elliott deployed his pent up energy to such outdoor tasks as prying up field rocks, and using his skid sledge and mule to drag them to pile into walls. Or he added to the firewood supply. The skid sledge was a homemade sled of poles and planks that was mostly used without snow. Snow days were put to better use skidding long logs down the hillsides to the woodpile for sawing. Lucy mostly stayed inside through the winter, busying herself with knitting, sewing and mending—along with the many chores of housekeeping and motherhood.

The greening of spring creeping up the slopes brought the mountains back to life. Gardens were put out and the cabbage, potato, bean and corn patches were planted. Wild greens and mushrooms were gathered and pasture was burned off. The Hawlins cow birthed her calf and the milk pail came full again.

When the soil was dry enough, Elliott hitched up the mule and went about plowing the garden and the several crop patches— the small, irregular cultivated areas wending around and between rocks too large to remove. The land was too rocky and uneven for regular squared-off fields. The drudgery of preparing the soil required a special skill to work the mule and the tireless stamina to keep up with the animal as it pulled and jerked the hand plow through rough soil.

Some spots had so many rocks that the soil around them could only be chopped up with a grubbing hoe.

While plowing, Elliott barked out mule calls—"Git up! now, Ho! now, Gee!, Haw!"—the commands to go forward, stop, go right, go left, as he lurched along behind the single bottom plow, his hands gripping the wooden handles and his boots stomping the clods turned over by the iron blade. Prying a modest measure of productivity out of stubborn land was rugged and exhausting work.

One evening, after a day of heavy labor, a soft twilight fell with an eyelash moon and the evening star hanging close in the sky above the mountain. In the stillness of the fading day, Lucy joined Elliott on the porch and stood beside him at the rocking chair in serene communion.

"I'm in a family way," she said in a muted voice, putting her hand on his shoulder. "I'm sure of it." She didn't expect excitement or any strong reaction from him. Pregnancy was life's natural progression, and not a cause for celebration.

Elliott contemplated the news for a silent minute before saying, "Wahl, it'll make one family out of two pushed together."

A warm glow of contentment came over Lucy. She felt the merger had gone well, but his sentiment now struck a comforting chord. She well knew about the husbands who took so little interest in pregnancy that there was no point in the wife even announcing it. It was women's business. She could not imagine a better outcome from her precarious transition to womanhood.

Elliott liked to do a little late season raccoon hunting in the spring, before the trees fully leafed out. Hunting season for most game was during fall and winter. There were no official hunting seasons in the mountains at that time, but it didn't matter much, for little game was left in the mountains. Large animals had been hunted nearly to elimination. Bears were extremely rare and deer were quite scarce. With so few deer, the cougars had completely vanished. A few foxes and bobcats remained, but the game had mostly dwindled down to raccoons, opossums, squirrels and rabbits. There were plenty of skunks, but no one hunted skunks.

Raccoons are nocturnal foragers, so hunting them was done at night with dogs. Saturday moonlit nights were for 'coon hunting, and 'coon hunting was Elliott's passion. As the moon waxed toward full, he looked forward to a Saturday night of pursuing the furry masked creatures.

After supper, Elliott walked down to his dog pen. Two figures approached the cabin from the other direction.

"Evenin', Lucy!" called one of the two men, as she started for the spring with a crock of fresh milk. "Whar's that thar man of yourn!"

"He right down thar to the dog pen," she yelled, pointing toward the small log barn.

The two turned toward the pen, each being tugged along by an exuberant hound on a rope leash. Elliott was retrieving his own black and tan hound dog. The three of them returned to the porch and tied off their dogs, which calmed them down. The coonhounds had become conditioned to expect a hunt whenever the leash rope went on, and it excited their predator instincts.

Jake and Odie had come up from the Hannah's Run side of Nickerson Hollow to hunt with Elliott. Both were slim wiry fellows—not bone skinny, but looking like they had more stringy sinew than bulk muscle on their frames. They were both taller and a few years younger than Elliott. The two looked like brothers, but weren't. The main distinguishing difference between them was that Odie's britches were a couple inches short, exposing his ankles, while Jake's were long and rumpled on his boots—as if the two wore misfit hand-me-downs. They actually were related, though neither knew exactly how or through which of their many Nickerson kin.

The three of them were sitting on the porch passing a jug when Lucy walked back from the spring.

THE TALE OF A WOODS COLT

"Whar abouts you boys huntin' tonight?" she queried, looking at no one.

"Reckon we gon' start over thar below the Hot Top, soon's the moon gits riz up," said Elliott from the rocker. A 'coon chase could range over hill and hollow, going until the fleeing raccoon either evaded the dogs or tired and climbed a tree.

There was still nearly a half hour until dark so the hunters bided the time by amusing themselves with the highlights of memorable earlier hunts. Hunting talk was for men only and Lucy anyway had little interest in it, so she left them to their tales.

Odie began with a story about a 'coon hunt gone awry.

"I cain't hardly git over the time that ol' dog of Lester's done treed and Lester, he see'd this li'l furry thang out on a branch in the dark and figgered he done had him a young 'coon," said Odie. "Lester, he fahred his gun, but the shot hit the branch and outen the tree drops this li'l ol' spotty pole cat skunk. Afore ol' Lester or the dogs can do ary a thang, that pole cat stands right up on his hands and sprays Lester down!"

They all let out a laugh at Lester's expense. Odie went on.

"Dogs done hung back and li'l pole cat, he just run off in the brush. Lester, he smelt so bad you had to stand on the upwind side to git near him!" said Odie, to more laughing.

Odie continued.

"Wahl, ol' Lester, he goes to cussin' and kickin', and we's just laughin' at him and all. Then he goes stompin' on home, so dang mad at us and that pole cat you hear't him cussin' clear across the holler!"

They all laughed and Odie finished the story.

"Lester, he dast not go in the house once't he got thar. No indeed. Instead, he shuck offen his clothes down by the branch and tried to wash it off, but it didn't come off too good. His woman, she made him sleep in the shed fer more'n a week—sarved him his vittles down thar and all. Even his dogs won't git near him! Ha! ha! ha, ha."

Everyone had a good laugh, with a few extra jokes tossed in about

Lester's wife's reaction to the ill-fated 'coon hunt.

In a bit Jake took a turn at telling a 'coon hunting tale.

"Ellitt, remember that thar time ol' Bennie wahr a-chasin' around back side the Hazel and got hisself all hung up in that thar ivy slick[4]?" Jake was talking to Elliott, but looking at Odie, who was not on the storied hunt and thus was the main audience of the tale.

"The dogs done struck[5] and ol' Bennie, he got to runnin' down so fast he went right over the edge of that ol' rock face afore he could git hisself stopped, and he dropped right smack in the ivy brush. He wahr all hung up and stuck in thar up offen the ground and cain't git hisself freed up or nothin'."

Odie let out a laugh, Elliott chucked and Jake went on with it.

"Bennie, he done gone to hollerin' but the dogs, they was a-yelpin' so loud you couldn't hear ol' Bennie atall. We just follered the dogs till they done treed the 'coon a right smart piece down from whar ol' Bennie wahr caught up in the ivy."

Jake paused for effect.

"Ol' Charlie, he done shot the 'coon outen the tree when I looked around and see'd thar wharn't no Bennie thar with us atall. We all holler't at him, but we didn't hear nary a thang. We took off up the mountain hollerin' 'Yee-ar! Bennie!!' loud as we could yell. We got us up the hill a piece to whar we done hear't him a-cryin'—'Over h'yar! I'm over h'yar in the ivy slick! I cain't git loose!! Hurry boys! I'm bodaciously ruin't![6]"

That got a little laugh out of both Odie and Elliott.

"Next thang, we got over to him and see'd his shirt wahr all tore open and he's a-bleedin' some, but he wahrn't actual ruin't atall. Mostly he's just cussin' up one side and down t'other."

Elliott chucked at the memory of it.

---

4 A dense mountainside stand of mountain laurel, an evergreen shrub related to Rhododendron, having stiff twisted intertwined branches.
5 Detected an animal's scent trail.
6 Seriously injured.

"Remember, Ellitt, how you done said to him 'Bennie, we's goin' to come back in the mornin' to cut you loose, because its too dark now,' and how he went to cussin' you and sayin' about how he gon' cut yer gizzard out and all, iffen you don't git him loose from the ivy right away?!"

Elliott laughed, and finished the story.

"Yass indeed. I's just foolin' with him, but ol' Bennie, he wahrn't in no mind to be fool't with. Once't we done cut him out of the ivy, he just went on down the mountain all by his ownself–didn't say 'thank you' or nothin' to us. Ol' Bennie, he stayed mighty scarce after that– and he hain't been out huntin' no more, neither."

The three hunters had another good laugh at Bennie, and then went to idle chat and banter, mostly about the traits and merits of their various coonhounds.

Then Elliott started in with another story.

"Then thar's that night late in the springtime when ol' Buck, he runs right up on a big ol' rattler snake. The dogs, they strike a lead on a 'coon and whup off a-yelpin' up the mountain. Ol' Buck, he goes to chasin' up through the brush to whar that thar ol' blue tick hound of his'n done stopped dead up'par in the rough."

Seeing he had the rapt attention of Jake and Odie, Elliott goes on.

"His dog, it standin' thar just a-snarlin' and ol' Buck, he figgers they's a snake and then he puts his foot right thar by the querled up sarpent, because he cain't see nothin' atall in the dark. The snake, it strikes out and hits him on the leg and ol' Buck, he just goes to hoppin' and a-hollerin' 'I done been snake bit! I done been snake bit!'"

Jake and Odie are captivated by the story, so Elliott forges on through the rest of the snake tale.

"Now that big ol' snake, all it done was snag its fangs in Buck's britches. It went to flyin' around with ol' Buck hoppin' and a-jumpin' and tryin' to kick the snake loose. He figgers the rattler done had a solid bite on his leg and I hope to tell you, Ol' Buck, he mighty scare't.

Soon enough he kicks the snake loose and it goes a-flyin' on down in the brush. Buck, he cryin' loud as he could, 'I'm snake bit! Ol' rattler snake done bit me on the leg!'

"What done happen then?" asked Odie.

"We's all right scare't too because didn't none of us have nary a drop of liquor to give him, and we's way up'par on the Hot Top. We's all afear't Buck gon' surely die. Wahl, we gits right up thar to him and he's sittin' thar cryin', 'I'm gon' die! I'm gon' die!'"

"But ol' Buck, he hain't dead atall," said Jake, inviting the end of the story.

"I'm a-gitten to that," said Elliott. "We lifts up Buck's britches and we done see'd thar warn't no snakebite. Ol' rattler snake just got hooked on his britches but never did bite his leg atall. I said, 'Quit yer bawlin' Buck. You hain't been bit atall,' but he just keeps on a-cryin' 'I'm dyin'! Oh Lord! I'm dyin' from snakebite!'

"Wahl, right then we's all a-laughin' and a-hootin' at him and all. He looks down to his leg and sees he hain't got no bite. Right thar he gits real quiet and commences to lookin' all around—fer a hole to crawl into, I reckon. Then Ol' Buck, he gits so mad at us fer laughin' and funnin' at him, why I believe right thar he done wish't he actual *wahr* snake bit!" They all had a good belly laugh at Buck and the rattlesnake.

By then it was dark and the moon had risen, so off they went.

The dogs, straining at their ropes, pulled the three hunters down a rough road toward Hot Mountain. Once out of sight of any cabins, they turned the hounds loose. The dogs scattered out through the woods with noses to the ground.

Elliott's dog soon struck a lead and went to yelping, signaling the others to come that way. Every 'coon hunter knows the sound of his own dog. In a minute all three dogs were tracking the scent, with the hunters tramping behind, following by ear.

"C'mon, boys, they's a-headin' right around side of the Hot Top!" called Elliott, as the chase picked up and they went crashing through the woods in pursuit. There was no easy route. They'd listen to which way the dogs were going and then pick a little easier route for themselves, but it was rough going. Gripping their muzzle loading shotguns, the three stumbled through the forest, hopping over fallen logs and dodging around huge boulders in the pale moonlight.

"They's a-goin' down that thar rocky side!" hollered Jake.

The pack's frenzied yelping on the trail of the fleeing quarry brought the hunters' excitement to a fever pitch. The exhilaration of charging headlong through dimly lit, rock and log cluttered woods is something only 'coon hunters understand.

Elliott led the way. "It's takin' 'em right up the draw, boys! Let's git us on up' par!" His stocky legs and low center of gravity made him well adapted to charging up and down slopes, scrambling over fallen trees and around boulders and rockfalls.

"They's runnin' down to the branch!" cried Elliott, pointing the direction.

Raccoons are wily, mischievous and clever creatures that can often lose the hounds by running or swimming down the middle of a creek, or by climbing a tree and going tree-to-tree on limbs to break the scent trail. The 'coon this night was likely doomed, because the streams that high up in the hollow were too small to lose a scent. A big twenty-five pound racoon can fight off one dog, but not a pack.

"It must be a big 'un, fast as he's goin'!" exclaimed Elliott. Trying to keep up, Jake and Odie were too winded to say anything. The pursuit chased hither and yon, setting all adrenaline to high rush—the hunter's, the hound's and the raccoon's.

Then the noisy dogs were no longer moving.

"They got him treed, boys!" cried Elliott.

"Yee'ar!!" The whooping hunters barreled toward the dog's din, straddling fallen trees and sidestepping boulders as they stumbled along through the jumbled forest.

Elliott, soaked in sweat despite the chilly night, was first to the treed 'coon. Odie and Jake soon came thrashing up behind him. All three stood with heads rolled back, shifting and craning, trying to spot the animal up in the tree in the dim moonlight.

The 'coon had gone up high in a big solitary white pine, with no chance to jump to another tree, leaving the yelping hounds jumping and pawing up the bark at the base.

"Thar he is! Up'par on yer left, in that thar shady spot!" called Odie, pointing.

"I sees him." Elliott raised and cocked his musket, braced himself against a small tree, took careful aim in the low light and slowly squeezed his finger on the trigger.

It was customary to let the hunter whose dog struck the scent shoot the first 'coon.

Bam!!! The shot 'coon plummeted to the ground with a thud and was quickly grabbed up and bagged by Jake before the dogs got it and tore it apart.

"Yee'ar, it's a big ol' 'coon, Ellitt!" he cried, swinging the sack over his shoulder.

Altogether, they had bagged three raccoons by the time the weary party shuffled back to the Hawlins place in a wee hour. Jake and Odie headed for the trail to home with their dogs, guns and bagged 'coons.

One 'coon each, the night had been successful—except for the raccoons.

"Be good, Ellitt!"

"See you around, boys!" shouted Elliott, as he penned his hound. It was near daybreak when he slipped wearily into bed beside Lucy.

Lucy skinned and butchered the raccoon in the morning, carefully removing the scent glands and giving the scraps to the dogs. It put fresh meat on the table and the pelt could be traded at the store.

Spring yielded to summer, and in time summer's warmth gave way to the crisp air of autumn. The forests went to full blaze with bright colors crawling downslope from the mountaintops. Corn was cut, trees shed their leaves and hogs were butchered. Lucy, her belly bulging, knew it wouldn't be long now.

Lowlanders would be celebrating Thanksgiving, but not the mountain people, most of whom only barely recognized Christmas and New Year's day.

Lucy's pains started one afternoon just after the mid-day meal.

Elliott was at the barn chinking logs when he looked up and saw Lylie racing down the path toward him.

"Daddy! Lucy, she done got the pains!"

The two hustled up to the cabin to find Lucy lying on the bed. Eddie, Sue and little Robert stood next to her, all three crying. The older two remembered only one other birth, and that was just over a year before when they'd been sent away and then came home to find their mother gone forever. The children were afraid and so was Elliott. Little Robert was too young to understand. He was upset because the others were.

Elliott issued an order. "Lylie, take Eddie and Sue on down and tell Aunt Tilly Lucy done got the pains and Daddy'll come fer her once't the water's broke. Then git on down and tell Hannah. Stay down thar 'till Daddy comes fer you in the mornin', you hear me now?"

"Yass, Daddy," said Lylie obediently, her face showing her apprehension.

"Git on, now!"

Elliott watched from the porch as his progeny disappeared down the trail. He turned and went in to be with Lucy. Little Robert had stayed behind in the cabin. He was too small to walk the two miles and too young to take any real interest in the birth. Elliott sat on the bed holding Lucy's hand in his. She squeezed tightly and cried out at a sharp contraction, bringing little Robert to tears.

"What's wrong, Mama?" he blubbered.

She reassured him. "Nothin's wrong, darlin'. Mama's just havin' a baby, that's all."

That seemed to satisfy him so he went back to amusing himself, leaving Elliott to fret over the impending birth as he sat with Lucy, putting on a cheery front and trying to conceal his worry.

"This h'yar gon' be the child what ties our family together," he said with a warm smile, as he held her hand in his.

"Me'n the baby gon' be just fine," she said, sensing the fear behind his face.

It was late afternoon when, to Elliott's relief, Hannah and Jenny came through the door. Jenny had not yet dared to accept Tilly's year-old invitation to attend another birth. But Lucy was her sister so Hannah, seeing Jenny would suffer more staying at home than by coming, had let her come.

Elliott withdrew to the porch, where one side of him reassured that childbirth was routine but the other side gnawed at him with the fear of disaster.

Lucy's water broke as the waning sun was sinking behind the mountain. Elliott sprang into action and hurried down to fetch Tilly.

Ernest and Tilly had just finished the evening meal when Elliott's head popped in the door. "Lucy's water done broke." Elliott and the midwife scurried back up the trail by moonlight, as darkness closed in across the silent mountains. He took up his worry station on the dim porch and Tilly reached for the door.

Hannah looked up from the stove when Tilly stepped into the room. "I got's the water to bilen. It won't be long, Tilly."

Tilly examined the patient. Finding all in order, she put her hand on Lucy's and leaned in close with words of reassurance, "You goin' to be fine now, she said, just above a whisper. "Everthang goin' to be just fine."

Out on the porch, Elliott sat rocking nervously, puffing his cob pipe. Jenny came out and placed herself uneasily on the porch steps. Neither said anything. He recalled Jenny being at Pearl's catastrophe and the sudden shock she'd suffered.

THE TALE OF A WOODS COLT

He thought it over and decided that the girl was selecting a position for herself, rather than seeking his company. He was there on the porch because that was the closest a mountain man could get to a birth. She was there because that was the least uncomfortable distance from the birth. Further away and she'd have to worry about what happened. Any closer and she'd have to see it happen.

He sat taut and silent, trying to interpret the sounds escaping from inside. Was Lucy's screaming and moaning worse than usual? Was it all taking too long? What did Tilly just say? Did the baby cry yet?

Finally the door flew open and Hannah stepped out, wearing the grin she reserved for special occasions.

"It's a girl! And Lucy done real good!"

Elliott and Jenny's eyes met in a moment of melting anxiety. Then they both were on their feet and through the door. Jenny's eyes went from Lucy to Tilly to Hannah and then around again in a celebration of the arrival of new life and the banishment of old terrors.

Elliott went straight to Lucy's bedside and sat, holding her hand and basking in her soft gaze. She spoke in a feeble yet happy voice. "This h'yar li'l girl makes two families into one."

"Sure enough, Lucy," was all he could say.

Winter struck with the vengeance of a swirling snowstorm, followed by plunging temperatures. Life on the mountain went indoors and slowed down. These were the riskiest months for the newborn. But to Lucy's relief, her tiny one stayed healthy.

The mountains were largely free of infectious epidemics, mostly because people lived well spaced apart, had infrequent social contact and drank pristine spring water. Still, four children in ten died before age five, of one thing or another.

Winter gave way and the spring blossomed into summer, and the summer ripened into autumn apple season, a time of plenty in the mountains. Apples meant food and drink, socializing and a little cash money. Everyone had at least a few apple trees and some, like Morgan Dinkins, had fruit to sell, in one form or another.

Many a mountain man came down to pick the thousands of bushels of Winesaps, Staymans, Jonathans, Grimes Goldens, Yorks and Blacktwigs from the heavily laden trees in the many small commercial orchards that studded the low slopes around Nabors Mill, Sperryville, and all along the base of the Blue Ridge.

Apple picking paid fifty cents a day, or sometimes a penny a bushel. Working on piecework, an energetic picker could earn a dollar in a very long day. The money earned in a few weeks of picking apples was about the most cash any mountain family would ever see at one time.

They also had to process the apples from their own trees for their own use. The better fruit were cored, sliced and spread on the rooftops to dry in the sun. Whole families participated in apple drying to get it done on the sunny days.

The next best apples went to apple butter. Boiling apple butter was an outdoor event with a fire under a big copper kettle full of apple mush. It was sometimes a cooperative social occasion that brought together two families. Everyone down around Nabors Mill made apple butter, but the Hawlins and Nickersons were among the very few upper hollow mountaineers who could afford the investment needed to produce and put up the delicious spread, one of the delights in the diet of those that had it.

Finally, the bruised drops and stunted leftover apples were chopped and pressed into cider, which fermented into hard cider that then was mostly converted into apple jack, the distilled brandy for which the mountains were famous. Some of the mountain men's distilling skills were legendary.

The Hawlinses and the Nickersons alternated convening at each other's place for a day of boiling down apple butter and squeezing cider. The host family mother and daughters would spend the previous day washing, peeling, coring and quartering ten bushels of apples—filling up every tub, bucket, pot, pail, and kettle they could muster.

A brisk and blustery October day found them all up at the Hawlins place. A fire burned under the big copper kettle that held a stew of cut up apples and water.

Boiling apple butter involved only two tasks, leaving plenty of time to hobnob. The fire had to be kept at a steady heat, and the kettle had to be stirred non-stop with a big wooden spoon-billed paddle. Managing the fire wasn't hard, but it required constant attention to keep the oak and hickory burning at an even heat. Stirring the apples had to be continuous and consistent. It was working the paddle two times around and once across the big kettle, nonstop all day long. Arms tired quickly, so everyone big enough to stir took a turn, and then took more turns until it was done.

"Otis, git over h'yar and stir the kettle!" called Hannah, who had tired at her turn with the paddle.

"Aw, that thar hain't man's work atall," complained Otis good naturedly, defending the masculine dignity required by eighteen year-old boys, then taking hold of the paddle and turning the task to his credit by stirring longer than anyone else.

Richard stayed scarce until he finally yielded to temptation and peeked around the cabin corner, smirking at Otis as he stirred. Festus spotted him.

"Richard! Git out thar and stir that damn kettle!" barked his father, who then spit out a shot of tobacco spit and took a swig from his jug. Richard dragged his feet. "Git on now, afore I whack you upside the head," growled the tipsy Festus, threatening the twelve year-old into shuffling sullenly over to the kettle and taking his turn.

In a while, Lucy relieved her little brother at the kettle. Hannah balanced the baby on her hip while Lucy stirred a spell; then they swapped and Hannah stirred the pot while Lucy held Florie, occasionally letting her down to try a few steps on her ten month-old legs, while holding onto her hands. Lucy had named her Florence.

"Mama, I'm goin' to have another child," she confided to Hannah. "I hain't tolt Ellitt yet." Lucy was all of twenty years old. She didn't expect much reaction from Hannah. Her mother just cracked a thin smile and nodded approvingly.

The apple chunks softened and broke down into a bubbling sauce within a couple of hours, thickening gradually. Noontime dinner was an outdoor picnic, with someone stirring the kettle all the while. The sauce would quickly burn on the kettle bottom if stirring stopped for just a few minutes, ruining the entire batch.

Then the sugar was added. "Stir in the money!" called Elliott, making a joke.

"Pour in that money!" seconded Festus. About three pounds of sugar was added per gallon of apple butter, adding up to a hundred pound sack of sugar—six dollars at the Nabors store. That was serious money.

Elliott and Festus had busied themselves with the side job of grinding juice apples and squeezing the pulp, using a small, wood-slatted cider press. Their corn whiskey jug emptied as the cider jugs filled. By mid-day, the two of them had downed half the jug, were more than a little lit and in a spirited mood.

The apple butter was finally ready. The last step was to dip and pack the finished product into the glass Mason jars that had appeared in the local stores not long after the Civil War ended.

"We got enough jars, Lucy?" asked Hannah

"I got some more in the cellar. Lylie, fetch up them jars outen the cellar!"

"Yassum."

With the last of the thick brown apple butter packed into jars and sealed, the Nickersons went home, leaving cleanup to the Hawlins. Elliott was wiping the kettle out with corncobs, with Lucy standing alongside gently bouncing Florie on her hip. "I'm goin' to have another one, Ellitt," she announced, looking at the infant.

He looked up, broke a small smile, and went on cleaning the kettle.

Winter came and went. Spring brought new life to the mountains and to the Hawlins cabin—a baby boy. The tiny one was premature, and they hadn't yet settled on a name.

Within days, the infant fell ill. Lucy noticed a slight fever. Fevers and infections were very common, but also worrisome. Herbal remedies weren't possible for babies, and doctors weren't accessible. Natural healing was the only cure.

After dinner, Lucy sat nursing her little one when he started spitting up his milk. No amount of burping helped. By supper, he had bad diarrhea. The family was apprehensive when they turned in for the night, and Lucy was alarmed.

By lamplight, she sat up with the infant, keeping him clean and trying to nurse him. But he couldn't keep it down. In the night, diarrhea worsened into dysentery, and severe dehydration.

In the pale light of dawn, Lucy was sitting by the stove cradling her baby, slowly rocking and sobbing softly. He had died in the wee hours. All the children came down and began crying. In time, Elliott gently lifted the small bundle from her arms. "It wahr meant to be," he said to console her, but she was inconsolable.

Loss of infants and small children afflicted nearly all mountain families. It was expected, but that only made it more familiar, not less painful. Elliott devoted the morning to making a small pine board coffin and digging the tiny grave at the burying ground. Infants that died were given full funerals on the mountain, but with a closed coffin and no preacher. The tiny one with no name was laid to rest by those gathered upon the knoll, identified only by a pointed headstone and footstone planted a couple of feet apart.

TWELVE

Late 1881
The Fall

Fall was the finest time in the mountains. The promise of spring, nurtured by summer, came to fruitition in fall–crops, gardens, apples, hogs and calves and the joy of life. Once all the winter provisions had been laid in, and the forest had shed its spent leaves, many a mountain man's thoughts turned to 'coon hunting.

The Friday weather was splendid for early December. Calm and cold, the clear skies pointed to a perfect night for hunting. No lanterns would be needed in the light of a waxing moon just three days shy of full.

Twilight fell early. Morgan had come up to join Elliott and the two regulars, Jake and Odie. He was discreet enough to stay outside the Hawlins cabin, and Lucy returned his discretion by remaining inside with Robert and the other children.

The hunting party set out downhill, down into the Hannah's Run area of Nickerson Hollow. Morgan's blue tick hound struck a scent near Short Mountain and off dashed the dogs with noses to the ground, yelping up a commotion that only four frenzied coonhounds could make. As usual, Elliott led the group in whooping down one slope and up the next.

"Step it up boys, they's a-headin' fer the Catlett!" called Elliott, urging them on toward Catlett Mountain. The hunters tromped and stumbled their way along the mountainside, then down into the hollow where Hannah's Run was flowing full and cold. There they paused to listen for the hounds.

"They's a-runnin' down the branch!" yelled Elliott. "Ol' 'coon tryin' to lose the scent!" They all took off downstream. A ways down Elliott halted, cocked an ear and called out, "They's back on the scent, whuppin' up the mountain makin' fer the pinnacle! Let's git on up' par, boys! Yee'ar!!"

The others had neither Elliott's zeal nor the legs to pump straight up the steep pitch.

"You git on, Ellitt. Me'n the boys'll be along directly," said Morgan, catching his breath. Morgan didn't try to keep up with his exuberant friend. It suited him to just stay within earshot of the dogs, knowing that a treed 'coon could wait until he got there.

So off went Elliott alone, swinging his legs over downed trees and side-stepping around boulders as he charged straight uphill in a bee line behind the dogs, while the others followed, picking their way on a switchback route up the mountain.

The three had made the ridgeline when Morgan paused, "The dogs hain't runnin' no more. Must have driven ol' 'coon up a tree." The yelping pack was a ways out on the long razorback ridge. The trio worked their way along the crest, dodging around several large rock outcroppings.

Directly, they came to the hound dog pandemonium at the trunk of a chestnut oak tree, where the yelping dogs jumped and pawed up to feverishly scratch the bark. Sure enough, up in the tree sat the 'coon, hunched in a limb crotch near the top. It wasn't very far above the ground, less than fifty feet. The trees didn't grow tall that far up on the dry rocky ridges. The cowering fur ball was quite visible in the bright moonlight.

But there was no Elliott.

"Ellitt!!" called Morgan. *Hain't like Ellitt to be slow gittin' up the mountain*, he thought, worried that something had gone wrong.

"Ellitt!! ... Ellitt!!" hollered Jake and Odie, with hands cupped to mouths.

They heard nothing over the din of the dogs.

Morgan decided that they should spread out for a better chance to hear Elliott. "Jake, git on down the side a ways, and Odie, you git on down over thar a piece. I'll drop down the middle. Listen careful and see iffen we cain't hear him."

The three hunters put about a hundred yards between them, and slipped downslope far enough to put the canine racket into the background.

"Ellitt!! Ellitt!! E-e-l-litt!!" cried out all three as they went, cocking ears and craning necks with every call.

Nothing.

Finally Morgan hollered, "Let's git on back up boys!" They reconvened on the ridge at the treed 'coon, which Morgan promptly shot and Jake bagged. The 'coon chase was over. Now they had to find Elliott.

Morgan said what he thought they all were thinking. "He done got hisself hurt somewhar down thar. Broke a leg or somethin'. We's best find him afore daybreak." The sharp night air had dropped below freezing.

They didn't know Elliott's exact route up the mountainside. Had he come straight up from Hannah's Run toward the ridge? Or had he angled up from the stream toward their present position? Morgan offered a search strategy.

"Let's foller slaunchways all the way down to the branch where he left off. Iffen we hain't found him yet, we can make straight back up to the ridge from thar." The other two nodded and the search was set.

They spread out but stayed within sight of each other, and picked their way down at an angle to the slope, calling out and straining to see through the forest in the filtered moonlight. The hounds had chased off and were a distant din half a mountain away. Reaching the bottom, dismay fell across their faces as they pushed through the last bit of undergrowth to the stream.

Discouragement was papable in Morgan's voice. "Wahl boys, let's just take her slow right straight up to the ridge," he said, activating the second leg of the search plan.

Up they tramped, panting and pausing, directly up the steep pitch, but with no sign of Elliott. The searchers staggered onto the ridge in a profuse sweat, despite the frigid air. The mood was despondent. Now what?

Morgan had been evaluating the situation and, with neither sign nor sound of Elliott, had concluded that there were two possibilities: Elliott had hurt himself—maybe a broken arm—and, being out of earshot, went straight home; or Elliott was injured such that he couldn't call out. Morgan feared the latter but tried to put it in a positive light. "He might have just hurt his arm and done gone home, bein' how he didn't hear us hollerin'," he ventured, trying to keep hope alive.

Morgan turned it over in his mind for a long minute before deciding what to do.

"Thar hain't no use in us huntin' fer him no more till daylight. Let's git us on back to his place," he said. "Iffen he hain't thar, we all can come on back at first light." The party, with a sense of gloom tempered by hope, picked up the ridge trail and circled back around to the Hazel country as the moon leaned toward a far ridge.

Morgan despaired as they wearily approached the Hawlins cabin and he saw that all was dark and quiet. If an injured Elliott had returned, lamplight would glow in the window.

"Odie, slip on in and wake Lucy," said Morgan.

Odie slid the door peg and eased into the dark cabin. Lucy was a sleeping form under covers on the plank bed.

"Psst. Lucy," hissed Odie, as if he were afraid of waking her instead of trying to rouse her. He tried again, raising his voice. "Psst! Lucy," Then he called out, "Lucy!"

"Ellitt. That you Ellitt?"

"No, Lucy. It's Odie."

Lucy sat up in bed. "Odie! Whar's Ellitt, Odie?"

"We cain't find him, Lucy. He's somewhar on the mountain and we done hunt all up and down, We cain't find him nowhar. You best come on out," he said before slipping back through the door.

Lucy put a sweater over her nightshirt and quickly came out on the cold porch. The three men stood there looking grim and spent. She turned to Morgan, who spoke.

"We wahr chasin' the dogs down Hannah's Run when they took to whuppin' off up to the pinnacle. Ellitt, he done took off whoopin' straight up after 'em." He paused and then went on. "Me and the boys h'yar, we done circled around up to the ridge to whar the 'coon wahr treed but thar wahrn't no Ellitt thar."

These were the first words Morgan had spoken to Lucy since they parted at the foot of his lane some six and a half years before. Her face collapsed into a portrait of anxiety.

"We done holler't all along the ridge and we didn't hear nary a thang," continued Morgan. "Then we all done stepped on down the mountain, right slow like, hollerin' and callin'. We got down to the place we last see'd him, then we struck straight up to the ridge again, but thar wahrn't no Ellitt," said Morgan, shaking his head. "We's a-fear't he done got hisself hurt bad."

"It's too colt to be hurt and out on the mountain the entahr night," fretted Lucy, wringing her hands as she surveyed the glum faces.

"We's all goin' back up'par at first light. We's goin' to find him Lucy," promised Morgan, holding out a glimmer of hope. "But we's gon' need four mans to carry him out. I'm thinkin' to call on Festus."

"The three of you stay h'yar and rest," said Lucy, pulling on her boots and throwing on a coat. "I'll git on down and fetch Daddy," she said, and disappeared down the shadowy trail under the cold dying moon.

"Catch you some winks, boys. We's gon' git a soon start," said Morgan. Jake and Odie went inside, pulled some blankets onto the floor and nodded off into much needed naps.

Morgan went about pulling two fence gate poles, and finding some feed sacks and rope—material to fashion into a rescue sling. He staged the gear in the yard, then stretched his lanky length along the porch floor, pulled the sacks over himself and lapsed into fitful sleep.

Festus and Lucy came scurrying into the yard, their talk waking the slumbering Morgan, who roused the two. Father and daughter normally had very little to talk about, but the present crisis suspended past patterns.

The rescue party set off about an hour before dawn. Lucy wanted to go, but better judgment held her back to stay with the children. Morgan's plan was to retrace their steps via the ridge trail. Then, starting from the top, stage the four of them down part way. He reasoned that an accident was more likely in the very rough and rocky upper third of Pinnacle Ridge.

They arrived at where the 'coon was killed, just as the first glimmer of dawn edged the eastern sky. The slope faced east, so a little light went a long way.

"Wahl boys, he up h'yar somewhar," said Morgan. "We pintblank just gots to find him is all." He then issued directions. "I'll walk the ridge up h'yar and Festus, you orter slip on down to whar you can still see me. Jake and Odie, git on down below Festus. Just come on across the mountain on the level, right slow like." Morgan handed the sacks and rope to Festus, holding onto the poles himself. "Keep a sharp eye now, boys." Each man took up position and the four worked their way slowly across the slope.

Morgan came to the top of a very large rock outcropping that dropped off at a high precipice. Half way along the crest he spotted a gun lying on the rocks ahead.

"Yee'ar!!"

With pulse pounding, he dropped the poles and impulsively raced forward.

"Ahh!!"

Morgan's feet suddenly flew out from under him, his hip thumping down hard and sliding sideways. His legs slipped over the edge just as his big fists grabbed at a stiff laurel branch—all in a second's time. He threw his arms around the crooked laurel trunk in a desperate clutch, arresting his slide over the rock face, but with his legs dangling in open air.

His heart raced as a fearsome image flashed before him. His face contorted into a taut grimace as he strained to claw and squirm back to safety. Grunting and frantically grabbing for every desperate inch, he pulled all of himself back from the brink.

Lying hard upon black ice, his heaving chest panted heavy misted breaths in the cold air, and his whole body shook from his frightful brush with disaster. He took quick stock of what had just happened. He had not noticed the ice, a dark frozen patch lying in a depression on the stony cliff top.

He rolled over to one side, off the ice, and pulled himself into a careful position on bare rock. On hands and knees, he peered cautiously over the crag.

At the bottom of the shear drop, he saw Elliott's crumpled body, lying face down on jumbled rocks. With fear in his heart and a lump in his throat, Morgan cried out: "Up h-h'yar!! I d-done found him!! He's up h'yar boys!!" he yelled. "Festus!! G-git on up to the foot of the rock clift!!"

Morgan chucked the two poles to one side over the cliff, grabbed up Elliott's gun and scrambled down around one end of the rock face. He and Festus approached Elliott together.

"Ellitt!" ... "Ellitt!" called each man, in the vain hope he might be alive.

With trembling hands the two pulled the cold, still body onto its back.

Festus sucked in a tense gasp at the sight. A veil of horror fell across his blanched face.

"L-Lord a'mighty," uttered Morgan, in stunned disbelief at the

THE TALE OF A WOODS COLT

battered face. Jake and Odie came crashing up through the undergrowth and, seeing Elliott, froze in speechless shock, transfixed by the gruesome sight. It was abundantly evident that Elliott had died on impact, not from exposure.

"H-he wahr chasin' along top of the rock in the n-night when suddenly he done hit that thar ice p-patch and he went right on over," said Morgan in a cracking voice, looking up at the deadly cliff. "I d-done hit the ice up'par just now and dang near c-come over the clift edge my ownself. I near liked to got myself k-kilt," he said, pointing up with a shaky finger.

Morgan retrieved the poles and, with quivering hands, he and Festus went about the sad task of slipping the sacks over the body and roping it into a pole sling. The four set out in sorrow, each shouldering one end of a pole with Elliott's body suspended between them.

Back at the Hawlins cabin, Lucy was beside herself with worry. She had roused and fed the children at sun up. Lylie, Eddie and Sue were bundled off down to Hannah. Only Robert and little Florie remained.

Fearing the worst was unbearable. Lucy paced the porch with her hands to her cheeks, then wrung them together, then crossed her arms, back and forth until she was thoroughly chilled. Then she absent-mindedly busied herself inside, to warm up.

Robert, infected by his mother's distress, was upset. "What wrong Mama?" he whimpered. "What wrong?"

She tried to compose herself and reassure him. "Mama's just waitin' fer Daddy, that's all." Florie was too small to be affected, but Robert kept on crying as Lucy shifted between inside the cabin and pacing the porch, her hands and arms in constant motion, her mind in turmoil.

Minutes seemed like hours and an hour was an eternity. Lucy was back out on the porch when the recovery team came into view. She saw straight away that their load was wrapped *in* the sacks, not lying *on* the sacks.

She shrieked as she stumbled down the steps and out into the yard.

Lucy knew instantly that Elliott was dead. With fingers clawing her cheeks, she dashed headlong half way across the yard toward the four somber faces trudging toward her. The men paused as she collapsed to her knees beside them. Morgan motioned and they eased the sling to the ground.

"NO!!! Lord no!! No!!!" screamed Lucy in the horror of the moment, flailing her arms to the ground and up again, over and over. "He's dead!! Why Lord?!" she cried out in a torrent of uncontrollable sobbing.

"He's dead! He's dead! You done took my Ellitt!" She wailed on and on.

The hunters each went down on a knee to lend her some silent support. She was inconsolable, spread out on the ground next to Elliott, his battered body wrapped in feed sacks and his mournful friends forming a ring of solidarity. There would be the ceremonial farewell, the funeral. This moment was the real farewell.

Lucy's furious anguish weakened to choking and sobbing. Morgan helped her to her feet, and she clung to his arm as he led her slowly back to the porch, now bathed in sunlight. He settled her into the rocker with a blanket and went back into the yard to help the others move the burlap-wrapped body to a spot by the end of the porch.

As Lucy sobbed on, Morgan anticipated her thoughts, knelt down beside her and spoke quietly. "Best not be lookin' at him, Lucy. He's hurt real bad. He done slip on some ice up'par on the pinnacle. He went right over the clift and hit flat down on the rocks. It kilt him right thar, straight away," he said morosely. "I'm awful sorry, Lucy. I'm sorry it's Ellitt."

Festus came out of the cabin with Robert and little Florie, sat the little girl in Lucy's lap and put the frightened boy at her side. His mother's weeping set him and Florie to crying, while the two men lingered about the porch in solemn silence. Presently, Festus spoke.

"Wahl, I best be a'gitten on down to fetch Hannah up h'yar to be with Lucy." He had started down the path when Morgan called after him.

"Festus! See iffen you cain't git the preacher man up h'yar fer the funeral tomorrow about dinnertime," said Morgan. Festus nodded and disappeared.

Morgan turned to Jake and Odie, coming up from feeding the 'coon carcass to the dogs. "How abouts you boys git on around the hollers with the word about Ellitt, and about the wake this evenin' and the funeral tomorrow. I'm goin' down to the barn and nail up a coffin."

Jake and Odie trotted off in different directions.

Tomorrow would be Sunday. Morgan figured the preacher would be free to come up after morning church. He found some loose pine boards and used Elliott's tools to fashion a stout coffin, which he dragged to the porch.

He was going to lay it on its side and roll Elliott's body into it. Before he could do so, Lucy put Florie down and stood up. "I wants to help put him in, Morgan," she said, choking. Gripping the tightly wrapped rope, they managed to lift the wrapped corpse into the box. She went back up on the porch, and Morgan nailed on the lid. The wake and funeral would be closed casket.

Little Robert, not understanding, looked at her and asked "Whar's Daddy, Mama?"

Lucy went down on her knees, putting a hand on each child's arm. "Daddy done gone to the Lord."

"When he gon' come home?"

She pulled them to her breast. "Daddy's home with the Lord now, darlin's."

Robert was too small to understand, but she'd said it and that seemed to reassure him. Florie was too young to comprehend any of it.

Morgan looked up to see Hannah and the Hawlins children hurrying into the yard with tears streaming down every face. Hannah rushed to Lucy, threw her arms around her and they both fell to sobbing. Hannah tried to choke out some words but they got stuck in her throat.

Morgan could see that it was her mother's embrace, not words, that eased Lucy's tormented heart. And he thought it best to keep a distance, though Hannah had never revealed any hard feelings toward him. He found a pick and shovel, and set off to the burial ground to spend most of a lonely day at the sad task of digging the grave.

Back in the cabin, Lucy had composed herself well enough to speak.

"What done happened to Daddy?" asked a weeping Lylie.

"Daddy done gone to the Lord." It was Robert. Lylie looked at Lucy.

"Daddy was 'coon huntin' last night and he done hurt hisself real bad so the Lord, he done call Daddy to come on to him," said Lucy to the three children. It was enough explanation for the younger two, and later she could tell Lylie more.

Morgan returned to the cabin and, seeing nothing more he could do, decided to go home. He called from the yard. "I best be a-gitten on down now. Nellie and me'll be back up this evenin'," he said somberly. He turned and strode off with his muzzle-loader over one shoulder and Elliott's over the other.

In late afternoon, Rosie, Festus and Jenny, the Hobsons, Fosters and the Nickersons all poured into the yard at almost the same time, a gaggle of mournful older faces and bewildered younger ones. Jenny and the mothers gripped food kettles and some of the men dangled jugs from their fingers. The women and older girls, Nellie the first among them, rushed inside to embrace Lucy and the Hawlins children in a heartfelt release of grief.

The men positioned the coffin inside on two chairs, moved the table to the porch and then gravitated out to the woodpile where each sat on an upended log chunk. There they recounted the whole sorrowful story of how Elliott was lost.

The various children initially milled about, wondering what to do with themselves. But then more arrived, forming the critical mass to spark off a spontaneous burst of energetic outdoor chasing about in a youthful exuberance that refused to be dampened by death.

More neighbors and relatives came in from several directions, including a large Nickerson Hollow contingent led by Asa Nickerson, the eponymous patriarch of that populous area. Each new arrival set off a fresh round of tearful commiseration with Lucy and the children, and a retelling of the sad tale among the men around the woodpile, with nips from jugs embellishing the story until the fatal 'coon hunt took on legendary proportions.

"Why Ellitt, he smelt ol' 'coon's scent just like he wahr a dog!" claimed Festus.

"Ol' Ellitt, he just go to stompin' directly up the mountain about fast as the dogs was runnin'," declared Jake.

Odie chimed in. "Yassar. He done climbed straight up the face of that thar rock clift afore he hit the ice and went back over."

Morgan sat solemnly and listened, with little to say and no desire to correct the wild exaggerations. His sorrow gripped him in a somber reticence.

The mourners all helped themselves to the spread of food, digging into the ample victuals crowded onto the porch table. Nellie made a plate for Lucy and sat with her in consolation, urging her in her grief to eat a bite to keep up her strength. Seeing this, Morgan went over to Lucy and expressed his sincere condolences. The tragedy seemed to have erased any uneasiness between Lucy, Nellie and Morgan.

Darkness had fallen by the time neighbors began leaving the wake for home, their oil lanterns guiding them along the rough road, or down rocky paths. By the time the children were put to bed, only close friends and kin remained in the cabin to sit through the long night.

Sunday morning broke still and cool, with a solid ceiling of sullen overcast hanging heavily on the shrouded peaks and infiltrating the ghostly forests. From the gloom, neighbors dribbled in until a large group milled about the yard.

The preacher appeared and immediately made the rounds of

commiseration as though they were all his own parishioners, after which he took up his pulpit on the porch with the entire company gathered in front. The sermon revolved entirely around predestination and the Lord's will. He kept his prayers short and he knew better than to try to pull any of them into his circle of salvation.

Morgan had hitched Elliott's mule to the sledge. When the sermon was over, he nodded to Ernest and Festus, who elbowed Otis. Jake and Odie hopped up and joined them to carry the heavy coffin outside and place it on the sledge. All the women wailed as they went. The doleful procession made its way to the burial ground with as much outpouring of sorrow as had ever flowed from a group of mourners.

Rosie, Lucy and Lylie, overcome with grief, fell to their knees in a final farewell as the box was lowered. They each dropped a few handfuls of cold earth onto the coffin amid all the moaning and crying.

The dreary gray sky settled a cold mist around them, adding a dismal feeling of gloom to the grim day. Once the words were said, the mourners trudged off into thickening air—chilled, dampened and shivering in body and spirit. In cold silence, Morgan and Festus filled the grave with earth, set the head and footstones and planted the two shovels with crossed handles in the custom of the mountains.

Lucy's kith and kin escorted her and the children back to the cabin and, after words of compassion and commiseration, left for their own homes. Only Hannah and Rosie stayed on. The desolate day closed with a cloak of melancholy draped across the Hawlins place. A cold rain began, and fell throughout the long night.

The homestead itself was well stocked and prepared, but the long winter passed with a lethargic depression within the cabin. Lucy went through the motions of daily existence in joyless repetition, and it affected the children. From time to time Hannah would send up some treat she'd cooked to boost their spirits. Festus and Otis stopped by occasionally to check on the animals, load firewood onto the porch and such.

THE TALE OF A WOODS COLT

For Lucy, it was one cheerless day running into another, all through the cold months. Her happy life had collapsed into a despairing and unpromising widowhood. Mother to five, she found them her only consolation—and her responsibility.

Winter's tight grip finally relaxed and let spring burst forth at last. The climbing sun and warming days lured them out into a feeble but welcome revival of sunken spirits. Festus and Otis took over plowing and planting the corn patches, fence repair and most of what Elliott would have done. Lucy put herself and Lylie to work putting in the garden and tending to the animals.

But nights came down hard on Lucy. The sharp edge of grief still cut deeply. With the children asleep, her loneliness sometimes brought on a profound misery that left her weeping in the dim light of her oil lamp, followed by fitful sleep.

Lucy carried on, and time tempered the searing flare of grief, leaving only the smoldering embers of sorrow. In the rhythm of mountain life, all of the hardships were compounded by the enduring sadness hanging heavily on her heart. She went through the year utterly dejected, and into the next year with no verve for living.

THIRTEEN

1883
Resurrection

Sitting alone on the porch churning butter in the fresh spring air, Lucy was in a pensive mood. She saw her life's rhythm in the monotonous cranking of the churn handle, a repetitive motion that kept things in dull good order but devoid of interest, spirit and liveliness. She was a wistful widow gripped by despondency and longing for her past, with little heart for the future.

Though with a brood of five, Lucy was only twenty-three. Her youthful comeliness had caught the eyes of a couple of recently widowed men of the hollows, who had floated feelers her way. But they had received no encouragement whatsoever, deterring any further advances. Under her shroud of despair, Lucy was unavailable.

No one was up to devising an alchemy that would revive her spirit, or to divining a code that would lift her stiff veil of aloofness. On her infrequent visits to the Nabors store or mill, Lucy's persona presented her as very indrawn and fragile. People came to regard her as afflicted by some demon of doom. She was as unapproachable as the distant pale moon in the cold night sky.

The congeniality between Lucy's brother and Elliott's daughter was a bright spot. Otis often came up with his father to help with farm work. This put him into contact with Lylie, mostly at dinnertime. In time, a spark flickered between them. Before the burned-off pastures had fully greened with new spring grass, the two were talking, as courting was called.

Lucy had emptied the churn and packed the last of the fresh

butter into a wooden mold when two figures emerged from the shadowy forest trail into the sun-drenched pasture well below the cabin, catching her eye. She could make out a young barefoot couple, but not who it was.

The slender woman, her stringy hair blowing in the afternoon breeze, walked with a steady bearing behind a tall fellow with a gangly stride. Lucy studied the approaching pair for any clue to identity.

As they came closer, she recognized a very grown up Janie Dinkins and Luke, Brother Hobson's oldest boy. Lucy hadn't seen Janie since Elliott's funeral a year and a half earlier, and she felt cheered to now see her coming up the path.

" Mornin', Lucy," greeted Janie. "How you gitten' on?" The young man nodded politely, with a smile.

"I'm just gittin' by. Good to see you again, Janie." Lucy rose and poured a bucket of water into the butter churn. "So now what brings the two of you up h'yar on the mountain?"

"Lucy, me and Luke, we done got married," said Janie, beaming at Luke and trying to seem cheerful. Visits always began with a pleasantry.

"Wahl, I'm mighty pleased fer you," said Lucy, washing out the churn. "So, you two livin' in with yer mama and daddy, Janie?"

Luke chimed in. "No, Lucy. We's done moved onto Daddy's place," he said proudly. "In that li'l Juria cabin up in the back field." They were both in their late teens.

"That's mighty fine, Janie. Good of you to bring the happy news." Lucy was genuinely happy for Janie, but it didn't seem enough reason for the visit.

Luke and Janie exchanged worried looks before Janie spoke. "Um, Lucy, we actual done come up with some bad news." Lucy's brow wrinkled in apprehension. She'd already had enough bad news for a lifetime.

Janie continued in a subdued voice. "Mama's in a bad way, Lucy. She done took awful sick. She askin' fer you to come on down and set with her."

"Nellie got another spell of the wheezes, Janie?"

"Mama done got more'n the wheezes. She been coughin' up blood," said Janie. "We's all mighty scare't, Lucy."

Lucy stood and went inside, put some things in a sack and pulled Lylie away from the stove.

"Where we goin' to, Lucy?"

"I'm goin' down to set with Nellie," said Lucy, nudging Lylie out the door in front of her.

"What's wrong with Nellie?"

"Nellie done took sick real bad. Now git on down and fetch Mama up to be with you and the children," said Lucy, as the teenager plopped down on the porch steps and pulled on her shoes.

Lylie took off down the trail to the Nickersons and Lucy joined Luke and Janie to backtrack down the lower woods trail, a short cut to the Dinkins place.

Things were quiet at the house when they arrived. Janie slipped inside and came out with Morgan, who eased his tired body into the rocker while the other three found places on the porch steps. His drawn face and furrowed brow revealed the grave situation.

"Mighty glad to see you, Lucy. Mighty glad. Nellie done been a-callin' fer you. She been coughin' right smart fer nigh on a yahr, now. She done said it wahr just the wheezes and all. Then, week afore last, she done cough up some blood. I knowed right thar it wahrn't no wheezes. It wahr the wastin' cough."

Morgan paused and wiped his hand down across his tired face.

"I knowed I had to git me some snails. So I done gone straight down to that thar dampy spot in the branch by Arnold and found me a mess of snails," he said. "Arnold, he come on out and said let him send fer the doctor over to Sperryville. I done tolt him the snails wahr the onliest thang what could help my Nellie.

"Wahl, I done got Nellie to swaller one snail ever day fer nine days[7]." Tears welled in his eyes as he told more. "The problem wahr, I didn't start on the full moon. It hain't fer another week now. I figgered she might not have that long so I done give 'em to her anyhow. I might have knowed it didn't do no good." His faced contorted with barely repressed anguish.

Lucy sucked clipped breaths under her cupped hand, as she tried to hold back her own feelings behind her tear-streaked face while Morgan went on.

"Arnold, he done sent fer the doctor anyhow. The doctor, he come up and done check Nellie over right much and said it wahr the consumption and thar warn't nothin' he could do fer her."

He turned his face away and drifted off to some sad place, sitting there with a faraway look in his eyes. He was exhausted by worry and all the work of spring planting, leaving Janie to look after her mother and the household.

Lucy composed herself, and then slipped in alone to Nellie. She was lying in bed, dozing in the dim lamplight. Nellie's eyes were closed and her breathing short and shallow. Her pale countenance and frail form seemed poised between life and death. After a time she woke and her wan face expanded into a weak smile at seeing Lucy.

"I been a-wantin' to see you, Lucy," she whispered. "The sickness done got me laid awful low. I reckon I won't be pullin' through this time."

"Now Nellie, you goin' to..."

"Hain't no use in tryin' to lift my spirits," said Nellie. "I supposen I done lived out my days. I'm feelin' right close to the Lord now."

"Oh Nellie, don't you be talkin' like that, now. I'm goin' to..."

"I knows you done come down to help me, Lucy," said Nellie, interupting again. "But thar hain't much you can do fer me now. Just a sip of water now and again'll do."

---

7 The sovereign treatment, repeated if needed, for 'wastin' cough – tuberculosis. The snails must be swallowed live so the 'slime goes t' the lungs an' cures 'em'. Of course, the most effective treatment is useless if not administered on the full moon.

She let a moment pass before speaking again.

"Take care of Morgan and the children fer me, Lucy. Can you do that fer me?"

Nellie eased up on her elbow and leaned a bit toward Lucy.

"Course I can, Nellie. I'm right h'yar now," said Lucy, leaning in close to Nellie. "Course I'll look after Morgan and the children. That's why I done come down."

Nellie let out a hacking cough, wiped the bloody sputum from her lips, took a sip from the tin cup and, with pleading eyes, whispered, "I means ferever, Lucy. Yer the one to take care of my Morgan and my children, once't I'm gone."

Lucy felt the tears welling in her eyes.

"Yer the one fer him Lucy; I knowed it all along. Tell me you'll do it. Say you will, fer Nellie." She fell back on her pillow, exhausted by the exertion.

Nellie's words brought back the tension Lucy had felt at their parting eight years before. Pent-up feelings of guilt and deceitfulness now gave way like a dam bursting, flooding her with a gush of tearful sobbing. "Oh Nellie! Nellie!" was all Lucy could get out as she embraced, and pressed her cheek against Nellie's, and wept into her dying cousin's shoulder.

"Now now, Lucy." Lucy eased back into eye contact and Nellie went on. "It's all out now. We's done come full circle h'yar. I'm goin' to rest easy, Lucy, just knowin' yer goin' to be right h'yar with 'em. I done tolt Morgan."

Nellie closed her eyes and sunk a little into the bed. She whispered "I'm about ready to go to the Lord now." In the next moment she fell into a serene slumber.

Lucy sat with Nellie a while, feeling purged and relieved of an inner burden. Presently, she went back out to the porch. Morgan had returned to his work in the field, and Janie and Luke had gone home. She sat alone in the porch rocker, absorbing the sad yet cathartic heart-to-heart with Nellie, and orienting herself to the sudden new direction of her life.

In a while, Janie returned and the two of them went about supper preparations in the silence of sorrow. Morgan's table grace replaced the appeal for Nellie's recovery with an appeal for a "fine place fer her with the Lord." Supper was subdued, with Nellie only sipping some water, and everyone else picking and nibbling with little appetite.

Nellie drifted off and the others passed the evening around the wood stove, taking the chill off the cool evening. There was no talk. Each sat in private contemplation until the children finally retired to bed in the loft. Morgan, Lucy and Janie, slumped in chairs by the warm stove, finally nodded off into a doze where they sat.

A sound woke Lucy in a wee hour to see Morgan sitting at Nellie's bedside with her hand between his palms, his body swaying slowly back and forth, and moaning softly. Somewhere in the night Nellie's soul had slipped away.

Lucy and Janie washed and dressed the body, and arranged the wake at the Dinkins house. The beautiful day formed a lovely backdrop to an evening of outdoor dining and visiting with kin, friends and neighbors who came to give final farewell. Most of the women placed a kiss on Nellie's cheek.

All through the evening, Otis and Lylie were inseparable, their feelings of sadness offset by the spark of youthful promise. Morgan and Festus spent several private minutes together, after which Festus kept company with his wife, before gravitating off to the men's circle for a few nips.

Lucy led her mother to a corner of the yard.

"Mama, Nellie done ask me to come be with Morgan," she said. "She made me to promise I would take care of him and the children. Them wahr her last words."

Hannah nodded approval without comment, and Lucy didn't think she was surprised.

Later, Morgan and Lucy found a private moment together under a far tree in the early twilight.

"Nellie done ask me to come take care of you and the children," she said, looking up at Morgan with misty eyes. She dearly wanted to take his hands but, in view of all the company, kept hers at her side.

Tears streamed down Morgan's face. He started to say something but only a repressed moan came out. He gave himself a moment, then spoke quietly.

"I'm...I'm askin' fer yer hand, Lucy," he said, choking in his grief.

"I will make you a good wife, Morgan. And Nellie will always be in my heart."

Arnold called on the preacher from the Nabors Methodist Church to conduct the funeral the next day. The weather favored, with a spring shower giving way to rays of sunshine beaming down through parting clouds to warm a profusion of wild flowers to fresh fragrances.

The small graveyard occupied the lower corner of the Dinkins property just at the Nabors Mill road, in glorious view of majestic Ragged Mountain. The procession to the burial took under half an hour but with a full outpouring of sorrow and grief.

The funeral gathering was large, with much shared sadness at Nellie's passing in her mid-thirties. The preacher delivered a lengthy service, deftly weaving in the fatalism of the mountaineers with the prayers of his lower hollow flock, who made up half the mourners. As the preacher said his last words, friends, neighbors and kin filed by the opened coffin to give their final farewell.

Many of the gathered lingered afterwards to talk about life's concerns and exchange a little gossip. One matter that was not the subject of gossip was Morgan, Lucy and Robert. It was a forgone conclusion that they would be together from now on. Everyone, except the preacher, accepted that Morgan, Lucy and their children were now one family.

THE TALE OF A WOODS COLT

The next morning, breakfast found Lucy explaining to her brood that they would be moving. "We goin' to move down thar to take care of Morgan and them. He goin' be yer new daddy," she told the perplexed children. The four younger ones just looked back at her passively, but Lylie fidgeted nervously. Lucy figured she knew what the sixteen year-old's distraction was about, but the girl obviously wasn't ready to bring it out quite yet.

Shortly, someone clomped up onto the porch. In through the door came a grinning Otis in his best britches, a straw hat and new boots. Her eyes glittering with excitement, Lylie hopped up and pulled a chair over, obviously expecting him.

"How do, Lucy," he said with a polite smile, removing his hat and sitting beside Lylie.

Lucy, for the first time, saw an affable and able young man of twenty in place of her little brother Otis.

"Wahl now, hain't you a fine excuse fer a man, Otis!" she teased.

He chuckled. "We wants you to be the first to know, Lucy," he said, glancing at Lylie's beaming face. "Lylie and me's a-gittin' married!" he gushed.

"That thar's mighty fine news, now," said an unsurprised Lucy, flashing a knowing smile at Lylie. Lylie blushed and the children all giggled. "I actual been a-hopin' right smart that the two of you's would git married.

"And right h'yar you gots you a good place to live on. Lylie, this wahr yer daddy's place, and his daddy's place afore him, and his granddaddy's place afore that. I reckon it orter be yourn now," said Lucy, releasing her widow's claim to the Hawlins homestead. "And Otis, you done right good keepin' the place up nigh on two yahrs now. I reckon you can just keep on a-workin' it."

But Lucy's widow's claim and Lylie's rights as an heir were less than they appeared, a fact that would one day be very significant. Elliott had not actually owned the land. He had no deed. It was his because his grandfather had given it to him. The family had been on the place for close to a century, but with no title to show for it. The sixty acres was clearly marked, the lines running from blazed tree to rock pile to fence corner. But no Hawlins had ever possessed a deed. Elliott had been a fifth generation squatter.

The land was actually part of the Stony Man Tract, more than five thousand acres draped across the mountains and hollows from the four thousand foot high Stony Man Mountain over to Hazel Mountain. A defunct mining outfit called Miners Lode Copper Company, Inc. owned the big spread.

A copper rush had swept the Blue Ridge Mountains some twenty-five years earlier. It so happened that the small mine on Stony Man Mountain proved unproductive and unprofitable. The venture was abandoned by the late 1860's, with little attention given to the tract and its inhabitants by the company or its eastern city stockholders. Several lifelong squatters were left undisturbed.

The mountaineers were well aware that land was acquired by deed and not by piling rocks, blazing trees and running fences. Most of them had clear title to their land. Those who were squatters knew they had no deed, but just came to believe that possession by occupancy equated to ownership, a tenuous claim that might have been one reason for suspicion and wariness of outsiders entering their region.

Lucy did the morning chores and then gathered up the family's meager wardrobe and personal items into a couple of feed sacks. Lylie and Otis had gone down to break the news to his parents. The important part for Festus and Hannah was that the couple would be taking over the Hawlins place and not squeezing in with them.

"Eddie, you carry Florie; Sue, you carry this sack, and here's a li'l one for you Robert." They all set off down the woods trail to Morgan's at the same time Otis and Lylie were lugging his sacks up to the Hawlins cabin, an exercise in moving house so seamless that the fire in the Hawlins stove never went out.

"I been expectin' you," said Janie, looking up from the Dinkins cook stove. She had whipped up an ample dinner for all. Morgan and Lucy sat at the table ends while the rest of them squeezed uneasily onto the two benches, the two sets of children studying each other shyly across the table. Lucy felt the need of some introduction to get started.

Morgan clasped his hands together on the tabletop.

"Thank you, Lord, fer keepin' our Nellie safe up thar with you in heaven and fer our family down h'yar on the yarth, Amen."

Morgan filled his plate and, as the food bowls went around the table, he introduced his children to Lucy's. The seven youngsters had all played together at several funerals, which were like community picnics to them. But they hadn't learned, or didn't remember, one another's names.

"This h'yar's my boy John and my girl Carrie," said Morgan. "We calls her Birdie because she all the time tryin' to sing like a bird," he said, with a chuckle. "And that thar's Robert, my youngest."

Lucy went next. "This h'yar's Eddie and that thar's Sue. The li'l one's Florie and my boy h'yar's Robert E. Lee."

Everyone looked at Lucy's Robert. Morgan leaned back and put his eyes on the boy.

"Wahl now, that thar's a powerful big name fer a li'l feller," said he, with a grin. "I don't suppose we can go around callin' him Robert E. Lee, though. They actual wahr a Robert E. Lee, and he wahr the greatest man that ever did live."

"Now then, we done got two Roberts right h'yar in the family." Morgan said. "Wahl then, we goin' to call Nellie's Robert *Bob* and we goin' to call Lucy's Robert *Rob*. Hain't gon' be no more Roberts." Morgan had settled the matter and the dinner continued. Lucy sensed they all were feeling a little more at ease with one another.

Rain threatened so Morgan skipped his after-dinner doze and

headed back to his fieldwork with John at his side. Though only fifteen, he was a willing helper and up to a man's work.

Janie announced, "I best be a-gitten on home."

Lucy stepped out on the porch to see her off in the informal changing of command at the Dinkins home, for Janie had taken charge during her mother's illness.

"Janie, I'm goin' do my very best to take good care of the entahr family."

"Call on me iffen I can help ary way atall," were Janie's parting words, as she turned and strode off across the yard. Lucy watched the young woman disappear down the lane under gray skies.

Lucy was comfortable with Janie but had some lingering doubts about Janie's feelings toward her. Janie seemed genuinely friendly and she acted as though Lucy was now family. But then there was the incident eight years before when Janie had come into the barn while Lucy and Morgan were in the hay mow together. Now Janie had grown up and knew full well what she had walked in on and that Robert was her half brother. Her mother was gone and Lucy had taken her place. So Lucy felt a touch of discomfort, wondering if Janie might harbor some buried feelings of resentment toward her.

Lucy turned her gaze to survey the homestead, laid out before her in full spring blossom. She thought it the prettiest place, even in dull weather, and hoped she'd never have to leave it.

After a quiet supper, Morgan withdrew to his porch rocker. Once she'd seen the seven children up to bed, Lucy went out to the porch and took a place on the steps. It seemed the place for her to be, as light faded into dusk and then deepened into darkness. The day died to a pitch-black night devoid of moon or stars.

They sat in a quiet and pensive contemplation. In a while, they rose and made their way up to bed in the dark and silent loft where the children slumbered peacefully.

Soon Morgan was snoring in slow rhythm. Lucy lay in melancholy but contented stillness, thinking about her little Robert. He was Rob now, seven years old and living under his natural father's roof. After his inauspicious beginning, and all that had happened, she couldn't help feeling that finally his future might hold promise, a sweet hope she held until claimed by sleep.

PART TWO
YOUNG ROB

FOURTEEN
1884
A Fish

The blazing August sun bore down relentlessly from a cloudless sky, curling corn leaves and baking the pastures brown. A month had delivered not a drop of relief by storm or shower. A smothering haze hung over hill and hollow like a sultry smoke that refused to drift away.

The beastly heat and sticky mugginess sapped energy and appetites. Lucy had moved cooking to the lean-to, an extension with a slanted roof fitted against the shady rear wall of the house. Florie rocked Lizbeth's wooden cradle in the shadow of the open rear door, pausing only to fan the flushed infant. Li'l Liz was Lucy's newest, born in the spring.

The family had come to the dinner table with scant desire to eat, after which the fierce sun had driven the languid children into various shady places where they played listlessly. Lucy decided a treat would stimulate their interest in supper. *Apple pie'd be just the thang*, she thought.

On their knees in the moist earth down under the big maple tree, Rob and Bob hunched over the spring, amusing themselves by trying to catch salamanders in the cool water. They heard Lucy call from the house.

"Bob! Rob!"

They looked up to see her standing at the top of the porch steps with her hands cupped to her mouth.

"Git up h'yar, both of yous!"

Rob stood up and hesitated, loath to leave the cool and shady spring. But she insistently hooked the air with her hand, so he reluctantly shuffled up to the house behind Bob, assuming they were about to be assigned some onerous chore.

Lucy came down the steps and handed Bob an empty sack, putting the eleven-year-old in charge. Rob stood studying his bare feet. At only eight, he was never put in charge of anything. He was acutely aware of his junior status among the four boys. He chafed at always being the tag-along.

"The two of you git on over to Janie and fetch me them Rambo apples," she ordered. "Git on, now."

They drifted across the yard at a mopey pace, with Bob dragging the sack on the dusty ground behind. Rob looked back to see his mother standing in the sweltering heat, watching them.

"Don't be late gitten back now, you hear me!" she hollered.

Janie and Luke Hobson lived in an old cabin on his home place, a mountain farm that he worked with his father, Lloyd, whom everyone called Brother Hobson. Janie had offered Lucy some of the fruit from their Summer Rambo apple trees.

Rob dawdled his way down the dusty road with Bob, neither taking an interest in anything. It was too hot for their usual sport of flinging rocks at trees.

The boys squeezed between the fence gate bars into Brother's place and quickly walked single file through the sunburned pasture, the hot earth baking the bottoms of their bare feet. They scooted past Brother's colt, a young stallion loitering in the shade of a spreading tree, and on to the relief of splashing across the small stream.

The path led around the edge of a knoll into the Juriah field, a cove of open land named after a "granny woman" who had lived out her life there. In the shimmering heat, they made their way past a patch of tall corn in full tassel, and on up through a rough pasture toward where the cabin sat at the flared base of a forested hillside.

When the cabin came into view, Rob saw Janie sitting on the porch mending some piece of clothing. As they approached, she called out, "Wahl now, what brings you boys out on such a hot evenin'?"

"Lucy says can she have them Rambo apples," said Bob, holding out the sack.

"Why sure you can have some Rambos! Lord knows, we done got enough of them to feed the entahr holler." She took his sack and pulled a couple of dozen fruit from a large barrel on the porch. "Thar now, you tell Lucy to send you back fer ary more she wants."

"Yassum." Bob slung the sack over his shoulder, and they trudged back the way they'd come.

The stream came into view, a welcome sight that perked up their pace across the parched earth. The cool mountain water was the antidote to August and balm to their baked feet. They lingered in the shallow rivulet, reluctant to brave the scorching path through the pasture beyond.

"Let's git us on up to that hole yonder," said Rob.

Bob sat the apple sack in the weeds near the water's edge and followed Rob, stepping unsteadily up the stony streambed some dozens of yards to a shady pool a couple of feet deep. Rob found a seat on a flat rock at the edge while Bob balanced his bottom on a small fallen log that reached across the stream, each dabbling bare feet in cool relief.

The boy's dangling legs and wiggling feet attracted a small school of minnows to excitedly nibble at the tips of their toes. It was only a tickle, since none of the fish were longer than a couple of inches.

"Looky thar what a big ol' fish!" exclaimed Rob, pointing to a small trout no longer than five inches.

"He a sight bigger'n the others," said Bob, studying the fish. "Must be the minnows' ol' grand daddy."

The fish might have been attracted to the lively minnows, or maybe it was fixated on the waggling toes. It held itself steady in the water several feet out and a few inches below the surface.

"He lookin' fer a little fish he can eat," said Rob with a certitude that belied his knowledge of fish. He reached over and broke a dead branch off a sapling. "Bet I can git him out with this stick," he boasted, flashing Bob an elfish look.

"You cain't catch no fish with no stick!" said Bob, looking incredulously at Rob.

"Bet I can git him."

"Bet you cain't."

"I can do it sure enough."

"No you cain't neither."

"I can."

"You cain't."

"I can and I will."

"Iffen you can, then do it."

"I'll do it when I wants to."

"See thar. You cain't do it atall."

Rob couldn't let the challenge go unmet. He eased the stick into the water and slowly moved it to just under the fish. He paused... Flick! Up flipped the stick as fast as he could jerk it.

"Dang!" cried Rob. The fish had simply dodged and scooted under a rock. But it soon returned. He tried again without success. The fish darted away and hid, but then boldly came back. Rob then focused more attention to inching the stick in directly under the middle of the fish, as close as possible. Both boys leaned over in rapt concentration, engrossed in the challenge.

Suddenly Rob flipped the fish out of the water, but it flopped back in. "Yee'ar! I most nearly done got him!!"

"H'yar, give me a tarn with the stick!" demanded Bob as he reached over to grab it.

Rob pulled the stick back. "Cain't have it. It's my stick and my fish."

"C'mon Rob! Let me have a tarn!" pleaded Bob.

"Git yer own stick and git yer own fish."

"C'mon now. Give me a chance, Rob!"

Rob relented and handed over the stick.

Bob worked the stick in under the fish and jerked up. "Dang!" He tried again. No luck. A third failure subdued his enthusiasm.

But the fish kept coming back.

Rob took the stick. "I can do it," he said resolutely. "I knows I can." He eased the stick to just under the belly of the fish and paused.

The fish was motionless. Holding the stick motionless, Rob hunched over in intense concentration. Their eyes were riveted on that fish. Both held their breaths and time stood still.

Flick! The fish flipped from the water and arced into the air with the drop-jawed boys tracking its trajectory with awed eyes. It landed on a dry rock top with a plop and a couple of flops of its tail.

Speechless, the boys stared at each other with mouths agape. Rob spoke first.

"Thar now. I said I can do it and I done it," he declared proudly, claiming full credit in a matter-of-fact voice that tried to conceal his own amazement. He reached over and grabbed up the slippery wriggly creature with both hands.

"Let me holt it, Rob!" begged Bob. "Let me holt the fish!"

"I don't know. What if it got loose?" Rob said, reluctant to relinquish his prize. He had proven himself, and it was his trump moment. He wanted to make it last a bit longer, and it wouldn't do if Bob should let the fish escape.

"It won't git loose! Let me holt it just once't, Rob!"

"Wahl, alright then. You can holt it just once't." He carefully handed off his fish to the delighted Bob's cupped open hands. Bob's turn was soon over; Rob collected his now-stilled catch and stuffed it into his pants pocket.

"We's best be a-gitten on back," Bob said, with a hint of urgency. The two scurried across the pasture past the grazing colt, slipped through the gate bars and lit out up the road for home.

"Whar in tarnation you two been!?" yelled Lucy at them when

they showed at the house. "And whar's my apples!?" she demanded, her face flushed with heat and irritation.

Rob and Bob looked at each other, as if expecting the other to have the fruit. They looked up at Lucy in dread, realizing that the sack of apples was still where Bob had set it down in the weeds by the stream. Without a word, the panicked pair spun in unison and went tearing off down the lane as fast as their little legs could carry them, with Lucy yelling from behind.

"Git right on back now or I'll wear the both you out with a hickory!"

The panting runners dived through the fence bars, dashed across the pasture and came to an abrupt halt when they saw the sack.

"Oh Lord!" gasped Bob.

There stood the colt. Scattered about on the ground lay the apples, with a big bite taken from each one.

Bob, catching his breath and shaking his head in disbelief, blurted out, "Oh Lord, Lucy gon' be some kind of mad. She gon' whup us good." Bob did not call Lucy Mama, but he recognized her authority.

"She hain't never laced us yet," said Rob, trying to ease Bob's anguish.

"She goin' to do it this time fer sure," said Bob. "Reckon we best git 'em all up and carry 'em on up home," he said, in a resigned voice. "Might be she can still use a piece of 'em."

"No," countered Rob. "Let's just git us some more. Janie done said come fer more."

"We hain't got the time fer it."

"Mama, she hain't gon' want all them apples with no bite takin' out," said Rob. "Hain't nary bitty sense in carryin' 'em up to her."

"Janie, she hain't gon' want give us no more so soon now," groaned Bob despairingly.

"Sure she will! C'mon!" urged Rob, grabbing up the sack and starting toward the Juriah cabin, with Bob trailing behind.

Janie was still sitting on the porch, fanning herself. "What brings you boys back so soon, now?"

"Uh, might we have some more of them apples, Miz Janie?" begged Rob.

"*What* now? You boys done up and ate all the apples I done give you?"

"Brother's colt done ate 'em, Miz Janie," divulged Rob, his eyes cast down.

"Brother's colt! How'd the colt git yer apples?"

"Bob h'yar, he done set the sack down because we's a-fishin'. We done catch a fish and run on up home without no apples atall. We come back to git 'em but the colt, he done got 'em all," said Rob, in a discouraged voice.

"Fishin'?! They hain't no eatin' fish in that thar branch and, besides, you two hain't got no fishin' poles," said Janie in a tone of amused disbelief.

"Yee'ar they is too fish in thar, and Rob h'yar done flip one out with a stick," said Bob.

"Flip one out with a stick!" She laughed at the absurd claim. "You boys best quit tellin' tales now," she said, entertained by the story.

"Hain't no tale," said Rob. "I hope me die iffen it hain't so, Miz Janie." He reached into his pocket, pulled out the evidence and displayed it on his upturned palm.

"Lordy be! Hain't much of a fish but I cain't hardly believe you got it outen the branch with a stick! You two boys is somethin' awful!" she exclaimed with an amused smile, taking the bag to the apple barrel and stuffing in more of the lightly blushed green Rambos.

She handed the sack to Rob. "Thar you is now."

"Aw, thank you Miz Janie. Thank you," said a grateful Rob.

"Thank you Miz Janie. Thank you a heap!" echoed a relieved Bob.

"C'mon," said Rob. They turned and scurried back down the path.

"You boys mind that colt don't git yer new apples now, you hear!" called Janie.

"See thar. Warn't nothin' *to* it," bragged Rob, as he handed the sack off to the appreciative Bob. The two splattered across the stream and set for home at a run. Rob was so pleased with himself that his short legs were energized to the tiring task of keeping up with Bob in the race back up to the house. He was no longer just the little tag along.

Lucy looked out when she heard Rob and Bob scampering up the lane. The sweaty and exhausted boys ran up to her and handed over the apple sack. Already enervated by the heavy heat, she was exasperated.

"Land sakes! I's about to give up on the both of you!" she scolded. "You two done spent most the entahr evenin' fetchin' a sack of apples!" She pulled out a half dozen fruit and handed them to Carrie. "Birdie, peel and cut these up right quick now." The piecrust was already rolled and in the pan.

Lucy turned back to Rob, who blurted out, "Mama, we done see'd this big ol' fish down in the branch. And I done fished it out."

She stood with arms akimbo, staring down at him. "Fished it out? You hain't got no fishin' pole. How you done fished it out?"

"I done flip it out with a stick, Mama." He reached into his pocket.

"You done wha…?" she uttered as he produced the fish on his extended palm, startling both her and Carrie into leaning back away from the dead creature.

"Looky thar! It's a bitty li'l thang!" chirped Carrie, with a smirk.

Lucy looked down with amusement at the diminutive fish. "It hain't much to look at but I cain't hardly believe you done catched it with a stick!" she exclaimed.

She saw a rush of pride in Rob's eyes at her surprised appreciation for his newly revealed talent. His little chest swelled with her approval.

"Can you cook it fer supper?" he asked eagerly.

Carrie chimed in. "Hain't enough thar to…," Lucy quickly put a finger to her lips.

She whispered to Carrie, "This h'yar hain't about the size of the fish, Birdie."

She turned to Rob. "Wahl, thar hain't but two bites on it, but I reckon I can fix it fer you," she said, taking the little thing by its tail and putting it by Carrie. "Birdie, once't yer done with the apples, how abouts you clean the fish fer me? That's a good girl."

Lucy turned back around to see a grin spread across Rob's face. "Now git on outen h'yar, both yous," she said, shooing them away with a flick of her hand.

The two scuffed out into the last of the heavy afternoon. A fine sense of accomplishment suffused Rob as he and Bob cooled off on the shady grass down by the spring.

The sound of Morgan and John plodding up the barn path alerted the boys to suppertime.

Rob perked up and grinned when Carrie placed the fried fish in front of him. Lying bare in the middle of the small tin plate, the granddaddy fish now looked rather spare to Rob. He then noticed his father eyeing the fish.

"Hain't hardly enough fish fer the entahr family. Hain't but two bites on it!" remarked Morgan with amusement, throwing a curious grin at Lucy.

"The fish is fer Rob," she said. "He done catch it down to the branch on Brother."

Rob felt himself puff with pride as Morgan raised his eyebrows and looked curiously at him. "How you done catch a fish, boy? You hain't got no fishin' pole or nothin'." Everyone's eyes fell upon Rob.

"I done fished it out with a stick," said Rob, with a note of satisfaction.

"Fished it out with a stick?"

Rob looked at Bob.

"Yup. He done flick it outen the water with a stick. I done see'd it."

With his claim corroborated, Rob looked back at Morgan.

"Wahl that thar's the first I ever hear't of such a thang!" exclaimed Morgan to the table. "Rob h'yar's a right clever li'l feller!"

Morgan put his hands together on the table. "Thank you Lord fer our family and fer our vittles and thank you fer Rob's li'l fish, because I knows you done had a hand in him catchin' it, amen."

Rob beamed with joy as he nibbled the meager flesh from the tiny fried trout.

"Now we gots apple pie fer ary one what eats all they supper," announced Lucy, reclaiming the children's attention with the lure of a special treat.

FIFTEEN

Revelation

On a mild autumn morning, Rob sat alone on the porch floor with his legs dangling over the edge, in the way of a boy wondering what to do with himself. Nothing had caught his interest yet so, kicking his feet back and forth, he waited for something to turn up.

The invigorating breezes of fall had broken the oppressive grip of summer heat. After a bountiful apple harvest, the sale of the fruit and couple of steers had added several coveted twenty-dollar Double Eagle gold coins to Morgan's stash, and his pocket jingled with some extra Morgans, as the ubiquitous silver dollars were called.

Down at the barn, Morgan haltered the mule and balanced three sacks of shelled corn over its back, the most weight he dared load on to the aging beast. Rob watched as his father brought the animal up to the house, hitched it to the porch post and sat down next to him.

"You be wantin' to git on down to the mill with me, boy?" asked Morgan, raising his eyebrows expectantly.

"Yassar!" Rob was excited to go. He had never been to the Nabors mill or store.

"H'yar then, you can carry the sacks." Morgan handed Rob a couple of folded burlap feed sacks. "We just waitin' fer yer mama and Birdie, now." The words had no sooner fallen from Morgan's lips than Lucy and the thirteen-year-old emerged from the house in their store-bought dresses, ready to go.

Rob hopped off the porch and took up position at Morgan's side, opposite the mule, and the foursome set out down the lane.

The Nabors mill and store served as the community center of a rugged and scenic landscape of subsistence farming and simple living.

THE TALE OF A WOODS COLT

Everyone gravitated to the store porch to loiter, mingle and to share news and gossip. Women exchanged the latest tittle-tattle, and the men weren't above doing a little bragging, one to the another.

The Dinkins party arrived at the store and mill to find a hubbub of activity. Mid-autumn Saturdays were always bustling. Corn that had been cut, pulled and shelled now needed to be ground into meal. Apples had been picked and sold. Store accounts needed to be settled, and money left over needed to be spent. There was news to exchange, rumors to share and stories to tell, all of which flowed as freely as the rippling mountain creek water just across the road.

The skies had blessed the land and the crops were all in. Yields and prices were up a smidgen, adding a few extra coins to the pockets of the mountain farmers, corn cutters and apple pickers.

Folk had flocked in from the far hollows and ridges, filling the store to overflowing. Customers waited at the counter while the two clerks bustled about collecting goods from shelves. The porch benches and floor fringes were full of chattering people.

Lucy and Carrie went straight for the store. Morgan hitched the mule to a post and flopped his three sacks of corn onto the mill porch, just across from the store. He noticed that Rob's attention had turned to the mysteries of the mill. The sweet smell of freshly ground corn meal wafted from the open door. The clatter from within drew Rob to the opening, and to the strange sounds emanating from the building. Morgan followed.

They peered into the dim, dusty space to see a ballet of rotating wooden shafts, gears and axles. Two slapping drive belts were running the two grinding stations flat out. The large pairs of thick, round grindstones rotated, crushing and crunching the kernels between their weight, spilling the coarsely ground cornmeal off their edges and down a short chute through the floor. At each station, one sweaty man poured corn into a hopper that fed into the center of the grinding stones, and another man bagged the meal as it poured out a chute into the room below.

Rob and Morgan could see through to the other side, where water spilled continuously onto the top of a big iron and wooden water wheel, turning it slowly, its axle driving the entire works. To Morgan, Rob seemed awestruck at viewing an intriguing new world.

The miller saw their silhouettes in the door opening and came out.

" Mornin' Tee," said Morgan, greeting the miller. Tee was Tommy Nabors who had taken over running the mill when his uncle Arnold retired five years earlier.

"Mornin' Morgan. It'll be a spell afore I git's the three sacks ground fer you." There were many sacks of grain piled up ahead of Morgan's. "And besides, the boss man wants to talk to you. He tolt me to send you on over when you come down," said Tee. "He over there to the house right now."

"Got ary idea what he want, Tee?"

"Ain't got nary idea, Morgan." Tee went back to his milling.

Morgan put his hand on Rob's shoulder as they stood there in the mill door, marveling at the action within. "Thinkin' you wants to be a mill hand, boy?" he asked. "Them's some hart workin' mans in thar."

Rob look up with earnest eyes. "I wants to be a hart workin' man."

Morgan met his gaze for a long moment, and then said, "Let's go find yer mama." He led Rob across the road and into the dim light of the store where they joined Lucy and Carrie at a pile of goods on the counter.

"Somethin' else fer you now, Lucy?" asked the young clerk.

"Just a box of flake soap'll be the last of it, Clancy."

The clerk used a long stick with a hooked end to tip the soapbox off the highest shelf, deftly catching it in his right hand.

Clancy was a natural clerk. All of his aptitude was concentrated in his head, and in his nimble fingers that drummed the countertop when they didn't have anything else to do. He wouldn't have been any good at farming, for his body was built backwards. He was broad across his beam and narrow at the chest. His torso tapered inward from spreading hips up to shoulders too slender to properly carry his large wobbly head. His chest slumped down to a belly bulge that gave him the shape of a pear on stilts.

Clancy added the soap to the tab and then, with the Dinkinses staring in their usual amazement, toted up the entire list in his head and wrote the total on the bill. They would have been no more astounded if he'd been a sorcerer conjuring up a miracle. Literacy and numeracy *were* mysterious miracles to the illiterate mountain people.

"Comes to a dollar and eight cent, Lucy," he said. Then he looked at the man of the family. "Would you be wantin' to settle up, Morgan?" he asked.

"Reckon I orter close her out, Clancy." Morgan, like everyone else, always paid off his store debt at this time of year.

Clancy fetched over the ledger book, sat it on the counter and flipped it open to Morgan's page. "Eleven dollar and eleven cent, includin' today, Morgan."

Morgan dug into his pocket, pulled out a handful of coins and deposited the pile on the counter. "Pull out the lebenty leben thar, Clancy."

Clancy spread the coins out and selected the correct amount. "Ten dollar, four quarter, a dime and a penny," he totaled, sweeping the ten silver Morgans and the smaller coins into his hand and pushing the remaining money back toward his customer.

Morgan pocketed his change, looked down at Rob and said, "Give Clancy them sacks, boy."

As Clancy bagged up the goods, he remarked to Lucy, "They got a new schoolmarm done opened school down to the church." Morgan could almost see Lucy's ears perk up with interest. "It's been goin' ever day fer nigh on two month now–exceptin' Saturday and Sunday, of course. Reckoned I orter mention it to you," he added, casting his eyes downward to Rob.

It wasn't the first school near Nabors Mill, but it was the only one at the time. News of its opening had not spread far, due to the indifference of many mountain people to education. The Methodist Church had sponsored the school and interest was largely confined to the parishioners in that lower hollow.

A school had opened twelve years earlier a mile or so above Nabors Mill, also in a small church. It had operated intermittently, giving a couple years of schooling to some, before closing for lack of a teacher. Clancy, along with the preacher's sons and a few other lower hollow children, had managed to acquire a primary education at the one-room public school three miles further down.

"C'mon now. Let's git on," said Morgan, signaling his disinterest in school as he took hold of the two sacks and turned toward the door. They filed out past the porch crowd, giving a nod here and a greeting there, and stepped down and across to the mill.

"That boy Clancy thar, he done got the biggest arse and the li'lest chest of ary man in the county," said Morgan derisively, as he strapped the store sacks onto the mule.

"Yass, but he eddicated, and that thar puts him ahead of most mans around h'yar," said Lucy.

Morgan scowled as he cinched down the load. "You and Birdie can git on up home. Rob and me'll be along in a spell," he said. "Arnold's wantin' a word with me."

Lucy and Carrie set off up the road and Morgan, with Rob behind him, stepped up onto the mill porch where he peeked inside and saw that his corn had not been ground yet. "C'mon boy," he said, turning to go. Leaving the mule hitched, they hopped off the porch steps and walked the few paces to the Hughes River, as the creek was called.

The Arnold Nabors home sat across the river. Rob followed Morgan across a narrow and rickety wooden footbridge, stepping with one quick but careful foot in front of the other, and holding out an arm for balance.

Sycamore trees leaned from the banks, the white smooth-skinned upper limbs reaching to a cloudless azure sky and swaying in the brisk autumn breeze, casting a shifting filigree of dappled light onto the bridge and the rippling water beneath.

Big curled brown leaves fluttered down, some landing on the water to bob along on the shimmering wavelets, their pointy lobes seeming to claw the air in protest at being so soon spent. Morgan and Rob took no notice of the seasonal effect as they hurried across. They had business at hand and then chores to do at home before dark.

The log cabin faced the creek, and sat a stone's throw from the water's edge. Arnold was a lord by local standards, but he had no manor house. He'd lived his entire life and raised his large family in the log cabin of his birth, a dwelling smaller than Morgan's modest home.

Wondering what Arnold wanted to talk about, Rob trailed Morgan across the yard to find Arnold sitting in his rocker on the front porch, relaxing his sturdy but worn body of sixty something years. The patriarch, bothered by arthritis from a life of hard labor, was mostly retired, though no one around there ever completely retired from work.

" Mornin', Arnold," said Morgan, approaching the porch.

"Mornin' Morgan. Pull up a chair," said Arnold, swinging his cane toward an old ladderback chair. "Set and talk a spell."

Rob took up a position expected of an eight year-old—on the floorboards at the end of the porch, where he could sit and listen.

"How you been gittin' on, Morgan?" asked Arnold, for openers.

"Been gittin' on fair to middlin'," said Morgan modestly.

"Why, with the big apple crop and prices up a mite, I figgered you done had you a right smart good year, Morgan."

"Hain't been a bad yahr atall, not bad atall. How you been gittin' on, Arnold?"

"I ain't too bad, exceptin' fer all my pains. I cain't do much of nothin' no more. I just keep a hand on the store and mill, and I make a li'l jack, now and again," said the older man. "Yer lookin' right strappin'

Morgan, and them boys of yourn'll soon be up to a man's work," he said, edging toward his reason for summoning Morgan.

"Yassar, the boys is comin' up right good, Arnold," agreed Morgan. "Them thar's some good boys. Yass indeed."

Mention of the boys got Rob's attention. He watched as Arnold picked up a pair of tin cups, reached over to a small keg with a bung tap, and drew off a measure of clear liquid into each.

"Here, have you a li'l nip of jack with me, Morgan," said Arnold, holding out a cup. "I generally usually takes me a dram most mornin's. Just run this keg off yesterday," he said, referring to the freshly distilled apple brandy.

"Don't mind if I do," said Morgan, taking a sip and smacking his lips. "That thar's some fine apple liquor, Arnold. Yer jack's about the best in the entahr holler and the mountain."

This was high praise. Distilling good applejack was an art to which many a mountain man aspired, and not a few attained.

Arnold leaned back in his rocker, stroked his chin under his drooped white moustache, and relaxed his gaze out across the creek to the mill and the store.

"Morgan," he said, staring outward. "I'm thinkin' I'm down to my last years. Once't I'm gone, my land'll git split up amongst the family. Before I pass on, I want to offer you that tract up'par against yer place," he said, shifting his eyes to Morgan. "You know yer ownself it's got some good grass and good timber. And one of them boys of yourn might could fix up that ol' cabin one day, Morgan," he added, pressing the sale. "I don't want but a hunnert forty dollar fer it."

Rob looked at Arnold to see his head tilted and eyebrows raised in an expectant look toward Morgan. Rob looked at Morgan. Arnold's offer seemed to have something to do with Morgan's "boys comin' up."

"Waahhl Arnold," said Morgan in slow response, his elbow on the chair rest and a finger stroking the side of his nose as he considered the proposition. "I done had a right good crop sure enough, with the apples and all. But a hunnert forty dollar'll clean me clear out."

"Put forty dollar on it, Morgan, and I'll go yer note on the hunnert fer three year," said Arnold. "I'd go you longer, exceptin' I most likely ain't got more'n that left." He ran his fingers back through his thinning white hair.

Morgan was silent, but Rob could see he was thinking hard about it.

"You got you a brood to feed and four boys comin' up, Morgan," said Arnold, looking straight at Morgan to wrap up the deal. "You needs you a bigger place. I reckon it's nigh on twenty acre in that parcel of land."

Rob, hearing the "boys" mentioned again, studied Morgan's face, while Morgan pondered the proposition.

"Merr'man's been worryin' me to sell to him, iffen you don't want it, that is," said Arnold, referring to Merriman Hobson, who owned a large mountain tract above the Morgan Dinkins place.

Just then Rob saw a figure of a man balancing himself across the footbridge, catching Arnold's eye and reprieving Morgan from an immediate decision.

"Look at who's a-comin' across the bridge!" exclaimed Arnold with a grin and a glint. "I knew he'd be along directly. He shows here ever Saturday mornin', rain or shine."

As the visitor strode closer, Rob could see a bearded, barefoot man a bit younger than Arnold, with a full shock of white hair on his head, a pair of shoes in his hand and a frown on his face.

The man marched up onto the porch and, with neither word nor nod nor glance to anyone, dropped his shoes and helped himself to a cup of applejack from Arnold's keg. He swallowed the first and drew a second. As he drained the cup, Arnold spoke.

"How you feelin' this mornin', Bob?"

The man smacked his lips and growled, "Like a crosscut saw—it'll take two mans to handle me." He then broke a grin at the amused Arnold.

"You know Morgan Dinkins here, don't you, Bob?"

"I seen him around the mill and store, time and again. Mornin', Morgan," said Bob with a nod.

"Mornin', Bob," said Morgan. "Reckon you hain't never see'd my boy h'yar, has you, Bob? This h'yar's my son, Rob," he said, pointing and looking over at Rob.

Rob riveted his eyes on Morgan, as a tingle went up his spine. Morgan had never actually referred to him as his son. It was always Rob or boy. Stepchildren were always called boy or girl. Rob felt both comforted and confused.

Bob looked at Rob. "Course he is. He look zackly like you, Morgan."

Bob so closely resembled Arnold that he could have been his younger brother. The slender face, the closely set eyes, the straight nose, the pursed lips, the long ear lobes, the ruddy complexion and the loose skin under the chin were all features shared by the two men. He sat down on the porch end next to Rob to pull his shoes onto thickly calloused feet.

Rob's curiosity overcame his diffidence and he asked, "Why you didn't put yer shoes on afore?"

"Ha! Ha, ha," laughed Arnold. "Ol' Bob there don't never put his shoes on in the mornin' until he done had himself two drams of liquor!" exclaimed Arnold, in good humor. "He got himself plenty of liquor over to his place on the Champe Plain, but he always comes over here Saturdays because he ain't workin' and my liquor's a sight better'n his!"

Bob said nothing.

"Bob, he cain't make his wheels round until he done had his drinks!" said Arnold, pressing the tease and looking at his friend mischievously. "Ain't that so, Bob?"

Bob offered no word of self-defense.

Bob Parsten was a wheelwright, a prized trade in those days of wagons, buggies and coaches. He lived on the upper edge of the Champe

Plain estate, where the land flared at the base of Ragged Mountain, a couple miles from Nabors Mill in the opposite direction from the Dinkins place.

"Bob, I just been tryin' to sell Morgan here a tract of good grass and timber before I have to go to the Lord," said Arnold, looking back over at Morgan. Parsten raised his eyebrows in an inquisitive look at Morgan, prompting Rob to look up at his father, the three of their gazes expecting a response out of him.

"Wahl Arnold, I reckon I orter buy it while'st I gots me the chance. You gots yerself a deal."

"There now, I'll git the deed and the note made up directly," said Arnold, quickly closing the sale. "You done come to the right decision, Morgan."

Morgan stood up. "Reckon Tee most likely got my meal ground by now," he said, signaling that the business talk was concluded. "We's best be a-gittin' on." Rob slid off the porch. "Arnold, Bob," said Morgan with a departing nod to each.

"Be good, Morgan," called Arnold, as the pair headed for the bridge.

Morgan loaded his sacks of meal onto the mule and they headed for home. They hadn't passed more than half a mile when he heard Rob speak.

"Ellitt wahr my actual daddy."

Morgan turned it over in his mind for a while as they walked up the dirt road. He finally spoke.

"Ellitt wahr yer daddy and then I'm yer next daddy. But I actual wahr yer first daddy and Ellitt, he wahr yer next daddy," he said, bringing a look of confusion to Rob's face. "Now I'm yer daddy again," he said, trying to explain it.

Rob asked no more questions, but Morgan knew the boy found it too puzzling to understand. He offered no more explanation, and they made their way home in silence.

SIXTEEN

The Next Day
School

On Sunday, the Dinkinses and Nickersons convened up at the Hawlins place with Lylie and Otis for a cheerful day of apple butter boiling. There were so many hands available to tend the fire and stir the kettle that most of the sunny day passed in leisurely socializing amid the sweet fruity aroma of bubbling apple mush.

Morgan, Festus and Otis busied themselves with grinding the apples into pulp and squeezing the pulp into cider. When it was Lylie's turn to stir the kettle, Lucy and Hannah sat down together on a bench in the yard to chat about family matters.

"Mama, just yesterday I's down to the store," said Lucy. "Clancy thar, he done tolt me about the school what done open up down to the church. I'm a-thinkin' about sendin' Bob and Rob on down thar to school."

Hannah pondered the thought. "Hain't no harm in it, I reckon," she finally said. "The both of 'em hain't big enough to work much. A li'l book larnin' might do 'em some good."

"I'm goin' to send 'em on down in the mornin'," declared Lucy resolutely, reinforced by her mother's words of support. She called out to the two boys, who were swinging on a grapevine hanging from a large tree. "Bob! Rob! Git over h'yar!"

The pair scuffed over to the bench, their downcast eyes signaling protest at the interruption of their play.

"I'm a-sendin' the both of yous to school in the mornin'."

The boys looked at each other and back at Lucy.

"What's school?" asked Bob.

"School is whar you larns to read, write and figger."

"Whar's it?" inquired Rob.

"It's right down thar to the church. You two's goin' in the mornin'."

"What we gon' do once't we gits thar?" wondered Bob.

"You just sets thar and gits larn't."

"Who gon' larn us?" he asked.

"The schoolmarm larns you."

"How she gon' larn us?" persisted Bob.

"She just show you the readin', writin' and figgerin' so's you can do it."

"Whats figgerin'?" asked Bob, showing interest.

"It's numbers, like what Clancy do down to the store."

"Is it gon' hurt?" worried Rob.

"Course not," said Lucy. "Less'n you don't mind the schoolmarm and don't do what she say and she lace you fer it. Now git on back to yer grapevine." She dismissed the perplexed boys and turned to Hannah. "Mama, this h'yar's a chance to git a li'l eddication into the family." Lucy was keen to provide any advantage, and this was the best she could do for them now.

Monday dawned slowly under a leaden sky that cast a still and somber mood. After breakfast, Lucy fitted Bob and Rob into the shirts she'd made the prior winter and trussed them up in the better of their two pairs of britches. The boys pulled on their coarse cloth coats and the shoes they saved for cold weather.

"Now git on down to the church. Don't be stoppin' and foolin' around, you hear me now?"

"Yassum."

Class had not yet started when the boys arrived to find the other children scattered about in ones and twos, inside and outside the church-cum-schoolhouse. The teacher, a respectable looking young woman with her dark brown hair parted down the middle and pulled back to a tight bun, sat writing at the desk in front, just to the side of the blackboard.

Rob and Bob had just stepped inside the door when they saw her look up at them. She rose with pencil and paper in hand and, looking quite proper in a plain full-length long-sleeved dress, gray sweater and high button shoes, walked back to where they stood.

"Hello, boys. I'm Miss Pricilla," she said with smile, slipping onto the end of a bench that placed her at eye level with Bob.

"You the schoolmarm?"

"Yes, I'm the teacher, but you can call me Miss Pricilla," she said with a warmth belying her prim appearance. "Now, what are your names?"

"Bob."

"Yes, but we have another Bob. Which Bob are you?"

"I'm Nellie's Bob."

"I see. And what is your name?" she continued, looking at Rob.

"Rob."

"Yes, but Rob who?"

"Lucy's Rob."

"But what is your full name Rob?"

He hesitated a moment before blurting out, "Robert E. Lee!"

She tossed her head back and laughed. "There was only one Robert E. Lee and I don't think you're him, Rob," she said, chuckling. "Now what are your last names, boys?" she asked, looking at Bob.

"Dinkins."

"Robert Dinkins. There now, R-o-b-e-r-t D-i-n-k-i-n-s." She wrote on her paper.

"I hain't no Robert. I'm Bob."

"Well, Bob is just a nickname for Robert."

"I hain't no Robert no more. I'm just Bob now."

"Very well then, Bob." She scratched out Robert and wrote in Bob. "What's your last name, Rob?"

Rob stared self-consciously at his feet. "I don't know," he muttered.

She frowned, but for the moment accepted his answer.

"Now what are your ages?"

"What?" asked Bob, his face wrinkling in puzzlement.

"How old are you boys?"

Rob and Bob looked at each other. Then Bob answered. "Reckon I'm ten, or leben."

Miss Priscilla looked at Rob.

"Reckon I don't know," he admitted shyly.

"Well now Rob, I want you to ask your mother this evening, and you can tell me in the morning. Ask her your last name and your age. Can you do that for me?"

"Yassum."

"You boys can sit right here," she said, standing up and pointing to a bench. She turned and walked back to her desk in front.

Rob slid uneasily onto the seat beside Bob, as the teacher lifted a small bell from her desk and tinkled it vigorously. The dozen or so children arranged themselves onto the several benches behind low tables and, with quick glances at the newcomers, continued their chatter. The class included only two girls, who sat together. A couple of older boys, of about twelve, shuffled in and sat beside one another.

"Children! Class is starting. Please be quiet and pay attention. James Wilson, have you forgotten your chore?" she called out to one of the older boys, who rose and scooted outside as the classroom quieted down. James quickly returned with an armload of wood that he stuffed into the black iron pot-bellied stove.

"We have two new pupils today—Bob and Rob," she announced, looking to the rear of the room. Heads swiveled back and all eyes fell upon the two.

Rob felt a wave of uneasy self-consciousness break over him. He looked at Bob, whose face revealed a full dose of the same. Most of the other pupils were acquainted through attending church. The Dinkinses didn't go to church, so they were strangers to all the others. At least they were tolerably located in the back of the room.

"We're learning to say and write the alphabet and to count simple numbers," the teacher explained to the new boys. "Who can say the entire alphabet?"

A small hand went up.

"Mary."

The girl bounced up. "A-b-c-d-e-f-g-h-i-j-k-l-m-n-o-p-q-r-s-t-u-v-w-x-y-z," she recited at top speed.

The teacher rose. "Very good, Mary. Now I want each one of you to write the alphabet," she announced, and went around to place a sheet of paper in front of every pupil. "Write as much as you can remember." They all went to work, as she came back to Bob and Rob.

"Boys" she said, sitting on a bench facing them, "we speak and write in words but all words are made of letters. There are twenty-six letters and they are called the alphabet. You must learn the alphabet before you can learn to read and write."

She placed a sheet of paper in front of each and held up two pencils. "We write with pencils," she said, holding out one to each. It was the first writing instrument either boy had ever held.

"First, hold the pencil like this," she said, demonstrating.

Rob awkwardly fumbled his fingers on the slender shaft, and he noticed that Bob did too. Then the teacher stood and reached over his shoulder to help him grip his fingers well enough around the pencil to hold the point to the paper. She did the same with Bob.

"Good. Next you must learn to say and write the first three letters of the alphabet." She had written *a, b* and *c* across the top of each boy's paper. "This is *a*, this is *b* and this is *c*. Try to remember these three letters—*a, b*, and *c*," she repeated. "Say them, *a, b, c*."

Rob hesitated. Bob uttered "*a, b, c*." Rob repeated, "*a, b, c*."

"Now, you write *a, b* and *c* like this." She put her fingers around theirs, first Bob's then Rob's, and guided the pencil point to form the three letters. "There, now you do it. Just keep saying and writing *a-b-c*, *a-b-c, a-b-c.*" She rose and returned to the front of the room.

"Who can write the alphabet on the blackboard?"

Mary's hand shot up. "I can, Miss Pricilla!"

As little Mary chalked the letters across the board, the teacher called out, "James, please count down from ten." James held a hand in front of his face and started tapping fingers with his other finger. "Ten, nine, eight…"

"Without your fingers please, James."

His hands went down. "Ten, nine…, eight, uh.. seven…, six.., five, four, three, two, one!"

"Good. Now subtract three from ten."

James held out all fingers, folded three, and counted the rest under his breath. "Seven!"

"That's correct, James, but you must learn to do it without using your fingers. Now, subtract five from ten."

Rob was baffled. He knew what five and ten were, as in five or ten fingers, but subtraction? What was subtraction?

James closed his eyes. His lips moved. "Five!"

"Very good, James. Now do one more. Subtract five from five."

The boy's eyes rolled downward. Then he thrust up his closed fist. "Hain't nothin'!" he exclaimed.

"Yes, but remember, James, nothing is called *zero*." James had been lagging in arithmetic.

"Thank you, Mary," said Miss Priscilla. The child returned to her seat. "Now class, I want each of you to look at the alphabet on the board and at your alphabet on your paper. Write down all the letters you forgot to write on your paper."

She came back to Bob and Rob. They had written only a couple of poorly formed *a*'s, *b*'s and *c*'s on their papers. Rob had taken more interest in James' arithmetic.

"What letter is this, Bob?" she quizzed, leaning over the boy's shoulder and pointing.

"*A?*"

"That's correct. And this letter?"

"*B?*"

"No, Bob. This is *c*. The third letter is *c*."

"Rob, what letter is this?"

"*A?*"

"No Rob. This is the second letter. What is the second letter?"

"*B?*"

"Yes, the second letter is *b*—just think *a,b,c—1,2,3*. Now, write each letter just like this," she instructed for the second time, wrapping her fingers around theirs and patiently guiding each boy's pencil.

"I want you two to write many more a's, b's and c's on your papers." Miss Pricilla then worked her way back to the front, going from pupil to pupil. She looked over each shoulder at their papers. "You can do better than that, James. Try to keep your letters straight."

After several more alphabet drills, she said, "We will now practice phonics. I will point to a letter on the board and ask one of you to make the sound of the letter. Remember, all the vowels and some consonants have two sounds."

Bob and Rob sat hunched over with pencils to paper, ignoring the mysteries of Miss Pricilla's phonics drill.

"Very well. We will now review the two words we learned last Friday. Mary, come to the blackboard." The little girl scurried to the front. "What were the two words, Mary?"

"Dog and cat."

Rob and Bob looked up, the familiar words catching their ears.

"Yes, dog and cat. I'll make the sound and someone say the letter. If it's correct, Mary will write it on the board. We'll start with dog. *Duh, duh, duh.*"

"Arrff! Arrff! Arrff! Rrr-OW! Fffsst!" It was James imitating a dog and cat.

"That's enough James! What is *duh*, class?" The smirking smart aleck slouched on his bench, his head down and hands folded in mock contrition.

"*D!*" called out a pupil.

"That's correct. Now *aw, aw, aw.*"

"*O!*" cried another.

"*Aw?* I done thought it was *Oh*," interjected James.

"That's the long *o*, James. Remember, *o* is a vowel. It has a short and a long sound. Dog has the short *o—aw*. If it were the long *o*, it would be a doge instead of a dog." The class giggled at the doge. "Do you understand, James?"

"I reckon," he said unconvincingly.

"And the last letter is *guh, guh, guh.*"

"*G!*" came a call from the middle of the room.

"That's correct." Mary had written dog on the board. Miss Pricilla pointed to each letter. "*Duh…aw…guh. Duh-aw-guh. D-o-g. Dog.* Now Cat. The first letter is *kuh, kuh, kuh.*"

"*K!*" It was James.

"*Kuh* can be *k*, James, but *k* is not correct. There is another letter that can sound like *kuh*. What is it, James?" He bit his lip, furrowed his brow and looked baffled. "What is it class?"

"*C!*" yelled someone. They completed the sounding out and spelling of cat.

"James, come to the board and write the numerals zero through nine."

The boy reluctantly shuffled forward and took up the chalk.

"At the top of the board please, James."

He slowly formed the numerals at irregular spacing and with the *three* reversed. The teacher took the chalk and wrote the numerals in an even line under his. "The three is like this, James. You must practice writing your numerals. You may be seated."

Rob and Bob were now watching with rapt attention. Miss Pricilla proceeded to write the numbers ten through nineteen directly under the single character numerals. She explained that the new numbers, up to nineteen, were written by just placing a *1* in front of the numeral above it, because it was ten more; twenty was written with a *2* instead of a *1* because twenty was "two tens."

Rob intently studied the numerals on the board, though the concept of base ten eluded him.

"Children, we will learn to spell two new words tomorrow, *boy* and *girl*. That is all for today. Class is dismissed." It was nearly noon.

Rob and Bob didn't understand what dismissed meant but, seeing the others leaving, they stood up as the teacher approached them. She looked down at the papers where they'd scrawled *a*'s, *b*'s and *c*'s all over. The letters were poorly formed but they'd written them in the correct order. Additionally Rob had written *1, 2, 3* in several places.

"Very good, boys. Now don't forget—*a, b, c*. I'll give you three more letters tomorrow. And you also must learn the sounds for each letter. Take your papers but leave the pencils here."

Hunger kept Bob and Rob on a direct course up the road to home. The pair walked into the cabin just as Carrie and Lucy finished cooking. Lucy spotted their papers. "What's this?" she asked, holding up Rob's paper sideways. "You write this, Rob?"

"Yassum."

"What's it say?"

"It's just *a, b, c*. It don't actual say nothin'."

"What's *a, b, c*?"

"It's letters. Words is made from letters. *A, b, c* is the first letters in the alfeebet. It's like *1,2,3*," explained Rob.

She took Bob's paper and studied it upside down, with Carrie peeking in from the side. "Laws! I cain't hardly believe you done larn't all that the first day!" Morgan and the older boys came in. "Look h'yar Morgan. Bob and Rob, they done larn't how to write on paper!"

Morgan examined the paper. "What's it say?"

"It don't actual say nothin'," said Lucy

"Hain't these words writ down h'yar?"

"No, it's just letters," said Rob.

"What's the good in writin' iffen it don't say nothin'?"

Bob explained. "This h'yar's just three letters. Words is made from letters. The letters is the alfeebet. We gots to larn the entahr alfeebet first, afore we can larn ary words atall. They's twenty-six letters and they all gots a sound. Some gots two sounds."

Rob added, "We cain't read or write till we's done larn't the alfeebet and all the sounds."

"Why, that thar's goin' to be a right smart piece of book larnin'," said Morgan, looking impressed by what he'd heard.

The family seated themselves around the table. Morgan said the table grace. "Thank you Lord fer our family and fer the vittles, and…"

Lucy cut in. "And thank you Lord fer these h'yar boys and all the larnin' they's a-gitten, amen." She looked at Morgan, who showed more surprise than annoyance at her sudden interjection.

Rob lingered around the stove after dinner. "Mama, how olt I am?"

Lucy paused, looked at him and then silently counted on her fingers. "Yer eight yahr."

"That the same as my age?"

"I reckon. Yer eight yahr olt. Schoolmarm ask you that?"

"Yassum. And she done ask what's my last name."

"What you done tolt her?"

"I tolt her I'm Robert E. Lee and she done laugh and say I cain't be Robert E. Lee."

"Wahl, you *is* Robert E. Lee, but yer last name is Nickerson."

"Bob, he done say his last name Dinkins. Why hain't I Dinkins?"

"Because you wahr born't t'uther side of the hill and Bob, he wahr born't this side. Them's Nickersons over thar and they's Dinkins over h'yar."

Rob was puzzled but he let it drop.

"Does you like the schoolmarm, Rob?"

"Yassum. She's Miss Pricilla."

There was no afternoon class. Experience had shown that half the pupils did not return after dinner, and the teacher could not hold the attention of some who did. The students were drawn from the fifty-odd families living in the lower hollow that extended out about a mile or so from Nabors Mill. The Dinkins lived on the upper fringe of that range.

None of the mountaineers sent children down from the ridges or upper hollows, and not all of the lower hollow folk saw any value in sending a child to school, especially one with a female teacher. A stern old schoolmaster with a liberal switch was considered superior to any young schoolmarm with a soft voice and empathetic manner.

Rob's second day of school started out the same as the first, with Miss Priscilla approaching him and Bob. "Good morning boys. Rob, did you remember to ask your mother something for me?"

"Uh, uh..."

"Your age and your last name?"

"Uh, yassum. I'm eight yahr olt. My last name Nickerson."

"R-o-b-e-r-t N-i-c-k-e-r-s-o-n," she spelled aloud as she wrote it down. "Eight years old." She turned and moved to the front of the room.

Rob and Bob reclaimed the inconspicuous seats in the rear when the teacher rang the class to order.

"Children, I want to be sure you have memorized the alphabet." Walking around the room, she placed a paper before each pupil. "I have written most of the alphabet across your papers. Some letters are missing and all are out of order. You must write the letters in correct order and also find the missing letters. Try to write in a straight line."

As the class leaned into the assignment, she came to the back and placed papers in front of Bob and Rob. "What are the first three letters," she quizzed.

"*A, b, c,*" they answered in unison.

"Good. Now, the next three letters are *d, e,* and *f.* I have written the first six letters on your paper, *a, b, c, d, e, f.*" She drilled them in saying and writing *d, e,* and *f* as she had the day before with *a, b,* and *c.* "I want you to write *a, b, c, d, e,* and *f* in straight lines on your papers."

Rob and Bob put pencils to paper as the teacher went from pupil to pupil, peering over shoulders to check progress. In a while, Rob had completed five crudely formed six-letter sequences in crooked lines. He looked over to see that Bob had written only two and, with a vacant look on his face, sat doodling aimlessly with his pencil.

"You have done very well, children. Most of you found the missing letters and wrote the correct alphabet." She looked toward James. "James, you missed the *n*. *N* comes after *m*."

Turning her attention back to the class, she continued, "We will now count all the way up to one hundred." The numbers one through twenty were still on the blackboard from the day before. She pointed to one of the numerals. "James, what number is this?"

"Uh, uh, uh, seven!"

"That's correct, James, but you must memorize the numerals so you don't always have to count up from one. Mary, come to the board."

Mary was the preacher's daughter. She was the youngest and most advanced pupil in the class, so she served as teacher's assistant. She lived next to the church and was always early to school, where she received extra tutoring until class was called. Rob and Bob, like several others, lived in homes with no clock and no one who could tell time. Time was approximate and that is how they arrived at school. The teacher started class whenever most were present.

The mention of numbers caught Rob's attention.

"Yesterday we counted from one to twenty. Today we will count from twenty to one hundred. The class will say the next number out loud and Mary will write it on the board. What comes after twenty?"

"Twenty-one," answered a pupil. Mary wrote *21* under the *11*.

"Next is..."

"Twenty-two," called several pupils.

"And..."

"Twenty-three," said the class in unison. And on they went, with Mary forming ten rows of ten and ten columns of ten.

Rob sat transfixed by the repetitive sound of the count. He had noticed that there were only ten characters and that all numbers above nine were formed by two of the ten characters. He also noticed the repetitive sequence of the numbers in the vertical columns as well as in the lines. He had been struggling to learn his letters. Now, the logic and order of numbers had just leaped into his head. His uneasy feeling of ineptness gave way to the thrill of unexpected enlightenment.

"Ninety-nine," they all chimed.

"What comes after ninety-nine, class?"

Silence.

"Mary?"

"One hundred!" exclaimed the seven year-old, entering *100* under the *90* on the board as the other pupils lapsed into chatter.

Rob stared at the blackboard. He recognized *100* as the beginning of a new sequence with three characters forming each number. He glanced at Bob, who was still doodling with his pencil and ignoring the class.

"Children! Children!" called Miss Priscilla, regaining their attention. "We will now practice phonics. What are the two new words for today? I told you yesterday."

The class quieted and turned vacant looks to the teacher.

"Mary?"

"Boy and girl."

"Yes, *boy* and *girl*. We'll start with *boy*." They sounded out all the letters one by one. Rob busied himself with paper and pencil, giving no attention to the phonics drill.

"Next we will draw pictures. What were the two words yesterday?"

"Dog and cat," answered the class.

"What do dogs have that cats don't have?"

"Long nose!" offered James. "Long legs!" added someone. "Long ears!" called another. Most dogs around there were hunting hounds.

"And what do cats have that dogs don't have?"

"Whiskers!" came an answer.

"Children, draw a dog and a cat on your papers. Don't forget the dog's long legs, ears and nose, and the cat's whiskers."

Miss Pricilla came back to Bob and Rob. "Bob! You've only written a few letters! Why haven't you done your work?"

"I don't know," he mumbled.

"And what's all this scrawling?"

"I don't know," he repeated, looking up at her sheepishly.

"Let me see yours, Rob," she said, holding out her hand.

Rob handed over his paper, keeping his eyes on her as she looked it over. He had written a row of numerals in addition to letters.

"This is better," she said, nodding approval. "I see you're interested in numbers, Rob. Can you say these numbers?" she asked, putting the paper in front of the boy.

"Zeero, one, two, three, four, five, six, seven, eight, nine."

"That's very good, Rob. Now I want you to remember each numeral so you can write it when I say the number. Will you try to do that?"

"Yassum."

"Now you boys draw your dog and cat."

Rob put his pencil to the paper and sketched one of the animals. He glanced at Bob, who had drawn nothing and was fidgeting and looking all around the room, as if interested in nothing more than being done with school. Rob kept drawing while the other pupils finished their pictures and broke into chatter.

"Children! Take your papers home and ask your mother and father which is the dog and which is the cat! Class is dismissed!"

Bob, eager to go, held his seat for the minute or two it took Rob to put a final touch to his picture, his first drawing ever. Then they headed for the door.

Outside, the pupils had all dispersed except for the two older boys, who approached Bob and Rob.

"Give me a chaw!" demanded James, with his palm stretched out at Bob.

"Hain't got no chaw."

James turned to Rob. "You got a chaw?"

"Hain't got no chaw neither."

He looked back at Bob. "You best give me a chaw in the mornin'," he warned.

"We hain't got no chaws atall."

"Git one from yer pappy."

"Our daddy hain't got no chaws neither. He don't chew."

"Yer pappy don't chew? Then you best bring me *somethin'* in the mornin'."

Most of the men and older boys chewed tobacco, as did some women and children in the remote reaches of mountain and hollow.

Lucy eagerly awaited the boys as she and Carrie prepared dinner. When they came through the door, she took hold of both school papers.

"Bob! You hain't got hardly nothin' on h'yar! Didn't you larn nothin' today?"

"I don't know."

"And what's all this h'yar?" she asked, pointing to the aimless scrawling. "I can see it hain't no writin'."

"I don't know," he repeated, with a forlorn look on his face.

"Rob, I sees you done larn't more of them thar letters," his mother said, studying the paper.

"Yassum, three letters and I larn't numbers." He took the paper and turned it right side up. "Them right thar is numbers," he said, pointing to the row of numerals.

"Can you read them numbers?"

Rob pointed a finger at each numeral. "Zeero, one, two, three, four, five, six, seven, eight, nine."

THE TALE OF A WOODS COLT

Lucy and almost everyone unable to read or write numbers could at least count to ten or higher on their fingers. There was a mystery, however. "What's zee-ro?" she asked.

"It hain't nothin'," answered Rob.

"Hain't nothin'?" That wasn't enough of an explanation for her.

He went on. "It's when you hain't got no number but you gots to have it to write numbers and figger."

Lucy was astounded at her son's knowledge of such a mystery. "Lordy! You done larn't to read numbers and it hain't but the second day!"

"Look h'yar, Mama," said Rob, pointing to the drawings. "It's a dog and a cat."

Lucy studied the crude figures. She smiled at Rob and couldn't wait for Morgan to see his progress. Just then he came in for dinner.

"Looky h'yar, Morgan! Rob done larn't to write numbers!" she cried excitedly, holding up the paper.

"Do tell, now!" he exclaimed. "First thang you know, the boy'll be clarkin' down to the store," he said, as if wrapping his mild disdain of education in a cloak of humor.

"And he done draw't two pitchures. They's animals, Morgan," she said, handing him the paper.

Morgan furrowed his brow and studied the figures for a moment. "Why sure! It's a mule and a 'possum!" he declared, to the amusement of all—except for Rob.

SEVENTEEN

A Dust-Up

The next morning, James and his pal appeared as Bob and Rob approached the church. "Whar's my chaw?" demanded James.

"Done said I hain't got no chaw," said Bob warily.

"What you got fer me, then?"

"Hain't got nothin'."

"You best give me somethin'," snarled the older boy, crowding his chest to Bob's chin. James towered over Bob, but was ungainly in the way of a boy whose body had outgrown his coordination.

"Said I hain't got nothin'," repeated Bob curtly, taking a side step.

Rob and James' pal stood watching. Several other pupils came over as the standoff caught their notice.

"You got somethin' and I'm goin' to git it!" yelled James, curling his lip and side stepping to keep his chest in Bob's face.

"You hain't gon' git *nothin'*," retorted Bob through clenched teeth.

"I can *whup* you, iffen I wants to!" shouted James.

"You cain't neither," snapped Bob defiantly.

"I can and I will!!" bellowed the bully, shoving Bob's chest.

In a flash, fists were flying. They fell to the ground, scuffing up a little cloud of dust, with the bigger boy rolling on top. Rob leaped onto James' back, furiously jerking his collar. The other boy dragged Rob off and fell on him, pinning him to the ground.

Then the wiry Bob managed to roll on top of James, gaining the upper hand. His quick agility offset his smaller size. He pounded through James' flailing arms to relentlessly pummel his angry fists into the bully's face.

James' pal suddenly shrieked. Rob, on his back in the dirt under him, had thrust his head up and chomped the boy's ear as hard as he could, hanging on like a bulldog. Pal screamed as blood gushed from his lacerated ear.

The yelling and the howling brought Miss Pricilla rushing from the building into the road. "Stop it!! Stop fighting!!" she shouted. "Stop it right now!" She grabbed Bob's collar and pulled him back and off James.

James struggled to his feet. His bleeding nose was bent, both of his eyes blackened, his face bruised and his split lip oozed blood. His friend had gotten loose from Rob and stood with a hand covering his bloody ear, moaning.

"Why are you boys fighting?" demanded the teacher.

The boys didn't answer.

Then one of the other pupils spoke up. "James Wilson there, he tried to take somethin' from Bob. Bob, he don't give James nothin' and James, he done push Bob. Right then they's down in the road a-fightin'."

Miss Pricilla looked at James and his sniveling friend. James looked down and away, scuffing his feet in the dirt, as if shamed by the beating he'd taken.

"Very well, then. It serves you two bullies right for picking on smaller boys. Now go home and don't come back to school until your mothers have come to see me. Go on now!"

James shot a snarly look at Bob and then muttered to his pal, "C'mon." The two shuffled off down the road.

"Now the rest of you go inside. Class is about to start," ordered the teacher, grabbing some firewood and following them in.

During the class, Miss Pricilla could see that Bob was completely disengaged from the lesson. He just sat doodling and fidgeting through the entire session. She allowed that he was disturbed by the dust up, and so didn't press him.

It went better with Rob. He recited the first six letters and could identify five of them when written separately. He was able to identify about half the numerals she pointed to, and successfully wrote several of the ones she called out.

She gave the other pupils an assignment, and went back to drill Rob in the next three letters and coach him in numbers. *He does have interest and aptitude,* she thought. She reckoned Rob could, with daily tutoring, catch up to the rest of the class within a month or so.

This was the only school currently open around Nabors Mill. The teacher hoped to bring the pupils to the most basic level of reading, writing and arithmetic by the time the seven-month term ended.

After graduating from the Normal School for Girls, Miss Pricilla had volunteered through her Methodist Church to teach in a deprived area. The church could afford only a bare subsistence wage and boarded her with the preacher's family. There was no money for primers and supplies beyond pencils and paper. Her only available teaching method was drilling her students and encouraging their progress. The next year was in doubt, though. She would have to move on to a more secure position after the term, leaving the church to find another teacher.

After school, Bob and Rob dragged their feet on their way home, knowing they'd likely get into trouble over the fighting. Lucy rushed over to the dirty pair as soon as they came through the door. "Bob! Rob! You two been down rollin' in the dirt? And yer coat done got tore, Bob! What you boys been doin'?"

"Fightin'," said Bob. "Big ol' boy done shove me and I done whup him good."

"Fightin'?! What you fightin' about?! You suppose to be larnin'."

"Big ol' boy done say give him a chaw. I hain't got no chaw and he done push me. They was two of 'em. T'other one, he jump Rob h'yar. I done beat that big ol' boy's face and Rob, he done bit t'other boy's ear near half in two," said Bob, claiming victory.

Lucy looked to Rob, who nodded confirmation. She felt a flush of anger rise in her face. She lifted her arms with clenched fists. "I'm goin' to git right down thar in the mornin' and lace both them boys good!" she vowed, shaking her fist. I'm gon' tan they hides! I'm gon' lay the hickory on 'em 'til they cain't stand up!"

"They hain't thar no more. Schoolmarm done send 'em on home until they mamas comes to see her," said Bob. "And besides, they's more'n laced now. I done broke his nose and the both 'ems bleedin' right smart."

Lucy took a seat and let herself calm down. "Don't you git holt of no chaws now, you hear me?" she said, warning both boys. "Chewin' tobacker hain't good fer boys," she said. With Morgan setting the example, the two older boys, Eddie and John, had not taken up the habit.

The next morning Bob and Rob again walked down to the church, but Bob hesitated outside.

"You goin' in? asked Rob.

"I don't want be settin' in school today."

"What you gon' do?"

"I don't know. Reckon I'll git on up the river a piece," said Bob.

The Hughes River drained several hollows before flowing by the mill and on down right beside the church. It was more of a creek, but everyone called it the river.

"What about larnin'?"

"I don't want be larnin' nothin' today."

With that, Bob turned and drifted toward the creek bank. Rob called after him. "You gon' come back h'yar?!"

Bob turned, "I'll be back afore you gits out."

Rob went inside and took his seat.

Miss Pricilla called the class to order with a ring of her little bell. She had chalked half a dozen of the very simplest addition and subtraction problems on the board.

"Children, I want you to copy and complete each arithmetic problem. Write the answer under each line," she instructed while passing out fresh paper. When she got back to Rob she asked, "Where's Bob today?"

"He don't want larn nothin' today."

She wasn't much surprised. Bob seemed to have disengaged during his second day, before the fight. She proceeded to give Rob the next three letters and to drill him in writing, reading and sounding them. He was up to *i*, but his interest was weaker and he had difficulty remembering it all.

"Can I do numbers?" he asked, pointing to the board.

"I don't think you're ready for that yet, Rob."

"I likes the numbers," he said, persisting.

"Very well then." She drilled him in reading and writing the numerals without using fingers, and then using fingers in the simplest addition and subtraction. She held up her hand. "Here are five. Take away two," she said, folding two fingers, "and how many are left?"

"Three."

"Good. Here is how you write it." She formed a five and placed a two under it and then drew a line under the two. "This means take away— subtraction," she said as she marked down a minus sign next to the two. "The answer goes down here under the line," she said, writing a three below the line. Rob seemed puzzled by the geometry of the calculation.

She took another tack.

"Now let me show you something, Rob. When you count up from one, you're actually adding. You're adding one at a time." She put pencil to paper. "You start with one and you add one. That equals two. You add one more to equal three—all the way up. You can count down by taking away one. Ten minus one equals nine. Subtract one more to equal eight—all the way down. Do you see, Rob?"

"Yassum."

"You now must learn to add and subtract any number from any number, between one and ten. You may use your fingers for a while but then later you must learn and remember to do it without fingers. Do you understand?"

THE TALE OF A WOODS COLT

"Yassum," he said, sounding enthusiastic. She let him spend the remainder of the session adding and subtracting numbers on his fingers.

The class ended and Rob stepped out to find Bob standing in the churchyard with two sizable brook trout on a string dangling from his hand.

"Whar'd you git them fish?"

"Done catch 'em my own self," declared Bob proudly. "Ol' Tee up to the mill, he done see'd me standin' thar to the river. He let me use his fishin' pole and I done got right lucky and catch me two fish." They headed up the road, each pleased with their very different accomplishments.

"Whar's yer paper and whar'd you git them fish?!" demanded Lucy, looking at Bob.

"Hain't got no paper. I'm tahred of larnin'. I done gone fishin' thar to the mill. Ol' Tee, he let me use his pole and I done catch me two fish!" said Bob with a grin.

"Bob, you gots to stick with yer larnin'," chided Lucy. "In the mornin' you gots to be in the school, not out to the river fishin.' You hear me now?"

"Yassum," he muttered, looking glum.

The morning found both boys back in their seats at school. After giving assignments to the others, Miss Pricilla sat with them in the rear of the room. She could see that Bob's mind was wandering, and she felt it was unlikely she'd retrieve it. She started with Rob.

"Rob, say the alphabet up to *i*."

"*A, b, c, d, e*... uh, uh...*f?*"

"That's correct. Go on."

"Uh, uh...uh..."

"*guh, guh, guh*," she hinted.

"Uh, uh, *h?*"

"No. *h* is hah. This is guh," she coached.

"*I!*"

"No Rob, What is guh?"

"Uh…I don't know." His eyes fell as he gave up.

"It's *g* Rob. Guh is *g*. I want you to write the alphabet from *a* to *i*."

She went to check on the other pupils, leaving Rob to work on his paper. She glanced back to see Bob fidgeting and squirming in his seat, looking positively pained to be there.

She returned to check Rob's work. "Rob you left out a letter here," she pointed. "Which letter goes here?"

"I needs to git to the outhouse," declared Bob, shifting about on the bench. His squirming suggested than he couldn't hold it much longer. "Of course you may, Bob, but hurry back."

"Yassum." He raced off the bench and darted out the door.

She turned back to Rob. "What is the letter? Think now."

Rob studied the paper. She waited a moment and then gave in. "It's the *g* Rob. The *g* is after *f* and before the *h*, remember?"

"Yassum. I reckon. Can we count numbers now?" he asked, looking up with eager eyes.

"Yes, in a little bit."

She went to the board and chalked some more problems that added or subtracted single numerals. She noticed Rob watching her closely. She also noticed that Bob had not returned.

"I want each of you to write these on your papers and find the answers."

She went back to Rob and sat with him, going over how to count in twos and in fives. When she returned to the front, it was evident to her that Rob's aptitude ran to arithmetic far more than to reading and writing.

"It's Friday, children. I will see you all Monday morning. Class is dismissed."

Rob went out into the churchyard. There was no Bob. He lingered. Once the other chattering children had drifted off and it had grown quiet, he heard a sound from behind the church. Thwack. Thwack.

Thwack. He ventured back to find Bob swinging a stout stick, dueling with a briar patch.

Bob would whack a bramble stem that, often as not, would swing down and snag him with a thorn. He would then pull the thorn loose, grunt a curse and proceed to beat the offending cane to shreds.

Rob stood quietly, staring at Bob doing battle with the patch of prickly brambles.

Bob flailed on for a while and then paused, panting, to catch his breath. He noticed Rob. The bush fighter stared at the tangle of mangled briar canes and decided he'd had enough combat for the day. "C'mon," he said as he brushed past Rob.

The two struck for home in silence.

"Bob, you hain't larn't hardly a thang!" cried Lucy in dismay when the boy came in empty-handed. Bob hung his head and turned away. That was the end of it. Lucy saw no point in haranguing him any more about it. It was obvious that Bob would not be getting an education.

That weekend an early and sharp cold snap settled over the region. Frigid air held Monday morning in a frozen vice grip.

"Rob, it's too colt fer school," declared Lucy. "You stay h'yar until it warms a mite." She was reluctant to send him off alone anyway, and the frigid air eased her decision.

By Friday the cold had relented. Rob set out for school alone, with Lucy watching from the porch.

"Rob! We have missed you in class all week!" Miss Pricilla did not mention Bob.

"Mama done say it wahr too colt fer school."

"Rob, you must attend every day or you will never catch up. Do you understand?"

"Yassum."

Class commenced and Rob immediately felt lost, as though it were his first day all over again. The teacher went over letters and numbers with him. "Rob. You have forgotten nearly half of the letters you learned last week!"

Rob felt discouraged, and sat through the morning with little interest and no accomplishment. The teacher dismissed the class and came to him. "Rob, I will spend extra time with you on Monday and you will learn everything you forgot," she said. "Would you like that?"

"Yassum," he answered softly with eyes cast down.

Rob set out for home but paused just out in the road and looked back. Miss Pricilla stood watching him from the church door.

"Whar's yer paper, Rob?" asked Lucy as he came through the door.

"Hain't got no paper," he answered, without looking up.

"What you done larn't today?" she inquired, facing her son with arms akimbo.

"Hain't larn't nothin'," he said, standing there looking defeated.

Lucy considered the problem. She was disappointed, but it did not occur to her that education is a continuum. She did not understand the need to progress steadily and consistently, lest learning be lost. She saw no difference in the value of a certain number of consecutive school days compared with the same number of randomly attended days. To her, units of learning could simply be accumulated individually at any time.

"I reckon you done had about enough fer now. Stay out a spell and then you can git on back in fer some more larnin'," she counseled, trying to put the best face on it.

"But Miss Pricilla, she done said I gots to come ever day," said Rob. "I wants to larn the numbers, Mama."

"It gon' be gittin' too colt fer you to to be walkin' way down thar all by yer ownself," said Lucy. "You can git on back down to school when it warms a mite. I promise, Rob"

"Yassum," he said softly.

Toward the end of winter, Lucy made good on her promise. And it was with great surprise that Miss Pricilla looked up to see Rob standing in the church doorway just before class. She rushed to the rear.

"Rob! I thought I'd never see you again!"

"Mama done say I orter come on back fer some more larnin'."

"Rob, this is the last month of the session. There's not enough time left to do you any good." She put a hand on his shoulder. "Tell your mother to send you back on the first day of the next session in September. Will you do that, Rob?"

"Yassum." He turned and shuffled back up the road to home.

Surprised to learn that the school year ran only seven months, Lucy vowed to send Rob to the next session for another try, but she continued feeling unhappy over the boys' failure in school. And both Bob and Rob moped around, feeling guilty about it.

Morgan took notice. He didn't much value education, but he didn't like seeing the boys so dejected. One day he came home with a tiny puppy in each hand. "It's about time you boys had you a dog. Let me tell you boys somethin'. A dog, he knows more right thar in his nose than ary amount of book larnin'," he said, making the case for dogs over school. "This un's fer you Bob and this un's fer Rob," he said, handing over the fuzzy little creatures to the delighted boys.

Rob and Bob came back to life and became inseparable from their new companions. Rob named his dog Skinner and Bob called his Rocky.

For lack of a teacher, school did not open at the Methodist church that September, or the next year, or the next.

EIGHTEEN
1890
A Gun

In the Blue Ridge, the autumn palette progresses from the top down. Green forests transform into vivid reds, yellows, tans and orange-browns, first draping the mountain crests in early October and then taking the best part of a month to flow down the slopes and spread into the valley.

The composition of the Dinkins family had shifted during the six years from the time of Bob and Rob's brief encounter with school. John, Carrie and Eddie had each married and moved, while Sue had blossomed into a comely young miss attracting a couple of competing youths from around the hollow. Little Elliott had come into the world and, at three, was the family baby. With Aunt Tilly supervising, Lucy's sister Jenny had delivered him on the day Arnold Nabors died. Lucy named "li'l Ellitt" in memory of Elliott Hawlins.

One evening Morgan was in his rocker on the porch, with his elbow on the armrest and his puffy jaw cradled in his hand. His toothache had worsened.

"Best git that thar tooth fixed, Morgan," said Lucy.

"I'm a-gittin' on down in the mornin'," he assured her.

Morgan still had half his teeth and Lucy, at thirty, had most of hers. Nearly all of the upper mountain people had lost a good many of their teeth by her age. The most remote of them had never heard of dentists. They would just let their teeth rot and fall out.

The Dinkinses believed in taking care of their teeth, by which they meant having bad ones pulled promptly. The people around Nabors

Mill were aware of dentists but there were none nearby.

The next morning found Rob heading down to the mill with Morgan. The mill was humming, but was not backed up. Rob hitched the old mule to a post and Morgan pulled the two sacks of corn off and dropped them on the porch. Two sacks were all he now dared pile onto the old animal. Morgan had replaced his aged horse the prior year, and it was now about time for a new mule.

Tee came out into the bright fall sunshine, glanced at the two sacks and then noticed the rag wrapped around Morgan's swollen jaw. He needed no explanation. Not a week went by without Tee pulling a tooth or two.

"Got yer liquor, Morgan?"

Morgan pulled out a tin flask.

"Drink it up and I'll git to you right soon." Tee lugged the sacks in and disappeared, leaving Rob and Morgan standing on the mill porch. They sat down on the bench and leaned back against the sun-warmed siding boards. Morgan swigged from his flask, draining out all the corn whiskey in short order.

In a while, Tee came out to check on his patient. "How you comin', Morgan?"

"I'sh jesh fine, Tee, sheptin' I cain't shtand up and I cain't shee shtraight neither," slurred Morgan as he swayed on his seat, restrained from toppling over by Rob.

Seeing Morgan suitably anesthetized, Tee said, "I'll fetch my pillikins and be out directly."

Tee returned with a pair of tooth extraction pliers in his hand. "Git in thar behind him, boy, and holt him steady," he told Rob. Well-muscled at fourteen by hard work, Rob slid one end of the bench out, slipped in behind and locked his arms around his father's chest.

"Now let's git 'er dug out," said Tee. "Open up, Morgan."

Tee reached his pillikins in and took hold of the sore tooth.

Morgan stiffened and screeched in pain as Tee clamped down tightly.

"Holt him boy! Holt him down!!" yelled Tee. He gave a quick jerk and out came the pliers, gripping the molar. "I done got her out, Morgan," he said, showing the pillikins with the tooth in one hand while thrusting a rolled up rag into Morgan's mouth with the other. "Bite down now. Holt that in there until I come back and takes it out."

Tee went back inside to his milling, leaving Rob to keep the moaning Morgan upright for the next several hours.

In time, Tee came out to remove the tooth rag and have a look. "They ain't no more bleedin' in there, Morgan. Reckon yer done. Best set right here a spell until you can walk straight."

Morgan, half-sobered, reached into his pocket and pulled out a quarter. Twenty-five cents was Tee's standard fee. "You right handy with them pillikins, Tee. Yer warth ever penny," said Morgan as he handed over the coin. "Yassar, warth ever penny."

"Thank you, Morgan." Tee pocketed the money and then lugged out the two big sacks of freshly ground cornmeal.

The sun was well down in the western sky when Morgan and Rob rose, lashed the sacks on the mule and started up the road. Morgan's head had mostly cleared, and his jaw had stopped throbbing, as he paced the road home at a slight stagger.

A cold and gray late autumn day found Rob at his domain, the woodpile, whacking away at his favorite chore. His other chores were under Lucy's command; splitting wood was his alone. Skinner lay comfortably on a pile of wood chips, watching.

A few snowflakes fell as Rob split round log sections into stove-sized firewood chunks. He propped one piece up against another and, holding the bottom with one foot, smacked the top with his axe. It looked risky. If a weak chunk should split easily, the blade could shoot right through to slice his foot or take off a toe. But Rob had a deft hand with the axe, seeming always to know just how hard to hit the wood. He had never actually injured himself.

"Rob!" called Morgan. "C'mon down to the barn, boy!"

With a one-handed overhead swing, Rob bedded the axe in a log and strode off toward Morgan and the barn path, his dog at his heels. He followed Morgan through the barn door.

"Wait h'yar."

Morgan climbed up into the haymow and disappeared. He reappeared with a leather pouch and a musket. He slung the pouch around his shoulder and, holding the gun in one hand, descended the ladder using the other.

"It's time you larn't the gun."

Rob's eyes lit with excitement.

They moved over to the barn's open end, where Morgan began the lesson.

"I'll show you how to load," he said. From the pouch he pulled a powder horn, a bag of lead shot and some wadding.

"First you shakes in a li'l powder," said Morgan, carefully demonstrating. "Don't put too much and don't put too li'l. Then you drops in yer shot." He shook some small lead balls from the bag into the barrel. "Next, you stuffs in yer wad." He pushed a piece into the muzzle. "Now you rams it all down," he said, pulling out the ramrod and running it down the barrel to pack the load.

Morgan leaned the gun against the wall and picked up an old rusted out metal pail. He walked to the far side of the barnyard, sat the pail atop a fence post and strode back to the barn. He picked up the gun and put the stock to Rob's right shoulder.

Rob raised his arms and gripped the musket in the way he'd often seen it done. Morgan eased Rob's left hand out a bit under the barrel. "Line yer eye up on this h'yar spot and on that thar spot," he instructed, pointing to the top of the barrel at the rear and then at the front. "You orter be a-lookin' at the middle of the pail when you fahrs. The hart part is holtin' her steady."

Morgan took the gun and cocked the hammer back. "The last

thang is you puts on the cap." He pulled out a percussion cap and fitted it over a small prong under the hammer. He faced the barnyard, raised the stock to his shoulder, took aim and squeezed the trigger. BAM!! The pail flew off the fence post with a Twang!

Skinner yelped and dashed from sight around the end of the barn.

"Set her back up and you can take a tarn."

Rob trotted out and put the pail back on the post.

With Morgan coaching, Rob loaded the gun. He dribbled powder into the barrel. "Li'l more now. That's it right thar," guided Morgan. Then he shook in a few small balls of shot from the bag. "Not too many now. That's enough. Put yer wad in and ram her down," said Morgan. "That's it. Now holt her up and take yer aim."

Rob lined up his right eye and sighted down the top of the barrel at the pail, but the pail kept moving from in front of the barrel as the muzzle wandered noticeably.

Morgan said, "Step over h'yar, boy." He braced the gun barrel against a barn board. Now you can holt her steady. Cock her back."

Rob thumbed the hammer back until it clicked into cocked position. Morgan put a firing cap in place. "Holt yer bead on the pail and squeeze yer trigger right slow like." Several seconds passed until BAM!! The gun kicked back in a puff of smoke as the pail went flying end over end.

"Yee'ar!" cried Rob, flashing a wide grin of exhilaration. Morgan wore a wide grin too, well aware of the importance of this moment.

Morgan set the pail on a post at a more challenging distance and, standing amid the blended rank odors of acrid burned gunpowder and the fetid barnyard, he took one more shot, sending the pail flying. He then turned to Rob.

"This h'yar wahr Ellitt's gun. Now it's yourn," he declared solemnly, holding out the musket in one hand and the pouch in the other, in a ceremonial bestowal and a rite of passage from childhood to manhood.

With his eyes bonded to Morgan's, Rob reached out and took hold of the gun and pouch. Morgan held on for a second before letting loose, adding an air of formality to the transfer.

Before breaking eye contact, Rob spoke.

"Ellitt wahr my daddy. I knows how you's my daddy now but how wahr you my daddy afore Ellitt?" Rob had never learned any more about his origins in the six years since Bob Parsten noted his resemblance to Morgan, followed by Morgan's mystifying explanation. Now he was older and needed to know more.

Rob's sudden unexpected question seemed to catch his father off guard. He hesitated a minute as if struggling to fashion a suitable answer. "Wahl, I wahr yer daddy afore you wahr born't and Ellitt, he wahr yer daddy after you wahr born't."

This wasn't enough for Rob and his face must have showed it, for Morgan continued.

"Yer daddy afore yer born't puts a li'l his own seed in yer mama what grows to a baby and you git's born't. Hain't no more to it."

That aroused Rob's curiosity. *That make Daddy my real daddy?* he wondered. *Afore I gits born't or after I gits born't—which one my real daddy?* He wanted to ask, but he could see that Morgan had said as much as he cared to offer.

"Let's git on up to dinner now," said Morgan, ending the subject. Clutching his new prize, Rob strode up to the cabin with a confident bounce in his pace.

"What's all that shootin' about?" asked Lucy.

"I's larnin' Rob the gun," said Morgan. "The gun wahr Ellitt's. I done give it to Rob. It's his'n now," he said, looking pridefully at Rob's glowing face.

Lucy knew the matter was Morgan's prerogative—men's business—and that he had now promoted Rob from her team to his. Rob would henceforth primarily help his father work the farm rather than handle homestead chores at his mother's behest.

Lucy had mixed feelings about it. A young man should have a gun, but it was hunting that had killed Elliott nearly a decade earlier. She said, "Wahl, let's git the dinner on the table." She said no more about the gun.

After dinner, Rob whittled a couple of wooden pegs and bored holes for them into the log wall just under Morgan and Bob's guns. There he proudly hung his musket.

The following morning found an inch or two of fluffy snow covering the ground.

"Let's go huntin', Rob," said Morgan, seeing a good opportunity to initiate the boy into the man's world.

Rob tied Skinner to a porch post. He wasn't a hunting dog, and a little snow made it possible to track game without dogs. The two set out for the upper pasture and soon came across prints in the snow.

"Let's see iffen we cain't slip up on the rabbit," whispered Morgan with a frosty breath.

Excited to be hunting, Rob crept along behind as Morgan took a few slow steps, paused to scrutinize the terrain ahead, then moved forward again and paused once more.

Morgan spotted the cottontail feeding on some still-green honeysuckle leaves at the edge of the woods above. Rob held his breath as his father slowly raised his cocked musket and held a careful aim until BAM!!

The rabbit took a couple of hops before collapsing in the snow. "Got it!" cried Morgan. He strode up and bagged his kill, then reloaded his gun.

They continued onward into the woods, until scattered tracks revealed the presence of a squirrel digging up buried nuts.

"It's most likely thar in the walnut tree," said Morgan in a hushed tone. "Let's wait a spell."

The two sat quietly on a fallen log, with eyes raised up to the bare branches. In due course, a plump gray squirrel appeared from a crotch in the tree and proceeded to scold the humans as though it knew what they were up to. The fuzzy rodent scurried from limb to limb, up and down, in and out of sight, protesting continuously but without pausing long enough to get shot.

"Hain't likely to git no shot at ol' squirrel," concluded Morgan as he stood up. They brushed snow off their bottoms and continued on, working their way back into the open.

Another set of rabbit tracks pointed toward a brushy area. "You git this 'un," murmured Morgan, motioning Rob forward.

Rob inched his way ahead with his musket cocked and ready. He stopped, surveyed the landscape and spotted the rabbit at the edge of a briar patch. The creature sat motionless in the snow. The rabbit likely saw the hunters, but was too far away to panic and run.

Rob's heart raced as he eased his gun to his shoulder, took aim and BAM!! The rabbit bounded into the briar patch and vanished.

"Dang!" he cried in dismay. "Dang it!" Rob's spirits sank. Missing his first shot at live game made him feel he was already a failure at hunting.

"It wahr right smart far off. You orter git in a li'l closer," said Morgan as Rob, feeling disheartened, reloaded his gun. The thought of going home empty-handed was discouraging enough, but this was worse than empty-handed because he had his chance and had missed. Rob felt a sudden urgency to bag a quarry before the day was out. Failure at school had been bad enough. Failure at hunting would be worse, much worse.

They worked their way around the mountain slope to the branch. Rob led as the two eased slowly up the draw to where another rabbit track appeared. Rob cocked and capped his gun, and skulked slowly forward with bated breath, determined to get close enough for a sure shot.

The tracks led to a greenbrier thicket, in the middle of which Rob made out the light brown furry form of a hunched rabbit. He eased his gun up as he inched closer, trying to ignore his freezing fingers. His failure would be compounded if he shot from too far and missed, or if he tried to get too close and the rabbit scampered off.

The animal must have felt securely concealed, as it did not bolt when Rob, with a lump in his throat, finally took aim and pulled the trigger.

The cottontail hopped a couple of bounces and fell on the snow dead.

Rob rushed forward to where the large rabbit lay on a bright red stain in the snow. He grabbed his kill by the hind legs and held it up in proud display, his tension released as a rush of relief swept through him.

"Now yer shootin', boy!" praised Morgan, bagging the kill. Rob, beaming with pride, was buoyant in his final liberation from childhood.

"Reckon someday I'd like to git me a shot at a deer or a bahr, or maybe a wildcat," said Rob with an enthusiasm free from the grip of self-doubt.

"They hain't no more cougar in the mountain, and the deer and bobcat is right scarce. Thar's a bahr or two, but hain't been one kilt in a mighty long spell," said Morgan, on the scarcity of large game in the over-hunted mountains. "We's mostly down to squirrel, rabbit, 'possum and 'coon, or a bobcat iffen yer lucky."

"I'd sure like to git me a buck," said Rob.

"Wahl, you might have some luck up'par a piece in the mountain behind Brother," said Morgan. "They's a couple deer thar, but they shy. You cain't hardly git no shot at 'em."

"I'd sure like to lay me a bead on a big ol' buck," said Rob again.

"Iffen you sets real still like, right at last light, you got a chance to see 'em. But gittin' yer shot hain't easy," said Morgan. "Wahl, we's best be a-gittin' back to dinner," he said, ending the hunt.

The hunters crossed the branch and backtracked down the other side of the draw, with Morgan in the lead.

"I wants to go 'coon huntin'," said Rob from behind.

A silent minute went by with no response from his father. Just then a loud fluttering whoosh startled them both as a grouse suddenly launched itself into frantic flight from the ground just a few steps in front.

Morgan's gun came swiftly up with the muzzle following the flapping bird to BAM!!; the brown fowl fell to earth, all in a few seconds time. "Got her!" he shouted.

Rob was astonished at the swiftness of the action. He wanted to shoot like that.

"Just a lucky shot," said Morgan, bagging the bird.

The smell of wood smoke hung in the air as the cabin came into view.

"Wahl, the two of you must have kilt somethin', what with all the shootin' you done," said Lucy.

"Yee'ar, we's done kilt two rabbits and a grouse," boasted Rob, as he pulled the game from the sack. "I done shot that big ol' rabbit," he said, pointing to his first claim on manhood lying motionless on the table.

"You two done right good; kilt three with four shots. I'll git 'em skin't and plucked after dinner," said Lucy approvingly.

The two rabbits and the grouse made it a successful morning hunt and put fresh meat on the table. Mountain hunters often returned with nothing to show for their effort.

The weather softened, turning Rob's attention to what Morgan had said about the deer. The mild temperatures were conducive to sitting in the woods for several hours in the hope that an elusive deer might appear.

"Let's go huntin', Bob," suggested Rob one afternoon.

"What we gon' hunt this late in the evenin'?" asked Bob.

"Daddy done said they's deer in the mountain back of Brother. Let's go set out and might be we can git us one."

"The two of you git on back by supper now, you hear," said Lucy, as the pair pulled muskets from wall pegs and went out the door. The sun slid toward the western ridge as they set out down the lane.

They passed the Brother Hobson cabin and tramped on past Luke and Janie's cabin, following a steep draw up to where the high pasture met the forest on a saddle between two hills.

"How about you git up on that thar rise, and I'll git on the big rock," suggested Rob, pointing at a high spot on one side and an outcropping on the opposite side of the draw. Bob nodded and the two took up stations that looked out over a large field-of-fire of upper pasture and lower forest.

Twilight soon descended on the hills. The hunters sat like statues in the still silence, showing no more presence than a tree or a stone. But no deer appeared in the dimming light and forest shadows. As darkness closed in across the woods, Rob rose in disappointment and descended to join Bob. They picked their way down to the open pasture, then continued side-by-side down through the grass, with the last wink of light marking their route.

"Ever wish't you could see a nekked girl?" asked Rob.

Bob stopped and gave Rob a quizzical look.

"I means a growed-up girl," said Rob, seeing his brother's puzzled expression.

They continued on down in silence.

"No. Hain't never did," Bob finally answered. "Somethin' you thinks about?"

"Time and again I does. Night time, mostly."

"Cain't say as it never thoughted me afore," said Bob. "Reckon I hain't much fer girls."

Hunh? thought Rob. He'd become interested in girls and thought it odd that the older Bob had not.

Rob climbed over Brother's fence bars and noticed two small figures walking up the road from below in the starry darkness. He hopped back over and, motioning Bob to follow, crouched behind the rock wall by the bars.

"They's two children comin' up," whispered Rob. "Let's have some fun."

As the two small figures came abreast the bars, Rob knocked two rocks together with a tap-tap, tap-tap, tap-tap that brought the little ones to a halt in the road.

"You hear that?" asked one.

"What's it?" asked the other.

"I don't know but I hear't it."

Rob recognized his little sisters' voices.

Tap-tap, tap-tap, tap-tap.

"I h-hears it n-now!" confirmed Lizbeth, with a timid tremor in her six-year old voice.

"It's a ha'nt!" exclaimed Florie. "It's a ha'nt fer sure!"

"What w-we g-g-gon' do, Florie!" begged Lizbeth.

"I don't know. I hain't fer s-sure," said Florie, with fear cracking her voice.

A few steps ahead on the other side of the road lay the cemetery. Walking past a cemetery at night was known to excite a ha'nt, as ghosts were called, to greater mischief.

Rob dared a furtive peak over the wall. The girls stood in the dark road, frozen in fear of evil doings. Then, with obvious trepidation, they took a couple of steps. Rob ducked back down and rounded his lips. "Woo-woo! woo-woo!, woo-woo!"

He snuck another peak.

Little Lizbeth was gripping her eleven year-old sister's arm. "Florie I'm scar't! Ol' ha'nt gon' git us, Florie-e-e-e!" She burst into tears.

"Oh Lord! Oh Lord!!" cried Florie in panic. She grabbed her little sister's hand. "C'mon! Run! Run, Lizbeth!!"

The girls flew past the cemetery and chased up the road out of sight without looking back.

The boys hopped the bars, stepped out into the road and followed their fleeing sisters for a short stretch. "Woo-woo!! woo-woo!! woo-woo!!"

"Done scar't them two right smart!" said Rob, laughing mischievously.

"Wish't I'd see'd them faces!" said Bob, making merry fun of spooking the poor little girls. They hurried home, right behind the sisters.

Rob and Bob came through the house door to see Florie and teary-eyed Lizbeth clinging to their mother's skirt and being scolded.

"Why you two so late a-gittin' back?!" demanded Lucy. "Course they's gon' be a ha'nt down to the buryin' ground at night! I done send you down to Sis fer a li'l sugar and you hain't gittin' back until past dark. Whar you two *been*!"

Florie spoke up. "Sis, her dog done had puppies and we's a-playin' with the new puppies, Mama!"

"Puppies! I done tolt you to git right home, child! An whar's my sugar!" demanded Lucy.

A worried look came across Florie's face. In all the excitement, she had forgotten about the sugar. "I don't know, Mama," she answered with downcast eyes. "Reckon I done drop it."

Lucy looked up at the two boys. "The two of you done hear't ary ha'nts out thar?"

"No. Hain't hear't no ha'nts atall." answered Bob.

"No. We hain't hear't nary a one." said Rob.

Morgan spoke.

"Let's git supper on the table," he said, laying the ha'nts to rest.

The next morning, Morgan haltered up the old mule, hitched it to the porch post and went in to breakfast.

"Wahl, cain't hardy work the ol' beast no more; about time to turn the critter in and git a new one. We's gon' hafter skid them saw logs offen the mountain once't the snow flies. Gon' need a strong mule right soon now," he said, thinking aloud to the family.

Old horses and mules weren't retired to pasture; a mule is useless at stud. Worn out draft animals were sold to slaughterhouses or rendering plants.

After breakfast Morgan led the old animal away and returned before dark with a young mule. It was a well-formed spirited animal that looked just about perfect.

"I hain't paid but ten dollar fer it," bragged Morgan. The reason for the low price was soon revealed. The mule would not permit a crupper, a leather harness strap, to be fitted around its tail. Merely approaching its rear end with a crupper would set it to braying and kicking out wildly with its hind feet.

After several failed attempts, Morgan worked out a way to get the crupper on the beast. Three people were needed in the stable to do it. He put on the bridle and bit, then the harness and attached the driving lines.

"Bob, you git on t'other line and I'll be on this'un. Rob, you stand in front so's he don't bolt. Thar now, work the critter back in the corner."

They slowly backed the animal into the stable corner to where it couldn't kick out to the rear.

"Holt this h'yar line, Rob."

Rob grabbed the line and bridle and, with Bob holding onto the other side, held the mule tightly in the corner.

"Holt him in now, boys!"

The animal stomped and squealed and brayed frantically as Morgan looped the crupper around the tail and attached it to the harness on the mule's back.

"Ease him out now, boys."

Once the crupper was on, the mule calmed down. It turned out to be a very good draft animal, except for that one peculiarity.

Early December brought several clear nights and a full moon—ideal for 'coon hunting. But Morgan had been struggling with the matter since a couple of weeks before when Rob had said he wanted to hunt 'coon.

Morgan, now a little north of fifty, had lost his zest for stumbling through rough and rocky mountainside forests in the dark. He hadn't hunted raccoon for several years, and he'd been heard to say, "These h'yar ridges is a-gitten steeper ever yahr. Why, they's dang nigh straight up and down now! Time I hits sebenty, I reckon theys gon' be perpindic'lar!"

Yet Morgan knew Rob now looked to his father to take him out on nighttime hunts. Not yet fifteen, the boy was too young to be invited along by the other mountain men. Rob was eager and Morgan didn't want his son to think the old man wasn't up to the strenuous exertion of the hunt.

And then there was Lucy. It would be even worse if Rob thought his mother had vetoed his 'coon hunt. But, mindful of Elliott's tragic end, Morgan knew it would torture her with worry if he took Rob out chasing up and down treacherous slopes in the gloom of night.

As they finished supper, Morgan said, "Mighty good night fer 'coon huntin'."

The words lit up Rob's eyes in anticipation as a look of alarm flashed across Lucy's face.

"Wish't we could do it, but my dogs is done got too olt," he said. "They hain't got enough left in 'em to run down no 'coon."

Rob's face fell in disappointment. His own dog Skinner wasn't a coonhound.

Lucy relaxed with relief.

Morgan continued. "Reckon I gots to find me some new hounds," he said, removing the prospect of hunting from the present, while not foreclosing the future. He left it at that, hoping Rob would see it as a temporary delay, and Lucy would sense a permanent end.

Winter's coldest days saw all the Dinkinses indoors, sitting around the stove shelling corn, cracking out walnuts and mending things.

Milder weather drew Morgan and the boys out to pile up rocks in the upper pasture, repair crossed rail fences where trees had fallen across them, and patch ruts in the road.

Keeping up the firewood supply was Rob's responsibility, a daily chore that left him with ample free time. As the days slowly lengthened, he took to roaming the hills and hollows with Skinner and his gun, hunting for the elusive deer and searching for his emerging self.

NINETEEN
1895
Love

The advance of five years time had grown Rob into a trim young man of quiet disposition and reserved sensitivity, but had provided him scant social intercourse, particularly with girls.

The grip of winter had relaxed and then retreated, leaving the gentle hand of spring to transform the stark landscape into a lush panorama of living green.

Pastures had been burned off to make way for new grass, the slender blades of green pushing out from blackened earth. Gardens had been planted, the rows of tender sprouts shoving up through freshly turned earth. Trees and bushes and brambles had all come to life with swollen buds and tiny curled leaves breaking out on every branch, stem and twig to paint the country with green foliage garnished with brightly colored blossoms.

An overnight rain had left the morning air clear and pure, now warmed by a bright sun that set up a soft breeze. All the Dinkinses were about their tasks, with Morgan and Bob busily plowing the patches, and Lizbeth and Li'l Ellitt off to school. Lucy had put the two into class the previous fall. She'd learned her lesson ten years earlier with Rob and Bob, and now tolerated no truancy.

Lucy went down to the spring and found Rob crouched on his knees, repairing the wooden spring box. He raised his face, pushed back his sandy hair, and met her eyes.

"Rob, I'm most nearly outen coal oil. Can you git on down to the store and fetch me up a can?" she requested. Requested—she'd not ordered him about like a child for nearly five years.

He rose to his feet and cast his blue eyes down at her. At nineteen and several steps into manhood, he stood nearly a head higher than she.

"Reckon I can, Mama. Ary thang else yer needin'?"

"No, just the coal oil is all—but thank you fer askin'."

Rob ambled off down the lane and joined the road, content with his own company. A reticent youth given to few words, his adolescence had been cloaked in a comfortable loneliness that accorded with his withdrawn demeanor and natural shyness. He'd spent many a day alone, tramping the hills and hollows with his dog and gun. He lacked the self-assurance to be at ease among peers, especially girls. Though he thought well of himself, fear of humiliation in front of others had left him repressed.

Rob's social encounters had been limited to family and neighborly gatherings for hog killing, apple butter boiling, corn shucking, Christmas shooting matches and the occasional funeral. At such times he had mostly kept to himself. When approached, he had always been taciturn and inhibited, having had neither school nor church to temper his aloofness.

The store was quiet, the usual on weekday mornings. Rob stepped in, let his eyes adjust to the dim light and saw but one clerk and one customer at the counter, and no one else in the place, which now stretched a ways back to the rear. A new addition had doubled the size of the store building.

He stepped up behind the young woman at the counter to wait his turn, and found himself eyeing her wavy blond locks and admiring her shapely form. He had an appreciative eye for comely girls, whom he preferred to view from behind or at a distance. She took no notice of him as she spoke to the clerk.

"Just a can of coal oil and a box of matches is all I'll be needin'," she said.

Rob raised a finger to get the clerk's attention.

"Uh, while'st yer back thar, Clancy, can you draw me a can of coal oil, too?" he called over her shoulder, thinking to save the clerk the extra footsteps.

She turned to face him, and exclaimed with no inhibition, "Why now! This h'yar must be the day fer coal oil!"

She right perty, he thought. "Reckon so," he said diffidently.

"Hain't you Morgan's boy?" she asked. "I believe I done see'd you around time and again."

"Yass I am, and I believe I done see'd you at a corn shuckin' a few yahr back. I'm Rob and hain't you Mollie's girl?" He surprised himself with such a long response.

"That's right. I'm Mary Jane."

Her pert manner had momentarily loosened his self-consciousness, but now he again found himself tongue-tied. He yearned to continue the conversation, but his loss of words looked likely to let it wither and fade.

Just then Clancy returned with the two cans, giving Rob a brief reprieve and a second chance.

"There now, a can fer each of you."

Clancy recited aloud as he jotted out two sales slips. "Morgan Dinkins—coal oil— nine cent, and Harvey Folsom_coal oil—nine cent, box of matches—two cent." He turned the slips toward his customers and went to pull the accounts ledger.

Rob watched Mary Jane sign the Folsom slip. Embarrassed that he couldn't write, he made his X mark on the Dinkins slip, hoping she wouldn't take notice of it.

Clancy flipped open the ledger, made the entries and then looked up at the two of them. "It's a funny thang," he said, "but the two of you looks just like that Byer boy and his new wife, from up in the holler."

Mary Jane giggled, as if titillated by Clancy's comparison. It was just the opening Rob needed to recover his tongue.

"Wahl then, since we's dang near married, reckon I orter carry the both of 'em," he said in jest, claiming an opportunity by taking hold of the two cans. She giggled again and they headed for the door, she seeming amused, while he was surprised and delighted by his own forwardness.

They stood barefoot on the store porch looking at one another for a few beats, he enjoying the slightly awkward silence.

"Wahl, I'm goin' up'par, Rob," she said, tossing her head toward the road west and reaching for one of the cans.

"I can just as easy go that way and see you on up home now," said he quickly, as he pulled the can back, eager to extend the moment.

"Suits me, and thank you fer carryin' my coal oil," said she, enjoying the attention.

The two of them strolled lazily up the road, following the creek and chatting in an easy and desultory way.

"You goes to church atall, Rob?" she asked. "I ain't never see'd you at meetin'."

"No, I hain't never been." He'd never taken an interest in church. *I might could git inter'sted now, though,* he thought.

"You orter come to meetin' some time," she said. "They got a new preacher man what puts the Lord right directly into yer life."

"Reckon everbody can use some more of the Lord," he said agreeably, thinking about some more of Mary Jane instead of the Lord.

"And they's a dance up'par, time and again. The new preacher man, he allows it," she said. "Old preacher man, he didn't allow no dancin'. Called it twistifications—said it wahr the work of the devil." She let out a little laugh.

"Ha! I hain't never hear't nothin' called that afore!" exclaimed Rob at the odd term.

"You orter come, Rob!"

"Wahl, I hain't much fer dancin', Mary Jane."

"Aw, it's easy," she assured. "I'll show you how. Yer goin' to love it."

"Wahl, bein's as how yer goin' to show me..."

"Fer sure I will, Rob!"

They entered a lane and crossed the shallow creek at a rocky ford. He offered her his hand at the high stepping-stones up to a teetering log footbridge.

"Why thank you, Rob. Yer such a gentleman!"

Feeling her hand in his set his heart a-flutter. They continued around a low hill to the Folsom home.

The walk up had been the best part of a mile. It had seemed to Rob like a mere minute, but it had freed him and given him an ease and greater communion with a girl than he had ever felt.

"Can I come see you again, Mary Jane?" For once in his life, he felt comfortable with a girl, and willing to present himself.

"Can you come over early Sunday evenin'?"

"I most surely can and I will!" He was thrilled.

"I'll see you Sunday evenin' then," she said sweetly.

Rob floated blissfully home through field, orchard and forest. His unlocked heart let loose a joyful rush he'd never known. Sunday couldn't come fast enough.

Late in the week, Lucy and Morgan were sitting together on the porch, enjoying twilight. "Morgan, Rob just hain't been hisself lately," she said. He looked at her curiously. "Hain't nothin' bad," she added. "He just been talkin' more and he actual been smilin' some."

"I done see'd it too. Somethin' good done got into the boy," said Morgan. "Don't say nothin' to him about it. Might set him back to his ol' ways."

After Sunday dinner, Rob went up to the loft and came down wearing his best shirt, his good pants, newly cleaned boots and a wide grin. He opened the door to leave.

"Whar you off to now Rob, lookin' like that in yer good trousies and all," called Lucy.

"Wahl Mama, I'm gittin' over to see Mary Jane," he said in a buoyant tone. "You know, there to Harvey and Mollie's."

Lucy raised her eyebrows, looked at him askance and nodded knowingly. He ducked out the door.

Morgan came in from his perch on the porch just after Rob had tapped down the steps and skipped out across the yard.

"Wahr about's *he* goin' all dressed up?"

"It's a girl, Morgan. Rob's seein' that Folsom girl, Mary Jane," announced Lucy. "*That's* what done got in to him. He goin' over thar now."

"It's about time. I most nearly reckoned he don't got no interest in girls, like his brother."

"No, hain't that. He just mighty shy, that's all," she said.

The Folsom home was one of the area's more substantial dwellings. It was a clapboard timber-framed structure rather than a log cabin, and had two first floor rooms, a kitchen extension, two loft rooms and a lean-to. The Folsom farm was no larger than the Dinkins place, but the land was easier to work and more productive, pushing the Folsom family fortunes up a peg or two.

Rob's eyes lit and his heart quickened as he drew near and saw Mary Jane on the porch glider, humming softly as she swayed to and fro, beckoning him over.

"C'mon, Rob and sit right h'yar," she said, patting the space beside her.

Both exhilaration and awkwardness rose in Rob when he eased himself onto the swing beside her. Natural shyness made him a feel a bit ill at ease, along with the thrill of being so close he could feel her warm radiance.

"Right nice day, hain't it?" he uttered.

"It's special nice, Rob, havin' you right here beside me," she said sweetly. "I bet all the girls takes a shine to you."

"Wahl, I actual don't…"

"I know what you goin' to tell me," she said, touching a finger to his shoulder and sending a current up his spine. "You goin' to say you hain't lookin' at no girl exceptin' me, hain't you?" she said beguilingly

"You fer sure the onliest one, Mary Jane."

Mary Jane's ebullient disposition soon charmed the woodenness out of him, and an hour passed in easy chat and playful banter.

Finally she said, "They's somethin' I got to do now, but can you come next Sunday, Rob?"

"Course I can, Mary Jane. And I most surely will!" he rejoined, standing to leave. She smiled sweetly from the swing, as he stepped into the yard and walked backwards to keep her in his eyes for a long minute, before turning and setting for home at a light and jaunty pace, as if walking on an enchanted carpet.

Through the week, Rob could think of nothing but Mary Jane. She was a song in his head and a joy in his heart. He went about his tasks aching for Sunday. At last it came and he spent another delightful hour with her, followed by another the next Sunday, and another and another.

Her hand in his had opened his dream for a life filled with promise and all that is good. Euphoria had banished all his melancholy. His loneliness had dissolved and disappeared. He was a new man with new hope for a new world, freed from his niggling qualms and misgivings. His imagination filled his head with visions of his future with Mary Jane.

Rob's thoughts harked back to five years earlier, to when his half-sister Sue was courting. She had talked once with each of two young men, but then continued only with one. After several visits together, they announced their betrothal. She married soon after and moved to Wagley Hollow. *Mary Jane and me, we gon' get married fer sure*, he assured himself, feeling nothing but bright promise for the future.

He even thought about buying some land. He recalled a certain sixty acres that Arnold Nabors had bequeathed to a daughter, who now wanted to sell. *Could be Sarah'll go my note and I can pay fer it over time*, he mused, encouraging himself to believe that he could acquire a place of his own.

THE TALE OF A WOODS COLT

Mountain parents didn't intrude on their children's courting, but Lucy couldn't help herself. "How you and Mary Jane gittin' on?" she casually asked Rob, in a private moment.

"We's gittin' on awful good, Mama." said Rob, the words bringing a glow to his face. "She all the time sayin' how she like me being thar and all," he said. "She just the perdiest thang, Mama. I cain't think about nothin' else."

"Reckon marriage in the pitchure, son?"

"I hope so," he said, with a blushing smile. "I most surely do hope so."

Her eyes misted as she opened her arms. "I'm so happy for you, Rob," she said, wrapping him in a hug. She could imagine nothing better for him.

The following Sunday, Rob, with a melody in his heart and a bounce in his step, glided back through field and forest to the swing on the porch, and to Mary Jane.

His music stopped and his feet went dead when he saw her sitting there, not on the swing, but hunched on the porch steps. Gone were the lively eyes, the ready smile and the easy manner—replaced with a worried look, nervous fidgeting and an uncertain hesitancy. Rob felt a chilled breath of apprehension as he stood in his tracks in front of the porch, and Mary Jane.

Sitting uneasily and wringing her hands anxiously, she spoke first.

"I been a-waitin' fer you, Rob. I just don't know how to tell you this," she said, with her hands gripped together, both elbows pulled in tight and eyes cast down. "Yer such a good man and I think the world of you— truly I do. I hope you believe that, Rob." Her eyes lifted up to tentatively look at him.

His brow furrowed and a curtain of worry unfurled across his face.

She went on, "But, wahl, it's just that... I been a-talkin' to another man and all." She looked past him, out into the yard. "And I wish they was an easy way to, to..." Her words trailed off as though she was trying to find a way to break the news without breaking his heart.

Rob felt his face go taut and his body tense. An alarm sounded in his head. *Yass! Why sure!* It jumped out at him. *She always had somethin' else to do Sunday evenin's!*

And now, standing there and seeing her, he knew. Seeing it in her eyes and on her face, and hearing it in her voice, he knew that she was not to be his. He looked at her for a long moment, expecting to hear more. But she held back and seemed unable to continue.

"Who is it?" he asked, as all hope drained from his dreams. "What's his name?"

"Jimmy Wilson," she said simply, being too fretful to elaborate.

It's that dang James! Rob knew exactly who he was. He was James, the bully at school twelve years ago—the bully that his brother, Bob, had bloodied. He held no respect or regard for that despicable Jimmy Wilson.

"Wahl then I..." he started to mutter, feeling stunned that she was spurning him and stung that she would fall in with such a low person.

"Rob, this hain't easy fer me to say, but Jimmy, him and me's goin' to git married. He done ask me last Sunday," she said in a tone of trepidation, as if worried about salting his wound and fearing his reaction.

Her words stabbed him like a dagger. His insides tumbled under a flooding cascade that had caught him unawares and sent him reeling. Drawing heavy breaths, he tried to hold himself together against the assault battering his heart. He'd rather a mule had kicked him in the gut than this.

Rob grimaced and his chest heaved as he struggled to hold back. He took a few unsteady steps away from her.

Mary Jane chewed her thumbs, looking anguished at his distress, as though desperately wanting to ease his torment.

"Please don't go, Rob," she pleaded. "*Please.*"

Rob brought himself back by the porch, but his misery left no room for words.

"I hain't feelin' no less fer you, Rob," she said, tearfully. "They's other girls better'n me. Yer a fine man and you surely undoubtedly goin' to make one a fine husband."

But there was no balm in her words. He felt bereft, as if gutted and hollow. He stood silently, his shock turning to silent numbness as she tried to explain.

"It's just that Jimmy, wahl, he got that big ol' farm with his daddy, and he done built hisself a house what's got four rooms, and he goes to church and can read and write and all. Rob, I like you a whole heap. Indeed I do. I'm just thinkin' about my life, that's all."

In his mind, Rob knew she was trying to make him understand that she was not disaffected with him. He could see she had anguished over her decision and that she acutely felt the hurt he was trying to suppress, and that she earnestly wished to ease his pain. And he knew she sincerely hoped he would not feel rejected, since she was caught in the compromises of life, and was choosing another direction. He knew all this, but it didn't matter. His mind was swamped by the tumultuous emotions torturing his psyche.

He couldn't look at her, and anyway couldn't let her see his welling tears. He turned away with downcast eyes. The hard hammer of rejection had fallen heavily on him, and Mary Jane's explanation had not softened the impact.

Jimmy Wilson's family worked one of most substantial farms around Nabors Mill, placing them just a notch below valley prosperity. Rob lived on fringe land that put him only a couple of cuts above poverty. He had no house of his own, and he had failed to learn to read and write.

"*Please*, Rob. *Please* don't think so bad of me. Cain't we just be friends?" she pleaded. "I want to be yer friend, Rob, always. I hope me die iffen I don't."

It was all Rob could do to keep from falling apart in front of her. It didn't matter that she would likely have thought the better of him if he had let it all out right there, right then. But he could not.

He walked away without uttering a word, back into his former self, but now a wounded loner who had taken a risk on love—and had lost. His joyful world had collapsed into misery. He trudged slowly back on leaden legs. He took his time, pausing to let tears purge some of the grief that was consuming him. After a long while, he reached the safety of home.

When Rob came through the door, Lucy surmised what had happened with one glance at his miserable face. He disappeared straight up to the loft without a word. She took a couple steps toward the stairs, but then stopped. Her instinct was to give him support, but then she sensed he wouldn't be receptive right then. No need to make it worse, she told herself.

Through the next few months, Rob moped through the motions of daily life. He had no circle of friends to salve his stung ego, or distract him from self-pity. He took some comfort in once again tramping the hills and hollows with his musket and aging dog, distracting himself in quest of the elusive deer. Then one day another light went out in his life when he found old Skinner lying in the barn dead.

Rob lived at home, but he existed in a distant place. No one could reach through to him, not even Bob or his mother. Bob and he had always hunted together. But now, when Bob would suggest it, Rob always declined, preferring to tramp afield by himself.

Then one day Lucy discreetly approached her son.

"Rob, what can I do to help you put that Mary Jane behind you?"

"Hain't nothin' to do, Mama."

"But I cain't hardly stand to see you like this, son."

"Wahl, don't nobody need to do nothin' fer me," he said morosely.

She wrung her hands, knowing she wasn't piercing his veil of pessimism.

"You know I'm always here fer you, iffen you ever wants to talk."

"I know, Mama."

By autumn, time had smoothed the sharp edge of lost love. On a crisp day of crystal air and bright sunshine, Rob decided to load his musket with birdshot and set off up the hill. He had been hearing the call of bobwhite quail for days now, coming from the upper pasture area.

Surrounded by a full palette of fall color, he walked up the orchard edge to an area of waist high broom sedge, dense honeysuckle vines and tangled briar patches. From there he stalked slowly across the contour of the slope with his gun at his shoulder, cocked and ready to fire. He knew he'd have only a second or two, once he flushed a covey of quail.

A startling rush of flapping wings fluttered up to his right; his muzzle swung toward the fast birds and BAM!! A pair of the fowl fell from flight.

"Yee'ar!!" he cried out, cheering his good shot. He carefully noted where the birds had fallen and then walked slowly, keeping his eye on the two spots. He found one bird right away, but had to look more closely for the other. Quail are so well camouflaged that they can be difficult to spot in the course brown broom sedge and bushes. His shot was lucky. He usually bagged only one bird at each flush, or none at all.

Rob hunted through the afternoon, flushing several more coveys, each with close to a dozen birds. His bag held five and he was feeling pleased with himself when he started back down the hill in the last rays of the sun, as it slid below Hot Mountain.

His mother was delighted when he came through the door with a sack of quail in hand. The plump little fowl were a delicacy that found a ready welcome on the Dinkins table.

"Florie, scald and pluck Rob's birds," ordered Lucy. "I'll fix 'em fer dinner tomorrow."

Hunting sustained Rob. Bringing home some food proved his worth. Yet he had lost the consolation he had once felt in being alone.

Gradually, he became obsessed with the desire for a new life—or for no life at all.

The next day, Morgan and the boys came in from the orchard to dinner. "Wahl, boys, we's orter git the last of them apples picked this evenin'," he said. "The price is up a mite but it still right low. The fruit just barely warth the pickin'. That's more 'n I can say fer the last two crops." The Dinkins' small presence in the cash economy had been shrunken by several years of low agricultural prices.

Lucy served up the roasted quail. "Wahl, least we hain't agoin' to starve. Looky what a fine mess of birds Rob put on the table," she said.

Back in the orchard after dinner, Rob was pulling apples from a tree to one side of Morgan, and Bob plucked from a tree on the other side. Rob called over to Morgan's tree. "Daddy, whar wahr Ellitt kilt?" Over at his tree, Bob paused and cocked an ear.

Morgan hesitated, continuing to pull off apples and wondering where Rob's question would lead. He finally decided that now was as good a time as any for Rob to know.

"It wahr up'par on the Pinnacle. Thar's a big ol' rock clift about half way out the ridge. He wahr chasin' the dogs across the top when he done hit ice in the dark and went right on over the clift."

Morgan didn't offer any more of the sad story, and Rob didn't ask.

Supper was mostly silent. Rob was withdrawn and melancholy, and no one wanted to risk saying something to make him any worse. Afterwards, he and Bob went out to the porch, pulled out their jack knives and whiled the evening silently carving whimsies on sticks.

Rocking on the porch, Morgan and Lucy closed down the Indian summer twilight by enjoying watching their three youngest burn off the last of their energy chasing about the yard until darkness closed in.

"C'mon now!" called Lucy, as the last light drained away, "Bedtime!"

She and Morgan stood up and followed the three children inside, retiring to bed and leaving Bob and Rob sitting on the steps.

Bob folded his knife. "It still that li'l Mary Jane, hain't it, Rob?" he said.

"I reckon," conceded Rob curtly, in a tone resistant to further discussion.

"It's odd how a girl can git so far under a feller's skin, he cain't git her dug out," mused Bob to the settling night air.

Rob absorbed the thought, feeling protected by the shroud of darkness. If a repressed emotion got loose and showed in his face, Bob might not notice. But he knew that Bob was right.

"Truth be tolt, I hain't been no whar near my regular self since," confided Rob.

"Wahl Rob, gittin' hurt always goin' to git better, sooner or later," said Bob.

"Times are I just wants to lay me down and die, Bob," said Rob despondently.

"Aw, don't you go doin' nothin' plumb foolish now, Rob," said Bob, sounding a bit alarmed.

Rob shifted the subject. "Hain't you never been a-talkin' to no girls atall?"

"No, I hain't that much fer girls," replied Bob. "Hain't that I don't like 'em or nothin'. It's just I hain't much fer 'em is all."

The evening ended with the brothers sitting in quiet contemplation until after full night had claimed the porch. They went inside and up to the slumbering loft.

Rob lay awake as his imagination turned over images in his mind of Elliott's last 'coon hunt and tragic accident. Sleep finally came, but it was fitful. He awoke very early, rose before anyone else and quietly set out alone into a gray and heavy morning.

He followed a woods trail up the mountain to the Hazel road and walked the road for several miles, veering left onto the Pinnacle ridge trail. Only hunters used the track that traced the narrow spine of a rough razorback ridge far too steep and rocky for habitation.

After a mile or so, he arrived at the lonesome, secluded cliff top. He leaned his gun against a boulder and stood on the top of the precipice in the still air, absorbing the barren solitude of the place.

He made himself step to the edge. His knees quivered and weakened as he peered over, seeing the tops of the trees and the rocks far below. He thought of Elliott, and imagined the slip on the ice that had taken him over this very cliff, and he thought of him falling into the darkness. He imagined Elliott's broken body lying on rocks below.

He straightened up and took a deep breath. He inched forward a little, placing his toes at the very edge of the sheer drop. He leaned slowly forward again until he saw the jumbled boulders at the bottom. A shiver of fear went up his spine, and he shuddered as he imagined his own smashed body lying cold and still.

He backed away and sat down on a rock, putting his head in his hands in despair at the barrenness of his life that had drawn him to this forlorn crag of death. The urge to take the leap crept over him again.

He rose and stepped carefully to the edge, poised at the brink of his final plunge to eternity. He closed his eyes, breathed deeply and wondered how it would feel, the brief second of terror, plummeting into oblivion.

He suddenly felt dizzy and was gripped by fear. A rush of panic surged through him. He quickly stepped backwards to safety, his wish to end his empty life overcome by his visceral instinct to survive.

He paused to let his shaky knees recover their strength. After a few moments, he picked up his gun with trembling hands and continued out along the ridge trail. It was not his day to die. He had no idea where life's path might lead him but he knew he had to follow it and not cast himself into black nothingness.

TWENTY

Stony Man

Rob tracked the ridge trail down into Nickerson Hollow toward where it joined the rough road that followed the creek up the middle of the long hollow. The road was little more than a wide rocky trail barely navigable by wagon or cart.

His composure restored by the hike down from the cliff, Rob intended to continue on down the hollow once he reached the road. But when he came to the intersection, he glanced in the uphill direction to see a party of four men on horses at a walk, just as they rounded a bend and disappeared from sight. By their appearance, they were not mountain men. His curiosity aroused, he followed them up the hollow at a quick pace.

He caught up with the riders just as they came into Old Man Asa Nickerson's yard. The four dismounted in front of the porch, setting a couple of hounds to baying. Two of Asa's sons lived just below and had noticed the strangers passing. They had grabbed their muskets and hurriedly joined Rob at the edge of Asa's yard. Rob, taking his cue from them, put on a dark frown of suspicion.

An imposing figure of a man appeared in the doorway—tall and fine featured, with thinning white hair that bushed down his cheeks into a well-trimmed thick white beard. Seeing the visitors, he hollered at the dogs, "Git on back down now!" The barefoot Asa stepped off the porch and approached the strangers in his yard.

"What mighten yer names be?" he asked.

"I'm Judge Plakesley from over in Madison," replied the one with the long beard. "We're looking for Asa Nickerson."

"Wahl, you done found him. Now what mighten yer bizness be?"

"These men here are considering buying the Stony Man Tract, and I'm showing them the land," said the judge. "Mister Nickerson, who do you believe owns all this land around here?"

"That thar Stony Man spread don't drop down the holler this far. It's most all up on the mountain thar," said Asa with a sweep of his arm and flick of his hand.

"That's not what we've been told, Nickerson," stated the judge sternly. "We reckon we're standin' on it right now. We've been told you're just squatting on the Stony Man."

The old man's face flushed with anger as he bellowed, "Thar hain't no chance't atall of you gittin' ary bit of land around h'yar! It belongs to me!" He threw his arm out toward them and shook his finger. "Yer a-standin' on my property and don't you fergit it! I don't care what that damn Pollit done tolt you. He thinks he owns everthang!"

"Just how far does your land go, Mister Nickerson?"

"It runs nigh up to the ridge thar and a right far piece up the crick yonder, seventy-five acre in all," said Asa. "I done chop the line clear around, so don't you git to thinkin' yer gon' hunch over on me!"

The group glanced over at the three sinister mountain men standing tall and strong, feet apart and firmly planted, their muskets gripped at the ready and faces sullenly grim.

"Well, Mister Nickerson, how did you get title to it?" asked the judge.

Asa's face contorted with rage. "I done paid *good money* fer it and I gots me a *clear deed* to prove it!" yelled the old man. "I been h'yar nigh on forty yahr and hain't nobody goin' to take it away from me!!" he roared with clenched fists and jutted jaw. "Now you best be a-gittin' on outen the holler, iffen you knows what's good fer you!"

Rob and the two sons ominously pulled back the hammers on their guns and slipped on firing caps. All that stood between the unwelcome guests and sudden death was a squeeze on the triggers.

Asa's veiled threat and the cocked weapons were sufficient to put a look of alarm on the faces of the unarmed visitors. Feeling intimidated by the enraged patriarch and by the three glowering armed men, the intruders mounted their steeds and beat a hasty retreat down and out of Nickerson Hollow.

Asa had the authority of a feudal lord in his end of the hollow, owing more to being the patriarch amongst his many nearby relatives than to any sense of fealty among the hollow folk. Lowlanders commonly believed that local lawmen were reluctant to assert authority or enforce laws up in what had come to be called Free State Hollow by valley people. The lowlanders considered the mountaineers to be wild and woolly and sometimes a law unto themselves, though more by legend than reality.

Old Man Asa noticed Rob standing with his sons, Russ and Gust. He and Rob were both Nickersons but not directly related in any known way. Rob's wanderings had acquainted him with some of the patriarch's extended family, but he didn't know any of them very well.

"Come on in and git you some dinner, boy," said Asa, appreciative of Rob's presence in helping drive off the interlopers.

"Wahl, I best be a-gittin' on, Mister Asa."

"Oh come set now and eat you some dinner. My woman's about to sarve it up."

Rob followed the old man inside, and the brothers turned back toward their own cabins. "Take you a seat at the table," said the old man's wife. Bertha was a ruddy, round-faced, roly-poly woman of boisterous good cheer that was bolstered by the peaceable end of the hostile encounter.

"Eat up, boy!" prompted Asa, as the missus forked ham, beans, turnips and a chunk of corn bread onto Rob's plate.

"You likes sass don't you?" she asked cheerily, holding out a bowl of applesauce.

"Yassum. I'm a fool fer sass," said Rob, helping himself to several dollops. He was being treated as an honored guest.

"Yer Morgan Dinkins' boy, hain't you?" asked Asa.

"Yassar. Name's Rob." He was glad Asa hadn't called him Morgan's other boy.

"I done hear't you been a-huntin' right smart."

"Yassar. I done got my gun about five yahr now," said Rob. "But I hain't see'd nary a deer yet, and I hain't never hear't nothin' about no bahr."

"Truth be tolt, huntin' hain't the shadow of what it once't wahr," said Asa. "Most all the big game done been hunted outen the mountain." His gaze drifted to back to times gone by. Then he spoke again.

"When I's just a boy comin' up in the holler, they was deer, bahr and paint'er—and plenty of 'em," he said, leaning back in his chair and gazing out into distant memories.

"More'n fifty yahr done gone by, and now they's most all gone," he said, reminiscing pensively. "Hain't nothin' but the small critters left to put ary meat on the table. Bertha, git Rob h'yar another piece of meat!"

Hunting blurred property rights. Everyone, even the squatters, marked the boundaries of the land they owned, or claimed. Property rights were closely guarded and were generally respected—except with hunting, which included gathering anything wild. Hunting ranged all over, as though the entire span of hills and hollows was common domain. Venturing onto another's land to take game, fish, nuts, berries, mushrooms and such was not poaching. The land's wild bounty would go to waste if not gleaned. So it was free for the taking, as long as the owner didn't actively prevent it.

"Whar you suppose them mans done come from?" wondered Rob, changing the subject.

"I knows zackly whar they's come from," said Asa. "They's from over in Madison, but they's done come down h'yar from the Stony Man. Young feller name of Pollit done set hisself up a camp fer city folk up'par on the mountain, goin' on nigh six yahr now. That thar judge and them, they been up'par worryin' Pollit about his property.

"Pollit, he thinks he owns most everthang around h'yar but he hain't actual got no clear title to none of it, and ol' judge thar's a-thinkin' he can git aholt of the entahr tract. To git hisself shed of 'em, that li'l Pollit done send 'em down h'yar to worry me about my land. But I gots me clear title to mine."

"What's a camp fer city folk?" asked Rob.

"Why, it's fer city folk what wants to come up on the mountain whar the summer hain't so hot and whar they can walk around and have fun and such. Calls it Stony Man Camp. They's a cabin or three but they mostly sleeps in them tents. And they gives him good money fer it," said Asa. "Pollit, he done got him some mountain mans workin' fer him up'par."

Rob's interest was piqued. "Supposen he be needin' ary more mans to work?"

"Wahl, you can git on up'par and find out, boy. Just foller Indian Run up to the ridge and over to the Rag road, and on up to the camp. Just keep yer eye out fer that thar Fletcher feller, that's all."

The Stony Man Mountain was one area where Rob had not ventured. Fletcher the outlaw lived with his wife and two children in a rough cabin about a mile from the camp. He had mysteriously come onto the mountain a decade earlier, and squatted in an abandoned shack. The demonic looking outcast avoided contact, and he abused any mountain people who ventured anywhere near his squatter's domain. The villainous Fletcher and his horse pistol-toting wife were widely feared, and assumed to be hiding out from the law.

"Yassar Mister Asa, reckon I *will* be gittin' up'par to the Stony Man," said Rob, rising from the table. "I thank you fer the vittles." He nodded to Asa and his wife, who saw him out the door. He heard the old man's voice behind him as he hopped down the porch steps, "C'mon back and set with me sometime, boy!"

Rob struck off up the trail and soon found himself under a colorful canopy of fall foliage—the bright reds of the rock maples, the soft yellows of the towering tulip poplars, the rusty browns of the sturdy oaks and the mottled purples of the low hanging dogwoods, all vivid under the cloudy gray ceiling. Making his way up the rocky trail on a carpet of fresh fallen leaves, he sensed a magical presence in the mountain forest that portended a turn in his life.

After a couple of hours tramping up through the woods and along open ridgetop pastures, Rob came to a plateau high on the mountain. There the leaves had mostly fallen, exposing the naked forest that surrounded a flat grassy clearing under the looming rock profile of Stony Man Peak.

A picturesque cottage came into view. Unlike the usual square-hewn chestnut log cabin of the mountains, the trim wooden cottage was of clapboards, and had porch railings of bark-covered sticks, giving a most rustic appearance. Two men stood talking on the porch.

Rob approached and called out, "Is one of you gentamens Pollit?"

The two turned toward Rob, and the shorter one answered. "Yes, I'm George Pollock. What might I do for you?"

"Boy, you should call him *Mister* Pollock," interrupted the other man.

"Yassar. Mister Pollit, I'm a-lookin' fer some work. Does you need you another man to work? I'm a hart workin' man."

"No I don't. Not now. Stony Man Camp is closed for the season, and my guests have all gone home," said Pollock. "We won't open again until next summer. You can check with me then, if you want."

"Wahl, I'm a-lookin' fer somethin' now." Rob suddenly realized he'd made a decision when he'd stepped back from the cliff on Pinnacle Ridge, a decision that was now reaching out to change his life.

"Well, you might find some work in town, but times are still hard and it won't be easy," said Pollock. "My friend here and I are going down the mountain on Monday. We can give you a ride down to Luray, if you want."

"Yassar. I'll git on down with you," said Rob without hesitation, making his second major decision of the day to turn his life around.

"Be here by mid-morning Monday. Today's Thursday you know," said Pollock. "And you won't be needing your gun."

"Yassar! I'll be right h'yar!" said Rob. He walked away and the two on the porch returned to their conversation.

Retracing his route back down into and out of Nickerson Hollow, Rob started having second thoughts about leaving his mountain home. His mind was struggling with the decision when he plodded into the yard in the last glimmer of daylight. His fatigued legs had put twenty miles of mountain trails behind him.

Lucy was shuffling the supper pots on the stove when Rob stepped through the door. "Whar you been?" she asked. "You been gone the entahr day!"

"Aw, I's just over to Nickerson Holler. I done see'd ol' man Asa. They wahr some mans thar tryin' to git his land, but we done run 'em off."

Morgan and Bob came in and looked relieved to see him.

Toward the end of supper, Rob said, "Daddy, I'm a-thinkin' about maybe leavin' the mountain."

"Whar you got in head to go, boy?"

"Wahl, I'm a-thinkin' about gittin' on down to Luray to see iffen I cain't find me some work."

"How you gon' git to Luray?" asked Lucy, surprised at his announcement.

"They's some mans up'par on the Stony Man done tolt me I can ride on down to Luray with 'em."

"Work? You gots plenty work right h'yar, 'twixt this place and yer huntin'," said Morgan. "Hain't fer sure you gon' find ary work atall over thar."

"I know, Daddy. But I'm tahred of huntin'. I'm thinkin' about somethin' new."

"What mans on up'par on the Stony Man?" asked Lucy. "What you been doin' way up'par?"

"Ol' man Asa done tolt me about a feller name of Pollit what done got a camp fer city folk up'par on the Stony Man. I done walk up and see'd him."

Morgan pondered the matter as he studied his hands on the table. He looked up and said, "Wahl, I reckon Bob and me can keep up with the place, but you gon' be better off stayin' right h'yar, son."

"Now Morgan, you know how he been down in his mind," said Lucy. "Leavin' the mountain might could do him good."

She looked at Rob.

"Might be you can find some good work over thar. Iffen you cain't, you can always come on back home."

"I don't want leave you and Daddy and the family, Mama," said Rob. "It's just that I hain't..."

Lucy cut him off.

"Rob, I want you to make up yer own mind. It's the onliest way you can be happy," she said. "Lord knows, you hain't been happy fer nigh on half a yahr now. I want the best fer you, son." Her eyes misted. "I always wanted the best fer you."

Supper was over. Bob, who'd been quietly listening, rose and discreetly crooked a finger at Rob to follow him. He led Rob out to the woodpile behind the house where they'd be out of earshot of Morgan, taking his evening ease in his porch rocker. They sat down on log rounds, and Bob looked at Rob intently.

"You thought I was sleepin' this mornin' when you lit out early," said Bob. "But I see'd you headin' up toward the Hazel. Seems to me you done gone somewhar else afore you got yerself down in the holler to call on old man Asa." He held Rob in his gaze.

Rob fidgeted.

Bob repeated himself.

"I figger you done gone somewhar else—afore you got down to ol' man Asa."

Rob let a minute go by.

"I did sure enough," he admitted. "I walked out toward the Pinnacle thinkin' I might find me a deer up'par."

"Yesterday, in the orchard, you ask Daddy about where Ellitt got kilt, and he tolt you it wahr up'par on the Pinnacle," said Bob. "I figger you done went up'par for a look at that rock clift."

Rob sat silently staring at the porch floor. He took a deep breath. "Yer right, Bob. I actual done gone up'par to that rock clift, but it warn't just fer a look." He looked Bob straight in the eye. "I went up'par to jump off. I wanted to kill myself and die."

Bob drew a gasp.

Rob continued.

"But whil'st I's standin' on top lookin' down, I see'd my body all broke up and bloody on them rocks. I stepped back. I hain't ready yet to look forever in the eye."

"What you want do now?"

"I don't know. Daddy, he want me to stay on h'yar. Maybe I orter not leave."

"Rob, when you done step back from that rock clift, you actual was steppin' into a new life," said Bob. "Stop follerin' that deer in the mountain and foller yer dream in the valley. You can do it, Rob."

Bob's words brought light to Rob's eyes and perked him up.

"I can and I will, Bob," said Rob wholeheartedly, feeling a burden lifted.

"And don't fergit, Rob, you got a home and a family to come back to anytime."

"I'm leavin' Monday mornin'," said Rob at breakfast.

"Wahl, could be it's the best thang fer you, son," said Morgan. "And don't fergit, you can come back home any time atall."

Rob was relieved that Morgan seemed to understand and accept his decision. And the others were all smiles around the table.

On Monday morning, the Dinkinses all climbed out from under their covers well before dawn; Lucy made an early breakfast while Rob stuffed some clothes and a few personal items into a tow sack.

The meal passed in sleepy silence and then, when Rob stood to go, Lucy handed him a packet. "H'yar's some dinner fer you." She put her hands on his upper arms and looked up to meet his eyes. "Rob, I always tried to do best fer you. And now I wants you to do yer best fer yerself," she said, with tears welling in her eyes.

His mother's teary farewell made Rob self-conscious, but her sincere concern for him was comforting.

"I will, Mama. I surely will," he promised.

She followed him onto the porch where the rest of the family had gathered. Morgan placed a hand on his shoulder.

"Keep yer head up, boy, and don't let nobody git you down."

"Yassar, Daddy."

Bob stepped forward. "I always figgered you'd git the itch to go somewhar," he said, with a grin and a wink.

"Bob, you be sure Daddy keeps the place up proper now, you hear," said Rob, with a teasing smile. He turned to the younger ones.

"Li'l Ellitt, you gon' stay in school and git eddicated?"

The nine-year old's eyes lit. "I will, Rob. Fer sure I will!"

With a final hug from his mother, Rob stepped off the porch and turned to face the children. "Y'all be good and mind yer mama now."

He strode off under the first sliver of morning light.

"And don't fergit to come back and see us sometime," called Lucy, with liquid eyes and a hand to her tear-streaked cheek.

PART THREE
THE VALLEY

TWENTY-ONE
Riding the Rods

Rob left his family behind and walked purposefully along the rough track up through Nickerson Hollow and up toward a new life. After nearly four hours, he strode into Stony Man Camp, where he found Pollock cinching down a trunk to the bed of a buckboard wagon with a team of mules hitched to it.

"I see you made it," said Pollock. "What's your name?"

"I'm Rob Nickerson."

"You met my friend here last week. He is Mister Printz, he farms in the valley and will take us to Luray," said Pollock, by way of introduction.

" Mornin', Mister Printz," said Rob, nodding to the taller man.

The two men climbed up onto the wagon seat, while Rob tossed his sack in and hopped up on the wagon bed at the open rear end. Printz flicked the reins and they were off, out across the open grass and then on down into the forest below.

Pulled, or rather restrained, by the mules, the buckboard lurched down the steep, rugged and winding road, with Printz riding the brake with one foot and holding the reins back firmly with both of his fists. Pollock and Rob did their best to hang on to the swaying and bouncing buckboard. After jolting and jerking down the rough track for an hour that seemed like three, the ride finally eased when the road flared and then flattened into the Shenandoah Valley, where it smoothed out considerably. Rob leaned up from the wagon bed toward the men on the seat.

"Mister Pollit, what you gon' do in Luray?"

"I'm catching the train home to Washington City."

"What's Washin'ton City?"

"It's the capital of the United States, where our president lives."

Rob pondered this. *I done hear't about Virginny, it's in the New Nited States and they calls the man in charge the pres'dint*, he thought. "Wahl, I reckon you and him is good friends then, bein' neighbors and all."

Pollock chuckled. "Washington is a big city with thousands of people, Rob," he said, over his shoulder. "Not everyone knows everyone. I've never actually met President Cleveland."

Pollock turned to the driver and Rob heard him say, "You know, Printz, I did actually invite the president, by way of Colonel Howell, to come take in the glory of autumn here at Stony Man Camp."

"Hear anything back from him?"

"Not directly. The word was that camp's too rustic and the ride up the mountain too rough for the big man and his tender bride," said Pollock. "No surprise there, though. He has that big summer home on Cape Cod. Stony Man can't compete with the luxury of Buzzard's Bay."

Rob pondered new concepts. What's a city? How many were thousands? A train?

"Mister Pollit, what's a train?" he asked, hoping Pollock wouldn't mock his ignorance with a derisive answer.

But the question didn't appear to surprise Pollock, who'd spent half a dozen seasons up in the far realm of the mountain folk. He looked back at Rob.

"A train is a big long line of carriages all hooked together that carries people and cargo along a railroad. A railroad is a road made with iron rails. The train has iron wheels that roll on the rails and is pulled by a steam locomotive," he said. "The locomotive burns black coal to make steam to pull all the carriages, and it goes very fast. Do you understand, Rob?"

"I reckon," said Rob, though he didn't know a thing about what Pollock was taking about. The only rails he knew were wooden fence rails. He had no idea what a locomotive was, and he couldn't even guess what a train looked like.

Luray came into view. Rob was awestruck. One house right after another lined both sides of the road as far as he could see. And there were other roads running off with houses along them, and most of the houses were white clapboard with windows all around and large porches. Some others were made of brick or stone, and had awnings—so many houses that some were built right against others.

Then they came to the stores with crates and barrels all over their porches. He saw buildings and he didn't know what the buildings were for. Wagons and carriages, and buggies and men on horses went in all directions. People were everywhere. It was a dizzying sight the likes of which Rob had never witnessed. He stared with widened eyes, agog at every passing thing before him.

Mr. Printz pulled the wagon to a halt in front of the depot and swiveled in his seat to face Rob. "This here's where you get off, boy. You might find work over at the livery stable there," he said, pointing to a nearby building. "Talk to Elmer."

Rob hopped off the wagon and into the beginnings of his new life. "Thank you a heap fer the ride," he said, swinging his tow sack over his shoulder and turning to go. The railroad tracks caught his eye. He walked over for a closer look. The two iron rails ran out of sight in both directions. He was puzzled. It did look like some kind of road, but he couldn't imagine what could run on it. He turned toward the livery stable.

Rob hadn't taken many steps when he heard the loudest and most awful shriek from the direction of the rails. He froze in his tracks, alarmed but also excited to see what made such a powerful noise. He cocked his ear to a faint pulsing sound from down the tracks, from out of sight.

The noise grew louder and louder, a strange din of forceful new sounds. He backed away from the rails, his heart racing with excitement and his eyes fixed toward the racket from down the track.

It came into view, a huge black iron monster chugging toward him on massive iron wheels, with a tall smokestack for a nose that belched great billows of black smoke out its top. Spent steam hissed from bulging side jowls and blossomed into puffs of white vapor that swirled and melted into the air along the row of tall wheels that rolled closer in a loud clatter.

Rob panicked and fled to safety behind a shed. He looked over to see Printz and Pollock break into loud guffaws at his fright. He felt shamefaced as he dared a peek around the shed corner to see the big thing shudder and screech to a halt.

It sat as if catching its breath, its big wheels at a standstill. The body of the great beast lay at rest in subdued whiffs of steam, releasing a drift of lazy smoke from its long nose of a stack.

Behind the massive iron machine stretched a row of long odd-looking coaches all hooked together, each with windows along the sides and a door at both ends. He saw Pollock step down from the buckboard, walk over to one of the coaches and turn to exchange a wave with Printz before going up the steps and disappearing inside.

Rob stared at the train in amazement. Several other people climbed on and, after a minute, a jet of steam shrieked from the top of the mighty engine. With new puffs of black smoke and fresh bursts of hissing steam, the wheels started to turn, moving the iron hulk and trailing coaches slowly up the rails, then picking up speed and disappearing.

With the train gone, Rob headed for the livery stable to find Elmer. He entered the dim light and approached a man removing harness from a horse.

"Might you be Mister Elmer?"

"Yes, I'm Elmer. What can I do for you?"

"Wahl, Mister Printz, he done said you might be needin' a man to work."

Elmer shook his head. "I ain't needin' no help right now, boy." He hesitated in thought and then added, "My brother Jack runs the livery stable down in Elkton. He might be needin' a man, if you can get yourself on down there."

"Whar about's Elkton?" Rob felt a small spark of encouragement. It did not occur to him that he would be pursuing nothing more than Elmer's idle speculation.

"It's about twenty-five miles south. The next train'll take you right to it. It'll be here in less'n an hour," said Elmer. "Go over to the station and get yourself a ticket."

"Whar about's the station, Mister Elmer?"

"It's that building right over there by the tracks." Elmer's eyes narrowed as he looked at Rob. "You just come down off the mountain, boy?"

"Yassir."

"I figured that."

"Uh, what's a ticket?" asked Rob hesitantly, aware that he was revealing more of his profound ignorance. He also didn't know what twenty-five miles meant or how to measure an hour, but he didn't feel the need to sacrifice any more dignity to find out.

"Why, it's a li'l piece of paper that lets you ride the train, boy. I thought everybody knowed that," said Elmer. "When you get down there, his name's Jack. Tell him Elmer sent you."

Rob went over to the station, paused at the door, peeked and then ventured in. He walked up to a clerk who was seated behind a small window reading something through narrow spectacles perched on the tip of his nose. "I wants to go to Elkton," he said timidly.

"One way or round trip?" droned the clerk without looking up.

"Uh, uh, I..."

"Do you want to go and come back or do you just want to go?" translated the clerk, raising his eyes and peering out over his glasses.

"I just wants to go."

"Very well, that'll be thirty-five cents."

"Uh, I hain't got no money."

"A train ticket costs money, son. I'm sorry, I can't just *give* you a ticket."

Dejected, Rob turned away and walked out the rear door, wondering what to do next. He slowly kicked along beside the tracks out past the water tank, with his head down in contemplation of his situation.

He heard a sound.

"Pssst! Pssst!! Hey buddy!"

Rob looked up and across the tracks to see a thin bony face with paddles for ears peeking out around the edge of a wooden storage shed. Narrow lips moved under a pointy nose. "Come over here, will you?" they whispered loudly. A skinny finger reached out and hooked the air.

Rob stepped across the tracks to find a wiry little man crouched behind the shed in the narrow space between the building and a high wall of stone.

"Help me get this board off of here, will you?" asked the narrow face in a hushed voice. The small fellow had pulled one of the shed's vertical planks loose at the bottom, but he lacked the strength to get it all the way off. He had only one arm.

Rob reached down, grabbed the plank and the pair of them pulled outward until the board popped loose.

"Good," said the one-armed man, his edgy, closely set eyes flicking a thanks to Rob. "Live around here, buddy?" he asked, his tense, worried expression suggesting a life of little promise and large uncertainties.

"No. I'm just wantin' to git on down to Elkton, but I hain't got no money," said Rob in a subdued voice.

"Well then, you can ride down there with me. Here, help me pull off another board. Pull it slow now. Don't make no noise. Nobody'll miss 'em off this back side."

"You gots you money fer the ticket?" wondered Rob aloud.

"No, I ain't got no money. You don't need no money to ride the rods, buddy."

Rob was mystified, but before he could ask, the board thief went on.

"That's what these here boards is for. We lay the boards across the rods and we lay ourselves on the boards," he said. "You goin' to be down to Elkton in no time!"

"What's rods?"

"The iron rods is hangin' under all the boxcars. They ain't but a little bit above the rails. You got to be right careful because you can get hurt or killed real easy. Ridin' the rods is how I lost my arm. That's why they all call me Wingy. What's *your* name?"

"I'm Rob. Uh, how you actual done lost yer arm, Wingy?"

"I fell to sleep when the train was movin' real slow through a town. I slipped off the rods and the wheel ran right over my arm—cut it clean off.

"Lordy," said Rob. "Why you hain't died right thar?"

"Ol' boy dragged me off the tracks, twisted a rope tight around the stump and carried me to the hospital. Saved my life, he did."

"Wahl, I'm right sorry you done lost yer arm, Wingy."

"I ain't so bad off, Rob. Lots of 'em loses their life. Used to ride inside the boxcars, but then the railroad got tough. Times been hard for couple years now and there's too many train tramps hoppin' the freights. The ol' Norfolk and Western been lockin' up the cars, and they laid on extra bulls.[8]"

"I'm not fer sure I wants to ride them rods, Wingy."

"The freight'll pull in here right soon now. We got to stay hid back here till both the brakeman and the bull passes by. Then we run for the train just as she starts to pull out," coached Wingy, ignoring Rob's reluctance to join him on the open rods under a boxcar. "The brakeman'll have a pick-axe handle. He'll pass first. The bull will be carryin' a gun and he'll pass next. We stay hid here until the whistle blows. Then we run for the last car. Just foller me and do what I do."

---

8   Railroad police. Armed security guards hired to keep trespassing freeloaders off trains.

"Whar about's you goin' to, Wingy?" asked Rob, feeling a little reassured.

"I'm gettin' on down to Waynesboro to see if I can find some work," said Wingy. "I don't live nowhere particular. I'm what they call a hobo. I just go wherever I can find work," he said. "Times is real hard right now. Work's been mighty scarce since the big Panic of '93. These days, a man's dang lucky to get a job cleanin' out stables and such. I can't even do that with only the one arm, so I ain't had much luck."

Rob knew nothing of big panics but Wingy sounded worryingly pessimistic about job prospects. Cleaning stables didn't seem so bad, though. He was ready for any job, any job at all.

"Wahl Wingy, I reckon I'm a hobo, too," said Rob. Then he remembered his food packet. He pulled it from the sack and opened it. "Have you a bite to eat, Wingy," he said, holding out half of his rations.

The little hobo's face softened and his eyes lit up at the sight of food. Not standing on ceremony, he immediately took what was offered and popped a piece into his mouth. "Mighty good," he said, savoring the fare as his tension relaxed. He appeared to be enjoying the finest meal of his life as he quickly devoured his portion. "I ain't had nothin' to eat since yesterday mornin'," he said, tucking in the last bite.

Suddenly Wingy's face came to full alert. He cupped a hand to his flap of an ear and leaned his head a bit beyond the shed corner. Rob leaned out from the end of the shed for a look.

"Believe I hear her comin'," hissed the hobo excitedly. Just then, a whistle shrieked and the train came into view chuffing up the tracks. Wingy pulled Rob back from the edge of the shack. "Stay hid! If they sees us, they'll run us off and we won't have no chance."

The train squeaked to a halt as the stealthy pair eased themselves against the middle of the shed's rear side to stay out of sight. Footsteps fell from the front of the train and came toward the rear, passing the shed. The two trespassers peeked furtively around the corner to see the brakeman disappear around the end of the train.

Soon they heard more footsteps that suddenly stopped beside the train opposite the shed, no more that twenty paces away. With bated breath, the two pressed their backs against the rear of the building. A stone banged loudly off the front of the shack, stiffening the backs and tensing the faces of the two motionless figures.

The bull took several more footsteps but stopped again, nearly panicking Rob into fleeing. But Wingy stood frozen in place, reinforcing Rob's nerve. The two held still as statues, urgently hoping the bull would move on.

BAM!!.

Rob jerked and started but Wingy grabbed his arm and threw a hand over his mouth. The bullet had smashed into the wall, splattering stone chips against the end of the shed. Rob stood motionless, rigid with a fright he'd never felt.

"Bulls eye!!" cried the bull to himself. The dreaded footsteps resumed, but were now receding. Rob and Wingy slowly released their breath and relaxed. A cautious peek revealed the bull rounding the end of the train and then his legs disappearing up along the other side. Wingy picked up his small duffle, slung the strap of it over his shoulder and held his position.

A scream blasted from the steam whistle, triggering Wingy into action.

"Let's go! Don't forget your board!" he cried, as he tucked his plank under his one arm. Rob took hold of his own board and sack and raced out on Wingy's heels to the rail car. As the train jerked slowly forward, Wingy deftly aimed and slid his board in across the two rods, thrust his duffle in and dove head first in onto the board.

Rob fumbled his plank and it slipped in under the second rod, almost hitting the moving rail ties. In the moments it took him to straighten up the board, he found himself walking at a quickly increasing pace.

"Wingy! I cain't git in!" he cried with alarm. "I cain't git in!!" The train's speed was picking up, panicking Rob.

"Push your sack in and dive in head first! Do it, Rob! Do it now!!"

With that, Rob crouched over as he trotted alongside the boxcar, extended his arms to shove his sack in first and then bellied in onto the plank.

As the train gained speed, he lay on his stomach panting, clutching his sack in one hand and gripping the board edge with the other. He hung on, his jaw clenched and brow beaded with anxious sweat, the rail bed flickering by just beneath him and then speeding up to a racing blur. His feet and half his legs still stuck out off the end of his plank. He could barely hear Wingy yelling over the clatter of iron wheels on iron rails.

"Rob! Ease yourself in on the board! Hold on to your board and ease yourself in!"

Rob gripped the plank edges and pulled, inching himself in until he was along side the relaxed hobo. He lay flat out on the board in tense dread as the countryside whizzed by, wondering how the one-armed man could seem so comfortable.

By and by Rob felt the train slowing. Wingy looked over at him. "This here's Elkton comin' up. The train'll stop before the station to take on water. We'll hop off just as she stops, and run straight to the trees."

The steam whistle blew and the train slowed to a walking pace. When it ground to a halt, the two rod-riders slithered out, pulled the planks and scurried into the treeline bordering the tracks. "Come this way," motioned Wingy. "The train'll soon pull up to the station. I got to get up to where I can get back on once the bull's had his look."

The tramp led Rob in picking their way through the trees and bushes to the edge of the rail yard. Wingy crouched down behind a stone wall, his eyes darting up and down the track. When he saw the area was clear, he turned, extended his hand and said, "Well, let's hope the both of us finds some work."

"I'm obliged to you, Wingy. You done larn't me to ride the rods," he said, clasping the hobo's bony hand and meeting his eyes in a moment of grateful appreciation.

"Good luck to you, Rob."

Rob turned and strode off onto a road and into the center of Elkton, a small burg with a single livery stable that he quickly found.

"I'm a-lookin' fer Mister Jack," he announced to an old man currying a bay mare in the first stall he came to.

"That'd be him right over there," said the groom, pointing toward a stocky middle-aged man who had just walked in and hitched a spirited young stallion.

Rob approached as the man pulled the saddle from the horse.

"Mister Jack. My name's Rob and I'm a-lookin' fer work."

The stablemaster put the saddle down and turned his gaze on Rob. With his black brush moustache, riding breeches, leather waistcoat and knee boots, Jack would have cut a dashing figure, had it not been for his ruddy bulbous nose and the dented derby on his head.

"Mister Elmer up to Luray done sent me."

"Is that a fact?" said Jack, scanning Rob head to toe. "Well now, I could use a good man. Ol' Gaston over there ain't up to what he once was," he said, nodding toward the groom. "Trouble is, times is tight and I can't pay hardly nothin' just now. Where do you call home, boy?"

"What?"

"Where's your home? Where do you live?"

"Wahl, I don't actual live nowhar, Mister Jack."

That got a laugh out of Jack. "You got to live somewhere, boy! Where does you eat and sleep?"

"I just come down h'yar today. I carried my dinner and I hain't slept yet."

"You come down off the mountain did you, boy?" asked Jack needlessly. Rob's every utterance pegged him as a mountaineer.

"Yassar." Rob was nervous, knowing that coming down off the mountain didn't help his chances.

"Well then, Rob, I'll put you up and feed you ober to the house, but I can't pay you but twenty-five cents a day. Two bits ain't much but I can't do no better."

"Yassar! You done gots yerself a hart workin' man, Mister Jack!"

Rob was thrilled, and he neither knew nor cared about how little two bits a day was. He'd never had any money of his own before.

"Well, it's about quittin' time," said Jack. "Let's get ober to the house."

Tow sack in hand, Rob followed Jack out and they walked a couple of blocks to a white clapboard cottage on a corner. They went in to the sight of a woman busily shuffling about in supper preparations. Clad in a full-length gingham dress, she turned turned to face them. "Who's this young man, Jack?"

"Lila, this here's Rob. Rob, this here's my wife, Lila."

"I'm very pleased to meet you, Rob."

"Yassum."

"I took him on at the stable today and he'll be stayin' here at the house. What's your last name, Rob?"

"Uh, Nickerson. I'm Robert E. Lee Nickerson," said Rob proudly.

"My lands! Robert E. Lee! You're named for the greatest man from Virginia!" exclaimed Lila. "We're the Wisemans. Our children are all grown up, so just the two of us here now. You can sleep in the upstairs room, Rob," she said, pointing at the stairs. Put your things up there and go wash up before supper."

"Yassum."

Warmed by Lila's kind words, Rob made his way upstairs to his room. He marveled at the bed. It was a far cry from the cornhusk ticks he'd slept on all of his life. He sat on the mattress and bounced a little, creaking the springs. He stroked his hand across the woolen blanket, and rubbed the soft flannel sheet between his fingers, steeped in the strange yet inviting comfort of his new surroundings. *Most surely my life already done took a tarn fer the better,* he thought.

He went back down and outside to flush his face and wash his hands at the well pump. *Fer sure I'm gon' git on good with Mister Jack and Miz Lila,* he told himself.

TWENTY-TWO

1896
A Stubborn Mule

Dinner after church was the main event at the Wiseman home, a leisurely and delectable repast that Rob looked forward to.

Jack handed the gravy boat to Rob.

"Hab some draby, boy."

Then he turned to Granny, a small wisp of a woman.

"Dranny, best hab you another pork chop before I eats 'em all up!" he said with a laugh, as he passed the platter. Lila's white-haired, sparkle-eyed mother always ate Sunday dinner with the Wisemans.

"Pass them dreens, Lila," said Jack.

"Is things pickin' up at all down to the stable, Jack?" she asked, handing him the bowl of cress. Land cress was the first salad green of the spring season and a welcome addition to the table after a winter of boiled cabbage and sauerkraut, potatoes and salted meat.

"It's picked up some, but the price of feed's gone up and I can't get no more for keepin' a horse, so we ain't makin' much money," said Jack, on a discouraged note. "I'm just hopin' better times comes to Wiseman's Stable before I have to cut back. I ain't nebber laid no one off and I don't want to start now."

"Jack, it's seemin' like Rob here's been a right good worker for you these past five months," said Lila, on a positive note.

"Yes indeed. The boy's a right good stable hand. And he got a berry good way with horses and mules," agreed Jack. "Wish I had more work for him. I been sendin' him ober to Cartwright's shop a day or two a week."

Despite nearly half a year with the Wisemans, Rob never spoke much at the table, preferring to just listen. And he was quite happy to be farmed out to the blacksmith shop next door. He had learned some of the basics of smithing from Lucas Cartwright and found it a welcome break from stable work.

"I sure hope you don't get too poor to put meat on the table, Jack," quipped Granny, with a snaggle-toothed grin.

Jack put on a grave look.

"Dranny, no matter how bad times are or how poor I may be, there will always be pork chops and a drate big ol' glass of buttermilk set in front of you on Sunday," he proclaimed, with an air of contrived solemnity. He wasn't inhibited by his odd speech impediment, the inability to pronounce *gr* or *v*.

Granny changed the subject.

"I sure do like that new preacher. It's a shame you can't never get this boy to go to church with us after all this time," she squeaked, looking across the table at Rob, who fidgeted a bit at the comment.

"Well Dranny, we took him the first Sunday he was here, back when you was down with the pleurisy. Pastor Hinebaugh come over to make him feel welcome but ebbery one in the congregation knew he come off the mountain soon as he opened his mouth," Jack said, glancing at Rob, who was feeling uneasy.

"Ebbery one of 'em had nothin' at all to say to him. And he don't know no prayers or hymns or nothin', and he can't read the Bible," said Jack, further discomfiting Rob. "There weren't nothin' for him to do but just sit there, so he didn't take to church much, Dranny."

Lila chimed in.

"Mama, you know Rob here's a tad shy," she said. "And you know most of them Methodists is a little high falutin'."

Rob felt the heat of his flushing face, as Lila went on.

"They're not as all-mighty welcomin' as they make out to be. I told Rob to try the Baptist church but he hasn't gone yet," she said. "I'm thinkin' of switchin' to the Baptists myself."

Rob wished they'd talk about something else. But Granny kept on with it.

"How's he ever goin' to be saved if he don't never go to church?" she demanded to know, emphasizing the gravity of the matter with her squinty gaze.

Rob felt the old lady's eyes boring in on him.

"Young man, you can't enter the Kingdom of God until you been saved," she intoned gravely, shaking her fuzzy white head. She raised a wagging finger at him. "And besides, there's some mighty pretty girls goes to church," she said, with a wink of her lively eye, sweetening her warning with a lure.

"Yassum," said Rob passively, as his face flushed again. Entering the Kingdom of God was much less immediate to a young man with little religious tradition than to a devout old woman who stood a good deal closer to the gates of heaven. Being saved from embarrassment was much more important to Rob than being saved from the fires of hell.

"Well, you're a good lookin' young fellow. You ought to be gettin' Jesus and a good wife into your life, and settle down respectable," said Granny, completing the guidance that the old always wish the young would seek from them, but never do.

Rob shifted nervously in his seat.

Lila spoke up.

"Yes, Mama, but like I said, Rob's shy and don't like to talk to folks much, so he don't get to know hardly anyone. We never bother him about it."

"Well, *someone* better bother him about it," insisted Granny.

"He's goin' to meet people when he wants to, Mama," rejoined Lila.

Then Jack stepped in.

"Now Dranny, don't worry yourself atall about it. This here's a fine young man and he'll get around to all that by and by. I'm sure he's goin' to lead a righteous life."

Dinner ended and Rob felt much relieved when everyone got up and left the table. He retreated outside for a long walk alone, as had become his habit on Sunday afternoons. It was his time for reflection upon his comfortable but lonely life. He missed his family. And, as he made his solitary way across meadows, through woodland and along back roads, he missed hunting with his gun.

On the edge of a forest, Rob spotted a slender sassafras sapling that had shaped its narrow trunk into a spiral by growing over an entwined honeysuckle vine. *Li'l twistified sassafras gon' make me the perfect walkin' stick,* he thought. He pulled out his Barlow knife and went about slicing the sapling to sever it at ground level, then nicked off the branches from the top part.

He held the sapling out at arm's length and decided to cut the top part off at a place where a twist bulged further out. The cut left the stick at shoulder height with an irregular knobby top a couple of inches across. *Hmm, I orter carve it out inter somethin',* he thought. *Stick's twisted kinder like a snake.* He studied the knobby top for a minute. "Rattler head," he said under his breath.

He sat himself on a fallen log and whiled the time away by carefully carving the stick top into the distinctive flattened wedge-shaped head of the sinister and venomous timber rattlesnake that infested the mountains. Below the snakehead he carved and shaped the twisted wood into a grip that fit his hand. When finished, he turned it to view his snakehead from all angles, and he was pleased with his handiwork. A dangerous serpent, normally killed on sight, was now his familiar companion in the unfamiliar world he had entered.

Two months later, a spring afternoon found Rob up in the stable mow forking down hay when he saw a man pull up out front in a black buggy with a gray mule tied to the rear. The man stepped down, untied the mule, led it into the stable, hitched the animal and approached Jack.

Though of average stature, the buggy driver looked a little different. Instead of the usual brown work clothes, he wore a blue shirt, dark trousers held up by wide black suspenders and a broad-brimmed straw hat that shadowed his clean-shaven face. Rob cocked an ear as he tossed down forkfuls of hay.

"Evenin' Jonas," said Jack. "What can I do for you today?"

"Yock, I yust a big chance taken and cheaply I bought diss mule, because it's broken not properly. He von't his tail let anyone near it, so deh crupper you can't put on. I only ten dollars for him paid, so anudder ten to get him broken for deh crupper I vill pay."

Rob, curious at the man's odd speech and interested in the mule, climbed down and approached the animal, a sturdy yearling.

Jack fetched a crupper and warily stepped toward the mule's rear, while Jonas held the halter. The animal's eyes lit and ears flipped back.

Jack paused, then eased toward the tail. The mule became skittish, then brayed and jerked its head and, squealing and squalling, kicked its hind feet out wildly, forcing Jack to back off.

"I don't know, Jonas. We might not get this one broke without him breakin' a leg or hurtin' somebody," said Jack, shaking his head.

"I can break the mule."

It was Rob, who stood looking intently at the two men.

"How can you do that, boy?" questioned Jack, arching his eyebrows in a skeptical tilt of face. "You know somethin' I don't know?"

"I can do it," declared Rob confidently. He turned and went to the tack room.

Jack and Jonas wore doubting looks when Rob returned carrying harness that he and Jack then cinched around and over the animal's back, taking care not to get behind the skittish creature.

"Mister Jack, holt this h'yar line and Mister Jonas, holt t'other line," instructed the stable hand, placing a man on each side of the recalcitrant beast. Rob positioned himself in front of the mule, grasping the halter.

"Work him back right slow-like into the corner thar," said Rob. "Git him in close whar he cain't kick out." Rob grabbed the crupper. "Holt him in tight now," he said. He slowly slid the crupper around the mule's tail.

The animal squalled and stomped furiously, but the two men held its jerking head down and back, frustrating its frantic efforts to evade that crupper.

"Thar now. Walk him on out," said Rob confidently. "He hain't goin' to be no trouble now." Rob tied the mule up to the hitching post and turned to the two men, a look of victory on his face.

"You gon' have to do it like that fer the best part of the season, but he won't kick and buck no more. It'll break him and then you can just strap him up regular."

Jack and Jonas were dumfounded. Jack looked at Jonas and then to Rob.

"Well if that don't beat the stuffin' out of ebbery thing I eber did see then I don't know what did!" exclaimed the stablemaster in astonishment.

Rob beamed with glory.

"Yock, you and me too soon get old and too late get shmart," said Jonas, laughing heartily. "Very clever diss young man is, yah? I should to him deh money give! Ha! Ha! Ha!"

Jonas' last remark perked Rob's attention, and he noticed that Jack looked a bit nervous.

"Yock, for you and Rob a good proposal I have," said Jonas. He turned to Rob. "Rob, you come to my farm for deh one season verking. For one day I pay you fifty cents—six dollars for deh veek. In my house you eat and sleep."

Jonas looked at Jack. "To you Yock, deh ten dollars I give now." He held up a gold Eagle between his fingers. "But only if my offer you both like. Maybe my offer you don't vant. But den I should to Rob deh money give, to be fair," he said with a nod at Rob. "Deh problem with my mule he did fix, you know. True, Yock?"

Rob looked at Jack who, eying the gold coin hungrily, said, "Well, Rob here's a right good worker but, truth be told, I really ain't got enough work for him. Fact is, I been sendin' him over to work with Lucas a couple days a week. But you're right, Jonas—about Rob and the mule and the money."

They both looked at Rob expectantly.

"Wahl, Mister Jack. I likes workin' fer you and all, and you done been right good to me. I cain't handily say I'm a-leavin' iffen you wants me to stay on."

"Ahem," uttered Jack, clearing his throat. "Well Rob, you been a good stable hand, but I don't mind lettin' you go if you want to, seein' as how business is so slow and all. I could take you back on at the end of the season, if things pick up."

Rob, looking down and scratching the dirt with the toe of his boot, considered the uneasiness he would have with Jack if he stayed on at the stable and took that gold Eagle that Jack had his eye on. By saving most of his pay, Rob possessed nearly thirty-five dollars already. He knew Jack needed the money. He looked up at Jonas.

"You gots yerself a man, Mister Jonas."

"Rob, on deh farm very hard deh verk is," cautioned Jonas.

"I'm a hart workin' man, Mister Jonas," said Rob forthrightly.

Jonas, with a broad smile, dropped the gold into Jack's hand.

"Thank you Jonas!" said Jack, quickly pocketing the coin. "Stop by the house to let Rob get his things and say goodbye to Lila."

Jonas tied the mule to the back of the buggy, and he and Rob climbed aboard under the afternoon sun.

"Don't ferget what I said about comin' back now, Rob," called Jack, waving as the buggy set off to the Wiseman home, where Rob quickly collected his few belongings and bid Lila goodbye.

Rob kept his silence and enjoyed the scenery as Jonas drove the buggy west, crossing the bridge over the Shennandoah River, and then turned south down a dusty road through the rolling countryside. Tender green shoots of corn, grain and hay patterned the fields. and the fragrance of roadside wildflowers filled the warm air.

Finally the farmer spoke up.

"Vat your last name iss, Rob?"

"Nickerson. I'm Robert E. Lee Nickerson."

Jonas glanced over at him with what Rob thought was a slight frown, but said no more as he drove on in studied silence. Rob held his tongue too. *Might could be Mister Jonas don't think much of Robert E. Lee,* he thought.

After a good while, Jonas steered the buggy into a lane leading down an easy slope between field fences, the zigzagging chestnut rails framing a large and handsome farm that dropped gently into the Shenandoah River bottomland. They followed their shadow down to the house.

The farmhouse was fitted onto a small lift of land part way down, where the slope flared. Jonas pulled the horse to a halt just by the ample yet unimposing white clapboard dwelling of plain design and tidy appearance. He turned to Rob.

"Schank. I am Yonas Schank, Rob. Come, my vife and children to meet."

As if on cue, a woman appeared from around the corner of the house just as the two buggy riders stepped to the ground. A girl and a small boy followed her at a close pace behind. The three stopped and stared at Rob.

"Ah, here now my vife is—Eleanor, and my daughter Rachel and my son Christian," said Jonas, with pride in his voice.

"Evenin'," muttered Rob, with a reserved nod, feeling self-conscious in the presence of a family unexpectedly confronting a stranger. He found them peculiar looking, clad as they were in strange garb unlike any he'd seen. He judged Eleanor to be a few years younger than Jonas, likely in her mid-thirties. Attired in an unadorned full-skirted grey dress, a tight bodice, snug long sleeves and a high collar, she was neatly dressed in a plain style. A simple black bonnet covered her head, black stockings sheathed her ankles and sturdy black shoes shod her feet, leaving only her hands and face bare.

Rachel, just showing the budding contours of puberty, was dressed like her mother, giving her more of an adult look. Tawny haired little Christian, with only his freckled face visible as he peeked from behind his mother's skirt, broke a shy grin revealing two missing front teeth.

Rob, feeling awkward and searching for something else to say, was suddenly startled to hear Jonas address Eleanor with words he found totally unintelligible. The only thing he understood was the utterance of his own name. Mystified, Rob stared at Jonas as the farmer's wife replied, "Ja, gut—sobald wie möglich."

She stepped forward to Rob. "Here Rob, let me take your things to your room." She reached for his tow sack and walking stick, as Jonas mounted the buggy.

"Come now Rob, to deh barn vee go."

Rob relinquished his possessions, hopped back up onto the buggy beside Jonas and off they rolled toward the large bank barn, beyond and below the house. A broad red-painted roof of ribbed metal sheltered the biggest barn Rob had ever seen. The building sat nested into a shallow slope, the basement open to the lower side and the front facing the uphill side, with an earthen ramp banked up to the big sliding main doors.

"Voh, dare!" Jonas pulled the horse to a stop under the lean-to roof of a wagon shed fitted against the end of the barn. He hopped down and proceeded to unhitch the horse while Rob, taking his lead from the farmer, untied the mule. "Diss vay. Come." Jonas led him to a group of stalls in the barn's basement level, where he motioned Rob and the mule into one stall and put the horse into another.

"Now, deh whole barn I show you," said Jonas, leading the way.

Rob marveled at the heavy timber-framed structure, set upon a massive stacked limestone foundation and covered all around with wide vertical boards, well-weathered and gray, a hundred feet long in all.

Jonas led Rob through the muddy cattle bay and the tidy milking parlor, past the tight feed bins and the tack room, and up steps to the granary, corncrib and the wide-open main floor. He pointed up at the haymows, empty cavernous spaces that reached to the roof and were connected to the main floor by built-in ladders, and to the lower-level milking parlor by vertical chutes. Tools, ropes, pails and hardware hung neatly from pegs on walls and beams, each in its own place. Rob had never been in a building with so many unique spaces, each so well fitted out to its purpose.

The grand tour ended back at the stalls, where Jonas poured oats into each animal's feed box. He handed Rob a grooming brush and some rags, and then started up the stairs to the main floor. He called back to Rob.

"Ven you is vit deh grooming all done, put dem out in deh pasture."

Rob tried, as he wiped and brushed down the two draft animals, to wrap his mind around his perplexing new surroundings—the big farm, their odd clothing, Jonas' strangely backwards way of talking and, most baffling, the unintelligible speech between the farmer and his wife.

Just as he was about to lead the horse and mule out to pasture, Rob heard the rhythmic dong-dong, dong-dong, dong-dong of an approaching cowbell. He took a few steps beyond the feed bin, in the direction of the sound.

In the next moment, the lead cow and seven other milkers plodded into the cattle bay, followed by two adolescent girls walking barefoot, the fetid barnyard mud oozing up between their toes. With switches in their hands, the two lightly flogged the cows into the dim light of the milking parlor and fastened each into a neck stanchion that held the animal in place for milking.

Rob watched them go about their task, studying both the milking and the girls with equal fascination. The chubby older one amply filled a worn replica of Eleanor's costume that, along with her rosy-cheeked moon face and round wire-rimmed spectacles, gave her an incongruous matronly appearance, as she went awkwardly about her tasks.

The younger was slender and more graceful, with lively blue eyes and curly blond locks. Sheathed in a faded yellow print dress to just below her knees, her movements hinted at her every svelte contour.

The milkmaids each grabbed a wooden bucket from the wall, turned, took a step toward the grain bins and stopped–arrested by the sight of the strange man in their presence.

Rob stood staring at the startled girls. He noticed that the larger one looked every bit as uneasy and self-conscious as he was. It took the smaller girl to break the awkward moment.

"Who are you?"

"Um, name's Rob," he said. Her look told him she wanted to know what he was about. "Mister Jonas, he done hahr'd me to work on the farm."

"Where did Father hire you?" inquired the older girl cautiously.

"Up'par to Elkton. I wahr workin' fer Mister Jack in the stable thar." Rob thought a bit of explanation would ease the girl's discomfort and give them the right impression of him. "Mister Jonas, he done come in with this h'yar mule what warn't broke proper," he said, nodding toward the animal. "And I done broke it fer him. Right thar Mister Jonas done hahr'd me on."

They looked at each other and then back at Rob.

"Well, I'm Sally and this here's Analiese," said the younger one confidently.

"We milk the cows," declared the older, announcing the obvious.

"Mornin' and evenin'," added Sally.

It then occurred to Rob that he was standing between the hesitant girls and the grain bins, blocking their way.

"Wahl, I best be a-gittin' these two critters out thar to the paster field."

He led the animals out from the end of the barn, pulled open the gate and turned them loose into the paddock. He shoved the gate to and lingered awhile, with his elbows on the top board and a foot on the bottom, looking out admiringly at a grazing pair of huge Belgian draft horses. He contemplated the milkmaids. *Black bonnet thar's Jonas' girl, but that li'l curly hair one cain't be in the same family. She belong to someone else fer sure,* he thought.

Hearing a sound, Rob pulled his foot off the gate and turned to see Jonas and another man rounding the end of the barn and coming toward him. As they walked up, Jonas spoke to the man.

"Diss young man is Rob Nickerson. He I told you about, vas deh mule breaking."

Jonas looked at Rob.

"Rob, diss is Earle Harman. Earle is viss me nine years now on deh farm verking. His family is in dat house living," he said, pointing a finger out across the field.

Rob looked out toward the tenant house, a small wooden structure that sat beyond the far edge of the field, and a ways back up from the riverbank.

"Earle, how about some days Rob viss you be verking?"

"Perfectly willin' Jonas, perfectly willin'." Harman looked at Rob. "Can you work a horse and mule, boy?"

"Yassar, Mister Arle."

"Just call me Earle. I ain't no sir or mister to nobody," said the farm hand in a hard-edged voice through tight lips that then spit out a sideways shot of tobacco juice.

In the way of a taciturn and distant man, Earle turned his gaze toward the field and the horses. Faded brown trousers and a tan shirt with sleeves rolled halfway up his forearms shrouded a ramrod body well hardened by continuous outdoor labor. He was about Jonas' age, but life had baked ten more years into his lean countenance.

Earle's old brown fedora shadowed a deeply lined leathery face with inscrutable eyes that were always squinting outward to infinite vistas, rather than looking at anyone in his presence. Standing next to Earle was like standing next to a statue—close enough to touch but beyond reach.

"Earle, tomorrow in deh cornfield, pumpkins vee plant," said Jonas, who then turned to Rob. "Come Rob. Almost suppertime."

"See you in the mornin' Jonas." Earle took out on the path that led along the fence to his home.

The farmer and his new hire struck for the main house. Rob thought, *Wahl, now. Thar 't is. That li'l Sally girl, she fer sure belong to Arle.*

TWENTY-THREE

Jesus

When he and Jonas reached the house, Rob paused in the yard to take a good look at the Schank home. Though lacking any ornamental woodwork, the clean two-story wood framed house was a common design found on family farms. His eyes went from the front section, where a center stair hall separated two rooms on each floor, to the rear extension that held the dining room and kitchen on the first floor, and three small bedrooms off a porch above.

The open-air stairway connecting the upper and lower side porches reminded him of the finest dwelling back home at Nabors Mill. "Looks kinder like Hettie's house," he said to himself, thinking of the Hettie Nabors home, right next to the Nabors store.

Rob went over and into the small building behind the house, where Jonas stood drying his face and hands. Working the pump handle, he drew up a basin of water from the cistern below, a masonry tank that collected rainwater from the roof because the limestone strata underlying the valley made all the well water so hard it couldn't be used with soap.

Rob flushed his face, washed his hands and, while drying himself, noticed a small iron stove, metal laundry tubs and a couple of washboards and scrub brushes on a table. *Right fine washroom,* he thought of the tidy and efficient-looking laundry.

"Come, Rob," said Jonas, leading the way into the kitchen, where Eleanor was busy pulling the evening meal together.

"Show Rob to his room, Rachel," she said, without looking up from stirring and turning the contents of several pots and pans on her big iron cook stove.

Rob followed the shy girl out and up the open porch stairs to a small room off the upper porch and above the kitchen. She opened the door and, without a word, stepped back and stood facing him. He stepped into the room, surveyed the space and then looked back out. She had vanished.

Paneled entirely in wooden boards, the room was whitewash clean and sparsely furnished with pieces of plain design—a single bed, straight chair, small chest, oil lamp and an end table with a Bible on it. Rob spied his walking stick against the chair and his sack on the bed, but it was the bedcover that caught his eye. Leaving the door open, he sat on the bed and studied the odd cover. He fingered the fabric curiously. Variously colored small swatches of cloth were sewn together to form a pattern. *Right perty*, he thought, but he wondered why such prosperous folks needed to save and sew every little scrap together to make a bedcover.

He pulled the Bible onto the bed and flipped it open in idle curiosity. Then it struck him. He had never in his life opened the cover of a book. The indecipherable words made it as impenetrable as a stone. Yet it was meaningful, for the unfathomable book reminded him of his failure at school—a memory as haunting as a bad dream.

Rob thought back twelve years to Miss Pricilla, whose class now seemed as if it had been a wagon of deliverance carrying the chosen few to be saved from dark ignorance. He had managed to clamber aboard her carriage of learning and enlightenment just before it went beyond reach. But, like a nightmare, he fell off and helplessly watched his salvation fade away into forever.

A twinge of regret shot through him. And the pang of love lost to illiteracy welled up a few tears into his private moment. *I might have stood a better chance with Mary Jane iffen only I'd....*

"Rob. Supper."

He looked up from the Bible and from his self-pity to see Rachel standing outside his door again, staring in at him as though she'd never left the spot. Then, in a blink, she was gone.

Rob stood beside the supper table, uncertain of where to sit. Two new freckly-faced boys had appeared and sat beside one another on a table bench. Little Christian slid onto the opposite bench with his two sisters, leaving an open place beside the two boys.

The table groaned with platters and bowls of steaming food that released strange and delicious aromas, setting Rob's mouth to watering.

Jonas stepped to the head of the table and motioned to Rob.

"Sit, Rob. Viss my sons you sit."

Jonas took his seat and looked at the two boys. "Samuel, Martin, diss man is Rob. He is for deh season verking on deh farm," he said to them.

Rob felt a little self-conscious under the boys' curious gazes, as he took his place on the bench. Samuel and Martin were dressed like Jonas, including the suspenders, which made them look like miniature men. It was the mop-head bowl haircuts and the impish grins on elfin faces that distinguished them as children. Rob followed their lead in tucking a napkin to his shirt.

Once seated, the family folded hands, closed eyes and bowed heads. Jonas' table grace was a good deal longer than anything Morgan had ever uttered, straining Rob's patience amid the whiffs of Eleanor's supper creations. Finally came, "In Yesus name, Amen."

Jonas helped himself to slices of juicy meat and passed the platter to Rob. Eleanor sawed thick slices of course dark bread from a heavy loaf at the foot of the table. All bowls and platters were set in motion, starting with Jonas and then to Rob and the boys, and to Eleanor, and around to the girls.

The food looked a little different to Rob. The pork was an unfamiliar cut, the sliced carrots floated in something unknown, and the peeled boiled potatoes had little flecks of green all over them. But it smelled so good that he eagerly took heaping helpings—until a bowl of mystery matter arrived in front of him. He hesitated to spoon out any of the lumpy balls and broth.

Eleanor spoke up. "Those are potato dumplings with paprika, Rob. Have you never had potato dumplings?"

"No'um, I hain't never and I cain't say as I ever done see'd it, neither."

"Well, they're made of potatoes, eggs and flour. Take some. They're very good with the meat."

Rob forked one of the dumplings onto his plate, figuring he could eat the one even if he didn't like it. He didn't want to offend. He felt the Schanks to be a bit strange but saw they were good people and he wanted them to think as well of him.

The mealtime passed with Eleanor asking the two boys about their day in school, and Jonas listening attentively.

The potato dumpling tasted better than he expected, so Rob helped himself to seconds, pleasing Eleanor.

She smiled warmly and said, "Rob, you needn't stay in your room evenings. You're welcome to join us in the parlor. Come to the parlor with us this evening."

"Uh, yassum, I reckon I can," he said tentatively, glancing toward Jonas.

Jonas wiped the napkin across his mouth and rose from the table. "I go deh animals to check now. You coming, Rob?"

"Uh, yassar. Yass I am." He pulled his napkin up to a quick wipe of his mouth, came to his feet and, with a nod to Eleanor, followed Jonas out the door.

They walked side-by-side toward the barn.

"Now you see vhy you are on my farm verking, Rob. My sons not yet big enough for verking deh farm."

"Yassar, Mister Jonas. I sees what yer sayin'."

"Samuel still in deh school going four more years. Martin six more years. Deh boys in deh school go for eight years. Deh girls only six years. In deh fall, Christian in deh school go first year."

Talk of school made Rob uneasy. It was a subject he avoided, lest he be asked about his own schooling. He wanted to delay revealing his illiteracy until he found a discreet time and setting to let it out with the least embarrassment to himself.

The mule, the bay and the big Belgians were standing patiently at the pasture gate. Rob and Jonas secured the draft animals in their stalls, and then stepped out into the evening light. Jonas paused and turned his eyes out toward the red ball of the sun as it sunk onto a silhouetted rail fence, throwing long shadows across the ground.

"Ya Rob, my vife I tink likes you. And I myself like you," he said, casting his gaze toward the horizon. "Ya, dat is good,...das ist gut. Alles ist gut, immer gut." His voice trailed off as he spoke first to Rob and then to the western sky, graying above the sunken sun. The glow of twilight saw them back up to the house.

Jonas waved Rob to follow him into the parlor, a first floor room in the front of the house. The family had gathered there after supper, as was their custom. Rob followed Jonas in, uneasily hoping he wouldn't blunder into something an ignorant mountaineer might say to embarrass himself or his hosts.

A low fire smoldered in the iron stove to temper the light chill of evening. A pair of oil lamps sent arcs of pale light washing up the walls, infusing the room in a soft and soothing yellow glow.

"Please sit, Rob," said Eleanor gently, extending her open palm toward an upholstered chair. Eleanor and the two girls, all now wearing white prayer kapps on their heads, sat with closed Bibles on their laps. The three boys were arranged in a line on a bench, showing unusual quietude.

Rob put his hand to the seat fabric, as if to test that it was safe to sit upon, before slowly settling onto the soft chair.

With a Bible in hand, Jonas sank himself into the rocker's thick pillow seat and opened the volume. After reading aloud a passage of scripture, Jonas folded his Bible and Eleanor opened hers. She selected and read a passage to the room, followed by the girls reading chosen verses.

Rob noticed the boys fidgeting a bit and was, himself, uneasy in the company of Bible readers. He was too sparsely acquainted with scripture to take any interest in it, and he felt self-conscious sitting amongst such a devout family.

"Rob, will you read us a verse or two?" asked Eleanor. With a serene smile, she held out her Bible.

Rob stiffened. His heart pounded and his mouth went dry, as he gripped the chair arms in rising anxiety.

"Uh, wahl, I hain't much fer pickin' readin's from the Bible and..."

"Oh, *please* do Rob. Please read a few lines, *won't* you?"

"Wahl, uh, uh Miz Eleanor, I, I hain't...," he stammered, in dread.

"Oh you must Rob. We do so want you to join our family in reading the Bible," she urged encouragingly, leaning over and laying her Bible on his lap.

Rob straightened the book and opened it, as panic swept through him. His mind raced to find a pretext to excuse himself from the room.

"Uh, uh, I hain't, uh, feelin' too good uh, Miz Eleanor," he stammered. "My throat's a mite sore and my mouth done gone dry. I expect I'm a-comin' down with a colt." He kept his eyes cast down to the open pages. "Reckon I best be a-gittin' in the bed to rest up," he said, feigning a small cough.

He rose and carefully placed the open Bible back on Eleanor's lap.

"Most likely I'll feel better in the mornin'," he said, and then quickly left the room, gently closing the door behind him. He felt both relieved and angry with himself as he stepped briskly across the porch, pattered up the porch stairs and ducked into the safety of his room. He closed the door behind him, paused, and took a deep breath before lighting the lamp with a shaking hand.

He paced the room, repeatedly punching one fist into the other palm. He felt sorry for himself, but was angry about what he had just done. He had sacrificed his dignity to save his dignity, but he didn't break even. He had never before held a secret with such power to steal away self-esteem and impose self-loathing.

He was sitting on the edge of his bed, with his head drooped in miserable self-pity, when a light knock came on the door. He looked up to see the door crack open.

"Rob? May I come in?" she asked softly. The door opened just enough to let Eleanor slip into the room. She held a steaming mug in one hand and eased the door shut with the other.

"I've made you a hot drink of cider vinegar and honey. It's very good for sore throats and for colds," she assured him, passing him the mug before sitting on the chair with her back straight, hands clasped and face in a pained expression.

"Rob, I'm very sorry. I didn't know. Rachel said she saw you reading the Bible and I thought…"

"I warn't readin'," he interjected. "I wahr just lookin' at it. It wahr the first book I ever actual helt in my own hands."

"Rob, would you like to learn to read?" she asked earnestly.

"How'd you know I cain't read?" he mumbled, his head still hung dejectedly.

"Well, when you opened the Bible on your lap, it was upside down, and you put it on my lap upside down," she said gently. "Rob, I can talk to the schoolmaster and maybe you can attend our school when it opens again in September. Would you want to do that?"

"Yassum, I reckon," he said, with downcast eyes, in a tone more polite than interested.

"If you learned to read, Rob, you could read the Bible. Wouldn't you like to be able to read the Bible?"

"Wahl, might be that I would. Hain't thar somethin' else warth the readin', besides the Bible?"

"Yes, of course there is. There are many good books, but the Bible is all you *need* to read, Rob. Everything to carry you through your life is in the Bible. The life and teachings of Jesus are the best guidance for leading our lives."

"Jesus done writ the Bible?"

"No, the Bible was written by many people, but not by Jesus. Jesus didn't write."

"Wahl, how he gon' larn me ary a thang iffen he didn't write nothin'?"

"Jesus only spoke his wisdom, Rob. Others wrote down his sayings many years later."

Rob's ears perked at this news. He assumed she was saying that Jesus was a fellow illiterate, and that encouraged him. If Jesus could be somebody despite illiteracy, maybe he could, too.

"You sayin' he wahr a great man what didn't write nothin' atall?"

"Jesus was the greatest man who ever lived."

"Wahr he greater than Robert E. Lee?"

"Yes, Rob, he was."

Rob was impressed, but he had one qualm, remembering Granny's warning at Sunday dinner with the Wisemans.

"Does I got to be saved?"

"No Rob. You need not be saved. Salvation is yours by the grace of God. You need only to follow the teachings of Jesus and live by His example."

Rob felt relieved, but he wasn't convinced. "Wahl, I hain't never follered no teachin's afore. What's teachin's good fer?"

"Rob, the teachings of Jesus will help you follow a righteous path and keep you from going astray."

"Yassum." Rob didn't understand the meaning of righteous and astray, but he assumed from context that the former was good and the latter bad. He didn't feel the need for further explanation, but he did have one more question.

"How Jesus done larn't so much, iffen he didn't read or nothin'?"

"God gave Jesus his wisdom. He was the son of the Lord God. The Lord in Heaven sent him down here to earth to teach the people to be good, so they can live peacefully and go to heaven when they die."

"Whar's Jesus now—or is he dead?"

"Jesus died, but he lives eternally. The Romans killed him for his teaching, but he rose from the grave. He's with his Heavenly Father now."

Rob wasn't very impressed by Jesus rising from the grave. He already knew that such things were ordinary. *Most nearly everone what died done riz from the grave,* he reminded himself. *To be a h'ant in the night to worry the livin' folk,* he thought, reflecting the common knowledge in his mountain home about ghosts.

It was those murderous Romans that bothered him. *Might be that larnin' and teachin's a mite risky, iffen you can git yerself kilt fer it,* he worried. *I'm fer sure I don't never want no truck with them Romans.* He wondered who they were, and where they were.

"Thank you, Miz Eleanor, fer the cider vinegar'n honey," he said.

She rose. "Goodnight Rob," she said, before easing out the door.

Rob snuffed the lamp and lay on the bed, staring up into the dark, contemplating Jesus and the parlor fiasco. Finally he curled into himself and pulled the patchwork bedcover up over his head.

Breakfast at the Schank table was a sumptuous affair, with boiled porridge and cream, hot biscuits and butter, fried eggs and scrapple, and slabs of smoked ham, all washed down with fresh milk and cool water.

Rob and Jonas rose, ready to confront a day of labor. Jonas disappeared into another room and returned with his straw hat and an old rumpled hat that he handed to Rob.

"For deh sun, Rob. To duh verk vee go now."

Donning headgear, they stepped out and made for the barn. The rising sun sent slanting rays glancing up off the shimmering river, bathing the farmstead in a vivid celebration of the new day.

Spring had seen the seeds of corn, barley, buckwheat and oats going into fertile soil. Winter wheat, planted the prior autumn, was above knee high already. A light breeze pushed the green wheatgrass into undulating waves rolling across the broad field.

Earle had harnessed the big Belgian workhorses, and was cinching down the last harness strap on the mule when Jonas and Rob walked in. The three of them, using Rob's method, backed the beast into a corner and fitted on the crupper. Then they and the draft animals went out to the day's tasks of plowing and planting.

"Ever run the spring harrow or the planter, boy?" quizzed Earle.

"Nosir. I just done the plowin' behind a horse or mule," said Rob, not needing to explain that the Dinkins farm had no spring harrow or planter. Instead, the mountain plowmen stomped the clods behind the plow and then dragged a primitive chain harrow to break up the turned earth. And planting the crop patches on mountain farms was done by hand with a hoe.

"We'll start you off plowin' then," said Earle, who proceeded to coach Rob in commanding the two big horses and in the use of the riding plow. "I'll learn you the harrow and planter later."

Earle and Jonas then went off together to plant pumpkins in a cornfield, leaving Rob to finish the last of the plowing for a field of late corn.

Rob had never worked more than one horse before, but he soon got the hang of handling the team of massive draft animals. Each topping a ton, they were by far the largest horses he had ever seen, and they awed him with their drawing power. Yet, despite their prodigious strength, they were docile and very responsive to commands, making the plowing easy.

Rob was used to stumbling behind a jerking plow on rocky uneven ground. *This here's easy settin' down work*, he thought, while riding along in the seated luxury of a sulky plow behind the big tan animals, their hairy white ankles stepping smartly and white faces bobbing in unison. He began to feel like a modern farmer as he drove them back and forth across the flat bottomland, folding the rich soil.

And so it went. The workweek saw men and beasts arranged in different combinations according to the job at hand, each bending strenuously into their tasks.

Early evenings found Rob in the barn stable grooming and feeding the draft animals, when the cows lumbered in to be milked. He always greeted the milkmaids politely. "How do Miss Annie Leese. How do Miss Sally," he'd say, tipping his new old hat.

Analiese would blush shyly and turn away, muttering something he couldn't make out. Sally, on the other hand, would bounce up to him and cheerily chirp, "Hello Rob!" Then, as she scooped feed to the cows, she would say something nice to him, like, "You looked right good out there handlin' them big ol' horses today!"

Rob would think things such as, *Lord, them two girls is different as ice and fire!* and, *That Annie Leese can leave a feller colt as a stone, but just lookin' at li'l Sally can sure git man's sap to runnin'.*

Come Sunday, breakfast saw jam or honey, and buckwheat pancakes added to the table as a treat. Eleanor was clearing the dishes when Rob stood to leave the table.

"Rob, do you ever attend church?" she asked.

"No'um. I hain't never been to church but just the one time. It wahr up'par to Elkton with Mister Jack and Miz Lila."

"Well, did you like church, Rob? Do you think you might want to go again?"

"No'um, I reckon not. Miz Lila done said them Meth'dists is a li'l high falutin' fer me. She done said I orter git on to the Baptist church, but I hain't never gone."

"But wouldn't you like to believe in Jesus, Rob?"

"Wahl, I don't actual know nothin' about Jesus, exceptin' what you done tolt me, but I believes in the Lord. Might be I could believe in Jesus–iffen he believes in me."

"Of course Jesus believes in you. He loves you, Rob," she said sincerely. "The Harmans go to a very nice Baptist church, and I'm sure they would be very happy to take you with them if you wanted to go."

"Wahl, I hain't fer sure I wants to go to church, Miz Eleanor."

THE TALE OF A WOODS COLT

"Well, if you change your mind, I'll speak to Eliza Harman for you, Rob."

Jonas had been sitting at the table, listening quietly. He rose as Rob wandered off. "Vell, I tink venn he Yesus need, den he Yesus find," he said.

TWENTY-FOUR

Sally

The Schanks departed for church, leaving Rob sitting on the side porch steps and feeling quite alone. He got up and strolled down toward the river. Passing within hailing distance of the Harman home, he saw the family boarding their wagon for the drive to the Baptist church.

He paused to watch and was spotted by Sally, who waved a hand high and let out a "Hello Rob!" which, in that mere moment, shaved an edge off his aloneness. He waved back, and then stood watching the cloud of dust close in behind the wagon as it slowly disappeared down the river road.

Rob felt comfortable with his situation at the Schank farm, but he wondered what his future held. Were his prospects leaving him behind and vanishing into the swirling dust like the Harmans' wagon? Or would the new things he'd learned lead him to a bright and promising life? He spent the afternoon ambling along the shady riverbank in the sylvan solitude, tossing stones at the occasional tree branch drifting by in the slow current.

He saw a floating limb that looked like it had a hand reaching out of the water; he called out to it as it drifted along near shore. "Whar about's you goin' to, ol' branch?!" He paced it and called again. "You don't know or you just hain't sayin'?!" He stopped, letting the water carry the limb on its way. *Ol' branch, he's just like me*, he thought. *"Goin' somewhar but don't got nary idea whar to.*

The hot and heavy early June air imbued the barn with a stinking miasma, a rank blend of wafting animal odors—pungent sweat, sour urine and fetid dung. Rob was finishing his day at the stables, in the routine he'd formed during his month on the farm, when in plodded the cows with only one milkmaid behind them.

"Whar's yer friend?" he inquired, as Sally drew near.

"She took sick. I'm milkin' alone this evenin'," said Sally as she clamped the animals into their stanchions.

"How abouts I help you git it done," he offered.

"You can if you want," she said over her shoulder, as she scooped a bucket of feed from the bin. "If you can milk."

"Sure I can milk!" He grabbed the other bucket and dug out a measure of the dry grain. "Now, I most likely cain't milk *fast* as you does but I can milk," he said, qualifying his claim, as they shook the feed grain out into the trough in front of each hungry cow's nose.

"Then you take them three there and I'll take these here five," she said, handing him a milk pail and a wash bucket before plopping herself down on a squat three-legged stool.

Sally washed off the cow's udder, held the milk pail between her knees and took hold of two of the four teets. The squeeze of her practiced hands shot the milk splashing into the pail in quick alternating bursts.

Rob squatted down on the other stool and went to work, squeezing out long lines of milk and thinking, *Them Schanks is powerful good folks and all, but you cain't hardly git to know 'em. Arle, he hain't bad to work fer but he don't never say too much of nothin'. Li'l Sally h'yar's most surely the friendliest one on the place.*

Rob followed Sally's lead in carrying each filled pail to a closet just outside the milking parlor, where they emptied their pails into a pair of ten gallon milk cans that went daily to the cheese factory.

He was pouring his third pail just as she lugged in her fifth. The tight space was close. Her sweaty warmth and the hint of her scent quickened his breath. "H'yar, let me git it," he offered, reaching for her pail, his arm just brushing hers. A sudden tingling current skittered through him, as he poured out the milk.

Holding the empty pail, he turned to see her looking up at him, smiling coyly. His instinct was to set the pail aside and savor the moment, but then an alarm in his head set off an anxiety, breaking the spell.

"We's best be a-gittin' the last of it," he said uneasily, tappng the lids into place on the cans.

Sally emptied the udder of her last cow and then, after pouring some eagerly awaited milk into the pans of the barn cats, helped Rob finish his last cow by milking from the opposite side. The last two pails of evening milk were kept for home use. They turned the cows back out to pasture and returned to fetch their full pails. She looked up at him.

"Thank you, Rob, for helpin' me with the milkin'," she said in her perky way.

"Wahrn't nothin' Miss Sally," he said modestly, picking up his pail. Calling her Miss put a space between them, keeping a safe distance. She let her pail sit, seeming to want to linger and chat, which made him nervous. He looked away.

"Well Rob, you can help me any ol' time at all," she said warmly, lifting her pail. They went out into the bright evening sun and parted for home.

'Lordy Lord, she just like Mary Jane, thought Rob, feeling at once both excited and apprehensive. As he toted the fresh milk up to the house, his memory flashed back to little more than a year before, and to how badly it had ended with Mary Jane. He'd put that episode firmly behind him, and he didn't want to repeat it.

Sunday afternoon found Rob lolling on the riverbank again, sitting on a sandy patch with his back leaned against a washed up log, watching the water drift slowly by. He always avoided Sunday dinner at the house on account of all the church and bible talk at the table. Instead, before the Schanks returned from church, he would scrounge up a bit of leftover food to nibble alone, here in the sanctity of the riverbank.

Cattle stood in river water to their knees, finding some relief from the early heat wave. Broad and shallow, the Shenandoah was the largest river Rob had ever seen. Like his own life, it was flowing to somewhere but he had no idea where, so he deemed it a friend and fellow traveler.

His solitude was broken by the loud whooping and yelping of young boys coming his way. In a minute, three boisterous youngsters broke through the weeds, and came to an abrupt standstill when they spied Rob propped against the log in front of them. They stared at him for a few seconds, until a figure emerged from the foliage behind them. It was Sally.

"Why Rob! I might have knowed I'd find you down here on such a hot evenin'!" she exclaimed.

The boys looked to her for an explanation.

"Boys, this here is Rob. He's the new man been workin' with Daddy and Mister Jonas." She looked at Rob. "These are my li'l brothers. I bring 'em down here to get in the water on hot evenin's."

Reassured, the three lads dashed and splashed exuberantly into the river, splattering as much as possible onto one another in their high-spirited antics. The sluggish summer current reached only to the little six-year-old's waist, and so didn't threaten or diminish their frolicking.

Sally plopped herself down cross-legged on the sand next to Rob, where she could keep an eye on her charges.

"Can you swim, Rob?"

"Sartainly not," he said forthrightly, his eyes drawn to hers. "They hain't got no deep water whar I comes from. Hain't nobody thar can swim and hardy none ever gits in the water atall. Most of 'em's a-fear't of the water," he said, a pleasant warmth coming over him.

"Well, I can't swim and neither can them three," she admitted, tossing her head toward the splashing trio. "But the river right along this stretch ain't got no deep holes in it, so they can't drown or nothin'." She gave herself half a moment and then looked at him intently.

"Rob, how come you don't go to church Sundays?"

"Wahl, it hain't hardly in me to go to church, I reckon," he confessed, turning his gaze to the river.

"You ever go to church? Even once?"

"I did go once't, with Mister Jack and Miz Lila up'par to Elkton. But them church folks wahr Meth'dists and I didn't git on with 'em too good. Miz Lila, she done tolt me I best be a-gittin' down to the Baptist church but I hain't gone yet."

"We all go to a Baptist church. You ought to come on with us Sunday, Rob."

"Wahl, I hain't much fer church goin'."

"Well, you just ain't goin' to get saved unless you go to church, Rob," she warned. "Don't you want to be saved?"

"Wahl, I hain't fer sure I actual needs to be saved."

"Course you need to be saved!" she exclaimed.

"Why I need to be saved?"

"Rob, everybody needs to be saved."

"How I'm gon' git saved?" he asked, looking back at her questioningly.

"It's easy. You just accept Jesus to be your personal Lord and Savior."

Iffen it hain't no more'n that to it, I might orter go ahead and git saved, he thought, and then asked, "Can I git saved right h'yar right now?"

"Well, no. You have to get saved in church with a preacher," she said. "You stand up and you walk forward and say you accept Christ as your Lord and Savior and then you get baptized. And then you have to go to church regular, of course."

"What's Christ?"

"Christ is *Jesus*, Rob. His first name is *Jesus* and his last name is *Christ*. Lord, you don't know *nothin'* about religion, do you?"

"Hardy nothin', I reckon," he said, and then ventured another question about something that had him worried. "Ary them Romans around h'yar, Miss Sally?"

"Romans?" She wrinkled her nose and tilted her head quizzically.

'Miz Eleanor, she tolt me them Romans done kilt Jesus just fer larnin' people."

Sally still looked baffled.

"Wish't it thought me to ask her about what Romans looks like," he said with concern. "I sure don't want no truck with none of 'em."

"Ohhh!" It dawned on her. "*Them* Romans! That was in the Holy Land, Rob. It's very far away—way over beyond the other side of Europe. So don't you worry none."

"You ever see'd ary Romans?"

"No. Ain't none of them around here," she assured. "And that was anyhow a very long time ago. Almost two thousand years."

Two thousand was beyond Rob's ken, but it sounded reassuring.

"Rob, do you know what year this is?"

He looked away, pausing long enough to expose some more of his ignorance.

"Hain't fer sure," he uttered to the air. Then he looked back at her. "I just knows the seven days and the twelve months. Hain't it always just *this* yahr?"

"Yes, of course its always this year, but each year has a number."

This aroused his interest.

"This year is eighteen-ninety-six. And it all began with Jesus, Rob. Jesus was born and that was the first year."

"Wahrn't they no yahrs atall afore Jesus wahr born't?"

"Sure there were years before, but it means it's been *eighteen hundred and ninety six years* since Jesus was born."

He turned it over in his mind. He visualized ten piles of ten and tried to imagine what eighteen of *those* piles looked like.

"That thar's right many yahrs," he agreed.

"And they crucified Jesus when he was just thirty—accordin' to the Sunday school teacher, anyhow," she stated. "So, you see, Rob, them bad ol' Romans is long gone—hundreds and hundreds of years ago."

He was relieved to learn this.

"And it all...," she started to say.

"Crucified?" he questioned, cutting her off.

"It's how they killed Jesus," she said, in a hushed and serious tone.

He leaned toward her. "How they actual done it?" he asked, in a low voice.

"Oh, it was *horrible*, Rob. They hung him up on a big ol' wood cross...," she held up her fingers in a cross, "with *nails* hammered through his hands and feet. And then they *stabbed* him in his belly with a sword." Her eyes welled with tears.

She composed herself. "He died on the cross for you and me and for everyone," she said. "And that's why you see all them crosses in churches and everywhere."

Rob had seen crosses, and it now pleased him to know their meaning.

"But Jesus rose from the grave, and it was the beginnin' of religion—baptizin' and all that," she explained. "Jesus himself was baptized, you know."

"What's babtizin'?" he asked curiously.

She smiled, as if glad he finally was showing interest in religion.

"Baptizin' is when the preacher puts you in a big ol' tank of water and pushes your head under backwards, and then he talks to the Lord, and he tells the Lord all about how you give yourself to Jesus and everything; then he asks the Lord to forgive all your sins in the name of the Father and of the Son and of the Holy Spirit, and after that he goes on some more and asks the Lord to accept you into the Kingdom of God, and then he pulls your head up and, right there, you been baptized and all your sins is washed away—as long as you pray regular and ask forgiveness for your new sins."

Rob thought *'Lord! With all that tellin' and askin', I might git drownded afore I gits saved!'* Then he said, "Wahl, I don't know nothin' about no sins."

"Sins is all the bad things you done, Rob. But the Lord will forgive you if you ask in prayer, once you been saved and baptized, of course."

Rob thought it over. He could see she was surprised at his ignorance of important and elementary knowledge, and now there was the matter of sinning.

"I hain't done no bad thangs, or hardly none."

"Course you have!" she countered. "Ain't just you. Everyone's a sinner, Rob. Why, most everything you do is sinnin', some way or another. Just thinkin' things can be sinnin'."

"Wahl, I hain't fer sure I wants to be saved, Miss Sally."

"Listen to me, Rob." She looked him straight in the eye. "If you get saved then you go up to Heaven when you die, to be with the Lord in everlastin' bliss. But if you *ain't* been saved, you go down to hell to be with the devil in eternal damnation."

He turned his gaze toward the river.

"I don't know nothin' about no heaven and hay'll," he said. He also didn't understand "everlastin' bliss" or "eternal damnation," but he felt no need to inquire, being as how he didn't feel destined for either.

Her face showed alarm at his complacency about such a serious matter, as though he didn't recognize the great danger he was in.

"I can see you *don't* but *surely* you don't want to go to *hell*, Rob. Do you want to burn in the fires of pain and sufferin' for all eternity?" she asked incredulously. "I sure *hope* you don't."

"Miz Eleanor, she done tolt me I don't need to git saved, long as I follers Jesus," said he. "And she hain't said nary a thang about no fires of hay'll."

"That's because they's *Mennonites*, Rob. Mennonites is different. They don't *need* to get saved because they don't *believe* in gettin' saved."

"What's Mennonites?" His curiosity was aroused.

"It's a religion, like Baptists and Methodists, exceptin' it ain't the same. They got different beliefs."

"Miz Eleanor, she fer sure believe in the Lord and Jesus. She done tolt me so her ownself," he asserted.

"*Course* they believe in Jesus! What religion *don't* believe in Jesus?!" she said, sounding a tad exasperated. But she went on. "The Mennonites is a little like Baptists, because they don't baptize no one until they's mostly growed up, but they's different because they don't believe in nowhere near as much sinnin' and such, so they don't need actual savin'. They believe they're saved just by followin' the teachin's of Jesus."

Rob hoped Sally wouldn't get discouraged with him over the extensive religious instruction she evidently believed he desperately needed.

"And most Mennonites can speak German," she said.

"What's Jarmin?"

Sally regained her patience. "It's a foreign language, Rob, like they speak over in Europe. Miz Eleanor, she told Mama their people came from Germany more'n a hundred fifty years ago, but they's still speakin' German.

Sally went on. "Miz Eleanor, she growed up around here speakin' German in the house and English in school, so she talks regular," she said. "But Mister Jonas, he growed up way up in Pennsylvania and went to the Mennonite school. Miz Eleanor told Mama he didn't hardly speak no English until he come down here about twenty years ago. That's why he talks funny and kind of backwards."

She paused and looked at him, as if waiting for more questions.

Rob now knew why he couldn't understand Jonas and Eleanor's conversation and why Jonas spoke strangely. But he wanted to know more. He didn't know where Europe, Germany and Pennsylvania were. But he was curious about something else.

"What's Anglish?"

"*What?* Rob! English is what *we* speak, silly!"

"Oh," he grunted. He was uncomfortably confronting his own ignorance again. "Wahl then, say somethin' in Jarmin."

"I can't say nothin' in German. It's a foreign language that nobody around here learns, except for the Mennonites. Rob, why don't you come to church with us next Sunday? Mama and Daddy's all the time trying to get new people in the church."

"Wahl, I don't know," he muttered vacantly, pinching his lower lip as his mind dwelt on something else. Then he looked into her eyes and spoke.

"Uh, Miss Sally, I cain't read or write atall," he said to her, and then looked down, feeling embarrassed. "I cain't read the Bible or nothin', and I don't know no church songs, no how."

She was quiet for a minute.

"Oh well, that don't make no difference, Rob. You can just listen, and you'll learn the prayers and hymns. There's another one or two of 'em in church that can't read neither. Pastor Goochnor, he don't care if you can't read, long as you come and pray—and leave a li'l money behind."

"I don't rightly know nothin' about prayin'," he admitted. "How am I gon' pray?"

"Prayin's easy, Rob. You just look down, close your eyes and talk to the Lord."

"My pappy talks to the Lord afore eatin'," he said. "That the same as prayin'?"

She paused for a moment.

"Well, table grace is like prayin', but it's just givin' thanks for the food and such," she explained, making a careful distinction. "Actual prayin' is askin' the Lord to forgive your sins or to get you well, or to straight out ask for somethin' you need, and all like that," she said, on a note of satisfaction with her answer.

Rob had expected Sally to react more strongly to his revelation, and he felt relieved that she didn't seem too surprised to know he was illiterate. He was suddenly much more comfortable in her presence. "What's hymns?" he wanted to know next.

"Hymns is the church songs. They're mostly about sinnin', savin', prayin' and goin' to heaven," she said. "And praisin' the Lord, of course."

"Can you sang me one, Sally?"

"Sure I can." She thought a moment. "Here's a good one for right here where we's at now. It's called *Shall We Gather at the River.*"

She started in.

"Shall we gather at the river, where bright angel feet have trod,
With its crystal tide forever, flowing by the throne of God.

"Yes we'll gather at the river, the beautiful the beautiful river,
Gather with the saints at the river that flows by the throne of God.

"On the margin of the river, washing up its silver spray,
We will walk and worship ever, all the happy golden day.

"Yes we'll gather at the river, the beautiful the beautiful river,
Gather with the saints at the river that flows by the throne of God."

Rob's eyes were closed and he was at peace, soothed by her mellow voice and the narcotic melody. When she finished, he straightened his head and opened his eyes to meet hers.

"You sang so perty, Sally," he said quietly. "Wish't I could sang that good."

"Come to church with us Sunday, Rob," she urged. "And learn to sing hymns."

He was tempted, but equivocated. "Wahl, reckon I best be a-thinkin' on it a spell."

Sally was quiet, as if seeing she wasn't going to close the sale, and contemplating calling it a day. "Well, guess I best be gettin' back up to the house," she announced, rising and brushing the sand off her bottom. She turned toward the river.

"You boys get out of the water now!" she yelled. "Time to get up to the house!"

THE TALE OF A WOODS COLT

The three dripping youngsters stumbled out and disappeared through the brush with Sally on their heels, leaving Rob alone again at his riverbank refuge.

The week passed with Rob working the fields, except for the rainy day when he joined Earle in the small blacksmith shop below the barn. Though a reserved man, Earle seemed pleased to mentor Rob in the farming arts. He was surprised to see the young mountaineer's able hand with the blacksmith's tools.

"Where'd you learn your smithin', boy?"

"Aw, I done work some with Mister Lucas, up'par to Elkton," said Rob.

"I see you got you a right good hand on the forge. Ol' Cartwright must have learned you right smart," said Earle approvingly. "Well, I'll learn you a mite more. Can you shoe a horse, boy?"

"Nosir, I hain't never larn't the shoein'."

"Them Belgians'll need shod again in a couple months. You'll get a chance to see how it's done," promised Earle. The day passed with the two of them heating the iron and hammering out the cherry-red metal into various repair parts and pieces for the farm.

TWENTY-FIVE
Rousing Mind and Body

The next Sunday, Rob retreated to his riverbank haven, but not before lingering in the safety of his room after breakfast, to let the families get off to church before he ventured out. He knew Eleanor and Sally were well intentioned, but he didn't want to find himself having to ward off their exhortations at the very moment of departing for church.

Once they were all gone, he slipped into the kitchen and helped himself to a crust of black bread and a hunk of hard cheese. He made his way down to the river, where he idled away the morning hours in his own company.

He found a place on the bank to sit and eat his simple fare. Watching the current flow by, he bit off hunks of course bread, gnawed the dense cheese and indulged some idle river thoughts.

"You just a-goin' all the time ol' feller," he said to the water. "You ever git yerself to somewhar?" he asked the silent river—and himself.

By late afternoon, he was sitting on his hands on the driftwood log, thinking about nothing in particular, when Sally and the boys popped through the bushes.

"Sally!" he called with a smile. He was glad to see her.

"Missed you in church this mornin'," she said breezily, as she swung her leg over and straddled the log to face Rob. The squealing boys splattered out into the cool water.

"You'd have liked the hymns."

"Wahl, I hain't up to gittin' myself in to church just yet," he said, in a self-deprecating way.

Then his heart spoke for itself.

"Sally, this right h'yar's the onliest church I'm a-needin', just settin' down h'yar to the river with you, and all," he said, surprising himself with his own forthrightness. But right away he regretted blurting out his feelings, for he feared she'd be offended by his disregard for religion.

His sudden frankness seemed to take her aback, dissolving her light and airy mood. But then her eyes softened and an angelic smile spread across her face.

"Rob, that's the sweetest thing anyone ever said to me," she said, looking warmly into his eyes.

His eyes embraced hers, but he worried that she might dismiss him as an unrepentant bumpkin. He desperately wished he knew how she saw him.

"Sally, I knows that I hain't got no eddication and all but…"

"Rob, I weren't one bit surprised last Sunday when you said you can't read and write. Mountain people can't, mostly. Everyone knows that. And they know you're a mountain man soon as you open your mouth," she said pointedly. "But you're way smarter than lot of folks that *can* read and write. You can learn to read but you need to learn to talk regular, too."

"I know I don't talk the same as valley folks, but what's actual wrong with my talkin'?" he asked, sensing she might be moved to help free him from his stigma and isolation.

"Well, to begin with, you put all those aitches on the front of words."

"What's aitches?"

"It's the letter *h*. It's like *heh, heh*. You say all these words with aitches that don't have no aitch in 'em."

"What words you talkin' about, Sally?"

"Well, like you all the time sayin' *hain't*. The actual word, Rob, is *ain't*. Say *ain't*, now," she told him, leaning his way with an expectant look on her face. A focused vitality had entered the dialogue. The sentimental moment had become a class, and the driftwood log was the classroom.

"*Ain't*," said he.

"There now. I knowed you could do it," she said, straightening herself and swaying a bit on the log. "Now next thing, you're all the time sayin' *ahr* when it should be *air*." She leaned closer to him. "Don't say *whar* and *thar*, Rob. The words is *where* and *there*."

"And here's another one," she said, leaning closer. "You always say *h'yar*. You got *yar* instead of *ere*. The word is *here*. Now say *where, there* and *here* for me," she demanded, looking straight into his eyes.

"*Where, there* and uh, uh, *here*," he repeated, distracted by her closeness.

"See! Ain't nothin' *to* it!" she exclaimed, throwing her body back and her palms into the air. You just got to learn to talk different. You can do it, Rob. I know you can."

"Here's another one. Don't say *wahr*, say *were*. And then there's *entahr*. It"s *entire*, Rob. Say *were* and *entire* for me.

"*Were* and *entire*. Sally, I'm a-hopin' you ain't gittin' tahred of me."

There's another one. It's not *tahred*, Rob. Say *tired*. And no, I ain't gettin' tired of you." She continued presenting corrections, and he continued repeating them.

Rob could see that Sally was on to something. If he could just sound less like a mountaineer, people might then think a little better of him. And he especially wanted Sally to think better of him. *She must think somethin' of me, or she'd not took no trouble to larn me,* he thought. He didn't want to let her down.

"Sally, I'm oblige to you fer larnin' me to talk more proper," he said, with sincere appreciation. He tried to ignore the tingling in his body.

"Well, I'm happy to learn you, Rob, but say *learnin'*, not *larnin'*; I'm *learnin'* you to talk proper. Say it, now. Say *learnin'*," she instructed, leaning toward him to where he could feel her steamy warmth radiating through the thin shift she wore.

"L-l-learnin'," he stuttered.

He didn't dare show the stimulation and excitement he was feeling. Her bare legs straddling the log, and her lithesome animation propelled him into a sensuous distraction. His head began to swirl, clouding his mental focus with carnal sensations, and he started to fumble his answers.

'Well, that's about enough school for today," she said, seeing that his attention span for elocution class was played out. "How about we meet here next Sunday, if it ain't rainin'? You goin' to be here, Rob?"

"Yass indeed. I most surely will, Sally!"

"Good, but don't say *yass* any more, Rob. Say *yes*. Say it now."

"Yes, Sally."

She slid off the log and stepped to the water's edge.

"Come on now! Let's get on up to the house!"

The boys waded ashore and the four young Harmans disappeared through the underbrush, leaving Rob sitting on his driftwood, dizzy with delight.

The next Sunday afternoon was sultry. Rob and Sally sat facing each other, cross-legged on the sand.

"Now Rob, say the first three words from last Sunday."

"Uh, *ain't...where* and uh, uh...I cain't remember."

"It started with *h* like *heh, heh,*" she prompted.

"Uh, *h'yar*, I means *here*," he said, quickly correcting himself.

"Now Rob, I don't want to hear you sayin' *h'yar* and *whar* and *hain't* no more," she admonished, and then she more or less repeated the previous exercise. "And don't say *wahr* and *larn*, neither." Then she asked, "Rob, did you ever go to school at all?"

"Uh, wahl...," he hesitated. *Lord, she a perty li'l thang,* he thought.

"Now right there's another one! Say *well*, Rob. Don't say *wahl*, say *well*. Say it."

"*Way'll*," he uttered. He couldn't keep his eyes off her. Her firm bosom, the hint of her nipples, and her barely covered crossed legs scrambled his thinking.

"No, Rob It's *well*. Say *well*."

"Way'll," he repeated. *Wish't I could holt her hand*, he thought, *or holt her...*

"No. It's *well*, Rob. *W-eh-ll*."

"Way-e'll," he uttered.

"Alright, close enough. Now, back to goin' to school. Did you never go to school?"

"I done gone to school once't, fer about a week is all. I done larn't, uh, learn't a piece of the alfeebet and some numbers."

"Say the alphabet for me."

"A, b, c....d....e....uh,..g....I cain't remember no more, Sally."

"Well, that ain't much, Rob. Can't do nothin' with that li'l bit. Can you count?"

"One, two, three, four, five..." he got up to thirty-seven on the way to a hundred.

"That's good. How about four plus five. Add five to four, Rob."

He tapped his fingers, "Nine."

"How about eight minus three. Subtract three from eight."

His fingers found the answer. "Five."

"Good, Rob! Whats seven times eight, now."

"I don't know nothin' about no times," he admitted, revealing the limit of his numeracy.

"Well, you got enough numbers there for farmin' and to mind your money, but it still ain't much. You ought to know more, Rob, and you goin' to have to learn some readin' and writin'."

"I reckon you done gone to school right smart. Can you larn me, Sally?" he asked sincerely.

"I finished school a few years ago," she said, referring to the usual six years of primary education. "And yes, I can learn you if you want to learn, Rob. But there you go again. Stop sayin' *larn*. It's *learn*, remember?"

"How's about right h'ya.., right here, ever Sunday, Sally?"

She scissor-legged herself up, called the boys in, and looked down at him.

"Alright, then. Every Sunday, long as you remember what I learn you."

They left, leaving Rob alone on the riverbank. He felt the glow of hope for himself. Now he could enjoy Sally's company and get a little education to boot. Maybe, he mused, somehow Sally could someday look up to him and admire him as a man, rather than down at him as a remedial pupil.

The following Sunday found Rob shedding a little more of his mountain accent, resisting the alphabet but learning simple multiplication. But he retained only a little of his lesson, devoting more of his attention to Sally than to her tutoring. He wanted to learn and to please her, but his hungry body interfered and distracted him. His mind wandered but his eyes stayed fixed on her.

"Now then, what letter comes after *l* Rob?"

He pondered and then guessed, " *n* ?"

"No. It's *m*."

"Sally, you gots ary brothers besides them three there?"

"Nope. Just the three brothers, but I got a li'l sister."

"Why ain't she down here?"

"She mostly stays in the house. She's afflicted. Mama and me takes care of her. Let me hear you say the alphabet up to *m*."

He started in, "*A, b, c, d, e, f, g, h, i, k, l, m*." She used a stick to write the letters in the sand for him to see.

"You left out *j*. It goes right here," she said, scratching a *j* into the sand. "Now, what's two times two, two times three and three times three?"

"Uh, four, six and uh,uh..eight?" His mind was on something else.

"Four is right and six is right but three times three is nine, Rob."

"Sally, you talkin' to ary mans atall?"

"Talkin'? I ain't seein' no one, if that's what you mean. Say *any*, not *ary*, Rob."

Her correction went right past him. He was chaffing under a stigma of inferiority, tempered only by the patience she showed and evident satisfaction that she took in trying to teach him.

"Rob?" she said, getting his attention back. "Don't say *ary*. That's old time talk. Say *any*. Now say *any ol' time at all*."

"Any ol' time atall."

"Good. Now that's enough for today." In a blink, she and the boys were gone.

The next Sunday lesson found them on their knees beside the log, with Sally trying to teach Rob to write the letters he'd memorized. She handed him the stick and instructed, "write *a*, *b*, and *c*."

He shifted onto his knees and, leaning forward a bit, scratched three crudely formed letters in the sand.

"No, you wrote *d*, not *b*, Rob," she said, pointing to his second letter. She smoothed the sand and took the stick. "*b* is like this."

"Next," she continued, "remember how I said every letter has a small and a big?"

He nodded.

"This here's the small *a*, *b*, and *c*. Now I'm goin' to show you how to write the big *A*, *B*, and *C*."

She handed him the stick and slid closer to him, shoulder-to-shoulder on the warm sand. She wrapped her arm inside his and clasped her hand onto his stick hand, sending a titillating ripple coursing through him. He tried to conceal a small gasp. Sweat beaded on his brow. His craving body yearned to embrace her.

"I'll help you do it, now," she said, leaning into him a little.

His addled mind paid little attention to her words. Her touch and scent sent a rush of pleasuring sensations through him.

Her hand guided the stick where he pressed the tip into the sand. "*A*....*B*....*C*," she called off, as warm waves of desire swept over him.

"There now," she declared, jumping to her feet. "I want you to remember them three big letters, Rob." She turned toward the water.

"Time to get on home, boys!"

"Cain't you stay just a li'l longer, Sally?" pleaded Rob, still crouched on his knees, not yet ready to stand up.

"We got to get back. Mama'll be wonderin' where we's at."

That night Rob drifted into bad dreams in which he reached out to touch her but she was always beyond reach and touch, and the frustration of it forced him awake. He lay fretting until his longing imagination took over and drew her into his tight embrace, the comfort of it allowing him some easy rest.

Sally's aura had invaded Rob's psyche. For the next few days it disturbed his focus by day and stirred him to restless sleep at night. He yearned that she could hold him in esteem and not pity, and would come to see the man and not the rube.

Thursday morning found Rob and Earle out in the wheat field, a broad golden sea of tall grass undulating in the wafting wind, like waves upon water. Sunlight danced on the ripened heads, bulging with seed and tossing in the breeze. The crop was ready for reaping. All the farmers were preparing to harvest their mellow winter wheat, the first grain of the season.

Jonas was a modern farmer and possessed a J.I. Case binder, a machine able to cut and wrap his thirty acres of wheat in three days time, after which he would loan the device to his neighbors. The harvest began with Earle and Rob each swinging a cradle scythe to cut the perimeter swath around the field, making space for the binder horses to walk without trampling the crop. It was most of a morning's hard labor.

Cradling one against each breast, Sally carried down two jugs of cool wellwater to where Rob was rhythmically cutting the wheat under the mid-morning sun, his steel scythe blade slicing the stalks that the wooden arm laid evenly over into neat windrows. Heavy exertion in the hot humid weather demanded frequent refreshment. Fieldwork was always punctuated by morning and afternoon water delivery to slake the sweaty men's thirst.

"Bet you're more than ready for a cool drink there, mister!" she quipped.

"I hope to tell you!" he said, panting. "Yer just in the nick of time thar, er, there, Sally!"

"Ha! I'm goin' to fix your tongue yet, Mister Rob! Here, have a drink," she said, coming closer.

Rob hooked his finger into the loop of a jug and, in a continuous movement, pulled the vessel from its nest against her breast and swung it on to his own raised arm. He wrapped his lips around the mouth of the jug and raised it with his bent elbow, swallowing great gulps, the leakage dribbling off his chin onto his sweat-soaked shirt.

Sally moved on, carrying the other jug to her father at the opposite side of the field. Rob stood still with the water jug dangling from his finger, staring at her supple form receding down the field edge until she turned the corner.

The sight of Sally struck a thirst in him that water could not quench. He sat the jug against the shady side of a fence post and took hold of his scythe, imagining himself passionately embracing her as he swept the blade back and forth in mesmerizing strokes, his pace and pulse increasing until he came face-to-face with....Earle, breaking the hypnotic spell. Panting, Rob paused.

"Good Lord, boy! Slow her down or you won't last out the day!" exclaimed Earle. The two scythers had completed the perimeter swath and had laid out their cut wheat along the field edge. Rob leaned on his scythe handle, catching his breath. Until dinner and then after, the two went about twisting stalks to bind the cut wheat into sheaves, which they set up into shocks along the fence.

Later in the afternoon, Jonas appeared on the pasture path riding the binder seat behind the big horses. "Let's get on up to the corner," said Earle. He and Rob tracked back to the field entrance to meet up with the binder.

Jonas eased the rig onto the wheat field and pulled the team to a halt. "Ya, vee vill two or tree turns around deh field make before deh supper." With that, he set the control levers and flicked the horses forward. The slicing blade and rotating paddles waded into the wheat, with the Belgians plodding along on the cut swath as the machine cut, bundled and bound the crop into sheaves.

Earle and Rob walked behind, grabbing up the sheaves and stacking the bundles into shocks, the small stacks of sheaves set teepee style. They could barely keep up with the binder, allowing no time for Rob's mind to wander.

On they toiled for several days, their labors interrupted only by water breaks and dinner, transforming the expanse of waving golden wheat into a stubble field studded with shocks set in neatly spaced rows to dry for a couple of weeks before threshing.

July rolled around and it was time for one of the farm's biggest days.

"Tomorrow deh machine for deh treshing comes," announced Jonas at the Sunday breakfast table, referring to the large apparatus that flails the wheat plants, separating them into straw, chaff and seed kernels—the precious grain.

Threshing day was always a choreographed drama of heavy exertion and rapid production, with a cast that drew in every able body on the farm, plus the threshing crew and several neighboring farmers. Nearly half of the total labor to produce and harvest the wheat crop was expended in the single day of threshing.

TWENTY-SIX
Threshing Day

Rob heard it before he saw it. He'd come out into the dark after an early breakfast, eager to witness the arrival of the mysterious threshing machine. A faint rhythmic throbbing sound came over the rise and rolled down the lane from the road. It grew louder, a pulsing and pounding racket that echoed off the barn boards.

In the dimness, he first saw puffs of smoke, followed by the appearance of a smoke stack sitting atop the boiler of a traction engine. A hissing steam cylinder cranked a pair of large wheels, their steel cleats clawing the ground as they advanced the machine down the lane. The engine carried two men and pulled a large four-wheeled contraption behind it, from which hung three more men clinging to the sides. A wooden barrel-shaped water wagon trailed behind.

Rob took a reactive step backwards at the loud racket and strange look of the approaching apparatus, curiously eyeing the noisy rig as it chuffed its way down to the flat beside the barnyard. He was watching the threshing crew arrange the outfit for the day's work when Jonas joined him in the yard.

"Come, Rob! Time for deh treshing!"

They quick-timed down past the barn in the first peek of dawn, the sliver of light edging the horizon beyond the river. They approached to where they had left the empty grain wagon and the hayrack wagon, which was piled high with wheat sheaves previously collected. Earle had already hitched draft teams to the two wagons and was standing beside the wooden and steel threshing machine, talking with a man who stood a head higher and was half again as heavy.

The crew uncoupled all three of the wheeled implements, and

used the steam engine to pull the water wagon to a place alongside where the engine would be positioned. They then turned the big engine in a half circle and backed it up to a spot level with the thresher and about seventy-five feet away from it, to distance the steam and sparks from the wheat and straw.

The engine was a prized machine—an 1890 J.I. Case model with a big pulley wheel and a bigger flywheel that kept the sixteen horsepower coming at a steady and even rate. Two workmen went about fitting the long flat drive belt onto the engine and the thresher pulley wheels. The ten-inch wide belt was crossed in the middle in a very long figure eight, to help keep it on the pulleys and to run the thresher mechanism in the right direction.

"Goot morning, Bob!" said Jonas to the big man, with a hearty handshake.

"Mornin' Jonas. Lookin' like a decent day if it don't go to stormin' this evenin'," said Bob, his permanently worried eyes looking out from under the brim of his big straw hat to scan the morning sky.

"Ya Bob, for deh vetter I prayed already," said Jonas, momentarily casting his eyes skyward. "Bob, diss is Rob—deh new man on deh farm."

Bob extended his hand, "I'm Bob Thurston. They all call me Big Bob," he said, with a chuckle punctuating his booming voice.

Rob reached out and was clasped by the biggest, meatiest hand he'd ever seen. "How do, Mister Bob," he said, his knuckles crinkling under the tight squeeze.

"I do right good, long as the weather holds out," said Bob, in a deep baritone. "You ready for a day of hard work, boy?" he asked, or warned, looking intently out under his bushy eyebrows and still clamping Rob's hand in a vise grip.

"Yessir, Mister Bob. I'm a hart workin' man," said Rob, his steady eyes meeting the big man's gaze, as his locked hand was released.

"Ah, goot! Deh neighbors coming!" Jonas pointed to a trio of hayrack wagons rolling over the rise in the lane, each carrying two men and pulled by stout workhorses—a pair of gray Percherons in front, a team of black Shires drawing the next wagon, and two handsome Clydesdales pulling the rear one.

Threshing was a cooperative enterprise. No single farm needed or could afford a threshing machine. Thurston was a custom thresher, taking his rig and crew from farm to farm, usually spending a day at each. He charged twenty-five dollars for the day, so the plan was always to run as many sheaves through the machine and to bag as much grain as possible. The farmers all traded labor to make the most of threshing day.

Jonas stepped over to dispatch his farmer friends out into the field to gather in the wheat. Up on the engine, Thurston's engineer, seeing that the entire company had assembled, turned to stoke his firebox and build up a full head of steam. He eased the engine backward to pull slack from the drive belt, and then set the brake.

Threshing was about to begin. The eight farmers would use four hayrack wagons to collect the sheaves and shuttle them from field to thresher, where a two-man crew would help feed them continuously into the open-topped bundle feeder. A third man would bag the stream of kernels at the grain chute and sew up the sacks. The engineer had to devote his full attention to stoking, watering and managing the steam engine. Big Bob's job was to oversee the operation and fill in wherever needed.

Jonas assigned Rob the young man's work, the heavy lifting of loading the full sacks onto the grain wagon and carting them fifty at a time to the barn granary.

In the minutes it took to bring the first wagon loaded with sheaves alongside the thresher, the throbbing engine had spooled itself up to full running speed. The engineer eased a lever back to engage the big pulley wheel, setting the drive belt in motion and bringing the thresher to life. The engine, as if a straining and grunting animal, hissed and groaned, heaving into its task of driving an implement that had revolutionized grain farming.[9] Big Bob's thresher was a modern machine, a big Dixie model made by the Aultman & Taylor Company.

The entire apparatus cranked up to full uproar, blaring out a cacophonous din of diverse clatter, with its huffing engine, flapping belt, spinning driveshafts, whirring fan, whining cylinder, clanking gear chains and flailing innards.

Rob stood watching in fascination. *Lord!* he thought. *A man best have his head screwed on proper around this here thrasher thang, or he sure enough gon' git it knocked off!* The equipment had no safety features. The monster was perfectly willing to bite off a careless hand or, for that matter, eat a man whole.

"Come Rob!" called Jonas, breaking Rob's spell and waving him up onto one of the piled-high wagons to join Earle, who was already passing wheat bundles to the crewmen who stuffed them into the greedy maw of the feeder.

The hungry brute instantly began blasting out a great arc of straw, blowing it upward where it then arched downwind to form a growing pile on the open earth. The beast ejected the chaff from an orifice in its belly, spewing the waste out onto the ground. The precious wheat kernels spilled into the grain chute and flowed into a burlap sack. It was a process of feeding, separating, excreting and collecting.

The first wagon was soon emptied and the other newly filled ones were coming in. Rob hopped down and quickly led the Belgians to pull the empty grain wagon to the bagging station, positioning it to collect the full sacks of grain. He scooted back around to join Jonas and Earle on the empty hayrack wagon rolling toward the field, to help load sheaves while a steady stream of ripe grain filled the first bags.

So went the action, punctuated only by boys bringing jugs of cool water and re-filling empties, keeping a jug handy to each work station and wagon. The men slaked their thirst with frequent quick gulps, for

---

9 Modern machinery made possible the production of one hundred bushels (6000 lbs.) of wheat with a total of fifty hours labor in 1896. Sixty years earlier it took three hundred hours labor. By the end of the twentieth century, one hundred bushels was produced with less than three hours labor.

there were no breaks. Production was non-stop.

Men fed the thresher at a furious rate. The sheaves wagons hurried to keep up. Rob bent into the heavy task of hoisting filled sacks onto the grain wagon, and then offloading and stacking them neatly in the granary at the rear of the barn's main floor. His only relief was riding the wagon, driving the horses back and forth between thresher and barn.

Straw and chaff piled up and grain poured into sacks. As the morning matured, the sweat-soaked workmen strained to keep up the pace in the heavy heat under a climbing sun. Jonas and Earle had half emptied a sheaves wagon when, without warning, the noisy rhythm was broken by a loud *Bang!!! Klunk!!*

In an instant, the big thresher's commotion suddenly shuddered to silence. The machine had jerked to a halt, throwing the drive belt off its pulleys and leaving the engineer scrambling to throttle down the howling steam engine that had been suddenly relieved of its load.

Big Bob, his exasperation displayed in his contorted face, stomped around from the far side yelling, "Damnation! Now what the hell?!" The steam engine hissed at idle while he peered into the bowels of the stilled thresher. There, in the greasy shadows, he spotted a broken shear pin on the cylinder hub.

The big man fetched a drift and a hammer from his toolbox and reached both of his beefy paws into the mechanism. All the men had gathered around, wearing worried looks. Bob tap-tap-tapped and then pulled out the broken piece. "There's what broke," he said, turning and holding up the sheared pin.

He turned back, peered in and studied the failure point, then straightened, pivoted and spoke.

"Well, I got another shear pin, but it won't do no good to put it in. The shaft is bound up. It'll just shear off again."

He retrieved a wrench and returned to the inner workings by thrusting both his hands into the body of the machine up to his elbows.

Contorting his arms, he twisted his wrench and banged his hammer on the shaft. "Damn," he muttered. In a bit, he pulled out a couple of greasy metal parts.

"Here's the problem, alright," he declared, turning and holding up the two pieces. "Bushing clamp got cocked on the journal—seized up the shaft," he said to the group.

Bob then studied the parts and talked to himself. "Bolt hole's worn out to one side and the bolt won't hold the clamp on tight or straight."

He sat the bolt and bushing clamp down on a wagon tongue, then turned away and looked down, stroking his chin in contemplation of what to do next.

Unnoticed, Rob stepped to the wagon tongue and went down on one knee to look at the damaged parts. He slid the worn bolt into the deformed clamp hole to see the problem.

While Rob fingered the defective parts, Big Bob turned back and announced to the group, "Well, we're goin' to need another clamp and bolt. Ain't no other way."

He looked at Jonas. "Trouble is, it'll be a day or two gettin' the clamp and I'm promised to a different farm every day," he said in a tone that foretold the real problem. "Reckon we ain't goin' to get no more of your threshin' done, Jonas," he said discouragingly, fully aware of what that meant.

Disaster.

Jonas' face fell. He realized that he would lose more than half his wheat crop—a tremendous setback. He pulled his straw hat off and put his hand to his head, stunned at this stroke of bad luck.

Meanwhile, Rob was on his knees turning the clamp and bolt over in his hands— and in his mind. Then it struck him in an electric jerk. He widened his eyes in revelation. He leaped up and dashed off to the blacksmith shop beyond the barn, where he rummaged through a keg and grabbed a couple of tools.

He trotted back to the thresher, clutching a thick machine bolt, a flat file and a C clamp. All eyes fell on him curiously.

"What you got there, boy?" queried the big man.

"I can fix it, Mister Bob," declared Rob.

Bob and Jonas exchanged skeptical glances, as Rob clamped the new bolt tightly to the wagon tongue.

"This here ain't all that easy to fix, boy," cautioned Bob.

"I knows I can do it, Mister Bob," assured Rob confidently. He began to file furiously on the new bolt, a larger one than the original.

They all stood in silence, offering no other ideas while watching Rob filing metal off the bolt, and holding it against the deformed clamp hole every few minutes. Soon he had custom-shaped that bolt to fit snugly into the irregularly worn clamp hole.

"Give her a try now, Mister Bob," he said hopefully, handing over his handiwork.

Big Bob examined the new bolt and, without a word, fitted it and the clamp back into the machine, while the crew wrapped the thrown drive belt back on the pulley wheels. He turned, wrench in hand, and looked at Rob. "Well, I got her in there."

Rob stepped back and hollered at the engineer, "Start her up!"

The engine man looked to Thurston. "Boss?"

Big Bob nodded and the engineer opened the throttle. The engine spun up to speed, with smoke belching from the stack and steam whooshing from the cylinder. He eased in the drive lever, bringing the thresher alive, to grins and nods all around.

The test, however, would be when the wheat went in and loaded up the mechanism.

The big machine clanked and rattled, clamoring to be fed. Two crewmen quickly climbed up to the thresher feeder. Earle pulled himself up onto the half-full wagon and started passing bundles to them.

Jonas stood motionless, staring at the action with pleading eyes and fingers pinching his cheeks.

Rob held his breath as the bundles were fed in and the straw flew out. Then a stream of grain poured down the chute to the cheers and whoops of the entire company. Rob glanced over his shoulder to see a tear streaking down Jonas' face. The farmer dropped to his knees, clasped his raised hands, lifted his eyes to the sky and uttered something in German.

With his hat in his hand, Big Bob stood watching the action.

Rob turned to see Jonas rise and come straight toward him. The farmer stretched his arms out widely and wrapped Rob in a tight hug that almost squeezed the wind out of him.

"Mein Gott! I yust be Yesus tanking for sending diss miracle, Rob!" he gushed. "You are from deh heaven coming!" raved the overjoyed farmer in a moving expression of gratitude, as he released his young hero.

Thurston, seeing that the fix was holding as the wagon emptied, put his hat on and stepped over to a beaming Rob. The big man grabbed the wizard's arm and whacked him on the back with an enthusiasm that nearly knocked the rest of the air out of him.

"By God, boy, you done it!" he bellowed. "I didn't think you could do it but, God almighty, you got her runnin' again sure enough!" boomed Thurston, grinning ear-to-ear.

"Y-yessir, M-Mister Bob," choked Rob, trying to catch his departed breath.

Even Earle had a word of praise. He swung down off the empty wagon. "You got a right sharp eye for shapin' out the metal there, boy!" he said, with a wink and a nod.

Rob was ecstatic. He glided on air as he returned to his task of loading and moving sacks of wheat, while all the farmers went back to fetching in the sheaves. His feet seemed to barely touch the ground. He had just been rocketed up from ignorant mountaineer to miracle maker.

Back at the house, the dinner table had been set up on the open porch just outside the kitchen. It consisted of several wide planks laid out across sawhorses to form a long table. Threshing day dinner was a marvel of cooking that began at dawn and drew Eliza Harman, Sally, and the Schank girls into Eleanor's kitchen to turn out a feast to be proud of. The fourteen men would be fed first, and then all the women and children would sit second table.

The usual dinner bell couldn't be heard over the threshing racket, so one of the water boys announced dinner by tapping on Big Bob's bare arm. Thurston waved in the wagons, the feeder crew climbed down, and the engineer shut down the steam engine.

The hungry gang trooped up to the house and went directly to the long-handled well pump to clean up and flush a cooling splash of water over their heads. Once freshened, the ravenous men went straight to the table and took a seat on one of the side benches. Their table chatter revolved around Rob's amazing repair job, as the women laid out the food in a copious array of simple but varied and nourishing fare.

"Can't hardly believe he got her runnin' again," said one of the men. "Ain't never seen one of 'em yet what knowed a thing about machinery," said another. "Say what you want, he sure as hell fixed it," said a third.

Jonas took his place at the head of the table and motioned Rob to sit to his right on the first bench. Big Bob placed himself at Jonas' left, with Earle occupying the chair at the opposite end.

The women brought out the last of the platters and bowls, all piled high with heaps of steaming food—crispy fried chicken and thick slabs of ham, roasted potatoes and gravy, beans and peas and squash and fresh greens. There were loaves of warm bread fresh from the oven, and sweet butter and apple butter.

Sweating pitchers sat full of cool water and fresh milk, and there were pies for dessert. The table fairly groaned under a bountiful spread that sent up delicious aromas, setting the hungry workmen to licking their lips greedily.

Jonas knew to keep his table grace short. These men didn't stand on ceremony.

"Tank you Gott for your blessings and your bounty, and for our families and for deh food and and for deh goot vetter, and Gott, tank you special for diss man you are sending for deh saving of deh veet, amen."

The women, standing behind the seated men, raised their bowed heads and looked at each other, baffled. *What* man? God sent *who* to save the wheat? They were already perplexed at the earlier remarks they'd overheard.

The famished workmen dug right in, setting all platters and bowls into orbit around the table. The food flew off onto plates, to be devoured with little etiquette or decorum. The threshing gang had expended more energy than athletes in training. They were feeding, not dining. The women hovered behind, at the ready with refills.

Big Bob clarified the mystery for the women. He cocked his large head and rolled his eyes toward the farmer.

"Jonas, if it'd be me, I'd dang sure hang onto your man Rob, here," he said loudly, in his resonant baritone. "The boy's a dadgum genius is what he is, fixin' my thresher like he did," he said with enthusiasm, while nodding at the grinning Rob. "I don't know what your payin' him—but it ain't enough!" roared Bob, to Jonas's good-natured laugh and affirming nods and chuckles all around the table.

Rob swelled with more pride than he had ever felt. All the praise nearly buoyed him off his seat. In a stroke, he'd been promoted from hard-working junior farm hand to clever and quick-thinking key man. And Big Bob's tribute had instantly shot his stock up in the eyes of the women.

He snuck a glance over at Sally. His delight was doubled to see her beaming back at him. *Now*, he thought most gratifyingly, *fer once't she gon' look to me like a man.* He felt a quiver of excitement each time she reached in a fresh bowl or platter across his shoulder, which was several times during the course of the meal.

Rob breezed through the strenuous work in the shimmering heat of the afternoon, which saw the entire field cleaned out and all the grain threshed. He barely felt the heavy exertion of loading and unloading all of the bagged wheat. By day's end, he had stacked in over five hundred bushels, and had run out of burlap bags. The last eighty bushels were poured loose into the grain wagon, filling the bed with a mound of wheat heaped waist deep.

The sun was laying long shadows by the time Big Bob and his outfit chugged their retreat up the lane. Jonas and Rob rode the last wheat-laden wagon into the barn, parking it on the main floor. The entire crop was in. They hopped down, whereupon Jonas turned and put a hand to Rob's shoulder.

"Tank you," he said quietly, his sincerity glistening in his eyes. "From my heart, tank you." After a heartfelt pause, Jonas turned and headed to the house, leaving Rob to his regular chore of feeding and grooming the draft animals.

He unhitched and walked the Belgians around to the lower rear side, where Earle had already stabled the horse and mule and had gone home. The next two days would be devoted to second-cutting the hayfield and loading it into the barn, filling the haymows.

TWENTY-SEVEN

The Milking Parlor

After a day of loading new-cut hay into the barn, the evening milking hour found Rob just finishing his feeding and grooming when Sally came herding the cows in. She was alone. He came out of the stable just as she approached the feed bin.

"Hello Rob," she said in a charming way, stirring an excitement in him.

He moved toward to her, close enough to touch, but his arms hung at his sides. "I'm right glad to see you, Sally," he said, meeting her lively eyes.

"Analiese burnt her hand right bad on the stove, so I got all the milkin' to myself," she said, with a beguiling look. She leaned a little closer. "So you ready to squeeze some cow tits with me?"

A warm rush ran through him as he reached over and swung open the wooden feed bin cover. "Course I am," he said eagerly, bending into the bin, grasping a grain pail in each hand and digging out full measures into each. He handed her one and they spread the grain along the trough in front of each cow's face.

They found stools, milk pails and wipe rags, and went straight to the task. Rob milked a little faster than the time before, finishing his three cows to her four.

Together they milked the last cow, she on one side and he on the other, the milk streaming from all four teats at once. They could see only each other's lower legs and feet. She mischievously aimed a shot of milk straight onto his ankle.

"Hee, hee, hee, bet I got you good!" she taunted.

"Ha! I can git you back!" he rejoined, squeezing a jet toward her bare foot. She jerked her foot.

"Missed me, you missed me!" she sang, responding with another shot to his other foot.

"Dang!" cried he. "I'll git you sure enough!" He sent a white jet splattering onto her leg.

"Oww!" she cried out in mock pain. He saw her aim another teat his way and grabbed her hand before she squirted.

"I gots you now!" cried he, claiming victory.

"No you ain't!" cried she, wriggling her hand furiously. She aimed her other teat and shot a squirt against his leg. "Got you good, boy!"

At that, they both jumped up to see each other's laughing faces above the cow's back. It was great fun—except for the cow.

Rob was feeling completely at ease as he watched Sally give some milk to the cats. He closely trailed her to the shed where she poured half her bucket into a can, then swapped buckets and poured in half of his, leaving the rest for the houses. She turned to face him in the cramped space.

His pulse quickened in her close presence; her liquid eyes looked up at his expectantly. His hands eased out, his fingers softly touched the back of her upper arms, lightly stroking her smooth skin; her eyes half closed and her hands came around his waist, her breath deepening as she drew herself closer.

He let his lips touch her forehead and his hands slid to her waist, gently pulling her against him. Slowly he nuzzled his face into hers, his eyes closed, her breath warm and caressing, finding her moist lips, absorbed in desire.

Parting lips, he brushed his flushed cheek to hers and playfully nibbled her earlobe. "Hee, hee, eeew, that tickles!" she giggled, turning to pull her ear away and nuzzle her face to his in a kiss.

"I'd like to tickle you right much more, Sally," he half-whispered. "But we's best be gittin' on back."

"I suppose so or they'll be missin' us. I'll be alone again tomorrow, and I can come in earlier."

"I'll be waitin' fer you, Sally."

With that, they each took up a milk pail, stepped out into the shining evening sun, traded wistful looks and parted for separate houses.

Rob's head was filled with Sally through the evening. He paid little mind to what he did or ate, or to what was said. At bedtime he imagined himself passionately embracing her, and she swirled in his dreams. He could barely wait to see her.

The next evening, Rob fidgeted at the grain bin, possessed by anticipation. Finally he heard the lead cow's faintly dong-donging neck bell. After an eternity, the animals plodded into the milking parlor.

"Sally!" He hastened over to the stanchions to help her lock in each cow.

"There you are!" she said cheerily.

His hands fumbled with the cow's neck clamps.

She came closer.

"I see yer glad to see me," she said in an alluringly lowered voice, her tempting eyes reaching up to his. "You ready to squeeze out some milk with me?"

"I been a-waitin' fer you, Sally," he said in a blushing pant, trying to contain his ardor.

"Them cows is waitin' too," she said, suggesting work before play as she stepped past him toward the feed bin.

"Sally!" He turned and followed her straight to the bin where, instead of swinging open the lid, she turned to face him. He nearly fell over her.

"Oh Rob! Oh!..."

Impulsively, he embraced her, kissing her while her arms wrapped around his waist; his fingers fondled her back and drew her against him.

"Reckon we can't wait no longer," she half whispered, her breath husky with desire.

He felt her hand loosening his pants button, then a second and the third. Her uncertain fingers slipped in to touch and caress him.

"Awww Sally. I ain't never...," his voice trailed off as his throbbing surged and ached.

With rivulets of sweat streaking his flushed face, he slid his hands to her hips and behind to her firm bottom; her breath quickened, her fingers loosening and easing his britches to his shins.

Rob felt a rush of embarrassment that did little to temper his lust. He hurried to unbutton her dress, letting it slip to the floor. With his quivering hands at her back, he drew her breasts to touch and lightly brush his rippling muscles; she gave a quick gasp.

He dropped his shorts and her hands slid to his bare hips; she leaned back onto the sloping grain bin, holding him between her spreading thighs. He leaned over her heaving breast, loins pressing gently to her until.... suddenly a rush surged through him, pulsing and pulsing. He let out a long groan.

"Ohh! Oh Rob! Oh my!"

"I'm sorry, Sally! I cain't holt it!" he cried. "I'm sorry! It just done come on me!"

"It's alright. Ain't no need to be sorry." she said, recovering her composure.

"It just come up real sudden," he uttered. "I'm terrible sorry. I cain't hardly..."

"Oh, Rob. Don't be so dang hard on yourself. It ain't no problem, honest it ain't," she said, assuaging his wounded ego. "Now pass me that wash rag."

He reached down behind and picked up the damp cow teat rag from the water bucket and handed it to her, and she gently wiped them both.

"It ain't supposed to be like this," he lamented, pulling up his pants. "It ain't right. I knows a man orter be..."

"Rob, look at me now," she said tenderly, reaching up to nudge his cheek and bring his eyes to hers. "I reckon love ain't always perfect, but I'm feelin' so close to you. Truly I am."

He felt better. She wasn't rejecting him, and she said it was love.

"Was this your first time?" she asked quietly, as she buttoned her dress. She already knew the answer.

"Way'll..." Tucking in his shirt, he hesitated. "Yes. It were my first actual time," he admitted. "I reckon we can have another chance, cain't we Sally?" he asked, reconciling himself to the truth of the moment and trying to put it behind him.

"Course we can, and for sure we will, Rob. You was probably just nervous about maybe somebody walkin' in on us," she said soothingly. "Or maybe it was them cows lookin' at us," she quipped, laughing.

Rob looked over his shoulder at the patient beasts standing in their stanchions, staring at them as if wondering what had happened to delay their routine.

"C'mon. Let's get the milkin' done, now," she said in a back-to-business way.

Rob slept fitfully that night, haunted by self-doubt despite Sally's reassurances. He hoped Analiese's burned hand would keep her out of the barn for a while longer, giving him a chance to overcome his inadequacy and make good on his humiliating misfire.

Feeling he'd fallen short as a man, Rob went through the next day possessed by a driving urgency to prove himself. Little is lost from one failure amongst success. But with no success, fail once and all is lost.

In the barn late that afternoon, Rob paced the aisle, wondering how Sally would be after yesterday's debacle. He waited by the feed bin as she switched in the cows, worried about how she saw him—if she felt any differently from yesterday. A gnawing uncertainty had eaten away his self-confidence. He didn't know what to say or do, so he just slouched against the bin as if it offered some haven from his anxiety.

Sally seemed her usual buoyant self, but she steadied when her gaze met his. She came to him and took his hand.

"Well now, we just can't get you all worked up right away, can we?" she said light-heartedly.

Rob felt his fears subside.

"No, I reckon we cain't," he said, breaking a tentative smile.

"I say we get these cows milked and then we just set and talk a spell. What do you say to that, Mister Rob?"

"Way'll, I was a-thinkin' the very same thang, Sally," he lied, feeling much encouraged. Her welcome words were balm to his self-esteem.

His anxiety melted away as the milk pails filled. Sally's heartening nonchalance had almost relaxed him by the time all the cow udders were empty. He watched with amusement at the barn cats rushing the pans when she poured in their ration.

"Look a-there!" exclaimed Sally excitedly, squatting in front of the pusses lapping at their milk. "Ol' Molly cat done had her kittens!" she cried, looking around at Rob and pointing to a cat whose previous bulging belly had collapsed into freshened teats.

"Yes indeed. I see she done give up a litter," he said cheerfully, pleased that Sally's focus had shifted away from him.

"Where's your babies now, Queenie," teased Sally, leaning toward the cat, which paid her not a whit of attention. "Where you got 'em now, Molly?" she said, waving her fingers in front of the cat's face. The cat just kept lapping up the warm milk as fast as it could. A cat is not easily distracted from its cream.

"She done got 'em hid, is where they is," he said. "Might be we can foller her to the litter, iffen that we wants to see 'em."

Sally stood up. "Bet we can find 'em," she said, with a twinkle in her eye.

"Where we gon' look first?"

"Why, they's bound to be up in the haymow," she said knowingly. "They's all the time hidin' their kittens up there." She tilted her head up and raised her eyes. "C'mon. Let's go up and look for 'em."

He followed her up the ladder rungs to the barn's main floor. They squeezed in alongside the grain wagon to where she led the way up another built-in ladder toward the haymow. Ten feet up, he looked down to the mound of wheat in the wagon bed below.

"Sally!" he called, jumping out above the wagon and startling pigeons to flutter from one end of the cavernous barn to the other. He landed feet first in the loose grain, sinking to his knees. He laughed with excitement and looked up to see her stunned face turn to glee.

"Wee! Ooo!" She leaped with arms for wings, plummeting down and landing next to him, buried to her thighs. With her hands gripping his upper arm, she struggled to pull her legs out of the deep grain and to hold a shaky balance on the shifting kernels.

'C'mon! Let's jump again!" she cried. She wobbled to the wagon edge, got herself on the ladder and clambered back up.

Rob waded out of the loose grain and followed her up, excited by the new thrill of freefalling to a soft landing. He came up alongside her at a higher rung, increasing the drop and speed a notch. Side-by-side and facing the wagon, they clung to the ladder, each with one foot on a rung and a hand on a rail.

"Ready...Jump!" he called, and they leaped out in unison with an "Eee! Haa!" and a "Wee! Ooo!"

Their legs dug in on a forward slant and the two of them landed on their bottoms, cratering the mound and sending up a thin puff of grain dust.

"Ooo!! That was *fun*!" gushed Sally. "Let's go again!"

They made a half dozen more leaps, from ever higher rungs, before finally finding themselves at the top of the ladder, standing on a broad wooden beam.

"Bet Molly cat's nest is right up in here," said Sally confidently, waiving her hand out toward the top of the hay pile that reached to the heights of the mow. "Let's hunt around."

They stepped off the high beam onto the shaky footing of loose hay, laid up in layers and warmed by the sun-baked roof. Sally went left so Rob went right, each of them pawing hay aside in search of the litter, though putting more effort into staying upright as the dry grass gave way or shifted under foot. They searched their way around the perimeter, finally coming face-to-face on the far side.

"Reckon them kittens ain't up here atall," he concluded, the perspiration beaded across his face and brow.

"Well, could be the ol' mama cat…Ahhh!!" She lost her balance and fell headlong into Rob's startled arms, toppling him backwards.

He landed on his back into the soft hay, with her flopping into his chest and then rolling to the side onto one of his flung out arms, gasping and giggling.

He let out an easy laugh, feeling himself as loose as if he had turned to rubber. Anxiety's rigid grip had relaxed with every lively leap into the wheat, and now it melted and drained from his being.

"I surely ain't never had so much fun, Sally." Her face said the same.

They lay sunken into the warm grassy fragrance of new-dried hay, catching their sweaty breath and basking in the cozy pleasure of the moment. She cuddled close and he curled his arm around her supple form. They fell quiet, and drifted nearly to sleep, to where the conscious flickers and dreams awaken.

In a bit he sat up, let his hands loosen the buttons on his britches, and slipped from their captivity. Tumescent in the high solitude, he pushed off his undershorts and slid himself lightly over her drowsy form.

With eyes nearly closed, she eased up her dress, let her legs come apart and slipped her hands around his waist. He came against her, and lowered his cheek to hers in a tender touch.

"Don't move," she whispered. "This feels real good."

He held still—until his breath quickened and his hips awakened into slow rhythm and, nearly panting, he felt a surge suddenly rising. He paused, and let the rush subside under the soothing stroke of her hand

THE TALE OF A WOODS COLT

on his back, her soft purring slowing and deepening his breath, calming his ardor into another delicious delay.

The moment passed and his mind collapsed into his passion, pressing, then a push; she sucked a short breath, tensed with a clipped cry, and then released; he was enveloped in ecstasy, sending a new flood rising.

"I'm, I'm..," He froze with a quick gasp that brought her calming murmur softly to his ears.

"Hold still now. Hold real still."

She held a hand at his back and the other on his backside, chest to breast, his panting slowing to a paced and steady breath.

"Don't move," she whispered.

A moment passed and his rush receded.

Time vanished when her gentle pull eased all of him in, sending a new current rising.

"Stay like this," she said, with a nibble to his ear lobe. "You feel so good."

Her words sent a soothing wave coursing through him. He held stock-still, the lull tempering his fervor and letting him slip back from the surge. Slowly in unison, their rising rhythm lit flares of pleasure in his volatile body without igniting the explosion.

Primeval forces overtook him. She moaned faintly with his every thrust, tension rising with the tempo, driving to ecstasy pulsing…and then collapsing, slick, dripping and depleted.

Still panting, he eased off and rolled over onto his back to lie beside her on the limp hay.

"Lord, Lord," was all he could mutter, staring straight up and catching his breath. "I cain't hardly believe it."

She turned his face toward her to meet eyes, close and intimate, "You had it in you all along. I knowed you did," she cooed sweetly, her finger stroking his cheek. She took his undershorts to wipe herself and then him. He noticed a reddish spot.

"This here yer first time?"

"Yes," she said quietly, lying back on the hay.

His hand found hers, as they lay for a spell, spent and content. Time returned.

"It's gitten a mite late. Hope ain't no one lookin' fer us," he finally said, with some concern.

They pulled on their clothes and wobble-stepped across the hay. He stuffed his balled-up shorts into a pants pocket and followed her down the ladders, and out to the milk shed where they'd left the house milk. They each took a pail and stepped into the bright early evening for home.

"Tomorrow?"

"Tomorrow."

She filled his heart and his mind. She was all he could think of, and all he wanted to think of. That night, he drifted off to sleep with his arms wrapping her body and his fingers fondling her locks in dreamy fantasy.

Theirs was a hungry and ardent embrace by the feed bin the next evening. They made the lively climb up the ladders to where they stripped naked and pressed fervently together, heaving and panting and collapsing, glistening bodies in the sultry heat, soaked in shared sweat. Limp and expended, they lay with limbs entwined on the soft heap high in the haymow.

Back down in the milking parlor, Rob and Sally lingered, hand-in-hand, eyes locked in a long and tender moment before parting with their milk pails.

By the next day, Analiese still had not returned to milking.

"We're sinnin' somethin' awful, Rob, because we ain't married," said Sally, breaking the silence, as they lay on their backs, relaxing on the hay from passionate embrace in their lofty palace of delight.

She let a minute pass. "I mean, do you think you might want to get married?" she asked uneasily.

He rolled onto his side and smiled at her serenely.

"Sally, will you marry me. Will you be my wife?"

Her eyes lit up. "Oh Rob! Yes! Let's get married right away! Let's do!" she cried, her face radiant with joy. "We'll get married and I can have my very own baby! Oh, *yes*! I'll ask Mama and Daddy right after supper!"

"What you want to ask yer mama and daddy fer? They ain't got no say in it."

"Course they do, Rob! I can't get married without askin' Mama and Daddy. And besides, I want them to be right there in the church with us."

"Church? You wants to git married in a church?"

"Everybody gets married in church, Rob. Well, not everybody. But church is the best place for gettin' married. There ain't nowhere better and, besides, it might get you into goin' to church regular."

Rob thought about this and decided it didn't need immediate resolution.

"Wonder where we goin' to live?" she mused, her mind shifting to practical matters. "Our house ain't got but four rooms and a kitchen."

"I reckon Miss Eleanor'll let you move in the room with me," he said. "Once't we's married proper and all." He considered it further. "Least until a baby come. Sally, I cain't hardly wait to have you in the bed with me regular."

Sally thought about it. "I suppose we can, so long as Jonas and Eleanor say so." She pondered some more. "But we have to eat with Mama and Daddy, so I can help Mama, and take proper care of my sister. And besides, I don't like Mennonite cookin' near as much as Mama's."

"I won't hear a word of it!!" yelled Earle. "You *can't* marry that boy and that there's the *end* of it!" He tore a chaw off his tobacco plug, stuffed it into his cheek and stalked out of the room to his evening place on the front porch.

"But Daddy!!" cried Sally after him, turning in her chair at the kitchen table.

"Daddy's right, darlin'," said Eliza, putting her hand to her daughter's arm.

"*Why* Mama?! Why *not*?!" protested Sally, turning back to her mother.

"We wants the best for you, Sally. Rob can't even read and write. Daddy and me, we wants you to have better'n what we got, not less. How's he ever goin' to give you a proper home?"

"I love him Mama. We'll be happy together. And I can learn him to read and write. You'll see. Don't you want me to be happy, Mama?" pleaded Sally, falling to tears.

"Course I do, darlin'. But that's just it. Rob's a fine young man and all, but he ain't never goin' to be more'n a farm hand. You'll be poor like us all your life," said Eliza, trying to spur her daughter to a higher aspiration. "And remember, when Daddy and me get old and pass on, you'll be takin' the full care of your sister. Have you thought about that, Sally?"

"Mama, Rob's real smart and he can learn fast. He's goin' to make somethin' of himself for sure. I just know he will. You saw your own self how he fixed that big ol' thresher machine."

"Yes, he is clever and all, but them mountain people don't hardly never make much of themselves down here in the valley," said Eliza, conceding no ground. "And besides, he ain't even a Baptist. He don't go to church or nothin', Sally. I just wish you could get interested in one of them young men from church that's got a good payin' job or that farms his own place."

"I don't care for none of them men at church, and I'll for sure get Rob in church before too long. I *will*, Mama."

"You got plenty of time, darlin'. Look how young you are. You ain't hardly old enough to get married, no how."

"I *am* old enough, Mama!" insisted Sally. "And I want to marry him."

"Love can come on fast and fade away even faster, darlin'," said Eliza, trying to extend her worldly wisdom across a generation to temper youth's blind optimism. "Think about your whole life, Sally."

Eliza Harman was not swayed, but at least she listened to her daughter while her husband fumed in silence, sitting alone out on the porch. She fixed her gaze on Sally.

"How much you been seein' of Rob?" she asked, with a touch of worry on one edge of her voice and a trace of suspicion on the other. "Besides Sundays at the river."

Sally had told her mother about tutoring Rob during the swim outings for the boys. Since she hadn't been alone with him, it had aroused no worry or suspicion.

"Hardly none," mumbled Sally, turning away from her mother and casting her eyes down.

A look of alarm fell across Eliza's face. "What do you mean 'hardly none' girl?"

There was no response. Sally sullenly avoided the subject, and her mother's eyes.

Eliza was quickly agitated, and threw a grip onto Sally's upper arm.

"I *asked* you a question, Sally," she said sternly. "*Look* at me!" She searched her daughter's face for a clue. Then her eyes widened and her jaw dropped. Her body stiffened.

"Ah *ha*! In the barn! Yes!" she exclaimed, pointing a finger at Sally. "Annaliese burned her hand and didn't help with the milkin'. You and *that boy* was in the barn *all alone* this entire week!"

Sally looked down at the floor, and nervously bit the end of her thumb.

"I want to know *right now* what you did with him! If you get yourself…"

Sally burst into tears, sprang to her feet and fled up the stairs to the refuge of her bed. She heard the screen door slap and the voices on the porch, before crying herself into fitful sleep.

The next morning Rob found Earle cinching up harness on the Belgians outside the stables. The scowl on his face said it hadn't gone well with Sally and the parents. Rob thought it best not to speak first.

Earle looked up, shot out a sharp jet of tobacco spit from his twisted mouth, bored a stare into Rob and growled out a threat. "Best stay away from my girl, if you know what's good for you, boy," he snarled, in the malign tone of those who feel threatened.

"Yessir, Mister Arle," said Rob, in deference to anger, and to not challenge Earle.

Earle relaxed his sinister snarl into a sneer. "Don't get me wrong. I ain't got nothin' against you, boy," he said, softening slightly. "But I can't have your kind marryin' our kind, if you know what I mean."

"Nosir, Mister Arle," responded Rob, not knowing what Earle meant, since he didn't grasp the concept of intermarriage taboos.

Earle shifted his gaze out to the horizon and went on. "You're a good boy sure enough, and mighty handy around the farm, too," he said, letting the hard edge slip off his voice. "I just can't let you marry Sally is all. I just won't stand for it."

Rob held his tongue and listened, as Earle continued. "It ain't like there's somethin' wrong with you personal, because there ain't." He paused, as if to collect his next thought. "It just that it ain't right for valley womens to marry no mountaineer. It don't make no never mind about if he's a good man or what. It just ain't right for 'em to mix, is all."

Rob had never been actually called a mountaineer to his face before, but it was obvious from the context what Earle meant, and he knew he was being snubbed as a mountain man, not as a person.

Earle went on.

"It ain't like we's high tone people, because we ain't. But we ain't goin' to mix with no mountaineers, neither. You should keep to your place, boy, and not get above your raisin'."

"Yessir, Mister Arle." Rob could see that the subject was as closed as Earle's mind.

Earle, apparently satisfied that he'd effectively hammered his point home, led the big horses out into the day of labor, leaving Rob standing there tapping pebbles with his toe.

TWENTY- EIGHT

Running Away

Rob stood waiting by the grain bin when the cows came in. Sally caught sight of him, her face mirroring the distress written all over his. He took a step toward her and she quickly shook her head. He stopped with a twinge of anger, thinking she wouldn't talk to him. Then he saw she wasn't alone. He turned and stepped quickly away, and ducked into the stable, easing the heavy plank door closed behind him.

As milking progressed, he heard Sally's voice. He put his ear to the door.

"Annaliese, can you take both these pails to the can shed while I put some balm on this here cow's tit?"

He heard the older girl's footsteps leaving and Sally's rushing to the stable.

"Rob! Open up!"

He swung the door open and she flew into his arms.

"Daddy and Mama won't hear of it!" she blubbered. "Oh Rob! They won't let us get married!"

"I know, Sally. Arle, he done give me a big ol' piece of his mind this mornin'."

"What are we goin' to do? I want to be with you, always," she sniffled.

"Holt on now. We ain't got but a few minutes until she gits back. We gots to act fast," he said quickly, holding her face and her attention. "We got to git away. After supper, git yer thangs together, but don't let no one see you. Once't they's all sleepin', slip out quiet-like and come right here."

"Where we goin' to?" she asked, dabbing her eyes with her dress.

"Ain't got no idea," he confessed. "Just git yerself here tonight; you hear me now?"

"Yes. Yes, I'll be here," she said quickly, sealing the promise with a quick kiss. He closed the stable door behind her, as she scooted back to the cows.

Rob lay on his back on the bed in his dark room, his tow sack at his side, waiting for the night to advance. The last lamp had gone out, but still he waited, allowing time for all of the Schanks to fall asleep.

Jonas had paid him his weekly three dollars, bringing his cash hoard up to nearly sixty-five dollars, most of it in the leather coin purse tied inside his britches. Tomorrow was Sunday. He knew the families would sleep an extra hour or more, so he and Sally wouldn't be missed early. It was a perfect time to sneak away and put the most miles behind them before their flight was discovered.

After the eternity of an hour, he finally judged the way clear. He rose, put on his hat and, with sack in one hand and staff in the other, eased out the door and tiptoed slowly down the porch stairs. A gleaming newly risen half moon lit his path to the barn. He felt his way in, plopped his bag on the grain bin, and waited in the deep darkness. In a bit he heard a rustle and then the door squeaked open, admitting a glimmer of pale moonlight.

"Sally, I'm over here," he whispered loudly.

"Rob, I can't see you. I can't see nothin' in there."

"Don't move. Stay right there." He eased toward the door and Sally's moonlit silhouette. "Any one see you leave the house?"

"No, no. They're all fast asleep."

"Let's us git goin' then."

He took her sack and slung it over his shoulder with his own, and the two of them lit out up the lane side-by-side, as quietly as a brisk pace allowed, hunching forward a little as though that might make them less visible.

Once on the road they relaxed and struck a steady upright stride, chasing their moon shadows laid out on the road in front. No one traveled the country roads late at night. There was little chance of an encounter.

"Where we goin' to, Rob?" she asked, a touch of anxiety tempering her excitement. "Mama'll be all upset, and Daddy'll be mad as a hornet."

"We can just foller the moon," he said, flicking his hand at the waning radiance in a weak romantic flourish. He had no plan and nowhere to go. The only valley people he knew were the Wisemans in Elkton, but that's the first place searchers would look.

"I been thinkin', Rob. Daddy's got a brother, but them two don't get along. They ain't spoke since about half my life—somethin' about some land and a deed and such."

Rob looked at her expectantly.

"Anyhow, Uncle Bert, he played with me all the time and thought the world of me when I was little. He and Aunt Daisy had two boys but never did have no girls, and they'd treat me like I was their own child. It's been so long, I bet they'd be glad to see me," she said, looking at him hopefully.

"Whereabouts they livin'?"

"Over in West Virginia, other side of Franklin somewhere. It's that way," she said, pointing the direction they were already going.

"See there! West Virginny fer sure!" he declared. "The moon'll take us right to it."

Her idea showed possibility, and he had no other to offer. So on they went in the pale light, carried along through the shadowy summer night on the promise and optimism of youth.

The road led into the town of Harrisonburg, where they picked up the main road west and followed it into the wee hours, in the company of the guiding moon and the faint light of the stars. Their forced march was energized by the urgency to get themselves beyond where anyone might recognize Sally when the road came alive with church-bound traffic in the morning.

They were an improbable looking couple, walking their way along the deserted road. She hurried along with the straight posture and a quick step that fit her pert personality. He leaned slightly forward with a fist gripping his staff, nearly loping as his work boots stepped out to a stride longer than natural, as though his body hadn't fully outgrown adolescence.

Exhausted, their weary legs brought them to a roadhouse inn just as the lamps inside were being lit and the sky behind showed the first glow of day. They thought they'd put enough distance between themselves and the town to feel safely anonymous. They approached a teamster who was hitching up six massive horses to a heavy freight wagon in the faint light just by the corral, off the end of the building.

"Mornin', mister," said Rob. "We's a-lookin' to git on over to Franklin today."

Turning to face the runaways, the teamster appeared thirtyish and solidly built—not stout nor stocky, nor chunky nor burly, but sturdy. Full faced with a pug nose and curly brown hair, he studied them for a moment.

"You don't say?" he said, hooking his thumbs in his brown leather vest pockets and looking slightly upward to meet Rob's eyes.

"Yessir. Might you be knowin' anyone what's goin' that way and can take us on?"

"Well, well now. So happens Franklin's where I'm headin'. You can ride with me—so long as you don't mind buyin' my breakfast and dinner."

"You gots yerself a deal, mister!" said Rob, thrilled at the good luck and the prospect of getting off aching feet and resting tired bones. They didn't know the measure of a mile, but the more than twenty they'd covered through the night, with only brief rests, had left them near collapse.

"Well, c'mon then, boy! Let's get us on in to the breakfast table and tie on the ol' feed bag!" cried the teamster eagerly, with a pat to Rob's back.

The threesome stepped through the door and Rob hung his hat on a wall peg. They took seats on one of the benches at a long plank table holding a dozen other men who were chatting among themselves and paid little attention to the two new faces.

A ruddy-faced barrel of a woman with one squinty eye and a smile that revealed a complete row of very crooked teeth went about setting out pitchers of milk and pots of coffee on the table between the oil lamps.

"Who's your friends here Mack?" she asked, eyeing Rob and Sally.

Mack was a regular at the inn, stopping overnight as he plied the Rawley Pike on freight runs.

"Well, Patsy," said Mack, pointing to Rob, "He's uh..."

"I'm Rob uh, Harman and this here's my sister Sally. We's a-gitten on over to Franklin to visit our uncle and aunt," said Rob.

"You two ain't from around here, are you?" Patsy didn't wait for an answer. "Most strangers stays up to the Rawley Springs hotels, takin' the healin' waters for their health and such. Whereabouts you two been stayin'?" she inquired curiously, seeing they were well below the hotel class of people.

"We ain't actual been stayin' nowhere around here. We done walked out of town hopin' to find us a ride on to Franklin, and we done run up on Mister Mack here," explained Rob, trying to avoid arousing suspicion.

"Is that a fact, now?" said Patsy on a skeptical note, looking askance with a raised eyebrow. "You don't seem like town people, neither." After a long quiet second she got down to business. "Well, breakfast is ten cent a head, seein' as how your with *Mister* Mack here—in advance," she demanded, holding out her hand. "Regular price is fifteen cent."

Rob pulled three dimes from his pocket and dropped them into Patsy's open palm, whereupon she set a knife, fork, tin cup and tin plate in front of each of them. She rotated around the table collecting payments and putting out place settings before disappearing into the kitchen.

"Patsy there and her two older sisters have owned this place for right many years now," said Mack. "The other two is back there doin' the cookin' and she works the tables. She knows every teamster and drover runnin' the pike."

Patsy backed herself out of the kitchen, bumping the swinging door open with her ample backside, and turned to reveal a collection of full bowls and piled high platters crowded onto a wide tray in the grip of her stubby hands.

As she set out the dishes, several forks reached in and stabbed at the steamy food the moment it hit the table. "Hold your horses, boys!" she scolded. "There's a heap more where this come from."

A couple more trips to the kitchen, and the spread was complete. It was hot and hearty fare, a workingman's breakfast of porridge and buttermilk, fried eggs and bacon, scrapple and gravy, biscuits and butter, and thin slabs of ham that Patsy rationed by forking one onto each tin plate, with two for Mack.

"There now, two for you Mack," she said, reaching the meat in over his shoulder and shaking it off her fork onto his plate. "So I don't want to hear you complainin' none!"

"I think you must love me, Patsy," teased Mack, with a little elbow to her side. Or maybe it wasn't a tease. Rob and Sally, famished from marching all-night, were too busy loading their plates and tucking into their food to take much notice. They didn't take long to eat their fill.

Mack wiped up a smear of egg yolk and gravy with his last biscuit, and popped it into his mouth. He drew his sleeve across his lips, pushed his tin plate away, leaned back, folded his arms and opened his mouth as if to speak.

Instead of words, there issued from his throat a slow and deep, resonant, baritone burp that rumbled on and just didn't want to stop.

Heads turned, faces grinned and there was a whoop or two that passed for applause.

"Ain't no one can love a belch like that!" blurted Patsy from across the table, pausing from collecting dishes to let out a belly laugh at Mack's performance.

"When you goin' to marry me, Patsy?" asked the burper.

"You know dang well I can't marry you, *Mister* Mack."

"Tell me again why not, Patsy. I forgot," he said, with a mischievous look that advertised it was not his first proposal nor would it be his last rejection.

She leaned over the table and stared into his eyes.

"Because-you'd-never-be-home-is-why," she said deliberately, wagging a finger at his nose in a practiced gesture. "And besides, you're already married, Mack," she added, with a sly side wink at Sally.

Mack looked puzzled.

She straightened herself up and, with the sweep of an arm and the cast of her gaze toward the door, struck a pose and exclaimed, "To them horses out there!"

Her theatrics drew a round of guffaws and jabs at Mack from the much-amused crowd. Sally and Rob, wishing less attention had been drawn in their direction, laughed just enough to blend in, but not enough to seem impolite.

"Well now, *there's* one I ain't hear'd before!" said Mack, in good humor.

The breakfast crowd began to break up and make for the door. Mack stood up, nudged the bench back with his legs, stepped over it and went outside. Sally and Rob were close on his heels, with their possessions in hand.

The sun had just broken the hilltops on the horizon as Mack, in fluid motion, swung himself up onto the wagon and into the driver's seat. Rob boosted Sally up onto the load of sacks in the wagon bed, where she nested herself down into some empty burlap bags behind the seat, facing rearward. He reached up and wrapped his hand around the armrest, raised his foot up onto the wheel hub and, imitating Mack's form, pulled himself up and slid onto the seat next to the teamster.

The horses, bobbing and shaking their heads, and lightly stomping their feet impatiently, were ready to move out when Mack situated his broad-brimmed hat on his head, took up the reins and flicked them with a "Giddup now!"

The team leaned into the load, the harness creaking and tightening as the heavy wagon started rolling forward. Mack steered the rig out onto the road and they were underway.

"Mighty fine breakfast in there, Mister Mack," said Rob.

"Yes indeed. Ain't none better along the entire pike," said Mack. "I haul in some food for 'em, time-to-time. That's why she knocked a nickel off the price."

"Right smart ways over to Franklin, Mister Mack?"

"It's a long run over the mountain, but these is all young horses and we ain't got but two ton of load," said the teamster. "Ain't much traffic, bein' Sunday and all. And they keeps this road up real good." He looked down at a round watch he'd pulled from his vest pocket. "We should pull into Franklin about four or so."

Rattling along the 'pike, it occurred to Rob that Mack had a fine job. *Mack here, he done gots about the best job I ever did see,* he thought. *It don't look all that hart and he ain't got no one to boss him around neither,* he told himself, warming to the idea of maybe becoming a teamster. *And most likely he gits right many breakfasts and dinners paid fer, same as today.*

Rob imagined having the six big horses under his command, and being responsible for the wagon and the load. He wondered what it must be like to get to know the people and places all along the road, and it appealed to him. He thought about it.

"What's a man got to do to be a driver, Mister Mack?"

"Oh, mostly just get to know the road and such, as long as you can handle horses. Thinkin' you might want to take up drivin'?" he asked, glancing at Rob.

"I ain't fer sure about it. I'm just thinkin' about thangs," said Rob, trying not to reveal his strong interest.

"Well, you pretty much got to ride with someone to learn the road and the ropes," Mack said. "No one'll give you a job until you're experienced, and there ain't no pay in ridin' helper."

Then he laid it all out for Rob.

"My daddy was a driver and I rode with him, comin' up. Course now, if you got the money you can buy an outfit and hire yourself out. Wagon'll run you about a hunnert dollar and a good horse about the same. It's what I do. This rig belongs to me and I'm gettin' right good money for it—three dollar fifty cent a day."

That sounded good. As the big hooves clapped and the big wheels clanked along on the packed stone roadbed, Rob turned it over in his mind. *Ol' Mack here might take me on, iffen he takes a shine to me,* he told himself. *I done saved up right good money so I ain't needin' no pay fer a while.* He let the idea work on him. *Could be ol' Uncle Bert'll put us up fer a while,* he thought hopefully, adding a piece to the puzzle. *And then we might could git us a little house half way along the pike so's I'd only be gone a day or three at a stretch. And one day I might could git my own outfit,* he dreamily told himself. *Three dollar fifty cent a day!* He liked the prospect of pulling down that kind of money.

Rob was letting his enthusiasm to become a freight driver build up a little steam, when a low one-story building came into view, close to the road ahead. It had the usual white clapboards, and several windows along the side, but didn't quite look like a house because the end that faced the road had the door but no windows. There was no sign of life or activity.

As they drew closer, Rob asked, "What's in there, Mister Mack?"

"That there's the Tollgate School. I went there myself, until the fourth grade that is," said Mack. "It's closed down and locked up for the summer."

THE TALE OF A WOODS COLT

Rob watched the school drift by. His mind floated back into his own childhood and his memory of school, and of his lost chance, and the regrets that had plagued him. He sat quietly for a while, feeling sorry for himself.

He looked back and down at Sally sleeping soundly, her face gleaming in the early sunlight, and it cheered him and he felt better and his spirits lifted.

"How far you get in school?" asked Mack, with a little more than casual interest in the question.

"About a week is all. I can count money but I cain't read or nothin'," confessed Rob. He paused. Mack said nothing. "Does you need readin' and writin' to drive, Mister Mack?" he asked, trying not to sound uneasy.

Mack's hesitation made Rob worry that the answer was going to be bad.

"Well, you actual do need to read some—things like the bill-of-lading and such," said Mack. "And you has to write just a little, now and again. And, well, then there's a li'l 'rithmetic—figgerin' your counts and weights and all." He seemed to be trying to lighten the weight of words that still fell hard on Rob. And there was one more thing. "Can you tell time? You got to pick up your load on time."

Rob didn't answer. He sat silently, looking out at the road ahead.

"Well, I'm afraid you got to know how to tell time," said Mack in a tone of empathy to temper the bad news. He looked over at Rob.

Rob stared straight out and said nothing more after the hammer blow had landed on his aspiration. He knew Mack was reading the sharp disappointment written on his face. Mack had settled it. Rob's new dream quickly drained away. He would not become a driver. *Way'll,* he thought, further up the road, *somethin' bound to turn up fer me over in West Virginny.* He was a hard-working man and he had Sally. That's all he needed.

"Goin' to be a hot one today," said Mack, changing the subject.

The pike, a long pivoting pole that gave toll roads the name turnpike, appeared ahead and the subject changed again.

"Up here's the tollhouse," said Mack, pulling the team to the right and edging the wagon off the road and into a space between other wagons. He parked in front of a miniature building of thick, whitewashed stone walls, with a door and one window in front, a second window above and a wood shingled roof that sloped low to the rear.

Mack climbed down and Rob followed him into the tollhouse. A long-faced man of some years, with long ears and a long beard, sat on a tall stool behind a high counter, peering out over short lenses perched on the end of his nose.

"What you got, Mack?"

"Load of lime and a team of six, Vern. Plus a couple of pick-ups to Franklin."

The toll master dipped his quill pen into an inkwell and duly noted the entry in his logbook. "Be two bits plus five cent each on the extras."

Mack had his quarter ready and turned to Rob, as he placed the coin on the counter in front of the clerk. "Forgot to tell you about the toll," he said apologetically.

Rob was paying attention. "Ain't no problem atall, Mister Mack." He dug a dime from his pocket and flicked it on the counter. Mack collected his receipt and the two stepped back outside.

"I got to see a man about a horse," said Mack, ducking behind the little building to Rob's puzzlement. Seeing neither man nor horse, he peeked curiously around the corner to witness the teamster standing with his back turned, watering the pasture through a split rail fence. Rob reckoned it would be a good time to step over and consult his own "man about a horse" through the next fence section, before setting off up the road.

They were back on the wagon ready to go, with the snoozing Sally oblivious to the toll stop. Mack pulled the rig left and back onto the road for a few dozen yards and halted at the turnpike. He handed his receipt to the attendant, who swung the pike open to let them pass.

The team tugged forward; the wheels creaked and turned and rolled into the open road ahead. The rig soon got up to pace, passing a small herd of cattle and parting a large flock of sheep, all flowing in the opposite direction, their drovers taking them into town to be sold at the stock auction the next day.

They hadn't gone a mile when a team of four slick black horses pulling a handsome surrey with a liveried driver trotted up from behind, pranced smartly by on the left and pulled out in front, grabbing Rob's attention. The sprightly team of four veered the empty coach off to the right, angling into a curving, finely graveled lane that was neatly edged with cut cobblestones. The lane led into manicured grounds studded with stately trees, their spreading limbs affording a filtered view of an imposing building beyond.

"Right perty spread," remarked Rob.

"That there's the Rawley Springs Hotel," said Mack. "Coach is goin' in to pick up guests and run 'em down to church. Most all of 'ems fancy city folks. They come down here to 'take the waters,' as they call it."

"Where abouts they takin' the water to?" asked Rob.

"They ain't takin' it nowhere. They just gets themselves down in the water up to their chins, right there in the spring," said Mack. "They got a regular bath house for 'em."

"They comes way down here just to git down in the water?" asked Rob incredulously. "Ain't they got no water in the city to git down in?"

"Sure, they got plenty water in the city, but they say this here water's different. They say the Rawley Spring water cures what ails you."

"What? Just gittin' down in the water and you ain't sick no more?"

"That's what they say. I don't know if it's so or not," said Mack. "Could be just *thinkin'* the water'll cure you might make you get better, or maybe feel better. I don't know. All I know is they all pays big money for it. Five dollar a day is what I heard."

Lord! Rob thought. *Five dollars to do what a pinch of biled h'yarb can do a sight better!* Rob pondered how fancy folk could have so much money and know so little about treating ailments. *Them city folk must not know hardly a thang about curin' no ailment.* To him, it was elementary knowledge that herbal potions from wild plants, taken on the full moon, were what cured illnesses.

The wagon rolled on into the hill country, passing fewer and smaller homesteads, to where more of the forest reached down the slopes close to the road. The steady clanking of the iron wheel bands on the stone road and the rhythmic cloppity-clop of twenty-four ironshod hooves, together with the warming rays of the morning sun on his back, all conspired to lull Rob into a drowsy slump, his nodding head bobbing and wobbling

"Ahhh-Oww!" cried Rob, snapping back awake under the firm grip of Mack's meaty fist jerking his collar sharply.

"Sorry for the rough handlin', but you dang near went over the side, boy," said Mack, letting go as Rob straightened and composed himself. "Can't have you goin' under the wheels. You still owes me dinner!" said the teamster, with a grin. "And besides, I ain't never lost nobody and I ain't goin' to start today!"

Rob kept his eyes open for a little while longer, until the fatigue and sleeplessness of the prior night caught up with him again.

"You orter slip back and catch you forty winks," said Mack, looking over at him.

Rob climbed over the seat back, snuggled in against Sally, pulled his hat over his face and was quickly dead to the world.

They slumbered as miles passed beneath, and on they slept as the team huffed and strained uphill on a three-mile grade. When the wagon topped the crest and started over the brow into the downhill, Mack jammed the shoe brake lever forward, using all of his arm strength to squeeze it into the tightest ratchet notch.

With wooden brake shoes pressed tightly against rear wheels, the sound of the leather linings rubbing against iron rims roused the sleepers and stirred them back into the moment. Sally propped herself up facing rearward and pulled out a white bonnet to shield her face from the fierce sun. Rob threw his hat on his head and climbed back over into the seat beside Mack, who was leaning back in the seat, with both feet jammed tightly on the footboard and both hands pulling firmly back on the reins. With his fists almost in his face, the teamster called "Ho now!! Ho!" several times while he held the team back to restrain the wagon on the descent.

Rob looked at Mack anxiously, alarmed at the thought of a runaway rig. The teamster was working the reins hard, but he maintained full control and he looked unconcerned.

Rob relaxed and turned his attention to the scenery, which changed with every switchback of the twisting road. The forested mountains and the little cabins tucked into small clearings down in snug hollows reminded him of home, sparking a twinge of homesickness. But they also made him feel more at ease, as the wagon descended the mountain into a small valley.

The grade flared; Mack released the brake and relaxed in the seat. "We're in West Virginia now. Couple more miles down to dinner," he announced.

Rob was unsure what a mile was. Everyone else seemed to know, and he wanted to know but he never wanted to ask. He'd deduced that it was a distance longer than most any farm; maybe it was the length of several farms.

A ways down, they rounded a curve and came directly upon a long low building of squared log walls under a wood shingled roof. Mack steered the team off the road and into a space in the shade, pulling to a halt under the spreading limbs of a large white oak tree.

To Rob, the place looked very much alive for a Sunday. At least one of the heavy wagons or other conveyances was pulling in or out at any given moment. To one end he saw a line of saddled horses tied to hitching posts along the front porch. Smoke issued from a stone chimney, and enticing whiffs from the kitchen wafted over on the breeze.

"The horses come first," said Mack, hopping down and lifting a sack of feed off the rear end. "There's your buckets and yonder's the water," he said, assigning Rob a task and pointing to a long handled pump at the water trough by the porch. Mack pulled six canvas feed bags from a box. "Hold these open for me, now," he asked Sally. He untied the feed sack and poured a measure into each bag.

Rob watered the team with a full bucket per horse, after which Mack fitted the feedbags onto the animals' heads. While Mack was checking over the wagon and harness, he and Sally walked over to the pump to wash hands and flush their faces.

Refreshed, they gazed out over the picturesque vista of narrow bottomland hugging a winding, tree-lined creek. "West Virginny's lookin' right perty," he said, taking her hand in his, as they both drew in a long drink of scenery. This here's my kinder country."

"Uncle Bert and Aunt Daisy'll surely be glad to see me," she said.

"I sartainly hope they's willin' to help us out," he said.

Mack tossed his hat on the wagon seat, came over and stuck his head under the spout, pulled the handle down and gushed out a flood of cool water. He shook and wiped his wet face, stepped up beside Rob and pointed down the narrow valley to a handsome building set at the confluence of two streams.

"That there's the Livingston Hotel, where the carriage trade stops," he said. "Us regular folks eats up here at Samson's."

Inside were long plank tables rimmed by a raucous crowd of drivers seated on rustic wooden benches, some of whom were downing tankards of beer and had become a bit illuminated. The three new arrivals found bench space at one end, away from the rowdiest of the bunch. A young auburn-haired fellow appeared with a large tray balanced on his up-turned hand.

"You'uns all three together, Mack?"

THE TALE OF A WOODS COLT

"Yep," said Mack, looking at Rob, who took the hint. Rob held his hat on his lap over the hand that he wiggled into his britches and fished out a silver dollar from his coin purse.

"Two bits apiece; a dime more if you want beer," recited Red.

Mack declined. "No beer, Bobby. Makes me sleepy."

Rob handed over the dollar. The waiter dropped it into his apron pocket and produced change with his one hand while lowering the tray with the other, revealing a platter piled with meat and a stack of tin plates.

"Two bits is your change." He set out three tin plates and forked a generously thick and juicy chop onto each. Forks, spoons and tin cups were already on the table that was loaded with food and drink.

"Surprised they servin' beer in here on Sunday," remarked Sally.

"These roadhouses and half the teamsters don't pay no mind to all that temperance stuff," said Mack. "And no one worries 'em about it, long as they ain't near to a church."

Mid-summer was the time of plentiful bounty. They helped themselves to platters of fresh seasonal vegetables—hot sweet corn and cold sliced tomatoes with onions, and bowls of boiled potatoes, turnips, squash, green beans and lima beans, and there was coleslaw and salad.

A big basket held thick slices of fresh-baked bread, and next to it sat a tub of butter and a boat of brown gravy. Steam rose from carafes of hot coffee, and the metal pitchers of cold water sweated droplets.

When he'd feasted his fill, Mack let out another of his run-on burps that no one noticed, such was the boisterous uproar in the room. They didn't linger. They were back on the wagon in short order.

Sally rode up on her knees, holding on to the back of the seat and looking at the road ahead between the two men. The Livingston Hotel came into view, the symmetry of long windows set in red brick walls giving it a look of formality. She noticed a tidy white church set just across the road from the imposing hotel. As they passed, Sally looked at the sign on the right.

"It's a Methodist church. I would think most folks around here was Baptists," she said.

"Most of 'em along here *is* Baptists," said Mack. "Livingstons put up that church to draw in the refined class of people. They fill up Saturday nights with a stagecoach crowd that wants to get right in to church Sunday mornin', then set for a fancy dinner and get on over to Harrisonburg in the evening."

Rob's eyes had been drawn left, awed by the group of trim buggies and runabouts, and the smart surreys and coaches parked in front of the hotel. He couldn't take his eyes off all of the fancy conveyances.

"And then there's some of the finer folks of Franklin drives up Sundays just for the dinner," said Mack.

"Them people must be right well fixed," said Sally.

"You got that right," agreed Mack. "Them rooms in there all got papered walls, gas lights, lace on the windows and fancy wash basins and such. They even got bath tubs!" he said, on a note of ridicule. "Why, they got waiters to bring you everything and chamber maids to draw your bath water, and someone to do about anything for you except blow your nose!" He laughed, obviously enjoying poking fun at high-brow hotel patrons.

Rob had swiveled in his seat, staring back at the stylishly attired passengers boarding a stagecoach.

"You're lookin' at clean hands and fine clothes—every one of 'em," said Mack. "Yes indeed. And that there's a genuine Concord Coach. Yessir, nothin' but *quality* stops at Livingston's," he declared, in words iced with sarcasm. Then he added, "That place sure pulls in the money, though."

"I can't imagine what it must be like to stay in such a place," said Sally.

They clopped and creaked westward through a very narrow valley a couple miles to where it opened into a slightly wider one.

"You ever go to church, Mack," she asked.

"Not regular. There's a Baptist church I like, whenever I find myself over to Elkins Sunday mornin'," said the teamster. "The preacher ain't got no education, but he sure got what it takes to get 'em all fired up with the Holy Spirit."

The road turned north and a village appeared. "This here's Brandywine," announced Mack, as they rattled past the group of tidy houses. "You ever hear of Washington City?" he asked Rob, as the wagon approached a bridge.

Rob remembered what Pollock had told him in Luray and saw his chance to impress Mack. "Why sure. That there's where the pres'dint lives," he said, as though anyone would know it. He checked Mack's face for a reaction. The teamster showed none, but Rob scored a point with Sally, who looked at him in amazement.

"Now this right here," said Mack as the wagon rumbled across the bridge planks," is the Potomac River. It runs right on down to Washington City."

This news startled Rob. "Mister Mack, I been a-thinkin' we's goin' *up* the country, not down near no big city?"

Mack chuckled. "We ain't near no city, boy. It's a couple hunnert mile on down."

That sounded better to Rob. He didn't know how far that was, but a couple hundred was a lot of anything.

In a few miles, they turned west again and passed through a gap in a ridge. After crossing another narrow valley, they pulled over a hump and entered a tighter gap in a higher ridge. As they closely followed a creek through a narrow winding gorge between steep forests, Rob felt more and more secure in the close fortress-like terrain.

At the next bridge Rob asked, "What might this here river be, Mister Mack?"

"Potomac River," answered Mack, checking Rob's face for *his* reaction.

Rob was baffled. "Wern't that last one the Potomac?"

Mack's grin told Rob the teamster relished the moment of mystery. "Both of 'ems the Potomac!" teased Mack.

Rob was confused and he could see Mack was savoring his riddle.

"Two forks of the South Branch. The South Branch actually got three forks."

The turnpike followed the small river upstream into Franklin, a neatly laid out little county seat anchoring an idyllic vale between low ridges. Mack swung the rig onto Main Street and they clattered along past large handsome houses for several blocks to the commercial section. He turned the team right into a side lane by a large building with a big sign on the façade, above the front porch roof.

"Pendleton Mercantile," said Sally, looking up at the sign. The front of the place was deserted—no parked wagons, no hitched horses, no one on porch benches. The town was closed up on Sundays.

"End of the line," said Mack to his passengers. He pulled the team to a halt by a shed behind the building. He turned to Rob. "Where abouts your uncle livin'?"

Rob looked at Sally. "I ain't sure," she confessed. "It ain't in town. They lives on a farm, but I can't remember where."

"Back in a minute," said Mack, hopping down and walking over to a house that sat behind the store, leaving Rob and Sally on the wagon.

"Reckon Mack actual believes we's brother and sister?" wondered Rob, as Mack rapped on the door.

"Not hardly," said Sally. "I saw him lookin' at us holdin' hands back there by the well pump at Samson's."

Mack strode back to the wagon, followed by an older man and a couple of young fellows. The man spoke to his assistants. "Pull the load off and stack the sacks in the shed, boys." He turned and looked up at Rob on the wagon seat. "So you two are Harmans are you?"

Rob gave a little nod and looked at Sally, who answered. "Yes sir. We're goin' to visit Uncle Bert and Aunt Daisy. Ain't seen 'em since I.. uh..we was little."

"Well, your uncle and aunt live south of town. Go past the courthouse and follow the river road about two miles to Smith Creek—it's your first bridge. Their place is the farmhouse on the right just before the bridge." He turned to the teamster. "Here's your money, Mack. The boy's will load you up for the Elkins run so you can leave first thing in the mornin'." He disappeared back into the house.

Rob and Sally found their tow sacks and his walking stick, and hopped off the wagon. Rob extended his hand. "Mister Mack, we..."

Mack interrupted.

"I know what you're thinkin'," he said, looking Rob straight in the eye. "I don't know where you come from or who's after you, but don't you worry none. I ain't goin' to say nothin' to nobody about carryin' you over here to Franklin." He extended his hand for a shake.

"Thank you, Mister Mack," said Sally, releasing a breath of relief.

"Yessir, Mister Mack," said Rob, pumping the teamster's beefy hand. "Thank you a heap."

The two runaways turned and walked out to the street, down to the river road and put the town behind them in the heat of the late afternoon.

TWENTY-NINE

The Chase

The evening sun hung well above the western ridge when Rob and Sally saw the small bridge ahead and bore right into a tree-lined lane with a modest white farmhouse at the end. A yellow dog came off the porch into the yard and announced the visitors. The screen door eased open; a head with a thick shock of hair, heavy eyebrows and a pair of curious eyes leaned out.

"Who's there!? Who are you?"

"It's Sally!"

"Sally? Sally who?"

"Earle's Sally, Uncle Bert."

The screen door swung open and a tall man stepped out onto the porch.

"Little Sally! Why didn't you say so!?"

He stepped down into the yard where he stood in his baggy brown trousers and white Sunday shirt, scanning her top to bottom.

"Sally, is that you!? Lord, you're near all growed up! I'd not have knowed you had you not said who you was!"

"We come to pay you and Aunt Daisy a visit, Uncle Bert."

"Daisy! Get out here!" he hollered over his shoulder. "Earle's Sally come to see us!"

"Who's your friend there, Sally?" he asked, nodding at Rob.

"Uh, this here's Rob, Uncle Bert." She glanced at Rob and looked uneasily at her uncle, holding her breath for his reaction.

An ample woman, full in a flower print dress and a kitchen apron, bumped the screen door open, stepped out on the porch and, spying Sally, exclaimed, "Land sakes alive!"

She pinched her dress to pull her hem up, skittered down the steps and rushed to wrap Sally in an exuberant hug. "How long has it *been*!" She pushed apart and, holding Sally's shoulders, looked her niece up and down. "Look at you! You're almost growed up!"

Sally winced at the "almost."

"Why, the last time we saw you, you wasn't no higher than this," said Daisy, holding a hand above her waist. "Wasn't she, Bert? How long's it been? Must have been nine or ten years!"

"This here's Rob, Aunt Daisy."

Aunt Daisy looked at Rob. "Very happy to meet you, Rob," she said pleasantly with a little nod. "Bert, did you meet Rob?"

"I was fixin' to when you come bustin' out the door," he said, stepping up to Rob with a hand extended. "Rob, a friend of Sally's is a friend of mine, most likely."

"Yessir, Mister Bert. I'm right pleased to meet you," said Rob uneasily and with a short handshake.

An awkward moment of silence was broken by Daisy.

"Well now, I'm goin' right in to put more supper on the stove. Bert, won't you show Sally to a bedroom and Rob to another bedroom," she said, setting the moral standard before quickly disappearing back inside.

"Yes, indeed. Come on in the house," said Bert, turning and leading Sally and Rob through the door, up the stairs, and to a room at the end of the hall. He grasped the doorknob, paused and turned his eyes back toward Rob.

"This here was the hired man's room, back before my boys was big enough to work the place with me. It ain't big but it should do." With that, he swung the door open to reveal a snug cubicle that barely held its single bed, a chair, a small dresser and a window. The hooks on the back of the door served as the closet.

Rob, knowing what was expected, stepped in and sat himself and his sack on the bed. "Why, it's just perfect, Mister Bert."

"Sally, let's put you over here," said Uncle, stepping across the hall and swinging the door into a plain but comfortably furnished corner bedroom with two of everything—windows, beds, chairs. "Used to be the boys' room, back before they got married."

"Oh yes, I remember your boys."

"Guess it can be your room now, before *you* get married!" said Uncle Bert, amused at his own ironic quip and not-so-subtle hint. He picked up the basin pitcher and stepped back over to Rob's cramped cell. "You can get li'l Sally some wash water if you want to," he said, handing the pitcher to Rob. "The pump is out back."

"Yessir! Yes I will!" Rob took the pitcher, almost ran down the stairs and found his way out the back door.

"Uncle Bert, you still raisin' them turkeys?" asked Sally, as he was starting down the stairs. "I want to go see 'em if you still got 'em."

"Oh, yes. They're in the coop down below the house. Don't be too long. Aunt Daisy'll be settin' supper on the table in a short while." He disappeared downstairs.

Rob came up with the pitcher of water, put it on Sally's basin table, sat himself next to her on the bed and took her hand. "What you thinkin'?" he asked.

"Well, they's glad to see me, like I said they'd be. But they ain't too sure about you, Rob," she said. "I'm thinkin' we best tell 'em we's gettin' married. There ain't no other way to handle it."

"I reckon we best say somethin' to 'em," agreed Rob.

Sally jumped to her feet. "Come on! Lets go look at the turkeys."

"Lord, thank you for your bounty and for our family and for our health and thank you for sendin' li'l Sally to see us after these many years and Lord, please do be sure to take care of her right proper now, amen."

Uncle's table grace made his concerns clear. The atmosphere at the table was stiff, with each mind wondering how and when to broach the delicate details of the visit.

"Have some of Daisy's famous fried chicken here, Rob."

"Thank you, Mister Bert."

"Sally, seems I remember you liked succotash when you was little."

"Yes, Uncle Bert. I still love succotash."

"I just baked the bread this evenin', Rob."

"Thank you, Miz Daisy."

"Sally, will you start the potatoes around?"

"Yes, Aunt Daisy."

They filled their plates and ate in an uneasy silence. Thoughts flowed freely but questions went begging. Time slowed and no one knew just what to say next in the edginess of the moment.

Aunt spoke up first. "How's Eliza, Sally?"

"Oh, Mama's just fine, Aunt Daisy."

Then Uncle Bert spoke. "Uh, Rob. How you come to know li'l Sally here?"

"I been a-workin' fer Mister Jonas, there on the farm where Sally lives, Mister Bert."

Then Aunt Daisy posed a sensitive question. "Sally, if you don't mind me askin', does your folks know you come here?"

"Well, Aunt Daisy..."

Bert broke in. "What your aunt's getting at is, your daddy and me, we ain't got along since near ten years ago when our own daddy left the farm to me, and Earle didn't get no piece of it and he got all upset with me and everything, so after that..."

"Oh hush now, Bert," said Daisy. "We don't need to get back in to all that."

"Daisy and me wants the best for you, Sally, but we don't want to stir up no trouble with Earle and your mama, neither," said Bert, looking at Sally, then at his wife cautiously.

Daisy couldn't hold back any longer. "Oh Sally! *Do* tell us what's goin' on. *Please* do. Tell us about you and Rob."

Sally looked anxiously at Rob.

"I can tell you, Miz Daisy," said Rob. "Sally and me, we wants to git married. She done tolt Mister Arle and her mama, but they done said she cain't be marryin' no mountain man. And Arle, he done give me a piece of his mind about it. We come over here to git away from 'em and git us both married together anyhow."

"Hmmm," murmured Bert, stroking his chin. "Trouble is, by my reckoning you're only fifteen, Sally."

"I'm almost sixteen, Uncle Bert."

"But Sally," said Daisy, "at your age, you need your mama's and daddy's permission to get married."

Sally fell to tears. "They won't never give no permission, Aunt Daisy," she said, sniveling. "There must be *some* way we can get married." She started to sob into her napkin.

"Now, now, Sally. Bert and me want to help you. We just don't want to fall foul of the law, is all."

"But what can we do?" sniffed Sally, wiping her eyes.

"I suppose you could tell the clerk of the court you're older, and hope he believes it," mused Daisy, looking at Bert.

"If I know my brother, he's probably mad as a hornet and already out lookin' for you," he said.

"Think he'd come *here* lookin' for us, Uncle Bert?"

"Ain't no way to know for sure, Sally. Good chance of it, though."

They spent the twilight hour sitting on the front porch, as was the custom in the country, talking family and recalling old times, before turning in for the night. Rob lay awake until a late hour, then slipped quietly into Sally's room and slid into bed with her, the two of them silently comforting one another into a peaceful night's sleep.

The next day, Rob and Sally put themselves at the disposal of aunt and uncle to be useful around the house and farm. After supper they were all out on the porch when a one-horse buggy came up the lane at a trot. Rob recognized the man from the Pendleton Mercantile as he hopped off the buggy and walked quickly to the porch.

"What brings you out here so late in the evenin', Grayson?"

"Bert, I have some urgent news. That brother of yourn, Earle, has been nosing around town."

"You don't say? Anything else?"

"He came into the store this evenin' asking about anyone who might have seen his daughter, Sally, and some young buck named Rob," said the merchant. "Said she was a runaway. He had the deputy sheriff with him and he seemed right worked up about it, Bert." He glanced at Rob and Sally on the porch swing.

"You hear any more?"

"I overheard 'em talking. Said he bet they'd come out here. Said something about gettin' trackin' dogs."

"I do thank you, Grayson," said Bert appreciatively. "Thank you for comin' out."

Grayson climbed back onto his buggy and looked to the porch. "If it were me Bert, I'd expect a visit tonight." He flicked his horse and disappeared as quickly as he had come.

Sally had her fingers to her cheeks. "Ohhh, I hope Daddy don't come and take me away," she fretted.

Daisy furrowed her brow. "What are we goin' to do, Bert?"

Rob looked to Bert but didn't say anything.

Bert pondered for a minute and then stood up. "First thing, you two come with me," he said, motioning to Rob and Sally as he stepped off the porch. He walked them around the end of the house and through a gate into a small pasture. "You two might have to run tonight," he said, striding across the grass.

A short distance across the field brought them to a narrow rocky creek bordered by scattered low trees.

"If you have to run, come right here and then walk in the water down there to the river," he said, pointing down the tree line across the road to a higher tree line several hundred yards away.

"Then you walk in the river downstream, to the left," he instructed with a sweep of his hand. "Don't worry, the river's mostly shallow—just a little muddy in places is all." He paused a minute to let his charges absorb the prospect of flying by night.

They followed him back toward the house, where he stopped at a shed, reached in and pulled out a square tin can by the top handle. Then it was back to the porch in the first glow of twilight.

"Where you all been, Bert?" asked Daisy.

"Just showin' 'em where to go if there's dogs trackin'." Bert settled back into his porch rocker. "Now then, let me tell you how to lose trackin' hounds." he said, raising a finger. "They can't track you in the water but they'll run the bank to find where you come out." He looked at Rob to be sure he was paying attention. "Now that's where this coal oil comes in," he said, picking up the gallon can.

"What we gon' do with coal oil, Mister Bert?"

"You're goin' to splash it on your feet and ankles soon as you steps out of the water. It'll throw the hounds off scent. They won't track a coal oil scent."

"What we gon' do *then*?"

Bert fixed his gaze on Rob. "First thing, the dogs won't yelp when they's trackin'. If you hear 'em barkin', they ain't trackin' no more. You got that?"

"Yessir, Mister Bert."

"Second thing is, the safest place to be is right behind 'em. When the dogs lose the scent, they'll run 'em up and down the river bank some, but they won't double full back on themselves."

Rob and Sally took in Bert's bloodhound lore with rapt attention.

"When you come out of the water, hide first to let 'em get past you and then swing in around behind 'em. Keep back out of sight but stay behind 'em. When they give up and head back to town, the two of you can make your break up the road."

"Why we got to run, Uncle Bert?" asked Sally. "Why can't we

just stay here?"

"If your daddy and that deputy come with dogs, he'll carry some piece of your clothes. They'll pick up up your scent around the house and know you been here. If they don't find you tonight, they'll be back in the mornin'," said Bert soberly. "You can't stay here. Ain't no way we can keep you hid."

Sally's face fell as she looked pleadingly at Aunt Daisy.

"Uncle Bert's right, darlin'. If you stay here, you'll get caught for sure."

"Whereabouts can we go, Mister Bert?" asked Rob.

"I been thinkin' about that," said Uncle Bert. "Get on up to Monterey; go out the lane here and turn right to go south. The river road takes you right to it."

"What's in Monterey for us, Uncle Bert?" asked Sally.

"I got a cousin up there, Sally. Name's Vancouver—Vancouver Sexton. He runs the only sawmill right in town. Ain't hard to find. Town's real small," said Bert, who then looked at Rob. "Tell him Bert Harman sent you and might be he'll take you in and give you a job."

"How far a piece is it up to Monterey, Mister Bert?"

"It's about twenty miles; you can make it by early mornin', if you don't leave too late and you keep movin'. Won't be no one else on the road through the night."

"Reckon Arle might look fer us up'par?" asked Rob.

"Could be. But if he does, he'll have to get himself a new deputy. Monterey is in Virginia," said Bert, pointing out that they'd be crossing the state line. "Once you're there, keep your eyes and ears open. You might have to stay hid. Now the two of you go up and get your things together and come on back down."

After Rob and Sally returned to the porch with their towsacks, the four of them sat in silent darkness, the air tense with anticipation. The humid summer haze hung heavily about the place. Bert kept his eyes on the dim lane in the sultry night.

Finally Rob spoke. "Mister Bert, what if your cousin cain't take me on?"

"Well, I don't know. Ain't much in Monterey. A turnpike runs through there though. Suppose you might hitch on with a teamster who'd carry you over to Cheat Mountain where they're pullin' out a lot of timber. Word is they're hirin' loggers and such like."

An hour went by, then most of another. The dense moonless night weighed on field and forest. Thin wisps of fog materialized, floating in the flat open bottoms above the corn stalks.

"Well, they might not be comin' tonight," said Bert. "You two best go on up and get some sleep," he said. "We'll stay up and keep an eye out."

Rob and Sally stood up with their sacks and turned toward the door.

"Take the coal oil with you," said Bert.

They each lay on their beds in their clothes, unable to sleep. Shortly, they heard hurried footsteps rushing up the stairs. Daisy popped her head into Sally's room, and then Rob's.

"They're comin' and they got dogs! Quickly now! Go out the back door!"

Rob stuffed the can into his sack and the two pounded down the stairs and scurried out the back door. Gripping their tow sacks, they dashed through the darkness, over to the tree line and the misty creek. Muggy air had settled in over the low-lying watercourses, forming a band of fog just above.

"Why *Earle*! What a surprise!" said Bert from his rocking chair. "Fancy seein' you here! What brings you to Franklin and way out here this time of night?"

"I think you know why I'm here, Bert," said Earle coldly. "Mind if we look around?"

"Lookin' for what, Earle?" asked Bert calmly.

"You know damn well who I'm lookin' for, Bert," snarled Earle. "And you best not be hidin' 'em, if you know what's good for you."

"Got a search warrant, Earle?" asked Bert, keeping a steady composure.

The other man spoke up.

"Uh, Mister Harman, I'm Sheriff's Deputy Warren and I'm servin' this here search warrant on you," said he, stepping forward and presenting a paper. A couple of dogs yelped from a cage on the back of the small wagon.

Daisy came through the screen door, threw a glance at Bert and gave the slightest nod.

"What's this all about, Bert?" she asked, feigning ignorance, then pretended to just then notice it was her brother-in-law. "Earle! What are *you* doin' way over here, and so late at night?"

"They want to search the place, Daisy," said Bert. "Deputy Warren here served me a warrant."

"Why, I do declare!" she exclaimed to no one. "What nonsense is this?" Then she shot a cold-eyed dagger at her brother-in-law. "Of all the nerve, Earle! Who do you think you are?"

"I ain't goin' to talk rough to no woman but, Daisy, if you and Bert is hidin' my Sally and that boy, you goin' to find yourselves in a court of law. Because I'll sure as hell press charges," declared Earle curtly.

"You can't think you can just come in here and..."

Her husband cut her off. "What make you think they come here, Earle?" he asked, earning a little more time for the fleeing fugitives.

"Roadhouse crew see'd 'em leavin' out for Franklin. You two's the only ones she'd know way over here," said Earle assuredly. "So don't make like you don't know nothin' about it, because I know you does!" he growled, turning surly again.

"Well then, go on in and have your look, boys," said Bert, trying to sound both confident and condescending. He followed the intruders through the door while Daisy stalked retreat back to the kitchen.

Earle and Deputy Warren looked into each first floor room and then went upstairs, with Bert trailing behind. They checked the Harman's bedroom and then entered the corner bedroom.

"The bed's mussed and look here, the pitcher's got water in it!" exclaimed Earle. "Someone's been in here and it ain't been long."

"Don't prove nothin', Earle," noted Bert. "Want to see the other rooms?"

"Hell no!!" Earle was steaming.

"You served your warrant. Don't you want to finish your search?" asked Bert, trying to buy just a little more time.

"I seen enough. They done left the house but they's somewhere here close! I know they is!" yelled Earle. "Let's get the dogs!"

The two stomped down the stairs, followed by Bert, and charged out to their buckboard wagon.

In minutes, Earle scented the leashed hounds with a garment and started around the end of the house with the exuberant animals, followed by the deputy holding an oil lantern from his raised hand. The dogs struck scent behind the house. Earle released them and the pair of hounds ran through the pasture with noses to the ground. They came to the creek bank and let out a few yelps as they sniffed around the water's edge.

Earle and the deputy caught up. "They's in the water!" cried Earle. "Most likely headin' for the road!" He leashed the hounds and worked them east, down the stream bank, trying to regain the scent. The road was only a few hundred feet away.

But by then Rob and Sally had splashed their way east, ducked under the road bridge and splattered on down the creek to the river where, in near panic, they were furiously wading northward with the current in knee-deep water. Sally stumbled. "Rob!" she cried in a hushed voice, losing her balance.

He jabbed his snakehead staff into the muddy bottom and grabbed her arm before she fell. "Holt on now. Holt my arm," he said, pulling her back to her feet. He cocked his ear. "We don't need to rush no more. They's runnin' the sides of the road. Mister Earle must have figgered we struck fer the road."

They felt relieved to hear the sound of the barking dogs receding in the distance. In the time it took to run the hounds along a stretch of both sides of the road, and then both sides of the creek bank down to the river, Rob and Sally had put nearly half a mile between themselves and the trackers.

The pursuit arrived at the river, having found no scent along either side of the creek. Earle now reasoned that the runaways would likely flee upriver to the south, away from town, so they and the dogs searched up the river's open west bank.

Rob and Sally slogged slowly through the water, straining with exertion in the darkness. A wooded slope rose from the east bank on their right. Cornfields bordered the west bank on their left. He paused where the woods began to recede back from the river.

"We done got... right far in front ... of 'em!" he gasped, panting heavily. "Let's git out!" They stumbled out of the muck onto the forested bank. Rob opened the can and splashed the contents on their soaked shoes, socks and ankles.

They lurched up the mud-slicked riverbank. "Don't touch nothin'!" cautioned Rob. "Might leave a scent." They quickly struggled a hundred yards up through the woods and stopped at a large fallen tree. They clambered over the big trunk and sat themselves and their sacks on the ground, leaned back against the far side of the log and caught their breaths.

Rob listened for the dogs. The barking was going away from them. "Ol' Earle, he done guess wrong again. They's a-running *up* the river," he said with some satisfaction, but then added, "I expect they's gon' cross over and be back down this here side directly. The trees'll only slow 'em a little."

"Oh Lord! Daddy gon' kill me if we gets caught," she worried, gripping his hand tightly. "You think they'll find us?"

"Not hardly," he said, confidently. "Like Mister Bert done said, dogs won't track a coal oil scent, and the wind's a-comin' down river, so they cain't smell us."

The yelping grew louder. Finding no scent up the river, the searchers crossed over and were scouting the wooded east bank back downstream. They stopped about where the fugitives had left the water. Sally sucked her breath and whispered, "Rob, I'm scared! We'll get caught for sure!"

Rob took her hand and murmured in her ear. "Shhh. No we ain't. Set still, now. Don't say nary a thang," he reassured. "And don't smack no skeeters."

The search party waded the river again and started working their way back up the open west bank, back toward the creek.

"They was on this side. Now they's workin' the dogs back up t'other side," said Rob. "They ain't struck no scent." He stood up and pulled Sally to her feet. "Let's git us in behind 'em."

Clutching their sacks, they crept downhill through the trees and waded over to the cornfield on the west bank. Slipping stealthily between rows of tall cornstalks, they paced the barking dogs that were working their way back up river, busily nosing this way and that in a futile search for the scent. The evaders came to the edge of the cornfield, from where the outline of Bert and Daisy's darkened house was barely visible across the hayfield and road. There they paused, crouched in the concealing leafy shadows.

The lantern reached the mouth of the creek. Earle and the deputy had come full circle empty-handed. Rob and Sally watched furtively from the cornfield, as men and dogs gave up and turned back toward the house. They watched as the lantern light bobbed up through the field, crossed the road, climbed onto the buckboard, receded out the lane, and disappeared down the road toward town.

"They gone?" asked Sally. "They *are* gone, ain't they, Rob?"

"Reckon they is. Let's git us back up to the house."

They stole back up, darting across the road and slipping into the yard, wary of a trick. What if Earle had stayed behind to pounce on the unsuspecting runaways? They kept to the dark shadows of yard trees, straining to see any movement or sign of life. The house was completely dark. The only sounds were chirping katydids from high in the trees, and crickets in the grass.

A familiar voice came from the porch.

"Over here."

Rob and Sally came closer. They saw two shadowy figures in porch rockers. Uncle Bert and Aunt Daisy were sitting there in the dark, taking the night air as though nothing had happened.

"See there. You can beat tracker dogs if you knows a thing or two," said Uncle Bert, on a note of victory. "Problem is, they might come right on back and try to take you by surprise. Best get right on the road up to Monterey."

Daisy came out of her chair and off the porch. "Here," she said, handing Sally a package. "I fixed you some food for the road." She looked down. "Lord! Your shoes and socks is all soaked, and the two of you smell like oil lamps!"

She ran inside and quickly returned with towels. "Take them shoes and socks off." She wiped and dabbed feet and shoes, getting them as dry as she could. "Put these dry socks on."

"We ain't got time to completely dry your shoes," said Bert. "Put 'em on and get goin' before them two decides to come back for a second look."

Sally wrapped her aunt in a wholehearted hug. "I can't thank you enough, Aunt Daisy!" she gushed and then turned to her uncle. "You saved us, Uncle Bert. I'll never forget what you done for us tonight."

Rob chimed in. "Thank you, Miz Daisy and Mister Bert. Thank you a whole heap!"

"Remember, see Vancouver at the sawmill. Good luck to you now," said Bert, with a wave.

Rob and Sally strode out to the road, turned south and set a pace toward their future. The waning moon had not yet risen, leaving the night dark and heavy, but they could discern the open road. They were giddy from their successful evasion, and it stimulated a brisk pace for the first couple of hours. Then the exertions of the evening began to take a toll. They slowed, and rested regularly.

"I'm tired," said Sally.

"I'm tired too, but we gots to keep goin'," said Rob.

The country was asleep. No light shone from any direction. There were no animal sounds. Birds were quietly at roost. Even the ubiquitous crickets and katydids had mostly given up for the night. The silent road belonged to the two refugees.

But before long the western sky woke up with a few winks. It began as a faint flickering, then frequent flashing. Soon the sky was alive with bursts of light that backlit a towering cloud formation above silhouetted ridgelines.

Rob and Sally pressed on, watching the storm form up but unsure of its track. Soon they could hear the muffled grumbling in the distance. The angry rumble became louder. Lightning flashes lit the sky, each followed by a rolling peal of thunder churning the heavens.

"Storm looks like it's comin' this way," said Sally.

"Lookin' like a right smart powerful storm," said Rob. Forked branches of lightning split the night sky.

Within minutes the menacing turmoil was bearing down on them. Alarmed at the charging tempest, they picked up their pace, hoping to find shelter along the way. Soon a gust of cool air rushed out in front of the intense lightning and crashing thunder to sweep over them as they hurried on.

The mighty force broke into an onslaught. They could hear the growing roar as the torrent swept down from the hills on the right. Blinding bolts streaked and exploded in sharp cracks, spurring them to a panicky run.

A shape loomed into view just across a rail fence on the left. It appeared to have a small roof.

"Let's git us right over there right now!" yelled Rob, between brilliant bursts and crashing booms of celestial artillery.

They clambered over the fence just as pelting rain swept in. Jagged splinters of lightning sliced the sky and slashed down to shatter trees with ear-splitting cracks. The cannonade overtook them, pounding the ground with deafening blasts and blinding flashes as they sprinted and ducked in under the little canopy.

"Ain't much but it'll hafter do!" he yelled over the thrashing chaos. They squeezed up under the little shelter, a roofed salt lick box in a cattle pasture that afforded only partial protection from the lashing rain. They crouched in refuge, huddled together in the box under the roof, tormented by the driving downpour.

The tremendous storm swept swiftly by. The squall was gone as fast as it had arrived. In twenty minutes the two unfolded themselves and emerged from under the roof. They crawled back over the fence and continued their sodden march in the mud of the drizzly aftermath.

Several gloomy, cheerless hours brought the dismal pair straggling into the little town that was just awakening to a cool and misty morning. The sawmill came into view down a side lane.

They approached to find a man facing away and bent over, firing up an ancient steam engine. Rob motioned Sally to halt a dozen yards out, not wishing to startle the unwitting sawyer. He swallowed hard, knowing he and Sally were about to make a dreary appearance.

"Ahem. Mornin' there, mister."

The man, about to stuff a chunk of wood into the firebox, turned his head and then straightened himself up and studied the drenched duo standing before him.

"Ah, we's a-lookin' fer Mister Van?"

"My name's Vancouver, if that's who you mean," said the man. And who might you two be?"

"Ah, my name's Rob and this here's Sally and we…"

"You got business with me?"

"Ah, well, ah, Mister Van, ah, Mister Bert done sent us."

"Mister Bert? Who's Mister Bert? Do I know him?"

"Bert and Daisy Harman," said Sally.

"Oh, why *sure*! My *cousin* Bert. Why didn't you *say* so, boy?"

"Yessir. Way'll, Mister Bert, he done said you might take us in fer a spell and take me on at yer sawmill."

"Oh he did, did he?" Vancouver ranged his gaze up and down the two soaked stragglers.

"Well, you're a right sorry sight to see," he said. "Dang near pitiful as them Yankees runnin' from ol' Stonewall back in sixty-two!" He laughed at his own quip. Rob's quizzical look brought more. "Yes indeed. I's just a boy but I seen it with my own eyes—them Yankees runnin' for their lives!" he said, with undisguised delight.

Then he returned to the moment. He sniffed. "And you smells a little like a kettle of coal oil!" he said with a wry grin, making Rob feel a little less unwelcome.

"We done walked through the night and got hit by a right powerful storm."

"Yes indeed. Powerful storm it was, back in sixty-two. But the thunder and lightnin' was Gen'ral Jackson chasin' them Yankees clear down past Franklin," he reminisced, looking distant and savoring the memory. Then he focused his gaze back on Rob.

"Alright then. We can talk this evenin' after you're cleaned up, dried out and had you a good sleep," said Vancouver. "You got any food with you?"

"Yes we do," replied Sally, holding up the packet.

"Good, good. Now you two can clean up at the pump there," he said, nodding at the well. "You'll see the soap. Then get on up to the barn there," he said, pointing, "and get some sleep and dry out your clothes."

THE TALE OF A WOODS COLT

Rob and Sally flushed their faces and tried to scrub the oil odor from shoes, socks and his britches. They trudged up to the barn barefoot, squeaked the door open and stepped into a dim sanctum imbued with the pleasant smell of freshly dried hay. They dropped their shoes, found some horse blankets and laid them out on the loose grass. They stripped off their drippy garments and spread them out on the hay and then, nearly naked, plopped themselves down on the blankets.

Sally unwrapped the food, releasing delicious aromas. It was plain cold fare—hard cheese, liver sausage, smoked meat, a couple crusts of bread and a bottle of milk—which hunger transformed into a gourmet feast. They ate every crumb and then, exhausted, collapsed on to the horse blankets and fell immediately to sleep.

On they slept, as a man walked into the sheriff's office a few blocks away.

"What can I do for you today?" asked the sheriff from his seat at a desk.

The man spoke.

"I see," said the sheriff.

The man continued.

"Well, if that's what you want to do, you'll have to file a paper," said the sheriff, pulling a sheet from his desk drawer.

"What are the names?" asked the sheriff.

The man answered.

"Alright, Mister Harman," said the sheriff, filling out the form. "Sign right here," he pointed, handing the the man his pen.

THIRTY

Justice

Vancouver stood by his sawmill talking to two men. He pointed at the barn.

The two men, one with a double-barreled shotgun under his arm, strode straight to the barn door, eased it open and stepped in. They stood over the slumbering fugitives.

"That them?" whispered the one with the shotgun.

"That's them, and look just at 'em. They damn near nekked," hissed Earle, reaching down and grabbing the sleeping Sally by the wrist.

Jerked awake, she screamed. "Daddy!!" He tightened his grip. "No!! No, Daddy!!" she shrieked as he pulled her to her feet. "No!!" She tried to pull loose before bursting into sobs.

Rob was jolted out of his dream. "What?! What's goin' on?!" he exclaimed, and then looked up. "Mister Arle!! How you done got here?!" He sprang to his feet in his undershorts, and took a step toward Earle, who had Sally firmly in his grip.

"Hold it right there, boy!" barked the sheriff, raising his shotgun a little.

Rob froze.

"Don't do nothin' foolish, now," said the lawman gravely. "You're under arrest, son."

"Who are you!?" demanded Rob.

The sheriff flashed his badge. "Sheriff Wiley of Highland County and I have a warrant for your arrest. I'm takin' you into custody."

"Arrest!? Custody!? What I done wrong?" protested Rob, standing still out of respect for the gun. "What law I done broke?"

"Under the laws of the Commonwealth of Virginia and the charges

THE TALE OF A WOODS COLT

filed by Mister Harman here, I place you, Robert Nickerson, under arrest," recited the sheriff, slapping handcuffs onto Rob's wrists. "You're comin' with me, boy."

Earle sniffed the air. He reached down with his free hand, grabbed up Rob's trousers by a leg and put it to his nose.

"Coal oil!" he cried. "They put coal oil on their legs!" he yelled, shaking the pants in the air. "So *that's* how you throwed off the dogs!" He glared at Rob menacingly. "Why, I got half a mind to soak you in oil and put a match to you like a torch!" He jerked Sally further away from Rob.

"Easy, Harman. Let's not *you* go and do somethin' foolish, now," cautioned the sheriff. "He'll get what's comin' to him. Now give him his britches."

Earle contemptuously tossed the trousers at Rob.

"Put your britches and shoes on and get your stuff," ordered Wiley.

Earle grabbed up Sally's sack and loose garments in one hand and tugged her toward the door with the other.

"Sally!" cried Rob.

"Rob! Rob!!" she cried, trying to break loose.

"You're comin' home with me, girl!" snapped Earle, throwing his arm around her. She squirmed and struggled but he had her in an arm lock. "You ain't gon' see *him* n' more, unless we needs to have a jailhouse weddin'[10]," he barked, glowering back at Rob. "I ain't about to let you get ruined by the likes of *him*."

Outside, Vancouver stood wringing his hands when Earle pulled Sally, nearly naked, from the barn and the sheriff led the shirtless Rob out.

"I didn't have no choice about it," he called out to Rob, holding up both palms and shaking his head. "They said you was wanted. There weren't a thing I could do."

---

10 A.k.a. Shotgun wedding – a family-coerced marriage of a pregnant girl to keep her "respectable," sometimes to a desirable but reluctant paramour, or to an unacceptable lover from whom she'd be immediately separated and divorced.

They all ignored the sawyer. The sheriff turned to Earle. "How *did* you find 'em, Harman?" he asked. "Ain't many valley folks comes up this way."

"Weren't that hard," said Earle, "between them roadhouse people and knowin' where the kinfolk was at. I'm goin' to get her right on home and file charges against him in Harrisonburg."

Earle looked at Rob, narrowing his eyes to a steely glare. "And I'll see *you* in court, boy," he growled ominously, before turning and dragging Sally over to his buckboard.

Rob, his hands cuffed behind his back, trudged through town ahead of the sheriff, his head hung and spirit wilted, drawing a look here and a stare there.

The cuffs came off when he stepped into the holding cell and stood with his face drooped and eyes cast down woefully. The bars clanked shut behind him.

"You'll get supper at five-thirty," said a voice.

Then he was alone.

After a bowl of lukewarm porridge before dawn, Rob held out his hands and the cuffs went back on, this time in front. He was led outside to two saddled horses, beside which stood a stern-faced man in a leather vest and a felt fedora. He cradled a shotgun in the crotch of his arm.

"Deputy Bates here's goin' to take you over to Harrisonburg," said the sheriff. "You mind what he tells you, now. You hear me, boy?"

"Yessir."

The sheriff untied and held the reins. "Get on."

Rob slipped his foot into a stirrup, reached his cuffed hands to the saddle and swung himself up on the horse. His sack had been tied on behind the saddle. He thought about his snakehead walking staff, left behind in the barn.

Bates sheathed his shotgun in a saddle holster, mounted the other horse, took hold of Rob's reins and spurred his mount to a walk. With Rob in tow, the deputy guided his horse out onto the road heading east.

Rob looked back at the town receding into the cool mist of dawn and saw Sheriff Wiley still standing by the hitching post, watching him intently. Outside town, the turn pike swung open for them when Deputy Bates handed the attendant a slip of paper.

The deputy's back and the back of his head was all Rob saw of him, as the two horses clopped along in tandem. They passed a laden freight wagon here and a flock of driven sheep there, and were passed by a four-horse stagecoach stretching for speed on a straightaway. It was up one ridge and down, then another ridge and another, pausing only for water at a cool mountain stream.

Bates reined back to a mid-day halt at a watering trough by a roadhouse. He dismounted. When Rob leaned to do the same, he ordered, "Stay in your saddle, boy."

Rob reckoned it must be the dinner stop, but he didn't ask. He stayed put while the deputy worked the pump handle to flush a gush of cool water into the wooden trough. While the horses slaked their thirst, Bates pulled the two feedbags from behind his saddle and fitted one on each animal.

"Now you can dismount."

Bates took a long drink from a dipper, refilled it and handed it to Rob. After a second round of water, the deputy led the horses and the handcuffed prisoner into the shade. He reached into his saddlebag and pulled out a packet, unwrapped it and handed Rob a large crust of bread and a chunk of farm cheese.

Rob was taken aback. *This here dinner?* he wondered, but he didn't say anything.

Bates spoke.

"Like to sit down and eat like a man but there ain't no money for it and besides, they don't want no prisoners in there no how," he said, tossing his head toward the roadhouse. "So this here's all we get and right here's where we eat it."

Bates sat down on a low stone wall and began munching from his packet. Rob found himself a flat spot on the wall and eased his sore bottom down. Gripping his bread in one fist and the cheese in the other, he had to hold both cuffed hands to his mouth to take a bite of either. The mid-day meal was over in a quarter hour.

The relentless sun and the still air dragged out the sultry afternoon. Along the dusty turnpike, rank odors of fetid dung rose, and deer flies buzzed in the hope of getting a suck of blood from man or beast. The horses sweated and panted, and the men wiped stinging salty sweat from their eyes. Time slowed in the heavy heat hanging on the shimmering road. They paused at a brook for water and then forged on.

It was beyond forty miles and nearly five o'clock when the two weary riders and their exhausted horses arrived outside the sheriff's office in Staunton.

Rob was led inside and the handcuffs were removed. The cell bars clanked shut behind him.

"You'll get your supper at five-thirty."

Then he was alone in the cell, tired and very sore from the long ride. His supper was served in the cell, a large bowl of white bean soup with fat meat, a hunk of cornbread and water. He slept soundly that night with nothing but a thin tick to cushion the hard plank bed. Morning found him stiff and aching.

After thin porridge at dawn, the cuffs went on and Rob was led outside. Bates was standing there beside the saddled horses. Nothing was said. Rob pulled his sore bottom into the saddle. Bates swung onto his horse and they departed at a walk.

Mid-day brought the deputy and prisoner into Harrisonburg. Bates tied up outside the sheriff's office and led Rob inside, where he took the handcuffs off.

THE TALE OF A WOODS COLT

Rob rubbed his wrists and morosely surveyed the spartan cell. The bars slammed shut behind him. A voice announced, "You missed dinner. Supper at five-thirty." He didn't care. It felt good to just lie down. Stretched out on the bunk, he thought poignantly of Sally and how he might see her again—or if he'd ever see her again.

Ten miles from where Rob lay behind bars in morose solitude, Earle pulled the buckboard into his yard where Sally's little brothers stood silently on the porch, staring at her returning in the afternoon heat. Eliza rushed out to embrace her wayward daughter in a hug of tears.

Later, as Rob hungrily tucked into his jailhouse ration, the Harmans sat down to their own supper. Earle's palpable anger cast a pall of silence over the course of the meal. When he was finished eating he pushed back from the table, prompting the three boys to escape to the yard. He rose and cast a hard eye at Sally. "Your belly best not get no bigger or there'll be hell to pay," he said, causing her to burst into tears. He went out to the porch to sulk, leaving Sally sitting at the table beside her mother.

Eliza took her daughter's hand. "Now, now Sally, Daddy's just trying to protect you. We want the best for you, darlin'."

"Daddy and you, neither one, don't care about what *I* want," sniffled Sally.

"In time, you'll find you a good God-fearing boy and we can put that Rob behind us," said Eliza soothingly. Then her face darkened. "Unless he's got you in a..." She held her tongue.

"I hope I *am* in a family way," said Sally defiantly. "Then you and Daddy would *make* him marry me. And I'd get away from here before you could break us up again."

Eliza stiffened in her chair. "That boy's going to prison for what he done to you, Sally. And you will stay right here with us until you find a proper husband," she said with finality.

"What's your full name?" asked the justice of the peace, looking up across his desk at the sullen young man in handcuffs standing opposite.

"Rob Nickerson."

"I got that much already. Now is that your *full* name, boy? Or do you even have a middle name?"

"Robert E. Lee Nickerson."

"Well, well, well," said the justice, leaning back, stroking his chin and studying the prisoner. "Your mama must have thought you would go somewhere in this world–besides prison," he said with a sneer, and then rocked forward and put pen to paper.

"Robert E. Lee Nickerson," he said as he wrote. "Well, now Robert E. Lee Nickerson, Mister Earle Harman has filed criminal charges against you. Do you want to post bail?" he asked. "It's fifty dollars."

"What's bail?"

"Bail is money you put up to be sure you show up on court day," explained the justice. "Post bail and you go free until your court day, except for checkin' in with the sheriff every day. If you don't render bail, you'll be remanded to the county jail."

"When's my court day?"

"End of August–little less than a month."

Rob was torn. He didn't relish nearly a month in jail, but then he didn't know anyone in town, so the bail plus the cost of bed and board would nearly empty his purse. He worried that no one would even want to put up an accused stranger anyway, and he worried about never seeing his bail money again.

"Well? Which is it?"

" Uh, nosir. I ain't gon' put up no money."

"Very well then. Take him back to jail, deputy."

I might have come to the wrong decision, fretted Rob as he stepped into the gloomy cell and heard the bars locked behind him. He sat down on the lower bunkbed, leaned his elbows on his knees and buried his face in his hands.

The close, stifling cell was dark, dingy and airless. It contained a chamber pot, a basin, a cup, a pitcher of water and not much else. The brick wall held a small barred window set too high to see out. Solid plank walls separated the jail's four cells.

The sheriff, the deputy and the clerk sat where they could police the prohibition against talking among the several prisoners. The inmates only saw each other when they were cuffed, shackled and taken out to the rear yard to shuffle around the fence for an hour each day. Under the watchful eye of the armed guard, few words were spoken there.

The days crept by in a dull monotony of sitting and waiting, punctuated only by three dreary meals and plodding through the exercise hour. Sleep was Rob's only escape, but it came slowly and was disturbed whenever a drunk was tossed into the cell with him. When that happened, the minutes became hours, as he lay awake on the top bunk enduring wheezes and hacking coughs from below, along with the drunk inevitably heaving into the chamber pot.

"All Rise," called the bailiff.

A side door opened and the judge, draped in a long black robe, entered the courtroom. The bailiff announced "The circuit court for the county of Rockingham in the Commonwealth of Virginia is now in session with the honorable Judge James C. Johnston presiding."

The judge seated himself high behind the bench, fitted on his spectacles and looked out to the dozen or so spectators standing in front of wooden benches in his courtroom.

"You may be seated."

Earle and Eliza Harman and the others sat down.

"Call the first case."

"In the cause of the Commonwealth versus Robert E. Lee Nickerson," said the clerk.

The bailiff opened the opposite side door to admit the deputy, followed by the prisoner shuffling in short steps, his legs shackled at the ankles and cuffed hands at his waist. Rob, taking his cue from the deputy, shuffled between a table and chair and turned to face the judge.

A man seated at the other table rose and spoke. "Your honor, the Grand Jury has handed down a True Bill of Indictment against Mister Nickerson charging Seduction and also charging Unlawful Carnal Knowledge of a Minor Female."

The judge looked down at Rob. "State your full name for the record."

"Robert E. Lee Nickerson."

"What is your age?"

"What?"

"How old are you, Mister Nickerson?"

"Uh, twenty, or twenty-one, I reckon."

"You 'reckon', Mister Nickerson?"

"Yessir. I'm twenty or twenty-one."

The judge looked out at Rob over his glasses. "Did I hear you say twenty-one?"

"Yessir."

"Let the record show that the defendant has reached the age of majority," said the judge to the clerk. He turned his attention back to Rob. "Do you not have a lawyer, Mister Nickerson?"

"Nosir."

"You have the right to a lawyer. Do you want to hire a lawyer?"

"Don't know why I need a lawyer," said Rob. "I ain't got nothin' to hide."

"Very well then. You heard the charges. How do you plead, Mister Nickerson?"

"Uh, well, uh…I, I ain't fer sure," stammered Rob. "I don't know nary a thang about what he done said," said Rob, with a nod toward the prosecutor at the other table, who had recited the two charges.

The judge leaned forward and peered out over his lenses. "Mister Nickerson, you have been charged with the crimes of taking unlawful liberties with a fifteen-year-old girl. You can plead innocent and be tried by a jury, or you can plead guilty and be sentenced as prescribed by law," he explained patiently.

"Way'll judge, I don't think I done nothin' wrong," said Rob. "We was goin' to git married first chance we got."

"That goes to the charge of Seduction, Mister Nickerson. Did you promise her you'd marry her?"

"Way'll, she actual were the first one to say somethin' about gittin' married."

"So you didn't promise to marry Miss Harman before she spoke of marrying you?"

"Nosir. I did not."

"That brings us to the charge of Unlawful Carnal Knowledge of a Minor Female," said the judge. "Young man, it's not legal to have, ahem, relations before you're married, and girls her age need the parents' permission to get married. Her parents brought the charges against you."

"But judge, where I comes from women's all the time gittin' married when they's fifteen," said Rob, feeling more innocent. "Plenty of 'ems moves in together first and gits married later."

The judge leaned a little further toward Rob. "I understand that, son. But the complaint has been filed, and the law is the law. Do you understand the charge against you?"

"I reckon."

"Well then, did you or did you not have intimate relations with Miss Harman?"

"Way'll, uh, if you means did me and her uh, uh, git together private and, and did we actual do somethin' like mans does with womens, uh, uh..."

"Yes, that's *exactly* what I mean. Did you or didn't you?"

"Yessir, we done it, but uh, uh, but I never..."

"That will be all Mister Nickerson," said the judge, leaning back with satisfaction. "I accept your guilty plea." He turned to the clerk.

"Mister Nickerson has pleaded guilty to the charge of Unlawful Carnal Knowledge of a Minor Female. I find him not guilty of the charge of Seduction."

"But judge..."

"There's nothing more to say, young man," interjected Judge Johnston. "You are guilty as charged. Your crime is punishable by up to five years of incarceration. I sentence you to two years, to be served in a state penitentiary, plus two dollars court costs," he declared, rapping his gavel down with a bang. "Next case."

Rob stood stunned, staring at the judge.

The deputy nudged him. "C'mon."

As Rob shuffled behind the deputy toward the side door, Earle came out of his seat, stepped forward to the rail, leaned across toward Rob and, with angry daggers shooting from his eyes, said in a low but menacing tone, "You had it comin' to you boy. Now you best hope to God her belly don't get no bigger."

The story of Rob Nickerson and the Blue Ridge mountain people continues in *The Call of the Whippoorwill*, the second book of the trilogy. The third book, *The Crags of Old Rag*, carries the story through Rob's long and colorful life.

CPSIA information can be obtained
at www.ICGtesting.com
Printed in the USA
BVOW09s1942171117
500675BV00001B/101/P